PARIS
AND AROUND
D0628068

CHARMING SMALL HOTELS & RESTAURANTS

PARIS AND AROUND

EDITED BY

Fiona Duncan & Leonie Glass

Interlink Books
An imprint of Interlink Publishing Group, Inc.
New York • Northampton

Expanded & redesigned edition

First American edition published in 2004 by
Interlink Books
An Imprint of Interlink Publishing Group, Inc
46 Crosby Street, Northampton, Massachusetts 01060
www.interlinkbooks.com

This series is conceived, designed and produced by
Duncan Petersen Publishing Ltd,
31 Ceylon Road, London W14 OPY

Editorial director Andrew Duncan
Production editor Sarah Boyall
Art editor Don Macpherson
Production Sarah Hinks

Library of Congress Cataloging-in-Publication Data available
ISBN 1-56656-517-0

Printed and bound in Spain

CONTENTS

Introduction	6
Hotels by area and price	14
Orientation, getting around and hotel location map	21-34
First Arrondissement	35
Third Arrondissement	38
Fourth Arrondissement	39
Fifth Arrondissement	48
Sixth Arrondissement	58
Seventh Arrondissement	85
Eighth Arrondissement	94
Ninth Arrondissement	101
Twelfth Arrondissement	103
Thirteenth Arrondissement	104
Fourteenth Arrondissement	106
Sixteenth Arrondissement	107
Seventeenth Arrondissement	114
Eighteenth Arrondissement	117
Ile-de-France	120
Half-page entries	125
Index of hotel and restaurant names	196
Menu decoder	200
Confirming a booking	204

Don't leave for France without the perfect companion for this guide: *Charming Restaurant Guides, France* (UK title) or *Charming French Restaurants* (US title).

INTRODUCTION

IN THIS INTRODUCTORY SECTION

Our selection criteria *7*

Types of accommodation *11*

How to find an entry *9*

Reporting to the guide *13*

Maps *21-34*

Paris was the very first city to have its own guide in the *Charming Small Hotel* series which now covers more than a dozen countries and regions, including the long-established all-France guide, a guide to Southern France, a France bed-and-breakfast guide, and the only guide devoted entirely to hotels in Venice.

Paris is romantic, alluring and memorable. Space in this book can't be bought so it only lists the hotels which, in our inspectors' opinion, best live up to these expectations. And they are inspected: each and every one has been visited.

During their 2003 tour of inspection our team not only recorded the hotels' tangible attributes but also looked for the intangible ones. There is no formal way of measuring the warmth of a welcome, for example, but woe betide any hotelier who forgets how important it is to make their guests feel at home.

Having had a lean time in the mid-1990s, Paris hotels are now flourishing. We're pleased to report that prices have changed little in the past two years and, with only a few exceptions, standards of maintenance and housekeeping remain high.

WHICH PART OF PARIS TO STAY IN?

If you look at the location maps on pages 24-34, you will notice a huge concentration of hotels on the Left Bank, particularly in Saint-Germain-des-Prés and the Latin Quarter, whose quaint streets, ancient buildings and Bohemian and literary associations make a perfect setting for charming small hotels. Another district with a distinctive character and beautiful buildings is the fourth *arrondissement*, including the Marais and Ile Saint-Louis. Nearby, the Pompidou Centre and Les Halles are famous landmarks, but be aware that the surrounding streets are scruffy and down-market. Business people and tourists who are magnetically attracted to the Arc de Triomphe will find accommodation in the (to our mind) far less atmospheric environment of the Champs-Elysées quarter. But

Our criteria

Although this is a guide to city hotels rather than country hotels, the selection criteria remain the same. We aim to include only those places that are in some way captivating, with a distinctive personality, and which offer a truly personal service. Paris presents us with something of a dilemma, since we cannot be as selective as we may when compiling a country or regional guide. We found many hotels which easily attain our very high standards; but there are a significant number which, though basically recommendable, for one reason or another fall short of our ideal. The descriptions of each hotel makes this distinction clear. Be assured that the hotels in this guide are all, one way or another, true to the concept of the charming small hotel, and that they are the pick of the hundreds of small hotels in Paris. If you find any more, please let us know (see page 13).

Our ideal Paris hotel has a calm, attractive setting in an interesting *quartier*; the building itself is either handsome or historic, or at least has a distinct character. The bedrooms are well-proportioned with as much character as the public rooms below. The decorations and furnishings are harmonious, comfortable and impeccably maintained, and include antique pieces that are meant to be used, not revered. The proprietors and staff are dedicated, thoughtful and sensitive in the pursuit of their guests' happiness – friendly and welcoming without being intrusive. The breakfast should be freshly prepared and well presented. Ideally, the hotel will have less than 30 bedrooms; but this is not a rigid requirement – many hotels with more than 30 bedrooms feel much smaller, and you will find such places in this guide.

In making our selection, we have been careful to bear in mind the many different requirements of readers of this guide. Some will be backpackers; others will be millionaires; and the vast majority will fall between the two. They all have in common their preference for a small, intimate hotel rather than a large anonymous one. Whether the hotel be a one-star hostel or a four-star château, it has been included because it fulfils our criteria.

Charming Small Hotel Guides have made their mark not only because of the places they feature, but for the way in which they are edited, designed and produced. Our entries employ, above all, words; they contain not one symbol. They are written by people with something to say, not a bureaucracy which has long since lost the ability to distinguish the praiseworthy from the mediocre.

SO WHAT EXACTLY DO WE LOOK FOR?

- *A peaceful, attractive setting in an interesting and picturesque position.*

- *A building that is either handsome or interesting or historic, or at least with a distinct character.*

- *Bedrooms that are well proportioned with as much character as the public rooms below.*

- *Ideally, we look for adequate space, but on a human scale: we don't go for places that rely on grandeur, or that have pretensions that could intimidate.*

- *Decorations must be harmonious and in good taste, and the furnishings and facilities comfortable and well maintained. We like to see interesting antique furniture that is there because it can be used, not simply revered.*

- *The proprietors and staff need to be dedicated and thoughtful, offering a personal welcome, without being intrusive. The guest needs to feel like an individual.*

no location in the centre of Paris should be entirely discounted. The city has been beautifully preserved, and every district has its own charm. Don't rule out staying further afield – Montmartre or Gobelins – the prices are lower and the public transport is excellent. Some people may prefer to mix a trip to Paris with a stay in the countryside, and our selection of hotels in the Ile-de-France (the province in whose centre Paris lies) offers that oppportunity.

NO FEAR OR FAVOUR
This is an independent guide. None of the places featured has paid for their entry. Beware of imitators who accept a 'small fee' for inclusion.

Pet loves

These are some of the things that stand out for us in many of the hotels at which we stayed. Maybe they will strike you too.

Lovely warm and welcoming reception rooms, with beautiful flower arrangements, working fireplaces and original stone floors.

Ancient, charming and architecturally important buildings, with original staircases, masses of beams and stone-vaulted cellars (often serving as the ubiquitous breakfast room).

Original and very pretty wrought-iron lifts, often rib-ticklingly small.

Bedrooms with splendid views, either of a pretty courtyard or street, or across the roof tops to the famous landmarks.

Comfortable beds and excellent linen.

Spotless and sophisticated marble-clad bathrooms.

Pet hates

Moody or downright rude receptionists.

Claustrophobic stone-vaulted breakfast rooms.

Televisions blaring into empty *salons*.

Shoe-box sized bedrooms.

Bedrooms which are banal and which don't live up to the promise of the reception rooms.

Hideous minibars.

Endless white-tiled bathrooms.

Skimpy tea towels masquerading as bath towels.

Noise pollution, caused as much by the lack of sound-proofed windows as by paper-thin walls. Even in the most tranquil back street, beware the 5-am visit by one of the remarkably assiduous fleet of Parisian street-cleaning vehicles.

Mean breakfasts, consisting of one slightly stale croissant, one pat of butter, one mini pot of jam and a jug of luke-warm coffee. Orange juice at extra cost.

How to find an entry

In this guide, hotels appear as either full-page, with colour photographs, or as half-page entries, without a photo. Full-page entries are generally the hotels that we judge most attractive. Half-page entries are not, in our opinion, as special, but don't disregard them, particularly if your first choice is full, which can often be the case.

Full-page entries appear first, organized by *arrondissement* (the 20 administrative districts arranged by number into which Paris is divided). Within their arrondissement, entries are listed alphabetically. The half-page entries follow, arranged in the same way. Our selection of hotels outside Paris are listed at the end of each section.

How to read an entry

At the top of each entry is a heading telling you the *arrondissement*. Next comes a coloured bar highlighting the

name of the district in which the hotel is located – Saint-Germain-des-Prés, Marais, Montparnasse etc. Then comes the name of the hotel. By this means, you can find a hotel in a particular area by simply browsing through the headings at the top of the pages, or by using the maps following this introduction to locate the appropriate pages. To locate a specific hotel, use the indexes at the back, which list the entries alphabetically by name, or refer to pages 14-20, where the hotels are divided into districts.

FACT BOXES

The fact box given for each hotel follows a standard pattern; the explanation that follows is for full- and half-page entries.

Tel All French telephone numbers now have ten digits. If you are dialling within France, Paris and Ile-de-France numbers must be prefaced with 01; the rest of France is divided into four regional zones (02-05). If you are dialling from abroad, leave off the 0 at the start of the ten-digit number.

Fax The above also applies to fax numbers. The fax has become a standard and trouble-free way of making and comfirming bookings, especially helpful if your French is not up to a telephone call (although the majority of receptionists speak English, and other languages too).

E-mail and website Most hotels in Paris now have their own website, the best of which have a selection of photographs showing public rooms and bedrooms, an excellent way of judging if a hotel is to your taste. E-mail is a short and efficient method of making a booking or an enquiry.

Location Where it is helpful, we have indicated in which part of the street the hotel is located, and given pointers to where the street can be found on a map. **Parking** If your car can be easily parked in the street of the hotel, we have put 'in street'. If the hotel has its own garage (rare), we have put 'free private'. If the nearest parking is in a public car park, we have put the name of the street where you will find the entrance. **Metro** The nearest stations are listed. **RER** (Réseau Express Régional) is the fast suburban service which consists of three lines crossing Paris. The nearest RER station is listed only if it is within reasonable walking distance (with luggage) of the hotel.

Food It is very rare to find a small hotel in Paris which serves any meals other than breakfast. Where they do, we indicate it, giving a rough idea of the cost of dinner for one without wine, but not for lunch. Room service is more common, and if it is available, we have mentioned it under 'Food'.

Prices In this guide, we have given room and meal prices in euros, using price bands as we do in many of the other guides in the series. Our price bands are as follows, and refer to a standard double room in high season, with breakfast for two and taxes.

€	under 100 euros
€€	100-175 euros
€€€	175-250 euros
€€€€	over 250 euros

In most Paris hotels, prices vary considerably according to the season and the type of room. The prices we quote are for the most expensive periods of the year, and for a room type that falls in the middle of the range.

The price quoted is for continental breakfast, which may be just a simple croissant, bread and coffee or a slightly more elaborate affair. Cooked dishes may also be on offer at a higher price – check with the hotel.

In 1994 a taxe de séjour (daily fee) was imposed on Paris hotels by the City Council. At the time of writing, this ranges from 46 cents to just over one euro, depending on the hotel's tourist category (one to four stars). Some hotels include this tax in their quoted prices, others do not – if you would like to know, check when you book. We have tried to give up-to-date prices, but bear in mind that proprietors might have increased them by the time you come to use this book – always check first.

Please note: prices were correct at time of going to press, but hotels may raise their prices at any time. To avoid unpleasant or embarrassing surprises, *check the cost when making a booking*.

Rooms Under this heading we indicate the number and type – single, double, triple, family and suites – and whether the rooms have baths (usually with shower or shower attachment as well) or just showers. Unless stated, you can assume that the bath or shower room will include a WC and washbasin.

If you have a large number of people to accommodate, do ask the hotel if rooms can be arranged to suit you. Although hotels may have one or two suites, rooms are generally not large, but sometimes connecting rooms are available, often with their own separate entrance. Very often the hotel will be able to supply a third bed in a double or twin room for a supplement. The cost varies, but expect to pay around 15 euros.

Of the facilities we list in the rooms, in most cases the telephones will be direct-dial. In most hotels you will now find a fax/modem point. Most hotels have cable or satellite TV in addition to the normal terrestrial channels: check with the hotel as to which foreign channels are available. We have not listed central heating as a facility, as all the hotels have this; we do, however, indicate when a hotel has air-conditioning. More and more hotels are introducing individual air-conditioning units in their rooms.

Facilities Under facilities we list public rooms, and whether the hotel has a courtyard or garden.

Credit cards We use the following abbreviations:

AE	American Express
DC	Diners Club
MC	MasterCard (Access/Eurocard)
V	Visa (Barclaycard/Bank Americard/Carte Bleu, etc)

Children This heading is almost redundant in Paris because every hotel in this guide is happy to accept children; however, some are more child-friendly than others. Many of the hotels, being small and delicately furnished, are not necessarily suited to young children; the breakfast rooms in particular, with their small tables and chairs, can present a problem.

Disabled Paris hotels are not the most suitable for those in wheelchairs. There are steps everywhere, very few ramps, and the lifts/elevators are often tiny. Newly built or renovated hotels are now required to provide specially adapted rooms. Where facilities exist, they are indicated: also if it possesses a lift/elevator.

Pets 'Accepted' means that the hotel is happy to accommodate well-behaved small animals. Sometimes they stipulate that animals are not allowed in public rooms. Often a small daily fee will be charged, in the region of 5-15 euros.

Closed Paris hotels rarely close. A handful shut down for a short period in summer or at Christmas.

The final entry in a fact box is normally the name of the **Proprietor**(s). Where a hotel is run by a manager, we give his or her name instead.

Reporting to the Guide

Please write and tell us about your experiences of small hotels, guest houses and inns, whether good or bad, whether listed in this edition or not. As well as hotels in Paris, we are interested in hotels in France, Spain, Italy, Austria, Greece, Germany, Switzerland and the U.S.A. We assume that reporters have no objections to our publishing their views unpaid.

Readers whose reports prove particularly helpful may be invited to join our Travellers' Panel. Members give us notice of their own travel plans; we suggest hotels that they might inspect, and help with the cost of accommodation.

The address is:

Editor, *Charming Small Hotel Guide*s
Duncan Petersen Publishing Limited,
31 Ceylon Road,
London W14 0PY.

Checklist

Please use a separate sheet of paper for each report; include your name, address and telephone number on each report.

Your reports will be received with particular pleasure if they are typed, and if they are organized under the following headings:

Name of establishment
Town or village it is in, or nearest
Full address, including postcode
Telephone number
Time and duration of visit
The building and setting
The public rooms
The bedrooms and bathrooms
Physical comfort (chairs, beds, heat, light, hot water)
Standards of maintenance and housekeeping
Atmosphere, welcome and service
Food
Value for money

We assume that in writing you have no objections to your views being published unpaid, either verbatim or in an edited version. Names of major outside contributors are acknowledged, at the editor's discretion, in the guide.

Hotels by area and price

Price bands		
	€	under 100 euros
	€€	100-175 euros
	€€€	175-250 euros
	€€€€	over 250 euros

In this list hotels are arranged by district, and price bands given

District	Hotel name	Pg. no	Price band
Bastille Quarter	Hôtel le Pavillon Bastille	103	€€
Beaubourg Quarter	Hôtel Place du Louvre	126	€€
	Hôtel Britanique	125	€€€
	Grand Hôtel de Champaigne	125	€€€
	Hôtel Victoires Opéra	127	€€€€
Chaillot Quarter	Hôtel du Bois	107	€€
	Au Palais de Chaillot Hôtel	111	€€
	Hôtel Majestic	157	€€€€
	Saint James Paris	113	€€€€
Champs-Elysées	Hôtel Elysées Matignon	148	€€
	Hôtel Elysées-Mermoz	97	€€
	Hôtel Etoile-Maillot	108	€€
	Hôtel Etoile Park	158	€€
	Hôtel Résidence Lord Byron	149	€€
	Hôtel Mayflower	150	€€
	Hôtel de l'Elysée	96	€€
	Hôtel Galileo	98	€€
	Hôtel Chambiges Elysées	148	€€€
	Hôtel Libertel Argentine	110	€€€
	Hôtel San Regis	151	€€€€
	Hôtel de Vigny	100	€€€€
	Hôtel Franklin Roosevelt	149	€€€€

Hotels by area and price

District	Hotel name	Pg. no	Price band
Champs-Elysées	Lancaster	99	€€€€
Eiffel Tower Quarter	Hôtel du Bailli de Suffren	155	€€
	Hôtel Paris Saint Charles	155	€€
Gobelins Quarter	Residence les Gobelins	104	€
	Le Vert Galant	105	€€
Les Halles	Hôtel Saint-Merry	47	€
Ile de la Cité	Hospitel	129	€
Ile Saint-Louis	Hôtel des Deux Iles	41	€€
	Hôtel Saint-Louis	45	€€
	Hôtel de Jeu de Paume	43	€€€
Invalides Quarter	Hôtel Valadon	92	€
	Hôtel Latour-Maubourg	87	€€
	Hôtel de Suède	146	€€
	Hôtel de Varenne	147	€€
Invalides/Eiffel Tower Quarter	Hôtel Saint-Dominique	89	€€
	Champ-de-Mars	85	€€
	Hôtel Thoumieux	90	€€
	Hôtel de la Tulipe	147	€€
	Hôtel Le Tourville	146	€€€
Invalides/Saint-Germain-des-Prés	Hôtel de Nevers	144	€€
Jardin des Plantes Quarter	Timhotel Jardin des Plantes	57	€€
Latin Quarter	Hôtel Esmeralda	50	€
	Hôtel Saint Jacques	56	€–€€
	Hôtel des Grandes Ecoles	51	€€
	Hôtel des Trois Collèges	133	€€

Hotels by Area and Price

District	Hotel name	Pg. no	Price band
Latin Quarter	Hôtel Résidence Henri IV	131	€€
	Hôtel de Notre-Dame	131	€€
	Hôtel du Panthéon	132	€€
	Hôtel Parc Saint-Séverin	54	€€
	Hôtel Degres de Notre-Dame	49	€€
	Hôtel Sorbonne	133	€€
	Hôtel Les Rives de Notre Dame	55	€€
	Hôtel des Grands Hommes	52	€€€
	Hôtel Saint Jacques	132	€€€
	Hotel Melia Colbert	53	€€€€
	Bateau Jolia	148	€€€€
Luxembourg Quarter	Hôtel Perreyve	138	€€
	Hôtel le Régent	139	€€
	Régent's Hôtel	140	€€
Marais	Grand Hôtel Jeanne d'Arc	42	€
	Hôtel de Nice	44	€
	Hôtel du Septième Art	130	€
	Hôtel de la Place des Vosges	129	€€
	Hôtel de la Bretonnerie	39	€€
	Hôtel Caron de Beaumarchais	40	€€
	Hôtel Saint-Louis Marais	46	€€
	Hôtel Saint-Paul-Le-Marais	130	€€
	Hôtel du Bourg Tibourg	128	€€€
	Pavillion de la Reine	38	€€€€
Marais/Les Halles	Hôtel Beaubourg	128	€€

HOTELS BY AREA AND PRICE

District	Hotel name	Pg. no	Price band
Monceau Quarter	Hôtel Eber	115	€€
Montmartre	Hôtel Ermitage	117	€
	Style Hôtel	119	€
	Hôtel Prima Lepic	118	€€
Montparnasse	Hôtel Istria	106	€€
	L'Atelier Montparnasse Hôtel	134	€€
	Hôtel Danemark	135	€€
	Hôtel le Lenox Montparnasse	154	€€
	Hôtel Raspail Montparnasse	154	€€
	Hôtel Le Sainte-Beuve	81	€€€
North of Etoile	Hôtel Champerret-Héliopolis	158	€€
	Hôtel Flaubert	159	€€
	Hôtel Royal Opéra	151	€€
	Hôtel de Banville	114	€€€
	Hôtel de Neuville	116	€€€
	Hôtel Regent's garden	159	€€€
Opéra Quarter	Hôtel Chopin	101	€
	Hôtel de Beauharnais	152	€€
	Hôtel Favart	127	€€
	Hôtel du Léman	152	€€
	Langlois	102	€€
	Hôtel Queen Mary	150	€€
	Hôtel de l'Arcade	95	€€€
	Hôtel Amarante beau Manoir	94	€€€
Opéra/Montmartre	Hôtel Riboutté-Lafayette	153	€

Hotels by Area and Price

District	Hotel name	Pg. no	Price band
Opéra/Montmartre	Hôtel de la Tour d'Auvergne	153	€€
Passy	Hôtel Gavarni	109	€€
	Le Hameau de Passy	156	€€
	Hôtel Trocadero de la Tour	157	€€
Porte Maillot	L'Hôtel Pergolèse	112	€€€€
Porte Saint-Cloud	Hôtel Boileau	156	€
Saint-Germain-des-Prés	Hôtel de Nesle	76	€
	Hôtel Saint-André-des-Arts	141	€
	Grand Hôtel des Balcons	62	€€
	Hôtel de Beaune	142	€€
	Hôtel du Globe	69	€€
	Hôtel Louis II	72	€€
	Hôtel de Quai Voltaire	145	€€
	Hôtel Bersoly's Saint-Germain	143	€€
	Hôtel Lenox Saint-Germain	88	€€
	Hôtel de Lille	143	€€
	Hôtel d'Orsay	145	€€
	Hôtel le Recamier	139	€€
	Hôtel Prince de Conti	138	€€
	Hôtel Louis II	72	€€
	Hôtel de l'Académie	142	€€€
	Crystal Hôtel	134	€€€
	Hotel Delavigne	65	€€€
	Hôtel de Fleurie	68	€€€
	Hôtel des Marroniers	136	€€€

HOTELS BY AREA AND PRICE

District	Hotel name	Pg. no	Price band
Saint-Germain-des-Prés	Hôtel Saint-Paul	79	€€€
	Hôtel de Université	91	€€€
	Hôtel Verneuil	93	€€€
	Hôtel d'Angleterre	59	€€€
	Hôtel Artus	60	€€€
	Hôtel Milliséme	137	€€€
	Hôtel Jardin de l'Odéon	135	€€€
	Hôtel Left Bank	71	€€€
	Le Relais Médicis	136	€€€
	Au Manoir Saint-Germain-des -Prés	74	€€€
	Hôtel de l'Odéon	137	€€€
	Relais Saint-Sulpice	80	€€€
	Hôtel Saint-Germain-des -Prés	140	€€€
	Hôtel des Saints-Péres	82	€€€
	Hôtel Duc de Saint-Simon	86	€€€€
	L'Hôtel	70	€€€€
	Le Relais Saint-Germain	77	€€€€
	Hôtel Montalembert	144	€€€€
	La Villa	141	€€€€
	Hôtel d'Aubusson	61	€€€€
	Hôtel Relais Christine	63	€€€€
Saint-Germain-des-Prés/	Delhy's Hotel	66	€
Latin Quarter			
	Hôtel du Lys	73	€–€€
	Relais-Hôtel le Vieux Paris	84	€€€€

HOTELS BY AREA AND PRICE

District	Hotel name	Pg. no	Price band
Saint-Germain-des-Prés/ Latin Quarter	Hôtel Villa d'Estrées	83	€€€€
Saint-Germain-des-Prés/ LuxembourgQuarter	Pension les Marronniers	75	€
	Hôtel de l'Abbaye	58	€
Saint-Germain-des-Prés/ Montparnasse	Hôtel Ferrandi	67	€€
	Hôtel Le Saint Grégoire	73	€€€
Tuileries Quarter	Hôtel de la Tamise	126	€€
	Hôtel des Tuileries	37	€€€
	Hôtel Mansart	36	€€€
Tuileries/Beaubourg Quarter	Le Relais du Louvre	35	€€
OUTSIDE PARIS			
Angerville	Hôtel de France	160	€€
Barbizon	Hôtellerie du Bas-Bréau	160	€€€
Dampierre	Auberge du Chateau	120	€
Ermenonville	Hôtel le Prieuré	121	€€
Flagy	Hostellerie du Moulin	122	€€
Fontaine Chaalis	Auberge de Fontaine	161	€
Germigny L'Evêque	Hostellerie Le Gonfalon	123	€
Provins	Hostellerie Aux Vieux Remparts	124	€€
Saint-Germain-en-Laye	La Forestière	161	€€€
	Le Pavillon Henry IV	162	€€€
Senlis	Hostellerie de la Porte Bellon	162	€

PARIS ORIENTATION

USING THE LOCATION MAPS

On pages 24-34 you will find hotel location maps: they show the whereabouts of every hotel in the guide. Both the name of each hotel, and its page number, are shown on the maps.

The scale of the maps is large enough to show most streets in which hotels are situated; however it has not been possible to show their precise locations within the streets.

You can use the location maps either to identify a hotel in the particular area or street in which you want to stay, and then turn to its entry; or you can read about a hotel first, then look for its name on the map to learn its whereabouts. If in any doubt about finding a hotel, ask it to fax you detailed directions.

GEOGRAPHY

As we explain in our introduction, page 6, Paris is divided into 20 districts, known as *arrondissements*. They are called le premier (written 1er), le deuxième (written 2e) and so on. The hotels in this guide are arranged by *arrondissement*, and the map on this page shows how these lie.

Of course, the different neighbourhoods of Paris are also known by their more familiar names – Latin Quarter, Saint-Germain, Montmartre and so on – and in the hotel entries a sub-heading identifies these areas.

OUTSIDE PARIS

The map on page 32 shows Ile-de-France, the French government region in which the city lies, and the locations of our hotel selections surrounding the city. Don't overlook them: many are within easy commuting distance of the city and provide some interesting, pleasantly peaceful alternatives to staying within the city itself.

Getting Around

Extras

On pages 200-203 you will find a menu decoder, translating many names of dishes and ingredients from French into English. On page 204 is guidance on how to reserve a room in French.

Useful information

Tourist offices Paris Convention and Visitors Bureau (Office du Tourisme), 127, ave des Champs-Elysées, Paris 75008; tel. (01) 49 52 53 54; open daily 9 am - 8 pm.

Espace de Tourisme Ile-de-France au Carrousel du Louvre, Carrousel du Louvre, 99 rue de Rivoli, Paris 75001; tel. (01) 42 44 10 59; open daily 10 am - 7 pm except Tuesday.

Bureaux de change You will find late-opening bureaux de change at the following addresses:

5, rue Ancienne-Comédie, Paris 75006; tel. (01) 43 26 33 30; open daily 9 am - 9 pm.

117, ave Champs-Elysées, Paris 75008; tel (01) 40 70 27 22; open daily 10 am - 10 pm.

Public transport

The RAPT (Paris Transport Authority) operates an efficient and fully integrated network of underground/subway trains, buses and express trains running out into the suburbs. Look out for the route-finder machines providing information on the quickest way to reach your destination by whatever combination of transport suits you. Punch in the relevant data and out will come details of how to proceed.

The Metro

Paris's underground or subway system, officially the Métropolitain, but universally referred to as the Metro, is rightly admired. Service is fast and frequent (trains run at 90-second intervals for much of the day); carriages are generally clean and comfortable; and security, once a problem, is now much improved, with police patrols common at major interchanges (but beware pick-pockets, especially on crowded trains). Smoking is banned throughout the network.

Services start at 5.15 am (a little later on Sunday) and end at about 1.15 am.

Lines are officially numbered but are commonly known by the names of the stations at either end of the route. These termini names are also used on the orange signs indicating a connection to another line (correspondence). The system is easily mastered and clear maps in various formats are available at all Metro stations and at tourist offices.

As stations are close together and few are far underground, you will find the Metro a convenient way of getting about, even for short hops.

THE RER

This is Paris's three-line express system – the Réseau Express Régional (RER). The three lines, called A, B and C, are fully integrated into the Metro network but stretch far out into the suburbs, where they run overground, and sometimes in parallel with the SNCF (ordinary rail) suburban services.

The RER lines provide a fast way of getting across Paris, of getting out to the airports and of reaching interesting towns close to Paris such as Versailles or Saint-Germain-en-Laye. Maps are again available from Metro stations and tourist offices.

BUSES

The existence of bus lanes on many streets in central Paris means that buses move reasonably fast, except during the evening rush hour. They offer a useful means of seeing Paris, with some positively attractive routes, such as the 24, which takes in the Madeleine, the place de la Concorde, the Louvre, Pont-Neuf, Nôtre Dame and the Latin Quarter.

All buses operate a day-time service from 7 am to about 8.30 pm Monday to Saturday, but only about 20 lines run on Sundays. Some of these also operate an evening service through to about 12.30 am. And ten Noctambus lines, indicated by an owl sign, radiate out from the place du Châtelet between 1.30 and 5.30 am every night. Clear route plans are posted up at bus stops and full bus maps, with lists of evening and Sunday services, are available from Metro stations and tourist offices.

TICKETS

The ticketing system for public transport is straightforward and fares are generally value for money. The same yellow tickets are used for both buses and the Metro. The most economical way to buy them is in blocks of ten, called carnets, but single tickets are also available, as are a variety of special tourist tickets and passes. They are available from the ticket window at Metro stations and from cafés sporting the RAPT logo.

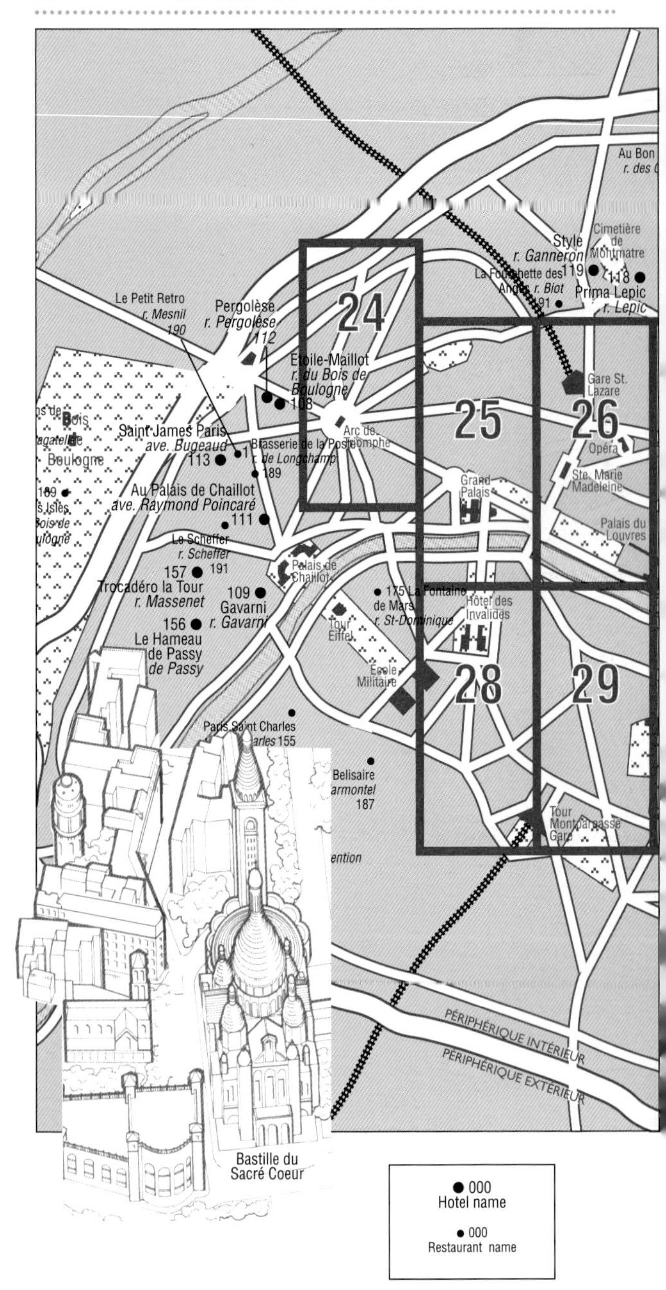

Au Bon
Cimetière de Montmatre
Style
r. Ganneron
119
118
Prima Lepic
r. Lepic
r. Biot
Le Petit Retro
r. Mesnil
190
Pergolèse
r. Pergolèse
112
24
Etoile-Maillot
r. du Bois de Boulogne
108
25
26
Gare St. Lazare
Opéra
Arc de Triomphe
Saint James Paris
ave. Bugeaud
113
Brasserie de la Poste
r. de Longchamp
189
Bois de Boulogne
Au Palais de Chaillot
ave. Raymond Poincaré
111
Grand Palais
Ste. Marie Madeleine
Palais du Louvres
Le Scheffer
r. Scheffer
157
191
Palais de Chaillot
Trocadéro la Tour
r. Massenet
109
Gavarni
r. Gavarni
156
Le Hameau de Passy
de Passy
175 La Fontaine de Mars
r. St-Dominique
Hôtel des Invalides
Tour Eiffel
Ecole Militaire
28
29
Paris Saint Charles
155
Belisaire
187
Tour Montparnasse Gare
PÉRIPHÉRIQUE INTÉRIEUR
PÉRIPHÉRIQUE EXTÉRIEUR
Bastille du Sacré Coeur
000
Hotel name
000
Restaurant name

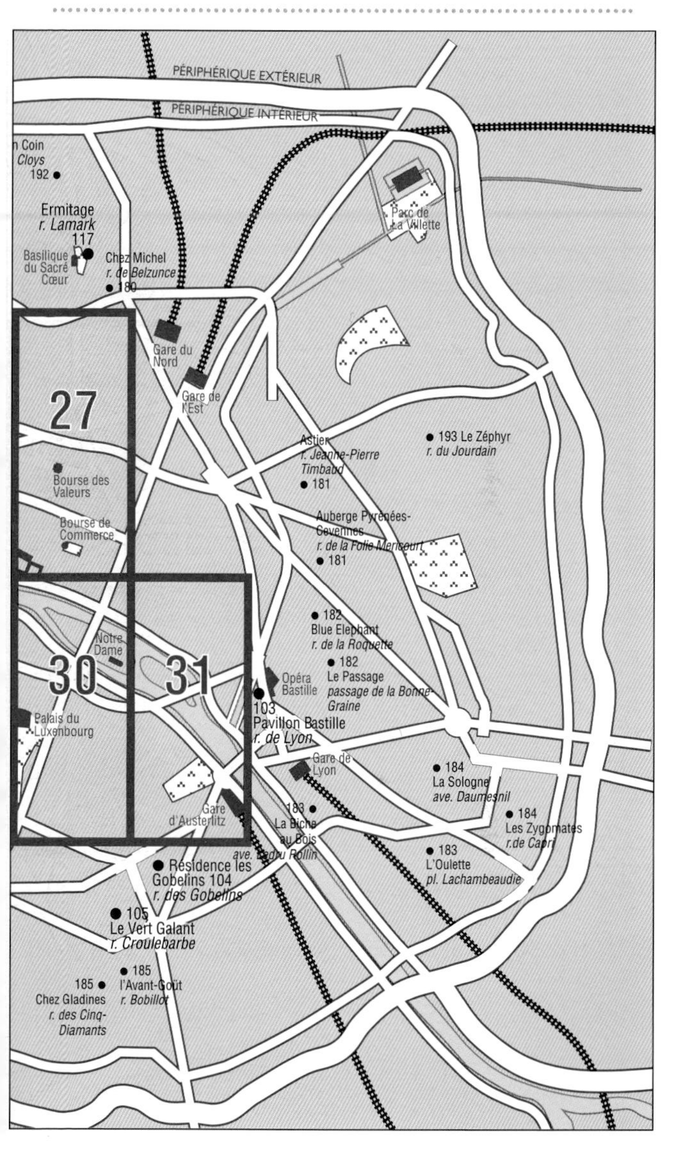
PÉRIPHÉRIQUE EXTÉRIEUR
PÉRIPHÉRIQUE INTÉRIEUR
n Coin
Cloys
192
Ermitage
r. Lamark
117
Basilique du Sacré Cœur
Chez Michel
r. de Belzunce
180
Parc de La Villette
Gare du Nord
Gare de l'Est
27
Bourse des Valeurs
Bourse de Commerce
Astier
r. Jeanne-Pierre Timbaud
181
193 Le Zéphyr
r. du Jourdain
Auberge Pyrénées-Cevennes
r. de la Folie Mericourt
181
182
Blue Elephant
r. de la Roquette
182
Le Passage
passage de la Bonne-Graine
Notre Dame
30
31
Opéra Bastille
103
Pavillon Bastille
r. de Lyon
Palais du Luxenbourg
Gare de Lyon
184
La Sologne
ave. Daumesnil
184
Les Zygomates
r.de Capri
Gare d'Austerlitz
183
La Biche au Bois
ave. Ledru Rollin
183
L'Oulette
pl. Lachambeaudie
Residence les Gobelins 104
r. des Gobelins
105
Le Vert Galant
r. Croulebarbe
185
l'Avant-Goût
r. Bobillot
185
Chez Gladines
r. des Cinq-Diamants

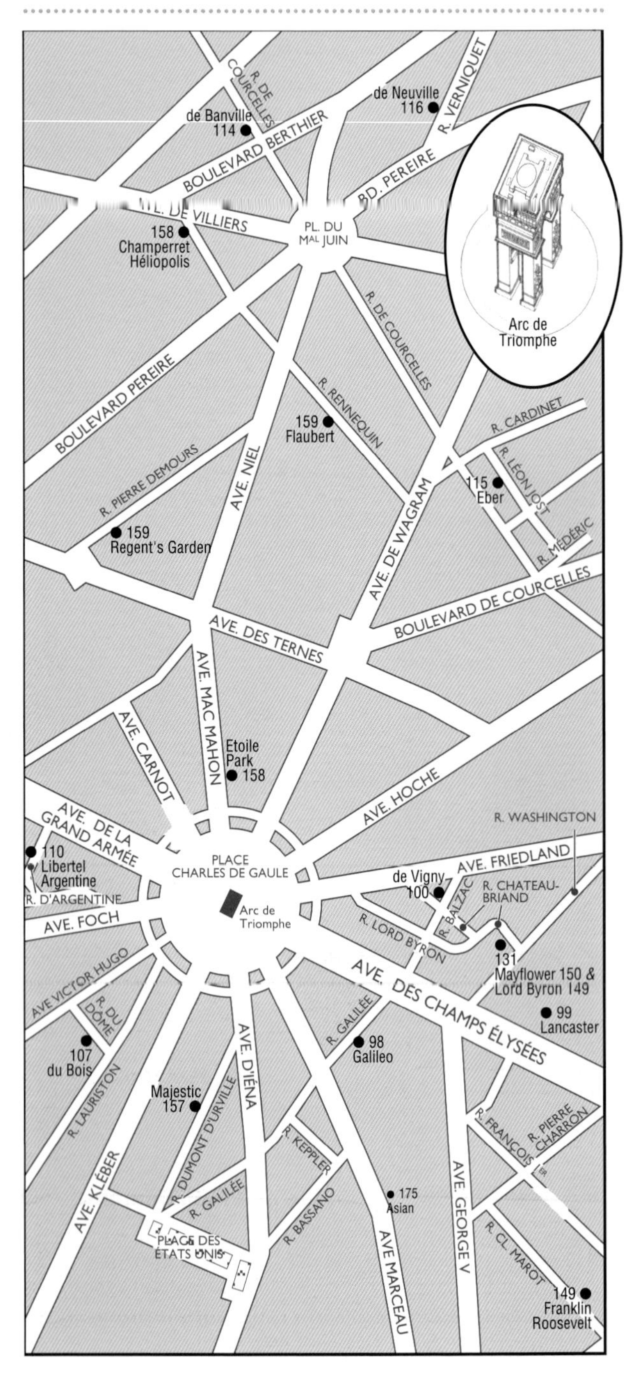
de Neuville
116
de Banville
114
R. DE COURCELLES
BOULEVARD BERTHIER
R. VERNIQUET
BD. PEREIRE
PL. DU Mal JUIN
158
Champerret Héliopolis
Arc de Triomphe
R. DE COURCELLES
R. RENNEQUIN
BOULEVARD PEREIRE
159
Flaubert
R. CARDINET
R. LÉON JOST
115
Eber
R. PIERRE DEMOURS
AVE. NIEL
AVE. DE WAGRAM
159
Regent's Garden
R. MÉDÉRIC
BOULEVARD DE COURCELLES
AVE. DES TERNES
AVE. MAC MAHON
AVE. CARNOT
Etoile Park
158
AVE. HOCHE
R. WASHINGTON
AVE. DE LA GRAND ARMÉE
110
Libertel Argentine
R. D'ARGENTINE
PLACE CHARLES DE GAULE
Arc de Triomphe
de Vigny
100
AVE. FRIEDLAND
R. CHATEAU-BRIAND
R. BALZAC
R. LORD BYRON
AVE. FOCH
131
Mayflower 150 &
Lord Byron 149
AVE. DES CHAMPS ÉLYSÉES
99
Lancaster
AVE VICTOR HUGO
R. DU DÔME
107
du Bois
R. GALILÉE
98
Galileo
R. LAURISTON
AVE. D'IÉNA
Majestic
157
R. DUMONT D'URVILLE
R. KEPPLER
R. FRANÇOIS Ier
R. PIERRE CHARRON
AVE. KLÉBER
R. GALILÉE
175
Asian
AVE. GEORGE V
R. BASSANO
PLACE DES ÉTATS UNIS
AVE MARCEAU
R. CL. MAROT
149
Franklin Roosevelt

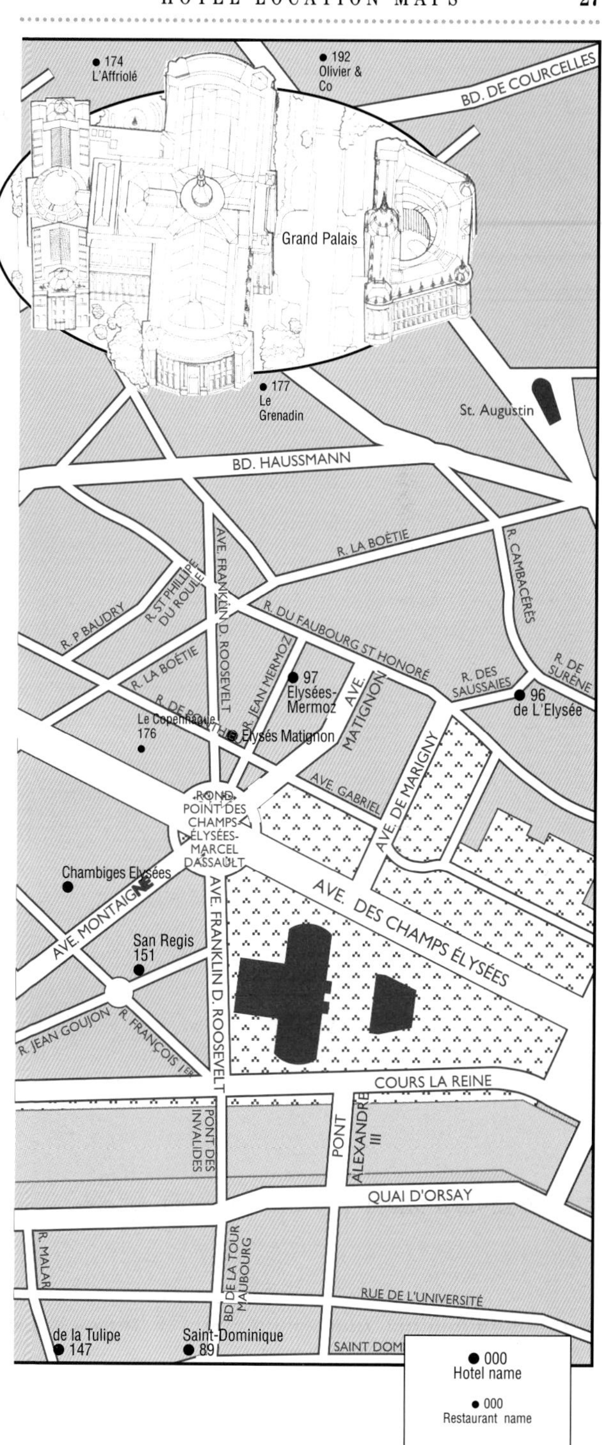

● 174
L'Affriolé
● 192
Olivier & Co
BD. DE COURCELLES
Grand Palais
● 177
Le Grenadin
St. Augustin
BD. HAUSSMANN
R. LA BOÉTIE
R. CAMBACÉRÈS
AVE. FRANKLIN D. ROOSEVELT
R. ST PHILIPPE DU ROULE
R. P BAUDRY
R. DU FAUBOURG ST HONORÉ
R. JEAN MERMOZ
R. LA BOÉTIE
R. DE SURÈNE
R. DES SAUSSAIES
● 97
Elysées-Mermoz
AVE. MATIGNON
● 96
de L'Elysée
Le Copenhague
176
Elysés Matignon
AVE. GABRIEL
AVE. DE MARIGNY
ROND POINT DES CHAMPS-ÉLYSÉES-MARCEL DASSAULT
Chambiges Elysées
AVE. MONTAIGNE
AVE. DES CHAMPS ÉLYSÉES
San Regis
151
R. JEAN GOUJON
R. FRANÇOIS Ier
AVE. FRANKLIN D. ROOSEVELT
COURS LA REINE
PONT DES INVALIDES
PONT ALEXANDRE III
QUAI D'ORSAY
R. MALAR
BD DE LA TOUR MAUBOURG
RUE DE L'UNIVERSITÉ
de la Tulipe
● 147
Saint-Dominique
● 89
SAINT DOM
● 000
Hotel name
● 000
Restaurant name

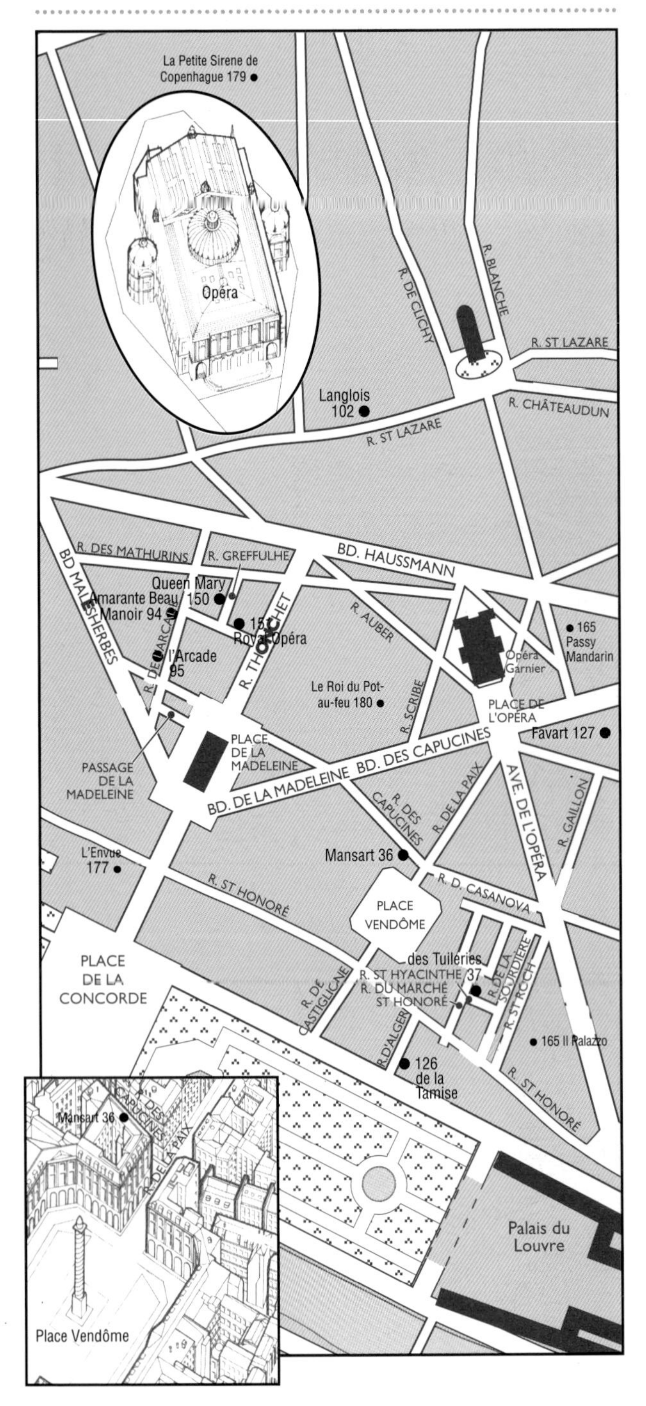

La Petite Sirene de Copenhague 179
Opéra
R. BLANCHE
R. DE CLICHY
R. ST LAZARE
R. CHÂTEAUDUN
Langlois 102
R. ST LAZARE
BD. HAUSSMANN
R. DES MATHURINS
R. GREFFULHE
BD MALESHERBES
Queen Mary 150
Amarante Beau Manoir 94
151 Royal Opéra
R. AUBER
165 Passy Mandarin
l'Arcade 95
Opéra Garnier
Le Roi du Pot-au-feu 180
R. SCRIBE
PLACE DE L'OPÉRA
Favart 127
PASSAGE DE LA MADELEINE
PLACE DE LA MADELEINE
BD. DES CAPUCINES
BD. DE LA MADELEINE
R. DES CAPUCINES
R. DE LA PAIX
AVE. DE L'OPÉRA
R. GAILLON
L'Envue 177
Mansart 36
R. ST HONORÉ
R. D. CASANOVA
PLACE VENDÔME
PLACE DE LA CONCORDE
des Tuileries
R. ST HYACINTHE 37
R. DU MARCHÉ ST HONORÉ
R. DE CASTIGLIONE
R. ST ROCH
R. D'ALGER
165 Il Palazzo
126 de la Tamise
R. ST HONORÉ
Mansart 36
R. DES CAPUCINES
R. DE LA PAIX
Palais du Louvre
Place Vendôme

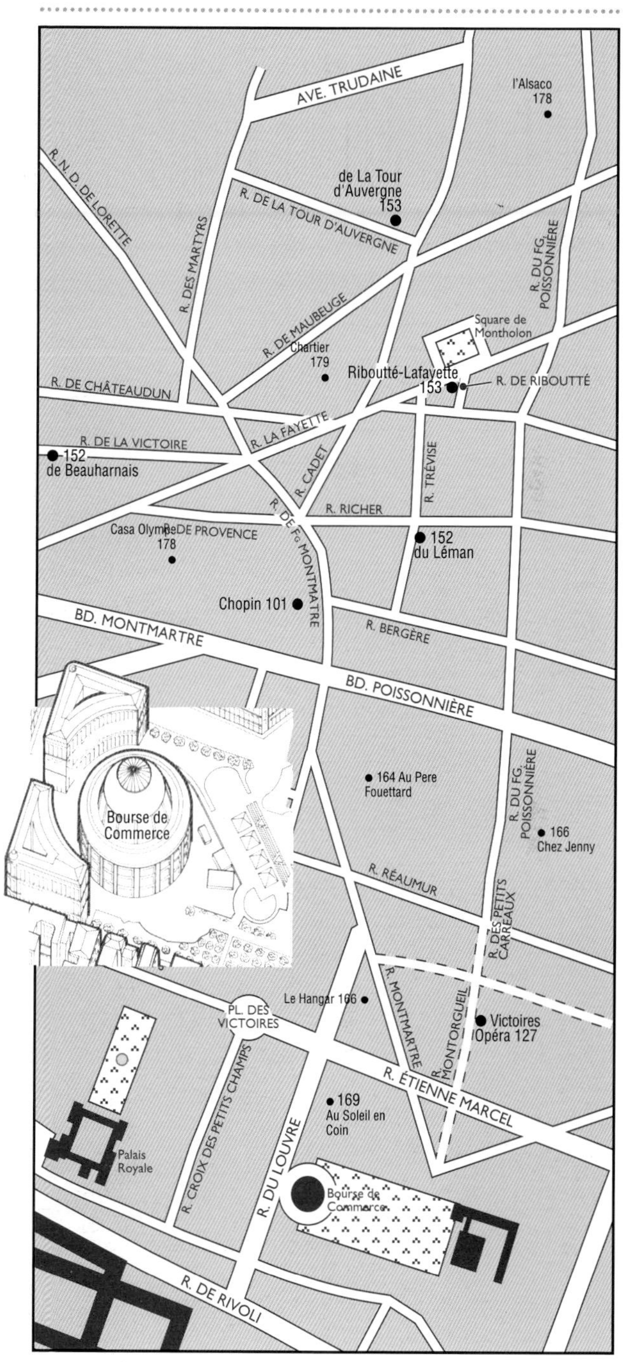
AVE. TRUDAINE
l'Alsaco
178
R. N. D. DE LORETTE
de La Tour
d'Auvergne
153
R. DE LA TOUR D'AUVERGNE
R. DES MARTYRS
R. DU FG. POISSONNIÈRE
R. DE MAUBEUGE
Square de
Montholon
Chartier
179
Riboutté-Lafayette
153
R. DE RIBOUTTÉ
R. DE CHÂTEAUDUN
R. LA FAYETTE
R. DE LA VICTOIRE
152
de Beauharnais
R. CADET
R. TRÉVISE
R. RICHER
Casa Olympe
R. DE PROVENCE
178
R. DE FG. MONTMARTRE
152
du Léman
Chopin 101
R. BERGÈRE
BD. MONTMARTRE
BD. POISSONNIÈRE
164 Au Pere
Fouettard
Bourse de
Commerce
R. DU FG. POISSONNIÈRE
166
Chez Jenny
R. RÉAUMUR
R. DES PETITS CARREAUX
Le Hangar 166
R. MONTMARTRE
R. MONTORGUEIL
Victoires
Opéra 127
PL. DES
VICTOIRES
R. CROIX DES PETITS CHAMPS
R. ÉTIENNE MARCEL
169
Au Soleil en
Coin
R. DU LOUVRE
Palais
Royale
Bourse de
Commerce
R. DE RIVOLI

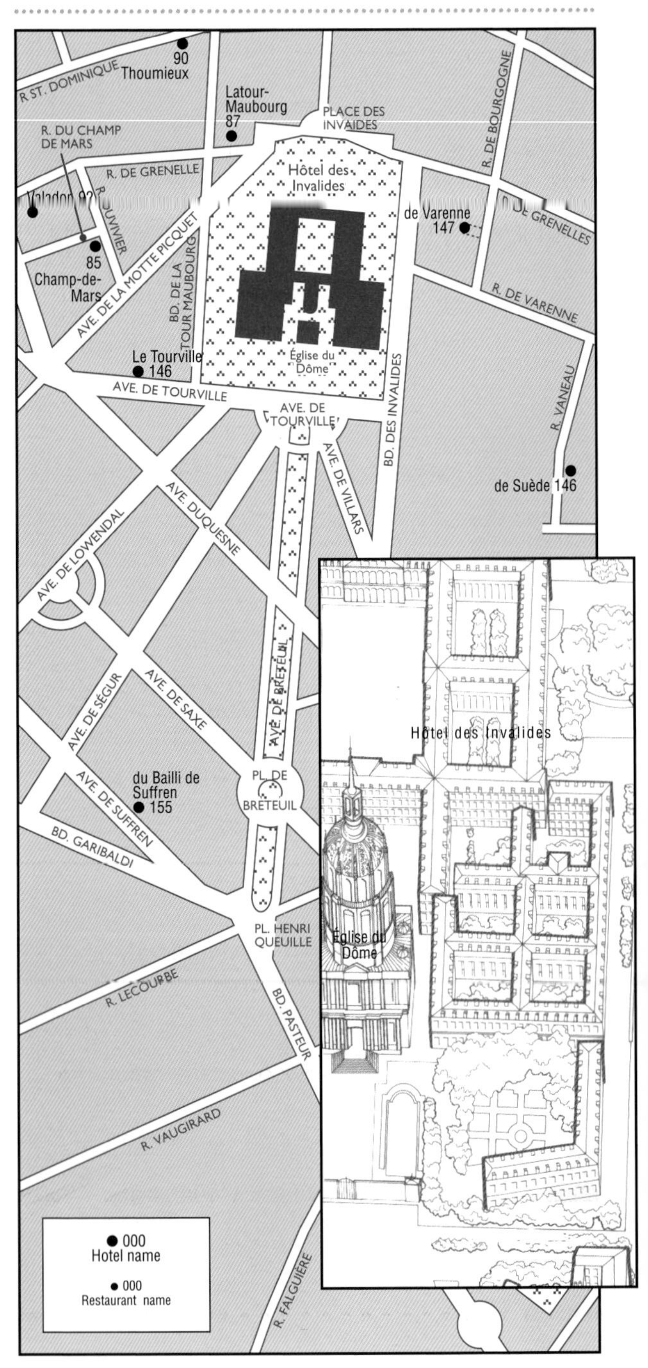

90
Thoumieux
R. ST. DOMINIQUE
Latour-Maubourg
87
PLACE DES INVALIDES
R. DU CHAMP DE MARS
R. DE GRENELLE
Hôtel des Invalides
R. DE BOURGOGNE
de Varenne
147
R. DE GRENELLE
85
Champ-de-Mars
R. DUVIVIER
AVE. DE LA MOTTE PICQUET
BD. DE LA TOUR MAUBOURG
R. DE VARENNE
Église du Dôme
Le Tourville
146
AVE. DE TOURVILLE
AVE. DE TOURVILLE
BD. DES INVALIDES
R. VANEAU
AVE. DE VILLARS
de Suède 146
AVE. DUQUESNE
AVE. DE LOWENDAL
AVE. DE BRETEUIL
Hôtel des Invalides
AVE. DE SÉGUR
AVE. DE SAXE
du Bailli de Suffren
155
AVE. DE SUFFREN
PL. DE BRETEUIL
BD. GARIBALDI
PL. HENRI QUEUILLE
Église du Dôme
R. LECOURBE
BD. PASTEUR
R. VAUGIRARD
000
Hotel name
000
Restaurant name
R. FALGUIÈRE

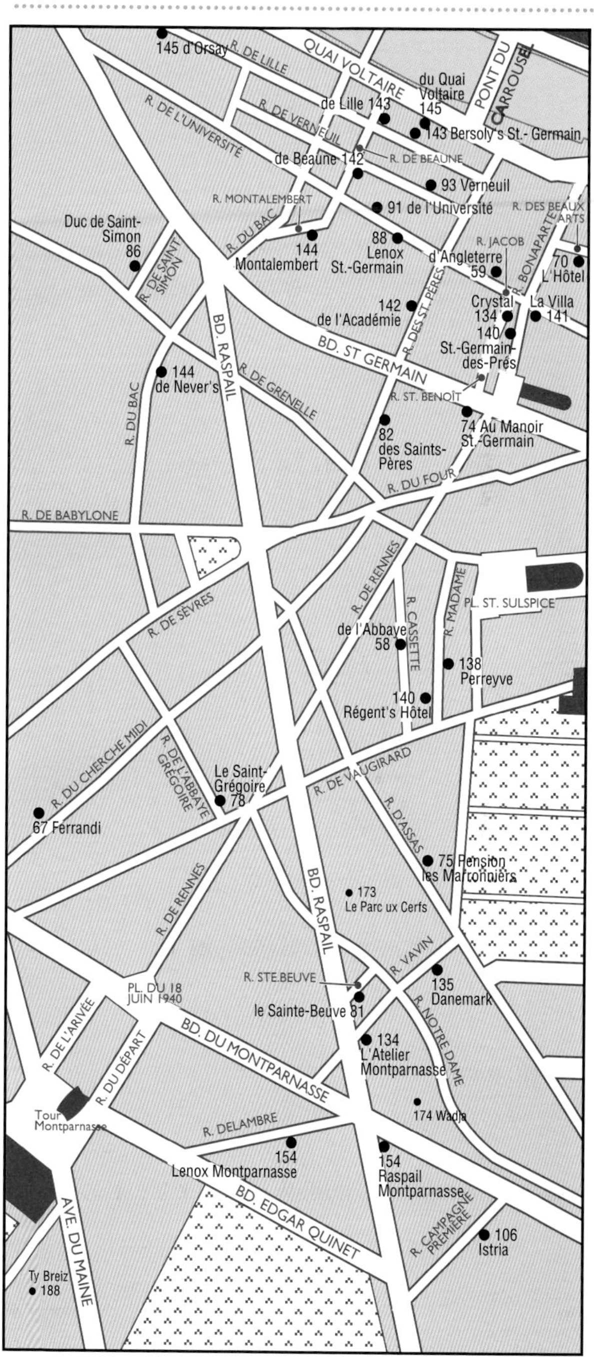
145 d'Orsay
R. DE LILLE
QUAI VOLTAIRE
du Quai Voltaire 145
PONT DU CARROUSEL
de Lille 143
R. DE VERNEUIL
143 Bersoly's St.-Germain
R. DE L'UNIVERSITÉ
de Beaune 142
R. DE BEAUNE
93 Verneuil
R. MONTALEMBERT
91 de l'Université
R. DES BEAUX ARTS
Duc de Saint-Simon 86
R. DU BAC
144 Montalembert
88 Lenox St.-Germain
R. JACOB
d'Angleterre 59
70 L'Hôtel
R. DE SAINT SIMON
R. BONAPARTE
142 de l'Académie
R. DES ST. PÈRES
Crystal 134
La Villa 141
140 St.-Germain-des-Prés
BD. RASPAIL
BD. ST GERMAIN
144 de Never's
R. DE GRENELLE
R. ST. BENOÎT
R. DU BAC
82 des Saints-Pères
74 Au Manoir St.-Germain
R. DU FOUR
R. DE BABYLONE
R. DE RENNES
R. MADAME
PL. ST. SULSPICE
R. CASSETTE
R. DE SÈVRES
de l'Abbaye 58
138 Perreyve
140 Régent's Hôtel
R. DU CHERCHE MIDI
R. DE L'ABBAYE GRÉGOIRE
Le Saint-Grégoire 78
R. DE VAUGIRARD
67 Ferrandi
R. D'ASSAS
75 Pension les Marronniers
BD. RASPAIL
173 Le Parc ux Cerfs
R. DE RENNES
R. VAVIN
135 Danemark
R. STE.BEUVE
PL. DU 18 JUIN 1940
le Sainte-Beuve 81
R. NOTRE DAME
R. DE L'ARIVÉE
BD. DU MONTPARNASSE
134 L'Atelier Montparnasse
R. DU DÉPART
174 Wadja
Tour Montparnasse
R. DELAMBRE
154 Lenox Montparnasse
154 Raspail Montparnasse
BD. EDGAR QUINET
R. CAMPAGNE PREMIÈRE
106 Istria
AVE. DU MAINE
Ty Breiz 188

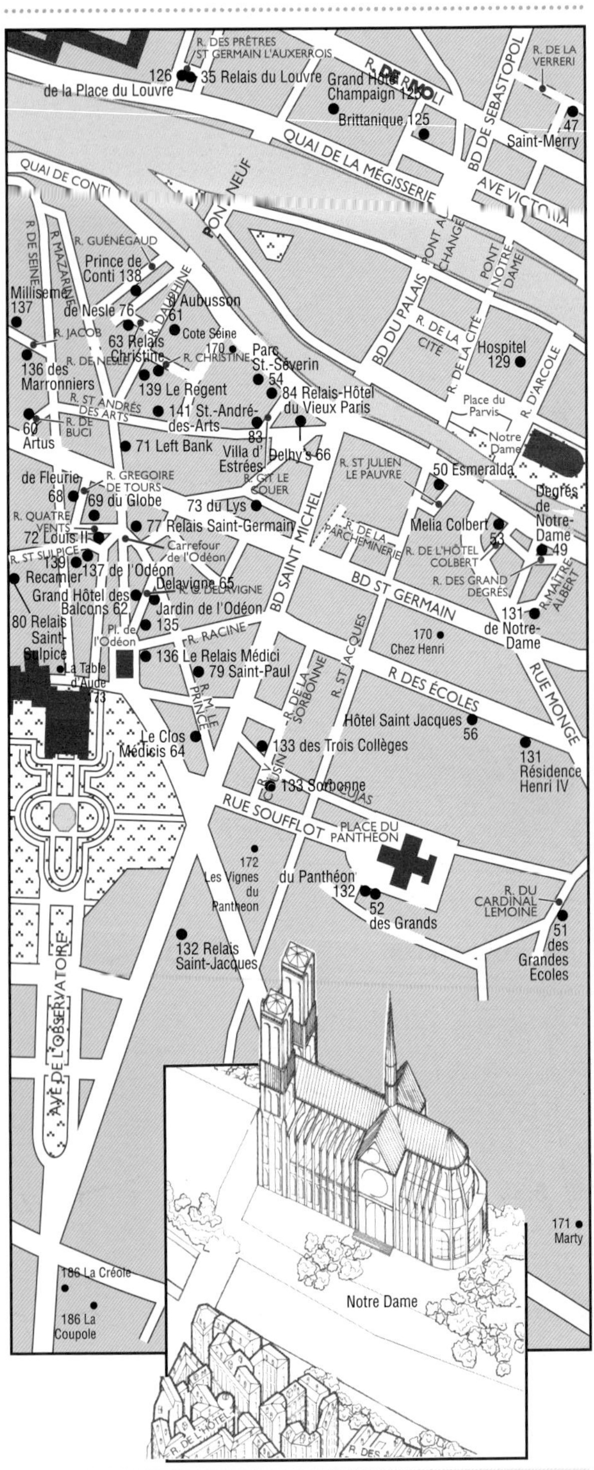

R. DES PRÊTRES ST GERMAIN L'AUXERROIS
126
35 Relais du Louvre
de la Place du Louvre
Grand Hôtel Champaign 125
Brittanique 125
BD DE SEBASTOPOL
R. DE LA VERRERI
47 Saint-Merry
QUAI DE LA MÉGISSERIE
AVE VICTORIA
QUAI DE CONTI
PONT NEUF
R. DE SEINE
R. MAZARINE
R. GUÉNÉGAUD
Prince de Conti 138
Millisieme 137
de Nesle 76
R. DAUPHINE
d'Aubusson 61
Cote Seine
R. JACOB
63 Relais Christine
R. DE NESLE
R. CHRISTINE
170
Parc St.-Séverin 54
136 des Marronniers
139 Le Regent
84 Relais-Hôtel du Vieux Paris
R. ST ANDRÉS DES ARTS
141 St.-André-des-Arts
R. DE BUCI
60 Artus
83
71 Left Bank
Villa d' Estrées
Delhy's 66
R. GIT LE COUER
R. GREGOIRE DE TOURS
de Fleurie 68
69 du Globe
73 du Lys
R. QUATRE VENTS
77 Relais Saint-Germain
72 Louis II
R. ST SULPICE
Carrefour de l'Odéon
139
137 de l'Odéon
Recamier
Delavigne 65
R. C. DELAVIGNE
Grand Hôtel des Balcons 62
Jardin de l'Odéon
80 Relais Saint-Sulpice
Pl. de l'Odéon
135
R. RACINE
136 Le Relais Médici
La Table d'Aude 173
79 Saint-Paul
R. M. LE PRINCE
Le Clos Médicis 64
BD SAINT MICHEL
PONT AU CHANGE
PONT NOTRE DAME
BD DU PALAIS
R. DE LA CITÉ
Hospitel 129
R. D'ARCOLE
Place du Parvis
Notre Dame
R. ST JULIEN LE PAUVRE
50 Esmeralda
Degrés de Notre-Dame
Melia Colbert 53
R. DE LA PARCHEMINERIE
R. DE L'HÔTEL COLBERT
49
R. DES GRAND DEGRÉS
R. MAÎTRE ALBERT
BD ST GERMAIN
170 Chez Henri
131 de Notre-Dame
R. ST JACQUES
R. DE LA SORBONNE
R DES ÉCOLES
RUE MONGE
Hôtel Saint Jacques 56
133 des Trois Collèges
131 Résidence Henri IV
R. V. COUSIN
133 Sorbonne
R. CUJAS
RUE SOUFFLOT
PLACE DU PANTHÉON
172 Les Vignes du Pantheon
du Panthéon 132
52 des Grands
R. DU CARDINAL LEMOINE
51 des Grandes Ecoles
132 Relais Saint-Jacques
AVE DE L'OBSERVATOIRE
171 Marty
186 La Créole
186 La Coupole
Notre Dame
R. DE L'HÔTEL
R. DES

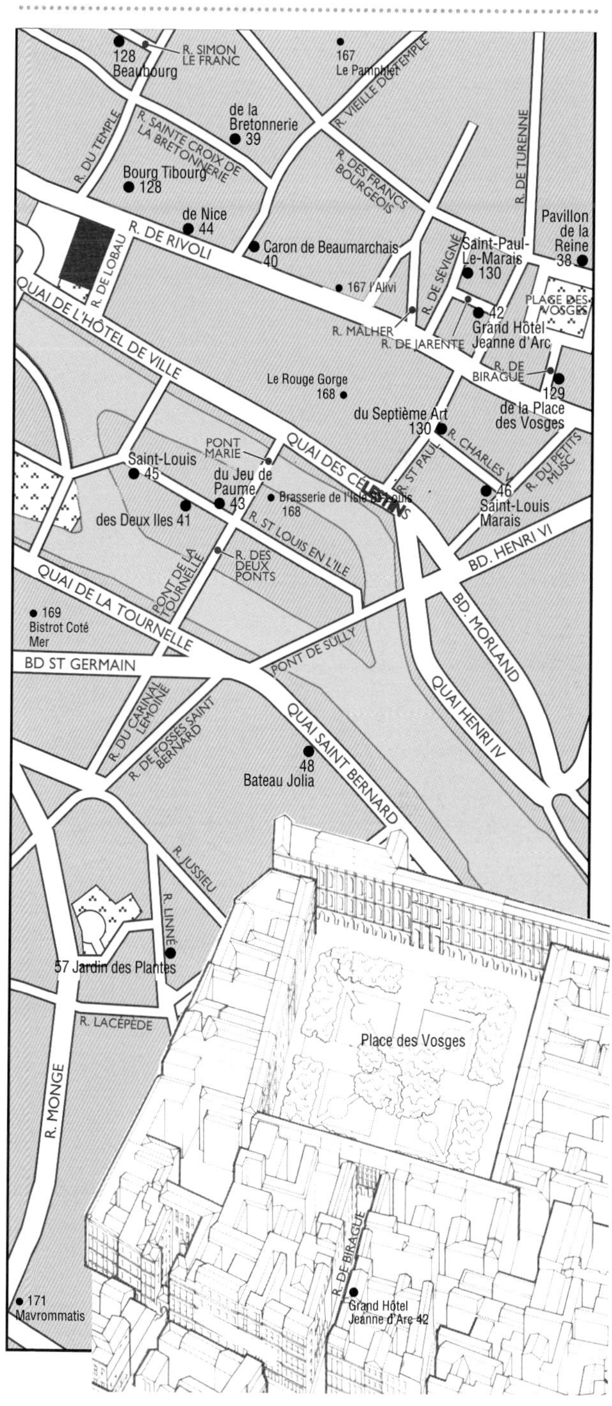

128 Beaubourg
R. SIMON LE FRANC
167 Le Pamphlet
R. VIEILLE DU TEMPLE
de la Bretonnerie 39
R. DU TEMPLE
R. SAINTE CROIX DE LA BRETONNERIE
Bourg Tibourg 128
R. DES FRANCS BOURGEOIS
R. DE TURENNE
de Nice 44
R. DE RIVOLI
Caron de Beaumarchais 40
Pavillon de la Reine 38
Saint-Paul-Le-Marais 130
R. DE LOBAU
167 l'Alivi
R. DE SÉVIGNÉ
PLACE DES VOSGES
42 Grand Hôtel Jeanne d'Arc
R. MALHER
R. DE JARENTE
QUAI DE L'HÔTEL DE VILLE
R. DE BIRAGUE
129 de la Place des Vosges
Le Rouge Gorge 168
du Septième Art 130
PONT MARIE
QUAI DES CÉLESTINS
R. CHARLES V
R. DU PETITS MUSC
R. ST PAUL
Saint-Louis 45
du Jeu de Paume 43
Brasserie de l'Isle St-Louis 168
46 Saint-Louis Marais
des Deux Iles 41
R. ST LOUIS EN L'ILE
BD. HENRI VI
R. DES DEUX PONTS
PONT DE LA TOURNELLE
QUAI DE LA TOURNELLE
169 Bistrot Coté Mer
BD. MORLAND
PONT DE SULLY
BD ST GERMAIN
QUAI HENRI IV
R. DU CARINAL LEMOINE
R. DE FOSSÉS SAINT BERNARD
QUAI SAINT BERNARD
48 Bateau Jolia
R. JUSSIEU
R. LINNÉ
57 Jardin des Plantes
R. LACÉPÈDE
R. MONGE
Place des Vosges
R. DE BIRAGUE
Grand Hôtel Jeanne d'Arc 42
171 Mavrommatis

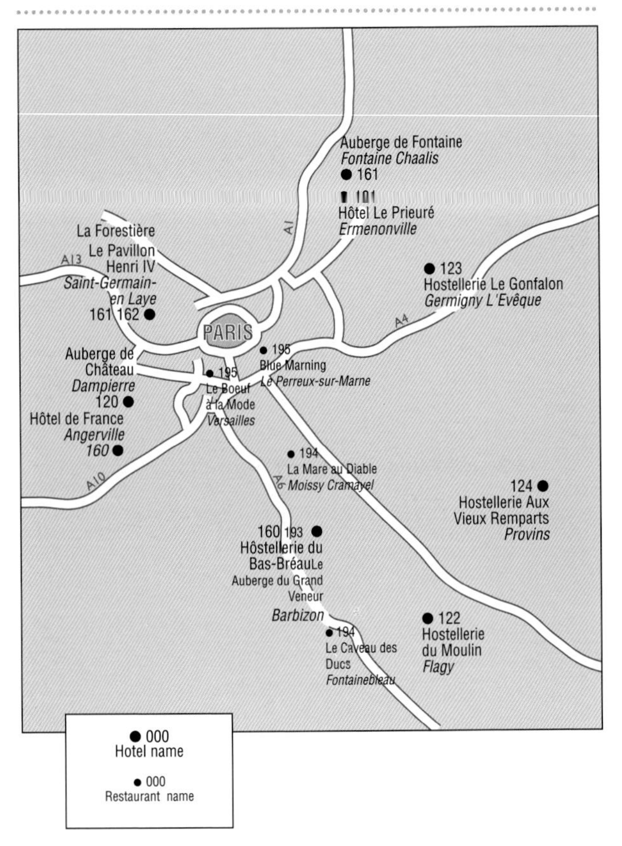

Auberge de Fontaine
Fontaine Chaalis
● 161
Hôtel Le Prieuré
Ermenonville
A1
La Forestière
Le Pavillon
Henri IV
Saint-Germain-
en Laye
161 162 ●
A13
● 123
Hostellerie Le Gonfalon
Germigny L'Evêque
A4
PARIS
● 195
Blue Marning
Le Perreux-sur-Marne
Auberge de
Château
Dampierre
120 ●
● 195
Le Boeuf
à la Mode
Versailles
Hôtel de France
Angerville
160 ●
A10
● 194
La Mare au Diable
Moissy Cramayel
A6
124 ●
Hostellerie Aux
Vieux Remparts
Provins
160 193 ●
Hôstellerie du
Bas-Bréau
Le
Auberge du Grand
Veneur
Barbizon
● 194
Le Caveau des
Ducs
Fontainebleau
● 122
Hostellerie
du Moulin
Flagy
● 000
Hotel name
● 000
Restaurant name

First Arrondissement

Tuileries/Beaubourg Quarter

Le Relais du Louvre

19 rue des Prêtres-Saint-Germain-l'Auxerrois, 75001 Paris
Tel (01) 40 41 96 42 **Fax** (01) 40 41 96 44
E-mail contact@relaisdulouvre.com **Website** www.relaisdulouvre.com

In a quiet side street hard by the Louvre and the river, this sophisticated, flexible little hotel proves that, in the right hands, even the most featureless of bedrooms can be made to feel charming and welcoming. Most are standard box-shape, no more than adequate in size, although some have the benefit of beamed ceilings and floor-length windows. Ours had a terrific view on to the gables and gargoyles of Saint-Germain-l'Auxerrois opposite and, though small, felt extremely welcoming and comforting, with its pink hydrangea curtains and matching bedspread, elegant desk and bedside tables, each with a decent-sized lamp. On the walls were pretty 19thC fashion plates, and the television could be popped away in the upholstered box on which it sat. Breakfast is served in your bedroom. Rooms are cleverly arranged so that a pair can be taken together, closed-off behind a communal front door; two rooms on the ground floor have access to a little patio. There is also a fabulous penthouse suite with fully equipped kitchen. The manageress, Sophie Aulnette, and her close-knit staff pride themselves on trying to accommodate clients in the best way and to help with budgets wherever possible.

Nearby Louvre; Ile de la Cité; Samaritaine store (roof-top view).
Location in quiet side street parallel to Quai du Louvre **Parking** opposite
Metro Pont-Neuf, Louvre-Rivoli
Food breakfast
Price €€
Rooms 19; 11 double and twin, all with bath; 5 single all with shower; 2 junior suites; 1 penthouse suite; all rooms have phone, modem point, TV, minibar, hairdrier, safe **Facilities** sitting area, internet booth
Credit cards AE, DC, MC, V **Children** accepted
Disabled 2 ground floor bedrooms, lift/elevator
Pets accepted **Closed** never
Manager Sophie Aulnette

First Arrondissement

Tuileries Quarter

Mansart

15 rue des Capucines, 75001 Paris
Tel (01) 42 61 50 28 **Fax** (01) 49 27 97 44
E-mail hotel.mansart@wanadoo.fr **Website** www.esprit-de-france.com

A superb location just a stone's throw from the Ritz, spacious bedrooms which recall an earlier, more gracious era, attentive service, fair prices – these were the principal reasons that we were first attracted to the Mansart, part of the Esprit de France group of hotels that also owns the d'Orsay (page 145) and the Saints-Pères (page 81). Unfortunately, a recent visit made us query our earlier high praise. The large modern lobby, with its marble floor and its walls boldly painted in geometric patterns based on Mansart's drawing for the gardens of Versailles (he was also the architect of place Vendôme) had somehow lost its sheen, and some of the bedrooms seemed tired, with signs of scuffed paint. Their dignified, old fashioned flavour continues to appeal, however, and we still enthused over No. 205, which feels like a private apartment, with its own entrance hall opening on to a large room with antique mirrors and regal prints on the white walls, the panelling picked out in gold. A cheaper option, though equally stately, is No. 212, a huge room with large gilt-framed mirrors and panelled walls – good value, we think, considering the size, and the hotel's location on the corner of place Vendôme.

Nearby place Vendôme; Opéra Garnier; Tuileries.
Location corner of place Vendôme **Parking** place Vendôme **Metro** Opéra, Madeleine
Food breakfast
Price €€€
Rooms 57; 53 double and twin, 50 with bath, 3 with shower; 4 single, all with bath; all rooms have phone, modem point,TV, minibar, hairdrier, safe
Facilities breakfast room, sitting area, internet booth
Credit cards AE, DC, MC, V
Children accepted
Disabled no special facilities
Pets not accepted **Closed** never
Manager M. Dupaen

First Arrondissement

Tuileries Quarter

Tuileries

10 rue Saint-Hyacinthe, 75001 Paris
Tel (01) 42 61 04 17 **Fax** (01) 49 27 91 56
E-mail hotel-des-tuileries@wanadoo.fr **Website** www.hotel-des-tuileries.com

This attractive 18thC mansion with Revolutionary associations offers the pleasant combination of a quiet but convenient setting, comfortable accommodation and – perhaps most important in a town where you can't count on it – a genuinely warm welcome. These privileges come at a price however, and our recent visits have made us feel that guests were paying somewhat over the odds for rooms.

Having said that, the hotel is very well placed both for sightseeing and shopping – close to beautiful place Vendôme and the exclusive shops of rue Faubourg Saint-Honoré. It has two small *salons*, recently redecorated, with velvet seats, paintings and tapestries on plain walls and Persian rugs on marble floors, with the addition of a small bar. There is a small breakfast room in the basement, and the cellar has been converted into a meeting room for up to 12 people. Bedrooms are individually decorated, often with a bold mix of styles and colours, which almost always comes off. One has a sky-and-clouds theme, another is in Japanese style, another has a four-poster bed and yellow drapes; antique, reproduction and modern furniture is successfully combined.

Nearby Tuileries; rue de Rivoli; Louvre; place de la Concorde.
Location just N of rue Saint-Honoré **Parking** place du Marché Saint-Honoré
Metro Tuileries, Pyramides
Food breakfast
Price €€€
Rooms 26, all double and twin, all with bath; all rooms have phone, modem point, TV, air-conditioning, minibar, trouser-press, hairdrier, safe
Facilities sitting room, bar, breakfast room, internet booth
Credit cards AE, DC, MC, V
Children accepted **Disabled** lift/elevator
Pets accepted **Closed** never
Proprietors Poulle-Vidal family

THIRD ARRONDISSEMENT

MARAIS

PAVILLON DE LA REINE

28 place des Vosges, 75003 Paris
TEL (01) 40 29 19 19 **FAX** (01) 40 29 19 20
E-MAIL contact@pavillon-de-la-reine.com **WEBSITE** www.pavillon-de-la-reine.com

SET BACK FROM the gloriously harmonious place des Vosges, approached through a calming courtyard garden, the Pavillon de la Reine has our vote for the most perfect location in Paris. Like its sister hotels, the Relais Christine (see page 63) and Saint James (see page 113), it is run with calm professionalism by a dedicated and friendly team, although, like them, perhaps it lacks the intimacy of a truly charming small hotel.

The fine 17thC mansion was once the residence of Anne of Austria, wife of Louis XIII. Rescued from near ruin, it now feels more like a baronial country house, with an impressive entrance hall and handsome deep red sitting room with furniture upholstered in smart stripes, an honesty bar and a huge stone fireplace complete with roaring log fire. There are two flowery courtyards and a stone-vaulted breakfast room, where a delicious, healthy buffet, including exotic fruits and freshly squeezed juice, is served each morning. Upstairs, via a wood-panelled lift, the smart, suitably luxurious bedrooms are all different, ranging from feminine *toile de jouy* to designer-decorated duplex suites in a Baroque riot of purple velvet and mauve silk. Whatever their outlook, they are all blissfully quiet.

NEARBY Musée Carnavalet; Musée Picasso; Ile Saint-Louis.
LOCATION entrance from N side of place des Vosges **PARKING** free private garage
METRO Saint-Paul
FOOD breakfast; room service
PRICE €€€€
ROOMS 55, all double and twin, including standard, deluxe and junior suites; all with bath; all rooms have phone, modem point, TV, air-conditioning, minibar, hairdrier
FACILITIES sitting room, breakfast room, internet booth, 2 courtyard gardens
CREDIT CARDS AE, DC, MC, V
CHILDREN accepted **DISABLED** ground floor bedrooms, lift/elevator **PETS** accepted
CLOSED never
MANAGER Véronique Ellinger

FOURTH ARRONDISSEMENT

MARAIS

HOTEL DE LA BRETONNERIE

22 rue Sainte-Croix-de-la-Bretonnerie, 75004 Paris
TEL (01) 48 87 77 63 **FAX** (01) 42 77 26 78
E-MAIL hotel@bretonnerie.com **WEBSITE** www.bretonnerie.com

A DISTINCTIVE 17THC townhouse, converted with sympathy, which, though conveniently placed in the middle of the picturesque and_fashionable Marais district, is – as a recent inspector points out – 'in a rather scruffy street', a little too close to the rowdy atmosphere of the Pompidou Centre. Fortunately, she continues, 'once in the hotel, all is calm and peaceful'.

The exposed beams in the public areas and the upper bedrooms are echoed throughout the house by the sturdy hardwood furniture. The small basement breakfast and sitting rooms attempt a Medieval flavour (which doesn't quite come off), with stone-vaulted ceilings, iron light fittings, richly coloured fabrics and polished tiled floors. Considering the apparent size of the hotel, the bedrooms are surprisingly roomy, also comfortable and pretty, and every one is different; some are arranged with the beds on a mezzanine gallery with the 'downstairs' used as a small sitting area. All have a glossy modern bathroom and guests will find no lack of comfort. Good-humoured staff extend a warm welcome, and cope admirably with such crises as the sudden arrival of all their guests at the same time.

NEARBY Hôtel de Ville; Pompidou Centre; Les Halles.
LOCATION between rue des Archives and rue Vieille du Temple **PARKING** Hôtel de Ville (rue de Lobau) **METRO** Saint-Paul/Hôtel de Ville/Rambuteau **RER** Châtelet-Les Halles
FOOD breakfast
PRICE €€
ROOMS 30; 27 double and twin, 3 suites, all with bath; all rooms have phone, TV, minibar, hairdrier, safe; some rooms have modem points
FACILITIES sitting area, breakfast room
CREDIT CARDS MC, V
CHILDREN accepted
DISABLED lift/elevator
PETS not accepted **CLOSED** never
MANAGER Valérie Sagot

FOURTH ARRONDISSEMENT

MARAIS

HOTEL CARON DE BEAUMARCHAIS

12 rue Vieille-du-Temple, 75004 Paris
TEL (01) 42 72 34 12 **FAX** (01) 42 72 34 63
E-MAIL hotel@carondebeaumarchais.com **WEBSITE** www.carondebeaumarchais.com

THE FRONTAGE CONSISTS of huge plate glass windows surrounded by electric blue paintwork, with the hotel's name emblazoned across the top. A glance inside reveals a square reception salon decorated in pretty pink and blue wallpaper with dainty period-style furniture, soft lighting and a huge flower arrangement. As we walked in, we had the fleeting impression that we were entering an upmarket *parfumerie*. The decoration might be a touch too chi-chi for our taste, but once inside, it is impossible not to be caught up in the warmth of this hotel and the staff who run it. Messieurs Bigeard *père et fils* genuinely want their guests to be contented and go to great lengths to ensure that they are.

The hotel's theme is the 18th century – colour schemes are based on the period and fabrics, taken from original designs – but more particularly Beaumarchais (he lived further down the street); there are framed pages from antique editions of the author's most famous work, *Marriage of Figaro*, in each of the small but pretty bedrooms. These have upholstered chairs, chandeliers and some pretty antiques, bought recently by the owners, which complement the 18thC style; some have walk-out balconies. Hand-painted tiles enliven the neat white bathrooms.

NEARBY Musée Carnavalet; place des Vosges; Notre-Dame.
LOCATION close to the rue de Rivoli **PARKING** Hôtel de Ville (rue de Lobau) **METRO** Hôtel de Ville/Saint-Paul
FOOD breakfast, brunch
PRICE €€
ROOMS 19 double and twin, 17 with bath, 2 with shower; all rooms have phone, modem point, TV, air conditioning, minibar, hairdrier
FACILITIES sitting area, breakfast room **CREDIT CARDS** AE, DC, MC, V
CHILDREN accepted **DISABLED** access difficult, lift/elevator
PETS accepted **CLOSED** never
PROPRIETORS Etienne and Alain Bigeard

FOURTH ARRONDISSEMENT

ILE SAINT-LOUIS

HOTEL DES DEUX ILES

59 rue Saint-Louis-en-l'Ile, 75004 Paris
TEL (01) 43 26 13 35 **FAX** (01)43 29 60 25
E-MAIL hotel.2iles@free.fr **WEBSITE** www.hotel-ile-saintlouis.com

IN ITS THIRD DECADE as an archetypal charming small hotel, Roland Buffat's well-known converted townhouse has had mixed reports from our readers recently. A couple of guests reported a rather 'uncaring' atmosphere during their stay; others complained of a minuscule room, although another was entirely satisfied.

Certainly first impressions are favourable. The inviting sofa and armchairs in the warm and welcoming sitting area have been attractively recovered in a striking red fabric with a yellow geometric design, although the acres of hessian which cover the walls remain a somewhat dated reminder of the hotel's 1970s origins. The plant-filled, glassed-in courtyard, which makes such a feature in the lobby, looks stunning, and there is another cosy sitting area in the cellar. Upstairs, the bedrooms are simple, very small and disappointingly bland. Bathrooms are given lift from boldly patterned ceramic tiles hand-painted in blue. (If you have seen as many Paris hotel bathrooms as we have, you will know that it's a positive thrill to see one that isn't uniformly clad in marble or white.) Overall, the effect of the Deux Iles is one of warmth, with very comfortable public rooms. Rolant Buffat also owns the Lutèce at 65 rue Saint-Louis-en-Ile, the Galiléo (page 98), and has recently opened the Henri IV at 9-11 rue Saint-Jacques.

NEARBY Les Halles; Hôtel de Ville; Notre-Dame.
LOCATION in Ile Saint-Louis' main street, between Pont Saint-Louis and rue des Deux Ponts **PARKING** Pont-Marie **METRO** Pont-Marie
FOOD breakfast
PRICE €€
ROOMS 17; 12 double and twin, 8 with bath, 4 with shower; 5 single, all with shower; all rooms have phone, modem point, TV, air-conditioning, hairdrier
FACILITIES 2 sitting rooms, breakfast room, internet booth, courtyard
CREDIT CARDS AE, MC, V **CHILDREN** accepted **DISABLED** access difficult, lift/elevator
PETS accepted **CLOSED** never **PROPRIETOR** Roland Buffat

FOURTH ARRONDISSEMENT

MARAIS

GRAND HOTEL JEANNE D'ARC

3 rue de Jarente, 75004 Paris
TEL (01) 48 87 62 11 **FAX** (01)48 87 37 31
E-MAIL information@hoteljeannedarc.com **WEBSITE** www.hoteljeannedarc.com

IN CONTRADICTION TO its name, this is a modest two-star hotel, fiercely popular with Americans, attracted by the 17thC building and unbeatable prices for this appealing area. Downstairs the decoration tends to be eclectic: witness the extraordinary 'fantasy' tiled mirror, which assaults you visually as you enter. Commissioned to embody the Joan of Arc theme, the frame is made of mosaic tiles and emblazoned with zinc *fleur de lys*, flags, coloured glass studs and an army of flashing candle lights. The breakfast room has wooden tables and chairs and sponged walls in a peachy colour with a frieze of painted trees. Clouds and stars are incorporated into the scheme of the tiny back sitting room.

Decoration in the simple, spotless bedrooms is fresh and less ambitious, though the furniture is uninspired. The best are the attic rooms, which have terrific views over the Marais. Bathrooms are generally spacious, some with startling blue splash effect tiles.

Most reports are complimentary, praising the excellent prices and great location in particular, although our inspector encountered one of the city's unfriendliest receptionists here; hopefully her manner improves when she's not busy. The hotel has a no-smoking policy.

NEARBY place des Vosges; Musée Carnavalet; Musée Picasso.
LOCATION N of rue de Rivoli, off rue de Sévigné **PARKING** rue Saint-Antoine **METRO** Saint-Paul/Bastille
FOOD breakfast
PRICE €
ROOMS 36; 24 double and twin, 12 family, all with bath or shower; all rooms have phone, TV **FACILITIES** sitting room, breakfast room
CREDIT CARDS MC, V
CHILDREN accepted **DISABLED** some rooms on ground floor, lift/elevator
PETS accepted **CLOSED** never
PROPRIETOR Mme Mesenge

FOURTH ARRONDISSEMENT

ILE SAINT-LOUIS

HOTEL DU JEU DE PAUME

54 rue Saint-Louis-en-l'Ile, 75004 Paris
TEL (01) 43 26 14 18 **FAX** (01)40 46 02 76
E-MAIL info@jeudepaumehotel.com **WEBSITE** www.jeudepaumehotel.com

WE FEATURE NO LESS than four hotels in the delightful rue Saint-Louis-en-l'Ile; but whereas the others are homely, this one is highly original and packs a stylish punch.

As its name implies, the building was the site of a 17thC *jeu de paume* court, built in the days when the 'palm game', forerunner to tennis, was all the rage; when the proprietors acquired it in the 1980s, however, it was a run-down warehouse. Monsieur Prache is an architect and he wrought something of a miracle on the building, opening out the heart of it, right up to the roof, exposing all the old timber construction and slinging mezzanine floors around a central well. The impression of light and transparency is reinforced by a glass-walled lift and glass balustrades around the upper floors. Stone walls and all those beams add a reasurringly rustic feel. The sitting area has the appearance of a sophisticated private apartment, with leather sofas, subtle lighting and a handsome stone fireplace. Nearby, at the reception desk, the chic, yet charming staff deal with the guests while a modish golden retriever pads around. Bedrooms are smallish, perfectly pleasant, but nothing like as exciting as the rest of the hotel.

NEARBY Marais; Notre-Dame; Latin Quarter.
LOCATION halfway along the island's main street, near the junction with rue des Deux Ponts **PARKING** Pont-Marie **METRO** Pont-Marie/Cité
FOOD breakfast
PRICE €€€
ROOMS 32 double, twin, suites and duplexes, all with bath; all rooms have phone, modem point, TV, minibar, hairdrier **FACILITIES** breakfast room, sitting room, bar, 2 conference rooms, sauna, internet booth, courtyard garden
CREDIT CARDS AE, DC, MC, V
CHILDREN accepted **DISABLED** access difficult, lift/elevator
PETS accepted **CLOSED** never
PROPRIETORS M. and Mme Prache

FOURTH ARRONDISSEMENT

MARAIS

HOTEL DE NICE

42 bis rue de Rivoli, 75004 Paris
TEL (01) 42 78 55 29 **FAX** (01) 42 78 36 07

HERE IS A WONDERFULLY wacky two star, every bit as comfortable and twice as enjoyable as many a more expensive three star. We thought it a terrific find, intrigued and not disappointed by what lay behind the vivid turquoise door and up the winding stairs.

The Nice is the enchanting creation of a previously high-flying professional couple who love both collecting and entertaining, although they have now passed on the running of the hotel to their daughter. The fruits of their hobby are everywhere – masses of period engravings and prints – particularly of Paris – mirrors, old doors, postcards, even a splendid portrait of Lady Diana Cooper. The effect is charming and highly individual – the panelled *salon*, for example, is a harmony of uncoordinated colours, fabrics and furniture: antique, painted, modern, garden. The use of wallpaper copied from French 18thC designs makes the compact bedrooms feel fresh and pretty, with the off-beat addition of Indian cotton bedspreads, and doors and skirtings boldly painted in turquoise, orange or pillar-box red. Two attic rooms on the top floor are particularly charming, with their own little balconies. Others look out on to a pretty square. You'll find only basic amenities here but plenty of character and youthful appeal.

NEARBY Musée Carnavalet; place des Vosges; Notre-Dame.
LOCATION near rue Vieille du Temple, on corner of rue de Rivoli and rue du Bourg Tibourg **PARKING** Hôtel de Ville (rue de Lobau) **METRO** Hôtel de Ville/Saint-Paul **RER** Châtelet-Les Halles
FOOD breakfast
PRICE €
ROOMS 23; 17 double and twin, one family, all with bath or shower; all rooms have phone, TV, hairdrier **FACILITIES** sitting/breakfast room
CREDIT CARDS MC, V **CHILDREN** accepted
DISABLED lift/elevator **PETS** accepted **CLOSED** never
PROPRIETORS M. and Mme Vaudoux

Fourth Arrondissement

Ile Saint-Louis

Hotel Saint-Louis

75 rue Saint-Louis-en-l'Ile, 75004 Paris
Tel (01) 46 34 04 80 **Fax** (01)46 34 02 13
E-mail slouis@cybercable.fr **Website** www.hotelsaintlouis.com

Ever since its development in the 17th century, Ile Saint-Louis has been one of the most sought-after residential areas in Paris; today it is both chic and picturesque and makes an ideal base for a stay, a peaceful backwater in the heart of the city. Hotels here naturally reflect the superior location in their prices, so if you can't resist, but need to watch the euros, the Saint-Louis makes the best choice, although we have had mixed reports from readers. Peering in from the street, the interior looks welcoming, cosy and dignified, with a small but comfortable sitting area; downstairs there is a more than usually attractive stone-vaulted breakfast room, complete with carved wall fountain and tables laid with pink cloths, flowers and pretty china. Renovation work in 1998 gave the Saint-Louis a fresher look, though bedrooms are still best described as dinky with chintz drapes and cane furniture.

The Saint-Louis has a long list of faithful clients, lured by the great location, unchanging standards and warm simplicity of the place. It is sad to note that the friendly 'hands-on' proprietors have bowed to pressure and revoked their 'no television' policy which used to reinforce the hotel's old-fashioned charm. More reports please.

Nearby Marais; Notre-Dame; Latin Quarter.
Location in Ile Saint-Louis' main street, near the Pont Saint-Louis end **Parking** Pont-Marie **Metro** Pont-Marie/Cité
Food breakfast
Price €€
Rooms 21 double and twin, 15 with bath, 6 with shower; all rooms have phone, modem point, TV, hairdrier, safe **Facilities** sitting area, breakfast room
Credit cards DC, MC, V
Children accepted **Disabled** 2 rooms on ground floor, lift/elevator
Pets accepted **Closed** never
Proprietors Andrée and Guy Record

Fourth Arrondissment

Marais

Hotel Saint-Louis Marais

1 rue Charles V, 75004 Paris
Tel (01) 48 87 87 04 **Fax** (01) 48 87 33 26
E-mail slmarais@noos.fr **Website** www.saintlouismarais.com

This attractive two-star in the heart of the Marais used to be a simple hotel with basic rooms and facilities and a cosy rustic feel. Long-time owners Andrée and Guy Record sold the hotel three years ago, having completed extensive work to upgrade it, and our latest inspection revealed a hotel with a rather different style. We felt it was no coincidence that we were greeted by a thrusting young man, full of ideas for change, who talked of little but websites. To our mind, not all the changes are for the better, for example the arrival of a hideous drinks dispenser in the reception area, which has otherwise been smartened up with Louis XIII-style furniture. The exposed beams, rough-stone walls and terracotta floor still lend a country flavour, which, glimpsed from the street through the glazed front door, looks inviting.

Another addition is the appealing stone-vaulted cellar breakfast room. But the most marked changes are in the bedrooms, redecorated in subtle colours or smart stripes, with antique furniture and muted fabrics; tapestry features strongly in wallhangings and upholstered chairs. They also have new sparkling white bathrooms.

Nearby place des Vosges; Musée Carnavalet; Ile Saint-Louis.
Location between rue du Petit Musc and rue Beautreillis, S of rue Saint-Antoine
Parking rue Saint-Antoine **Metro** Bastille/Sully Morland
Food breakfast
Price €€
Rooms 16 double and twin, all with bath or shower; all rooms have phone, modem point, TV, hairdrier, safe
Facilities sitting room, breakfast room, internet booth
Credit cards MC, V
Children accepted **Disabled** one room on ground floor
Pets accepted **Closed** never
Proprietor M. Le Guennec

FOURTH ARRONDISSMENT

LES HALLES

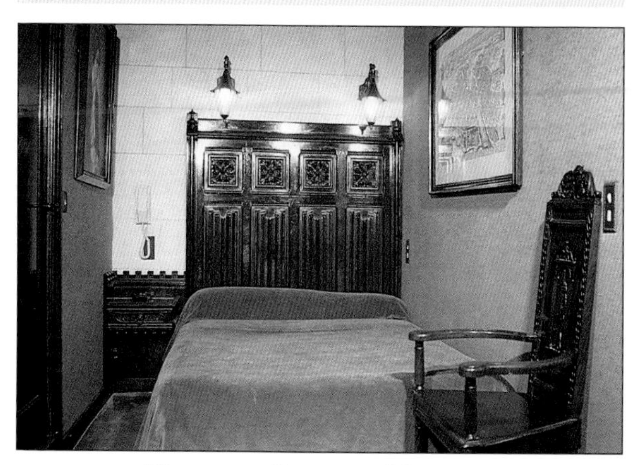

HOTEL SAINT-MERRY

78 rue de la Verrerie, 75004 Paris
TEL (01) 42 78 14 15 **FAX** (01) 40 29 06 82
E-MAIL hotelstmerry@wanadoo.fr **WEBSITE** www.hotelmarais.com

RECENTLY WE HAVE received conflicting reports of this distinctive small hotel. Some readers love its church-like, medieval atmosphere: its heavily beamed ceilings, pale stone walls, wrought-iron fittings and splendid carved wood neo-Gothic furnishings, and will not contemplate staying anywhere else. Others have complained of claustrophobically small bedrooms and low standards of housekeeping. There are no public rooms to speak of, and breakfast, which is brought to your room, is prepared in a tiny galley behind the reception; a spiralling staircase is the only means by which you can reach your room. The hotel was sold recently, and we would welcome more reports of it under the new management.

This former presbytery of the adjacent church of Saint-Merri became a private residence after the 1789 revolution, and served for a time as a brothel before it was rescued from decay by its former proprietor, Christian Crabbe, in the 1960s. He decided on its memorable – if sombre – style after acquiring some neo-Gothic furnishings which were languishing in the basement of the church. The hotel is famous for No. 9, where flying buttresses form a low canopy over the bed, while Nos. 12 and 17 have remarkable bedheads. There is also a charming suite under the eaves.

NEARBY Pompidou Centre; Hôtel de Ville; Marais; Notre-Dame.
LOCATION in pedestrianized zone, on the corner of rue de la Verrerie and rue Saint-Martin **PARKING** Hôtel de Ville (rue de Lobau) **METRO** Hôtel de Ville/Rambuteau **RER** Châtelet-Les Halles
FOOD breakfast
PRICE €
ROOMS 12; 11 double and twin, one suite, all with bath or shower; all rooms have phone, hairdrier **FACILITIES** small sitting area
CREDIT CARDS AE, MC, V **CHILDREN** accepted
DISABLED not suitable **PETS** accepted
CLOSED never **PROPRIETOR** Pierre Juin

Fifth Arrondissement

Latin Quarter

Bateau Jolia

face au 11 quai Saint-Bernard, 75005 Paris
Tel (01) 43 54 03 46 **Fax** (01) 43 29 79 15
E-mail ItsHip@la-vie-en-rose.com **Website** www.la-vie-en-rose.com

From the moment we discovered it four years ago, we couldn't resist including Bateau Jolia in the guide. It's a charming small hotel with a difference – a barge for two on the Seine. Moored in a prime spot for exploring the Iles and Latin Quarter, it's run by American couple, David and Laura Ann Novick. They bought the barge in 1997, and made their home in the bows. Their guests have the use of a beautifully designed saloon, a luxurious marble bathroom and – down a steep ladder, so not for the elderly or infirm – the stern cabin, panelled in pale wood and containing, according to our reporter, one of the most comfortable beds in Paris. "I loved being rocked to sleep by the river," she says.

Laura's passion for antiques is evident everywhere in the art deco furniture, lights and mirrors. It isn't cheap (1,950 dollars for three days), but drinks, snacks, cooked breakfast, museum passes, metro tickets and even long-distance phone calls are all thrown in. David prides himself on his gourmet breakfasts. He'll cook whatever you fancy – eggs, blinis, Toulouse sausage. David and Laura aim to give their guests "what we'd have liked when we came to Paris for a special weekend". And they deliver.

Nearby Ile Saint-Louis; Ile de la Cité; boulevard Saint-Germain.
Location moored just to the E of Pont de la Tournelle, below Quai de la Tournelle
Parking free parking on quai **Metro** Maubert Mutualité
Food breakfast, meals by arrangement
Price €€€€ 3-day minimum
Rooms one double room with bath, phone, modem point, TV, video, CD player, minibar, tea/coffee kit, hairdrier, safe
Facilities sitting room, sundeck
Credit cards not accepted
Children not accepted **Disabled** not suitable
Pets not accepted **Closed** never
Proprietors David and Laura Ann Novick

FIFTH ARRONDISSEMENT

LATIN QUARTER

HOTEL DEGRES DE NOTRE-DAME

10 rue des Grands Degrés, 75005 Paris
TEL (01) 55 42 88 88 **FAX** (01) 40 46 95 34

ALMOST ALL THE small hotels of Paris are without a dining room. Here, however, is an exception – the kind of family-run establishment well-known in the French countryside, but rarely found in the city: a restaurant with rooms. The building is charmingly sited on a little tree-filled square, and the restaurant has the feel of a simple *auberge*, serving correspondingly rustic food, nothing special, but honest and reasonably priced. This is where guests also take breakfast (served at any time), which features the freshest of bread, orange juice squeezed on the spot, and good coffee. A steep wooden staircase (staff carry your bags), decorated with charming murals, leads to the bedrooms, which are good value, well-equipped and distinctively decorated, with beamed ceilings, smart wooden furnishings and walls crammed with paintings, reflecting M. Tahir's passion for art. Some rooms have views over Notre-Dame; a few are tiny (it's worth paying 15-euros extra for a slightly bigger room); the ones at the front are the largest, most with triple windows on to the street; No. 24 is handsome, with an expansive desk in the centre; and the huge attic room has been totally revamped with its own little kitchen area. M. Tahir has also recently acquired and tastefully renovated a simple, but spacious studio apartment in the building next door.

NEARBY Notre-Dame; Musée de Cluny; Ile Saint-Louis.
LOCATION on tiny square at junction with rue Fréderic-Sauton, close to quai de Montebello **PARKING** place Maubert **METRO** Saint-Michel **RER** Saint-Michel
FOOD breakfast, lunch, dinner
PRICE €€
ROOMS 10 double, all with bath; all rooms have phone, modem point, TV, hairdrier; some rooms have minibar; 2 studio apartments **FACILITIES** restaurant, bar **CREDIT CARDS** MC, V **CHILDREN** accepted
DISABLED not suitable **PETS** accepted
CLOSED never **PROPRIETOR** M. Tahir

FIFTH ARRONDISSEMENT

LATIN QUARTER

HOTEL ESMERALDA

4 rue Saint-Julien-le-Pauvre, 75005 Paris
TEL (01) 43 54 19 20 **FAX** (01) 40 51 00 68

A HOTEL OF GREAT character, loved by legions of faithful guests as much for its charmingly eccentric owner as for its genuine Left Bank atmosphere and superb position. Sadly, its gentle decline started some years ago: witness the star, crudely whitewashed out on the tourist board plaque outside the hotel, testament to its demotion from a two- to a one-star establishment. Although a recent inspection revealed that little had changed, the hotel was still full to bursting and we witnessed prospective guests being turned away. (You really need to book several months ahead during busy periods.) So in this edition of our guide, we have decided to promote the Esmeralda to a long entry. The rooms, with their old beams, stone walls, undulating quarry tile or carpet floors and carefree assortment of furniture and fabrics, might be shabby, creaky, not spotlessly clean, and hard to recommend to newcomers, but they are also brimming with character, romantic and cheap. The best have views of Notre-Dame.

Don't even contemplate booking a room here if you're looking for deep comfort and mod cons; the Esmeralda is for devotees, prepared to turn a blind eye to the Quasimodo touches, time-worn decoration and antediluvian plumbing.

NEARBY Notre-Dame; Sainte-Chapelle; Musée de Cluny; Ile Saint-Louis.
LOCATION in side street off quai de Montebello, opposite a little public garden
PARKING place Maubert **METRO** Saint-Michel **RER** Saint-Michel
FOOD breakfast
PRICE €
ROOMS 20 double and twin, with bath, shower or washbasin; all rooms have phone
FACILITIES breakfast room, sitting area
CREDIT CARDS not accepted **CHILDREN** accepted
DISABLED not suitable **PETS** accepted
CLOSED never
PROPRIETOR Mme Bruel

Fifth Arrondissement

Latin Quarter

Hotel des Grandes Ecoles

75 rue du Cardinal Lemoine, 75005 Paris
Tel (01) 43 26 79 23 **Fax** (01) 43 25 28 15
E-mail Hotel.Grandes.Ecoles@wanadoo.fr **Website** www.hotel-grandes-ecoles.com

Tucked away in a peaceful corner off rue du Cardinal Lemoine and within spitting distance of the Sorbonne, to which its name refers, this hotel is a real find. Its pale pink, shuttered exterior and setting in a lovely courtyard garden lend it the ambience of a country villa. The homely interior is entirely in keeping: a polished wood floor extends from the reception area through to a large breakfast-room, and there is an abundance of mellow wood furniture, rush-seated chairs and lace-covered tables. There are a couple of drawbacks: it has no sitting room; and the modestly furnished bedrooms in the main building have rather immodestly thin walls. Most are decorated with faded flowery fabrics, lace bedspreads and tablecloths. The place exudes old-fashioned charm.

The recent renovation of a second building has given the hotel a further 15 large, bright bedrooms, done out in attractive *toile de jouy* style with fresh-looking bathrooms.

The owner, Madame Le Foch, also runs the hotel, and though she does not speak English, is cheerful and welcoming. A hotel whose simplicity and prices match its two stars, but which has the quiet good taste that few luxury hotels achieve.

Nearby Panthéon; Sorbonne; Musée de Cluny.
Location between rue Monge and rue Rollin, S of rue Clovis **Parking** rue Soufflot
Metro Cardinal Lemoine/Place Monge
Food breakfast; room service
Price €€
Rooms 51; 45 double and twin, 6 family, all with bath or shower; all rooms have phone, hairdrier **Facilities** breakfast room, garden
Credit cards MC, V **Children** accepted
Disabled 2 specially equipped rooms, lift/elevator
Pets accepted **Closed** never
Proprietor Mme Le Foch

Fifth Arrondissement

Latin Quarter

Hotel des Grands Hommes

17 place du Panthéon, 75005 Paris
Tel (01) 46 34 19 60 **Fax** (01) 43 26 67 32
E-mail reservation @hoteldesgrandshommes.com **Website** www.heartdesgrandshommes.com

It's worth putting up with some street noise to have one of the rooms at the front with a view of the Panthéon opposite. Lit up by night, it looks breathtaking – a sight shared by the Grands Hommes' sister hotel, the aptly-named Panthéon (page 132). The best of the two, des Grands Hommes occupies a handsome 18thC building, which retains some original features. The entrance/sitting area has been dramatically redecorated, swapping the warm, almost overwhelming peach colour scheme for a smart look, combining fresh white walls and paintwork with a marble floor, Empire-style furniture, including small upright sofas, and busts in niches. Lush green plants in the minute glassed-in garden provide a splash of contrasting colour. The little cellar breakfast-room has a low vaulted ceiling (no good for the seriously claustrophobic).

The small bedrooms have also been completely revamped. Busy 18thC-style papers cover the walls, chosen to co-ordinate with curtains and quilts. Clever built-in designs for cupboards and bedside tables make the maximum use of the space. Some rooms have beams, and some pretty arched French windows. There is one lovely large suite, which sleeps four.

Nearby Panthéon; Saint-Etienne-du-Mont; Sorbonne; boulevard Saint-Michel; Musée de Cluny.
Location on S side, between rue Clotaire and rue d'Ulm **Parking** rue Soufflot **Metro** Cardinal Lemoine/Place Monge **RER** Luxembourg
Food breakfast
Price €€€
Rooms 31 double and twin with bath; all rooms have phone, modem point, TV, air-conditioning, minibar, hairdrier
Facilities sitting room, breakfast room, conference room
Credit cards AE, DC, MC, V **Children** accepted
Disabled lift/elevator **Pets** not accepted **Closed** never
Proprietor Mme Moncelli

FIFTH ARRONDISSEMENT

LATIN QUARTER

HOTEL MELIA COLBERT

7 rue de l'Hôtel-Colbert, 75005 Paris
TEL (01) 56 81 19 00 **FAX** (01) 56 81 19 02
E-MAIL meliacolbert@hotels-of-paris.co.uk **WEBSITE** www.hotels-of-paris.co.uk/melia4

SET BACK FROM THE tiny rue de l'Hôtel-Colbert and approached through a wrought-iron gate and imaginatively planted courtyard, the Melia Colbert gives the impression of a private house rather than a hotel. A handsome building with its origins in the 17th century, it was converted in 1966 into this elegant, well-run three-star hotel which, despite its takeover by the Melia chain, retains its period atmosphere.

On the ground floor, the sunny *salon*-cum-bar with French windows on to the courtyard, ornate upholstered chairs and a host of small tables, is a perfect spot for having tea or a drink. Stairs lead down from here to an unusually spacious cellar breakfast room. A second cosy sitting room, tucked up under the eaves, enjoys a fine view of Notre-Dame.

Many of the bedrooms have floor-to-ceiling windows, *toile de jouy* wallpaper and traditional French-style furniture – velvet chairs and occasional tables; the north-facing rooms have the best views, and there are two fourth-floor suites with beams and sloping walls.

It has the double advantage of being close to the hub, ideally placed for visiting the Ile de la Cité and Saint-Germain, and beautifully quiet. We would welcome reports of this hotel under its new management.

NEARBY Ile de la Cité; blvd Saint-Germain; Musée de Cluny.
LOCATION between quai de Montebello and rue Lagrange **PARKING** rue Lagrange or place du Parvis Notre-Dame **METRO** Maubert Mutualité **RER** Saint-Michel
FOOD breakfast
PRICE €€€€
ROOMS 36; 34 double and twin, 2 suites, all with bath; all rooms have phone, modem point, TV, air-conditioning, minibar, hairdrier, safe
FACILITIES bar/sitting room, upstairs sitting room, breakfast room, conference room **CREDIT CARDS** AE, DC, MC, V **CHILDREN** accepted
DISABLED lift/elevator **PETS** not accepted
CLOSED never **MANAGER** Pascal Lacroix

FIFTH ARRONDISSEMENT

LATIN QUARTER

HOTEL PARC SAINT-SEVERIN

22 rue de la Parcheminerie, 75005 Paris
TEL (01) 43 54 32 17 **FAX** (01) 43 54 70 71
E-MAIL hotel.parc.severin@wanadoo.fr **WEBSITE** www.esprit-de-france.com

OF THE MANY BEDROOMS described in this book, No. 70 at the Parc Saint-Séverin (part of the Esprit de France group) remains this writer's favourite. And although it's an expensive choice, its assets are far greater than, say, a standard double room at the Pavillon de la Reine (page 38) or the Relais Christine (page 63), which cost some 80 euros per night more. Overall, of course, those are far superior hotels, but this room is special: a light, sophisticated and beautifully decorated penthouse suite which is entirely encircled by a broad private terrace affording breathtaking views across the rooftops of all the landmark buildings as far as the Eiffel Tower in one direction, Sacré-Coeur in another. Taking breakfast here on a warm summer morning is sheer bliss. Less expensive, but nonetheless very impressive, are two more rooms, each with a broad terrace on three sides. On lower floors, room Nos. 50 and 12 both have style and space. The rest are pleasant, unexceptional, pastel coloured, with predominantly grey modern furniture. The large ground floor lobby breakfast room is a disappointment, another example of contemporary colours – shades of orange and brown – abstract paintings and a mix of modern and reproduction furniture failing to inspire.

NEARBY Notre-Dame; Musée de Cluny; Saint-Séverin.
LOCATION in pedestrian area close to Saint-Séverin and junction with rue des Prêtres Saint-Séverin **PARKING** rue Lagrange **METRO** Saint-Michel **RER** Saint-Michel
FOOD breakfast
PRICE €€
ROOMS 22 double and twin, one family room, 4 single, all with bath; all rooms have phone, modem point, TV, air-conditioning, minibar, hairdrier, safe
FACILITIES breakfast room, sitting area, internet booth
CREDIT CARDS AE, DC, MC, V
CHILDREN accepted **DISABLED** lift/elevator
PETS not accepted **CLOSED** never
MANAGER Renoir Mulliez

Fifth Arrondissement

Latin Quarter

Les Rives de Notre-Dame

15 quai Saint-Michel, 75005 Paris
Tel (01) 43 54 81 16 **Fax** (01) 43 26 27 09
E-mail hotel@rivesdenotredame.com **Website** www.rivesdenotredame.com

The brochure speaks of the bureaucracy which almost prevented the owners of this pricey little hotel from transforming the run-down 16thC building which they had bought. Its outlook is the Ile de la Cité across the traffic-heavy quai Saint-Michel and the Seine, but the owners' hearts are firmly in Provence and Tuscany, and the decoration is designed to transport you to the south. In our case, the ground floor reception and glass-and-beam roofed sitting room managed to take us no further than a fashionable Paris flower shop, thanks to the banks of plants and dried flowers arranged on the tiled floor, the garden-style furniture and the floral collages decorating the walls.

By contrast, the well-proportioned bedrooms are stylish but less precious than downstairs and have a genuine feel of the sun, with Provençal fabrics, wood-framed windows shaded by the prettiest of white cotton curtains, and charming fabric bedheads held in a frame of verdigris ironwork flowers. All the rooms have a sofa that converts into an extra bed. The bathrooms are attractive, with terracotta floors and lovely basins. Breakfast in bed, brought by uniformed staff, feels like a treat.

Nearby Notre-Dame; Musée de Cluny; Ile Saint-Louis.
Location mid-way along quai **Parking** Notre-Dame **Metro** Saint-Michel
RER Saint-Michel
Food breakfast, room service
Price €€
Rooms 10; 6 double, 3 single, one suite, all with bath; all rooms have phone,_ modem point, TV, air-conditionin, minibar, hairdrier, safe
Facilities sitting room, breakfast room
Credit cards AE, DC, MC, V
Children accepted **Disabled** access difficult, lift/elevator
Pets accepted **Closed** never
Manager M. Martin

FIFTH ARRONDISSEMENT

LATIN QUARTER

HOTEL SAINT JACQUES

35 rue des Ecoles, 75005 Paris
TEL (01) 44 07 45 45 **FAX** (01) 43 25 65 50
E-MAIL hotelsaintjacques@wanadoo.fr **WEBSITE** www.hotel-saintjacques.com

JEAN-PAUL ROUSSEAU BOUGHT this imposing 19thC hotel six years ago, since when he has renovated it extensively. Though officially it only has two stars (with prices to match), it now offers all the comforts that you'd expect from a three-star establishment. The renovation has also given M. Rousseau the opportunity to indulge his passion for *trompe l'oeil* murals – they are everywhere: in bedrooms and reception rooms, on landings and stairs. Even the furniture is decorated, and clouds scud across most of the ceilings. You eat breakfast under a painted scene of Notre-Dame and the Seine, and your room might transport you to an English garden in midsummer, or into elegant 19thC American society. Some of the bedrooms still have fine original features: beautiful mouldings, fireplaces and, in a couple, 19thC frescoed ceilings, uncovered in the rebuilding work. The pastel colour schemes could have been picked from a bag of sugared almonds.

A charming and committed owner, Jean-Paul Rousseau has invested much time and energy into successfully revitalizing this hotel, assisted by his right-hand man, Joe, who speaks a fistful of foreign languages and can usually be found at the reception desk. Personal touches include a stand full of umbrellas for guests' use.

NEARBY Panthéon; Sorbonne; Musée de Cluny.
LOCATION on corner with rue des Carmes **PARKING** place Maubert
METRO Maubert-Mutualité
FOOD breakfast
PRICE €–€€
ROOMS 32; 14 double and twin, 15 triple, all with bath; 3 single, 2 with shower, one with basin; all rooms have phone, modem point, TV, hairdrier, safe
FACILITIES sitting room, breakfast room, internet booth
CREDIT CARDS AE, DC, MC, V **CHILDREN** accepted
DISABLED access possible, lift/elevator **PETS** accepted
CLOSED never **PROPRIETOR** Jean-Paul Rousseau

Fifth Arrondissement

Jardin des Plantes Quarter

Timhotel Jardin des Plantes

5 rue Linné, 75005 Paris
Tel (01) 47 07 06 20 **Fax** (01) 47 07 62 74
E-mail jardin-des-plantes@timhotel.fr **Website** timhotel.com

From each floor up, you can see a little further into the lovely green oasis of the Botanical Gardens opposite, until you reach the fifth floor, where the rooms not only have the best view, but lead out on to an attractive roof terrace. A botanical theme is carried throughout, from the flower-painted tiles on the reception desk to the buttercup and strawberry lights that illuminate the stairs. The decoration in each of the decent-sized bedrooms is devoted to a particular bloom: bright yellow mimosa, deep blue irises or pink geraniums. Fabrics co-ordinate, and the chosen flower is picked out in bathroom tiles. With simple, if dated, white cane furniture, the rooms all have a bright summery feel.

Don't be put off by the even more dated decoration downstairs: the cellar sitting room – a showcase for up-and-coming artists and a musical venue – is pure 1970s brown and beige. This two-star hotel (part of the Timhotel chain), is friendly and comfortable, and offers good value. Welcome extras include an ironing room and a sauna. Breakfast is served in the brasserie next door or on the roof terrace.

Nearby Jardin des Plantes; Musée National d'Histoire Naturelle.
Location opposite NW corner of Jardin des Plantes, between rue des Arènes and rue Lacépède **Parking** rue Censier **Metro** Jussieu/Place Monge **RER** Gare d'Austerlitz
Food breakfast, lunch
Price €€
Rooms 33; 32 double and twin, one family, all with bath or shower; all rooms have phone, TV, minibar, hairdrier; one room has modem point
Facilities sitting room, brasserie, ironing room, sauna, internet booth
Credit cards AE, DC, MC, V
Children accepted
Disabled lift/elevator
Pets accepted **Closed** never
Manager Mme Balatre

Sixth Arrondissement

Saint-Germain-des-Pres/Luxembourg Quarter

Hotel de l'Abbaye

10 rue Cassette, 75006 Paris
Tel (01) 45 44 38 11 **Fax** (01) 45 48 07 86
E-mail hotel.abbaye@wanadoo.fr **Website** www.hotel-abbaye.com

If we gave awards, this gorgeous hotel would be a very strong contender. Indeed, we find it hard to fault with the caveat that the standard bedrooms are fairly small (and feel even smaller compared to the spaciousness of the public rooms); you would do well to upgrade to a larger room if you can. One on the ground floor has its own terrace, as do the four duplex apartments. There are also three new '*suite salons*', in a different, more masculine style and equipped with an arsenal of high-tech gadgets.

The moment one walks into this skilfully converted former abbey, one feels calmed and cossetted. The hotel has a reputation for attentive yet unobtrusive service which it justly deserves: the courteous staff seem genuinely eager to be of help. The public rooms are inviting yet chic, filled with fresh flowers, with several sitting areas furnished with attractively upholstered sofas and armchairs and warmly lit by huge table lamps; in cool weather there's an open fire. The breakfast room/bar must be one of the most alluring in Paris, conservatory style, with walls covered in trellis and French doors which overlook a large courtyard garden complete with fountain. Here you can take breakfast or a drink in warm weather. Worth every penny.

Nearby Jardin du Luxembourg; Saint-Sulpice.
Location close to junction with rue de Meziers **Parking** Saint-Sulpice
Metro Saint-Sulpice
Food breakfast
Price €€€
Rooms 37 single, double and twin, 3 suites, 4 duplex apartments, all with bath; all rooms have phone, TV, modem point, air-conditioning, hairdrier
Facilities 2 sitting rooms, breakfast room, bar, courtyard garden, internet booth
Credit cards AE, DC, MC, V **Children** accepted
Disabled 2 ground floor bedrooms **Pets** not accepted
Closed never **Proprietors** M. and Mme Lafortune

SIXTH ARRONDISSEMENT

SAINT-GERMAIN-DES-PRES

HOTEL ANGLETERRE

44 rue Jacob, 75006 Paris
TEL (01) 42 60 34 72 **FAX** (01) 42 60 16 93
E-MAIL anglotel@wanadoo.fr

OH DEAR. We have long described this as one of the most comforting and gracious small hotels in Paris. With its faintly English air, befitting a building which was once the British Embassy, it has both charm and a story: in 1783, Benjamin Franklin refused to enter it to sign the Treaty of Paris because he considered it to be British soil. Had he done so, he would have found well-proportioned rooms, fine mantlepieces, a beautiful staircase with *trompe l'oeil* murals and a lovely courtyard garden.

So why the sigh? Because of the crop of adverse reports – mixed with some complementary ones – that we have received recently. Shabby bedrooms, intimidating desk staff, rip-off breakasts, say some. Lovely bedrooms, great atmosphere, say others. Confused? So are we, but it's obvious that some of the rooms require attention, while others – as we saw for ourselves – are fine. They certainly have great potential, being both spacious and elegant, many with original features. One deluxe one has an enormous bathroom, all marbled and mirrored glamour, based on one in the London Ritz. Another bathroom has a charming hand-painted suite, with the basin set into a wood and tiled washstand.

NEARBY boulevard Saint-Germain, Musée d'Orsay; Louvre.
LOCATION in the stretch of rue Jacob between rue Bonaparte and rue des Saints-Pères **PARKING** rue du Dragon **METRO** Saint-Germain-des-Prés
FOOD breakfast
PRICE €€€
ROOMS 24 double and twin, either small, standard or deluxe, all with bath; 3 apartments; all rooms have phone, modem point, TV, air-conditioning, hairdrier, safe **FACILITIES** sitting room, breakfast room, bar, courtyard garden
CREDIT CARDS AE, DC, MC, V
CHILDREN accepted **DISABLED** lift/elevator to some rooms only
PETS not accepted **CLOSED** never
MANAGER Mme Michèle Blouin

Sixth Arrondissement

Saint-Germain-des-Pres

Hotel Artus

34 rue de Buci, 75006 Paris
Tel (01) 43 29 07 20 **Fax** (01) 43 29 67 44
E-mail info@artushotel.com **Website** www.artushotel.com

Trendy hotels, however small, don't always make charming ones; character is often obliterated by the unrelenting quest to be hip, and what seems at first stylishly minimalist turns out to be sterile and dull. The Artus, however, which has recently changed its name from Buci Latin so as not to confuse it with the Hôtel Buci down the road, has enough characterful touches to give it a heart. One of these is the popular basement coffee shop from where delicious smells waft up to the reception room, enlivened by a collection of American painted metal toys. Here there are sensually curving walls, across one of which are the framed photographs of the hotel's 27 bedroom doors, each painted by one of three artists. There's more crazy painting up the stairwell, the work of a New York graffitti artist: be sure to look.

Rooms at the Artus are comfortable and employ good quality bedlinen simply draped over the beds, a predominantly terracotta and maroon colour scheme, *de rigueur* curvy fitted furniture, and bathrooms with prettily tiled floors. Neither bedrooms nor bathrooms are large, but if you crave space, consider the suite or duplex, with splendid Victorian cast-iron bath.

Nearby rue de Buci street market; boulevard Saint-Germain.
Location just off boulevard Saint-Germain **Parking** rue Mazarine **Metro** Mabillon
Food breakfast
Price €€€
Rooms 25 double and twin, 19 with bath, 6 with shower; one junior suite; one duplex; all rooms have phone, modem point, TV, air-conditioning, minibar, hairdrier.
Facilities sitting area, bar, coffee shop/breakfast room, internet booth
Credit cards AE, DC, MC, V **Children** accepted
Disabled 2 adapted rooms on ground floor, lift/elevator
Pets accepted
Closed never
Manager Laurence Raymond

SIXTH ARRONDISSEMENT

SAINT-GERMAIN-DES-PRES

HOTEL AUBUSSON

33 rue Dauphine, 75006 Paris
TEL (01) 43 29 43 43 **FAX** (01) 43 29 12 62
E-MAIL reservationmichael@hoteldaubusson.com **WEBSITE** www.hoteldaubusson.com

IF YOU PREFER your base in Paris to be a straightforward hotel, veering a little towards the anonymous, but with personal touches, rather than one with a distinct, enveloping personality, then the Aubusson is a good choice. On chilly days, a log fire crackles in the grate in the elegant sitting room; staff are welcoming and friendly; there is live jazz Thursday to Saturday nights; and prices remain reasonable for the four-star comfort offered.

The hotel – ten years old or so – occupies a 17thC honey-stone town house arranged around a large courtyard. A huge pair of double doors, formally a coach entrance, lead from the streeet into the airy lobby. To the right, Café Laurent – in various incarnations – has attracted the literati and glitterati since 1690. The sitting room manages to be cosy despite its grand proportions with a high beamed ceiling, Versailles parquet floor and pretty furniture, lamps and mirrors. Appropriately, two Aubusson tapestries hang in the breakfast room next door.

The bedrooms cocoon their inhabitants behind heavy doors in silence and restrained, if fairly unimaginative, luxury. The most expensive are massive and beamed, but even the smallest are large by local standards.

NEARBY boulevard Saint-Germain; Ile de la Cité; Latin Quarter.
LOCATION corner of rue Christine **PARKING** private garage **METRO** Saint-Michel/Odéon
FOOD breakfast; light meals; 24 hr room service
PRICE €€€€
ROOMS 49 double and twin, all with bath; all rooms have phone, modem point, TV, air conditioning, minibar, hairdrier, safe
FACILITIES sitting room, breakfast room, café/bar, courtyard garden, internet booth
CREDIT CARDS AE, DC, MC, V
CHILDREN accepted
DISABLED 2 rooms specially adapted, lift/elevator
PETS accepted
CLOSED never **MANAGER** Pascal Gimel

SIXTH ARRONDISSEMENT

SAINT-GERMAIN-DES-PRES

GRAND HOTEL DES BALCONS

3 rue Casimir-Delavigne, 75006 Paris
TEL (01) 46 34 78 50 **FAX** (01) 46 34 06 27
EMAIL resa@balcons.com **WEBSITE** www.balcons.com

FOR THE TRAVELLER WHO is searching for a budget hotel on the Left Bank, but wants to avoid one of the wackier enterprises on offer, this one should be of great interest. When you have heard about the bargain breakfast you might decide to look no further.

As its name implies, the magisterial façade of the hotel is covered in wrought-iron balconies. Inside, the reception room and large breakfast room are dignified and gleaming, obviously well cared for by the team of maids dressed in black with white aprons. Art Nouveau is the theme, to match the fine original stained-glass windows, and there is waist-high wooden panelling with an Art Nouveau motif and light fittings in the same style; walls and ceiling are painted bright yellow. The exotic flower arrangements are the handiwork of proprietor Madame Corroyer. Upstairs, bedrooms are spruce, with ample storage space, mirrors on the walls and neat bathrooms. Brightly coloured fabrics keep the blues at bay; our inspector's room had jolly red curtains, with pretty lace ones behind, and a crisp white bedspread. As for breakfast: you can have bacon, egg and sausage, plus ham, fruit, cheese and more for the same price you pay for a couple of croissants everywhere else.

NEARBY Saint-Sulpice; Jardin du Luxembourg; Latin Quarter.
LOCATION in a short street between place de l'Odéon and rue Monsieur le Prince
PARKING rue de l'Ecole de Médecine **METRO** Odéon
FOOD breakfast
PRICE €€
ROOMS 55; 35 double, twin and triple, 23 with bath, 12 with shower; 20 single, 15 with bath, 5 with shower; all rooms have phone, modem point, TV
FACILITIES sitting area, breakfast room **CREDIT CARDS** MC, V
CHILDREN accepted **DISABLED** 2 rooms on ground floor, lift/elevator **PETS** accepted
CLOSED never
PROPRIETORS M. and Mme Corroyer

SIXTH ARRONDISSEMENT

SAINT-GERMAIN-DES-PRES

RELAIS CHRISTINE

3 rue Christine, 75006 Paris
TEL (01) 40 51 60 80 **FAX** (01) 40 51 60 81
E-MAIL contact@relais-christine.com **WEBSITE** www.relais-christine.com

UNTIL THE ADVENT of the Aubusson almost next door (see page 61), and the re-incarnation of L'Hôtel nearby (see page 70), the Relais Christine was the sixième's most prestigious hotel; now, perhaps, it stands somewhat in their shadow. If you can afford it, though, you are unlikely to be disappointed: it has the calm, luxurious feel of a grand hotel but on a far more intimate scale; in this it is matched by its sister hotel, the Pavillon de la Reine (see page 38).

Approached through a handsome courtyard, the Relais Christine is an oasis of dignified calm. The reception hall is coolly tiled and strewn with Persian rugs, and the ceiling retains its original painted beams. In the handsome panelled sitting room, a help-yourself drinks table enhances the feel of a private room. Traces of the building's medieval roots are visible in the elegant stone-vaulted breakfast room, which has a huge hearth and a massive central pillar. Bedrooms are decorated with restrained luxury, with plenty of cupboard space, pretty pictures, and bathrooms in which it is a pleasure to idle away time.

NEARBY boulevard Saint-Germain; Ile de la Cité; Latin Quarter.
LOCATION in a short quiet street between rue Dauphine and rue des Grands Augustins **PARKING** private garage **METRO** Odéon
FOOD breakfast; room service
PRICE €€€€
ROOMS 38 double and twin, 13 suites, all with bath (separate WC); all rooms have phone, modem point, TV, air-conditioning, minibar, hairdrier, safe
FACILITIES sitting room, breakfast room, bar, meeting room
CREDIT CARDS AE, DC, MC, V
CHILDREN accepted
DISABLED access difficult, lift/elevator
PETS accepted **CLOSED** never
MANAGER M. Chomat

SIXTH ARRONDISSEMENT

SAINT-GERMAIN-DES-PRES/LATIN QUARTER

HOTEL LE CLOS MEDICIS

56 rue Monsieur-le-Prince, 75006 Paris
TEL (01) 43 29 10 80 **FAX** (01) 43 54 26 90
E-MAIL message@closmedicis.com **WEBSITE** www.closmedicis.com

THE CHARMING OWNER of this justly popular Left Bank hotel, Pascal Beherec, has departed for warmer climes, now living in Marrakech, where he has opened the luxurious Villa des Orangers. His Paris base, however, remains in the caring hands of his equally charming manager, Olivier Méallet and his hands-on staff, and, as a recent visit confirmed, continues to thrive. The ground floor, an artful mix of old and new, with split levels and curves giving a sense of style and space, has been further enhanced with comfortable seating. A wrought-iron balustrade separates the entrance from the sunken sitting area, where an exposed chimney with open fireplace is set between two chunks of original stone wall. The look is cool and contemporary, yet welcoming.

Bedrooms and bathrooms are no more than adequate in size, but thoughtfully decorated, using mostly plain fabrics and contemporary, but comfortable furnishings. A programme of refurbishment is in constant operation, with a few rooms being redecorated each year. Bathrooms have terracotta floors, pretty ceramic tiles, and matching basins. The courtyard, where you can breakfast, has recently been improved.

NEARBY Jardin du Luxembourg; Panthéon; Musée de Cluny.
LOCATION between rue Vaugirard and boulevard Saint-Michel **PARKING** rue Soufflot
METRO Cluny La Sorbonne/Odéon **RER** Luxembourg
FOOD breakfast
PRICE €€€
ROOMS 38, all double and twin, all with bath, 2 with private terrace; all rooms have phone, modem point, TV, air-conditioning, minibar, hairdrier, safe
FACILITIES sitting room, bar, breakfast room, courtyard, internet booth
CREDIT CARDS AE, DC, MC, V **CHILDREN** accepted
DISABLED one adapted room on ground floor, lift/elevator
PETS accepted **CLOSED** never
MANAGER Olivier Méallet

Sixth Arrondissement

Saint-Germain-des-Pres

Hotel Delavigne

1 rue Casimir-Delavigne, 75006 Paris
Tel (01) 43 29 31 50 **Fax** (01) 43 29 78 56
E-mail resa@hoteldelavigne.com **Website** www.hoteldelavigne.com

In a quiet street close to the Odéon Theatre, between the boulevard Saint-Germain and the Luxembourg Gardens, the Delavigne is an attractive, recently renovated and carefully decorated hotel, perhaps somewhat lacking in character and individuality but none the less a very comfortable base for a relaxing stay on the Left Bank. A little, at any rate, of its 18thC origins and personality has been retained.

Arriving at the handsome entrance, guests are greeted, through sliding glass doors, by a large and artful flower arrangement in the small entrance hall. A lovely winding wooden staircase with pretty stucco work on its underside leads to the bedrooms. The lobby is handsome and airy if a little bland, with louvred blinds, sculptures, leather sofas, prints on the walls and more colourful vases full of flowers.

Bedrooms are in much the same vein, tastefully decorated, if never quite shaking off that indefinable 'hotel' feel. Each one is different, however, some with delightful touches such as Spanish-style wrought-iron bedheads teamed with pretty floral bedspreads. Walls are covered in silk fabric or floral wallpapers and the well-chosen free standing furniture, including desks and armchairs, mixes reproduction antiques with the occasional old piece.

Nearby Jardin du Luxembourg; boulevard Saint Germain.
Location in a short street between rue Monsieur-le-Prince and place de l'Odéon
Parking rue de l'Ecole-de-Médecine **Metro** Saint-Michel/Odéon **RER** Luxembourg
Food breakfast
Price €€€
Rooms 34 double and twin, 30 with bath, 4 with shower; all rooms have phone, modem point, TV, safe, hairdrier **Facilities** sitting room, breakfast room
Credit cards MC, V **Children** accepted
Disabled lift/elevator
Pets accepted
Closed never **Propietor** Daniel Fraïoli

Sixth Arrondissement

Saint-Germain-des-Pres/Latin Quarter

Delhy's Hotel

22 rue de l'Hirondelle, 75006 Paris
Tel (01) 43 26 58 25 **Fax** (01) 43 26 51 06
E-mail delhys@wanadoo.fr

As we tramp the streets of Paris inspecting hotels we always keep an eye out for likely looking one-star establishments, precious few of which – unfortunately – make it into these pages. Delhy's looked spruce enough on the outside to invite exploration, and the interior did not, at any point, disappoint. The grouchy receptionist was much less welcoming, it has to be said, but we gather that the owner is friendly 'if quirky'.

We've never had recommendations for this hotel, and there has been no chance, as we go to press, for us to stay the night, so we can only go on what we saw of the place, but judging by other hotels in its class, its standards are impressively high. And it's location, in a quiet street on the borders of Saint-Germain and the Latin Quarter in the heart of the Rive Gauche, could not be better. First comes the reception room, neat as a pin and prettily painted in ochre yellow. Then the charming breakfast room, again neat and fresh, with unusual painted tables and bamboo stools, and café curtains hung at interior windows. A pretty staircase, with exposed stone walls, leads to the bedrooms, which are simple, but never tawdry, with unexpected touches such as good wooden furnishings and matching striped curtains and bedspreads. All rooms have a basin; some have a shower.

Nearby boulevard Saint-Germain; Notre-Dame; Latin Quarter.
Location in a short street off place Saint-Michel **Parking** place Saint-Michel,Ile de la Cité **Metro** Saint-Michel **RER** Saint-Michel
Food breakfast
Price €
Rooms 21 single, double, twin and triple, some with shower, some with basin only; communal showers and WCs; all rooms have phone, TV
Facilities breakfast room **Credit cards** MC, V
Children accepted
Disabled access difficult **Pets** not accepted
Closed never **Proprietor** M. Mehdy

SIXTH ARRONDISSEMENT

SAINT-GERMAIN-DES-PRES/MONTPARNASSE

HOTEL FERRANDI

44 rue Jacob, 75006 Paris
TEL (01) 42 22 97 40 **FAX** (01) 45 44 89 97
E-MAIL hotel.ferrandi@wanadoo.fr

NOT MANY OF THE CITY'S smaller hotels are particularly noteworthy from the exterior; the Ferrandi (and indeed its sister hotel, the Elysée, page 96) is an exception, being an immensely long and very gracious five-storey former 19thC private mansion. Indeed so long is it that all the rooms face the street.

The hotel was brought to our attention by a correspondent who had enjoyed the quiet, dignified atmosphere engendered by its elegant 18thC style of decoration. With his eyes directed firmly on the dominant white marble fireplace or the crystal chandelier, our enthusiast must have forgiven the brown swirly carpet in the salon (and in the sober leather-seated breakfast room) which reminded us of Edwardian resort hotels favoured by very old aunties. Still, old-world dignity is the key here. Bedrooms, in *toile de jouy*, display period furniture and generous beds, some canopied, with crisp white bedcovers. Rooms and bathrooms vary in size, although they are all good on storage space; the 'luxe' rooms are spacious, with room for table and chairs, and there is a rather too boldly decorated suite with ornate Venetian chandelier. No. 27 makes an excellent bedroom for one. Quaint, slightly shabby, but reasonably priced.

NEARBY boulevard Montparnasse; Jardin du Luxembourg.
LOCATION about halfway along the street, between boulevard Montparnasse and boulevard Raspail **PARKING** hotel garage **METRO** Vaneau/Saint-Placide
FOOD breakfast
PRICE €€
ROOMS 42, all double, 32 with bath, 9 with shower; one suite; all rooms have phone, modem point, TV, air-conditioning, hairdrier **FACILITIES** sitting room, bar, breakfast room, courtyard **CREDIT CARDS** AE, DC, MC, V
CHILDREN accepted
DISABLED lift/elevator **PETS** accepted
CLOSED never **MANAGER** Mme Lafond

SIXTH ARRONDISSEMENT

SAINT-GERMAIN-DES-PRES

HOTEL FLEURIE

32 rue Grégoire-de-Tours, 75006 Paris
TEL (01) 53 73 70 00 **FAX** (01) 53 73 70 20
E-MAIL bonjour@hotel-de-fleurie.tm.fr **WEBSITE** www.hotel-de-fleurie.tm.fr

A MODEL HOTEL, rightly very popular, where charm, efficiency and up-to-date comforts go hand-in-hand. Renovated in the 1980s by the Marolleau family, who once owned the well-known Latin Quarter brasserie, Balzar, it combines an immaculate appearance (not least the pretty façade, elegantly lit at night, complete with statues in the niches) with a cosy, intimate feel. The hands-on owners – parents and two sons – are determined to keep it so, and the place always feels well cared for.

Instantly eye-catching in the terracotta-tiled reception is a delightful *faience* stove picked up by Madame Marolleau in the flea market; the adjoining sitting room, with its exposed beams and section of ancient wall, has a discreet bar and little tables covered in Provençal cloths. The basement cave, where a generous breakfast is served, is equally cosy, cleverly lit by uplighters. The spotless bedrooms do not disappoint. You will find pretty billowing curtains, walls of panelled wood and grasspaper, period-style furniture, inviting beds and – a rare touch – fresh flowers. Bathrooms, all in pink-hued marble, are well equipped with thick towels on heated rails and towelling bathrobes.

NEARBY boulevard Saint-Germain; Saint-Sulpice; Jardin du Luxembourg.
LOCATION between boulevard Saint-Germain and rue des Quatres-Vents **PARKING** rue de l'Ecole de Médecine **METRO** Mabillon/Odéon
FOOD breakfast
PRICE €€€
ROOMS 29; 19 double and twin, 17 with bath, 2 with shower; 10 single, 5 with bath, 5 with shower; all rooms have phone, modem point, TV, air-conditioning, minibar, hairdrier, safe **FACILITIES** sitting room, bar, breakfast room, internet booth
CREDIT CARDS AE, DC, MC, V
CHILDREN accepted
DISABLED lift/elevator **PETS** not accepted
CLOSED never **PROPRIETORS** Marolleau family

SIXTH ARRONDISSEMENT

SAINT-GERMAIN-DES-PRES

HOTEL GLOBE

15 rue des Quatre-Vents, 75006 Paris
TEL (01) 43 26 35 50 **FAX** (01) 46 33 62 69

A GEM OF A HOTEL – tiny and quaint, with a caring team behind it. In the entrance – the building is 17thC, once part of the Abbey of Saint-Germain-des-Prés – a door set in a wrought-iron grille leads to perhaps the smallest *salon* in Paris, decorated with bird of paradise fabric on the walls and lorded over by a splendid suit of armour. Back in the hallway, a huge arrangement of flowers and a pretty *trompe l'oeil* mural cleverly reflected in a mirror, invite you to press on up the little staircase. Here on the first floor is the 'reception': simply a bureau in a cluttered private *salon*. There is no breakfast room – breakfast is brought to you.

All the bedooms have an old-fashioned charm, with an assortment of mainly period furniture, white crochet bedspreads, and pretty canopies over some beds. One, for example, has stone walls, a beamed ceiling and pretty floral fabrics. In other rooms, showers and loos are tucked away behind painted folding doors. Yet, though they are sweet, you might also find the bedrooms somewhat fusty, and after a couple of days our inspector reported a distinct yearning for space. Still, for the charm, location and price, he felt that the Globe was hard to beat.

NEARBY boulevard Saint-Germain; Saint-Sulpice; Jardin du Luxembourg.
LOCATION in a short street which crosses the rue de Tournon **PARKING** Saint-Sulpice
METRO Odéon
FOOD breakfast
PRICE €€
ROOMS 15, all double, 5 with bath, 9 with shower; all rooms have phone, TV
FACILITIES sitting area **CREDIT CARDS** MC, V
CHILDREN accepted
DISABLED one ground floor room
PETS accepted
CLOSED Aug
PROPRIETOR Mme Ressier

Sixth Arrondissement

Saint-Germain-des-Pres

L'Hotel

13 rue des Beaux-Arts, 75006 Paris
Tel (01) 44 41 99 00 **Fax** (01) 43 25 64 81
E-mail reservation@l-hotel.com **Website** www.l-hotel.com

If you hanker after the opulence of a Jacques Garcia interior, but prefer a more low-key atmosphere than at the famous designer's other Paris hotel, Costes – darling of the fashion and film crowd – then head for L'Hôtel. Famous for its astonishing six-storey circular atrium, its connection with Oscar Wilde and its reign - in the 1970s and '80s -- as the most louche and celebrity-studded hotel in town, L'Hôtel re-emerged two years ago from a period of tawdry decline. Garcia's opulent recreation of the hotel in its heyday conjures a mood of luxurious decadence, and in each of the 30 bedrooms he has created a different fantasy. Amongst the suites, lovers will adore Ottoman-inspired 'Pierre Loti' and 'Cardinal', with its pretty rooftop terrace. Those who can bear the *tristesse* can sleep in 'Oscar Wilde', the (now enlarged) room where the playwright expired beyond his means when the building was a crummy boarding house. Another amazing *chambre de luxe* contains the original mirrored art deco bedroom furniture of Mistinguett. The least expensive rooms are compact but dramatic, like sleeping in a velvet-lined jewel box. Best of all is the softly-lit stone-walled plunge pool, which guests can book exclusively for an hour at a time. Accompanied by champagne, candlelight and nothing more than a couple of bathrobes, it's impossibly romantic.

Nearby boulevard Saint-Germain; Musée d'Orsay, Ile de la Cité.
Location between rue Bonaparte and rue de Seine **Parking** boulevard Saint-Germain (rue du Dragon) **Metro** Saint-Germain-des-Prés
Food breakfast, lunch, dinner; room service
Price €€€€
Rooms 30 double, twin and suites, all with bath; all rooms have phone, modem point, TV, air-conditioning, minibar, safe, hairdrier
Facilities sitting room, bar, restaurant, courtyard, internet booth, plunge pool, beauty treatment room **Credit cards** AE, DC, MC, V
Children accepted **Disabled** lift/elevator
Pets not accepted **Closed** never **Manager** Fabienne Capelli

SIXTH ARRONDISSEMENT

SAINT-GERMAIN-DES-PRES

HOTEL LEFT BANK

9 rue de l'Ancienne-Comédie, 75006 Paris
TEL (01) 43 54 01 70 **FAX** (01) 43 26 17 14
E-MAIL lb@paris-hotels-charm.com **WEBSITE** www.paris-hotels-charm,com

IF THERE IS A DOWNSIDE to the Left Bank, it is the elevated prices and slightly impersonal feel that goes with its status as a Best Western hotel, despite the fact that it is run by hands-on hoteliers M. and Mme Teil, who own three other establishments featured in this guide (including Manoir Saint-Germain-des-Prés, page 74). As at those hotels, the Left Bank has a decorative theme which is carried throughout, in this case to charming effect. Downstairs there are tapestry chairs, a Persian rug, and an old stone wall adorned by a vast Aubusson tapestry. Bedrooms are delightful, with *toile de jouy* fabric on the walls, dark wood fittings, including charming old cupboard doors from Périgord, and pretty white crochet bedcovers. In the spacious triple rooms, the third bed is an elegant *bateau lit*, much appreciated by children. Bathrooms mix dark red with pale stone coloured marble. Some of the bedrooms are exceptional for their views. No. 604 has two windows on opposite sides of the room, one giving on to the Eiffel Tower, the other across the rooftops to Notre-Dame, Sainte-Chapelle and, further away, the bulging pipes of the Pompidou Centre. Other rooms share this view, but not the Eiffel Tower as well.

NEARBY boulevard Saint-Germain; Latin Quarter.
LOCATION next to Le Procope, halfway along the street, which leads from carrefour de l'Odéon **PARKING** rue Mazarine **METRO** Odéon
FOOD breakfast
PRICE €€€
ROOMS 31, 20 double and twin, 11 triple, all with bath; all rooms have phone, TV, modem point, air-conditioning, minibar, hairdrier, safe
FACILITIES sitting room, breakfast room, internet booth
CREDIT CARDS AE, DC, MC, V **CHILDREN** accepted
DISABLED specially adapted room on ground floor, lift/elevator
PETS accepted
CLOSED never **MANAGER** Fanny Desques

SIXTH ARRONDISSEMENT

SAINT-GERMAIN-DES-PRES

HOTEL LOUIS II

2 rue Saint-Sulpice, 75006 Paris
TEL (01) 46 33 13 80 **FAX** (01) 46 33 17 29
E-MAIL louis2@club-internet.fr **WEBSITE** www.hotel-louis2.com

WHEN WE LAST VISITED the Louis II we relegated it to the back pages of this guide because we felt it had become a little shabby and neglected. However, a recent visit has persuaded us to reinstate it. We were delighted to find that a new manager, the large, ebulliant and hands-on M. Meynant, had revived and spruced up this characterful hotel. Not that we are talking about a new look. With the same elderly owners as the Globe (page 69), this is a quaint, old-fashioned establishment with *mignon* bedrooms and '70s-style bathrooms, which might be too fusty for some people's tastes, but appeal to the nostalgic in others. They suffer somewhat, especially in summer, from a feeling of airlessness, although half have air-conditioning units, and the other half are provided with fans. But M. Meynant cares about the place, and has redecorated many of the rooms, each different, with pretty fabrics on the walls and elegant light fittings. The crochet bedspreads are specially made for the two hotels in Le Puy in the Auvergne and the handmade mattresses are carefully maintained. Breakfast, at 14 euros, seems astonishingly expensive for such a modest hotel, but it is a real feast, with bread from Mulot, 17 types of jam, nine types of tea, two of coffee, superb hot chocolate, fruit salad, fresh orange juice, cheese and so on.

NEARBY boulevard Saint-Germain; Saint-Sulpice; Jardin du Luxembourg.
LOCATION just off boulevard Saint-Germain near l'Odéon **PARKING** place Saint-Sulpice **METRO** Odéon
FOOD breakfast
PRICE €€
ROOMS 22; 20 double and twin, 2 triple, all with bath or shower; all rooms have phone, TV, minibar, hairdrier, safe; half have air-conditioning
FACILITIES sitting room/breakfast room **CREDIT CARDS** AE, DC, MC, V
CHILDREN accepted **DISABLED** not suitable **PETS** accepted **CLOSED** never
MANAGER François Meynant

SIXTH ARRONDISSEMENT

SAINT-GERMAIN-DES-PRES/LATIN QUARTER

HOTEL DU LYS

23 rue Serpente, 75006 Paris
TEL (01) 43 26 97 57 **FAX** (01) 44 07 34 90
E-MAIL hoteldulys@wanadoo.fr **WEBSITE** www.hoteldulys.com

FOR MORE THAN 50 years the Hôtel du Lys, ideally situated in a very quiet street parallel to the lively blvd Saint-Germain, has been a family-run hotel operated along *pension* lines. Nowadays it is in the hands of Marie-Helène Decharne, daughter of the original owners, and her husband. "We think of it more as a house than a hotel," she says. "Our guests are individuals; we give them a room and breakfast; after that they look after themselves, but when they are here, this is their home. Some of our clients have been returning regularly for 40 years."

In the 17th century the building was the *hôtel particulier* of loyal followers of the king, who proudly displayed the royal fleur de lys. Little has changed over the years. A venerable wooden staircase winds through the half-timbered stairwell to the bedrooms, all of which are individually decorated in pretty country-style fabrics. There are old wooden cupboard doors, beams, stone walls, a mixture of furniture and simple bathrooms. One room is tiny and pink, with a huge mirror behind the bed; another, next door, is just as sweet, with a jumble of beams in the ceiling. "We treat each room as if it were our own," says Mme Decharne.

NEARBY boulevard Saint-Germain; boulevard Saint-Michel, Musée de Cluny.
LOCATION parallel to boulevard Saint-Germain between rue Mignon and rue Hautefeuille **PARKING** rue de l'Ecole de Médecine **METRO** Odéon/Cluny La Sorbonne
FOOD breakfast
PRICE €–€€
ROOMS 22 single, double and triple, 6 with bath, 16 with shower; all rooms have phone, TV **FACILITIES** sitting room/breakfast room
CREDIT CARDS MC, V
CHILDREN accepted
DISABLED not suitable
PETS accepted **CLOSED** never
PROPRIETOR Mme Decharne

Sixth Arrondissement

Saint-Germain-des-Pres

Manoir Saint-Germain-des-Pres

153 bouldevard Saint-Germain-des-Prés, 75006 Paris
Tel (01) 42 22 21 65 **Fax** (01) 45 48 22 25
E-mail msg@paris-hotels-charm.com **Website** www.paris-hotels-charm.com

Located in a prime position opposite the famous cafés, Flore and Deux Magots, this hotel has undergone dramatic transformation in the last few years. From its incarnation as the Tonic Hôtel Taranne, only the bathrooms, including Jacuzzi baths, have been retained; the rest of the hideous modern decoration has been swept away and replaced with something quite different: reproduction 18thC painted panelling, called *boiserie*, executed by craftsmen from Périgord to resemble old wood, wormholes and all. Painted in two shades of pale green, it looks charming in the public rooms, where it is complemented by Aubusson tapestries and period furniture; it particularly suits the little conservatory with leaf-painted glass roof. But it's very artful – sedan chair, top hats displayed on a box, baskets of fake fruit on the breakfast tables, that sort of thing – and after a while it does begin to cloy. In the bedrooms the *boiserie* is mixed with *toile de jouy* fabric on the walls, and again, though pretty, its repetition makes the rooms seem uniform, even dull. Rooms are either 'standard', which means small, or 'large', which means fairly spacious. Most pleasant is No. 504, with steps leading down to the bathroom and a cosy attic feel; another has its own roof-top terrace.

Nearby Saint-Germain-des-Prés; Musée d'Orsay.
Location boulevard Saint-Germain at Saint-Germain-des-Prés, next to Brasserie Lipp, opposite Café Flore **Parking** rue du Dragon **Metro** Saint-Germain-des-Prés
Food breakfast; light meals also available
Price €€€
Rooms 32 single, double and twin, all with Jacuzzi bath; all rooms have phone, modem point, TV, minibar, hairdrier, safe
Facilities sitting room, bar, breakfast room, conservatory
Credit cards AE, DC, MC, V **Children** accepted
Disabled lift/elevator **Pets** accepted
Closed never **Manager** Mme Galichet

Sixth Arrondissement

Saint-Germain-des-Pres/Luxembourg

Pension Les Marronniers

78 rue d'Assas 75006 Paris
Tel (01) 43 26 37 71
E-mail o marro@club-internet.fr **Website** www.pension-marronniers.com

A throw back. A time warp. Walking through the big heavy front doors, up the plain wooden stairs and into Marie Poirier's *salon* is like walking into a Balzac novel, and this unchanged *pension* even has, amongst the guests who come and go, a permanent lodger who has been there for a quarter of a century. This is the last of a breed, a homely boarding house ('the guests help with the table and even the shopping') complete with characterful landlady, which hasn't changed since it opened for business in the late 19th century. Marie's mother ran it before her (her brother runs the Hôtel Résidence les Gobelins, page 104) and the *salon* still overflows with Victorian-style potted plants, sepia photos and pictures on the walls, cluttered tables, cosy sofas and objects everywhere. At dinner, everyone sits around the dining table for soup in winter, salad in summer; followed by meat and vegetables; and cheese and dessert served from the delightfully old-fashioned kitchen behind glass doors and café curtains. Marie herself is a commanding but kindly presence, with rings on every finger and a tendency to long black dresses and cowboy boots. The *salon* is great, the bedrooms are very humble, some with shower cubicles sitting in them. But they are very, very cheap. Perfect for young students whose parents want an eye kept on them, says Marie.

Nearby Jardin du Luxembourg; Saint-Sulpice.
Location near the corner of rue d'Assas and rue Vavin, beside the Jardin du Luxembourg **Parking** rue Auguste Comte **Metro** Vavin/Notre Dame-des-Champs
RER Luxembourg
Food breakfast, dinner
Price €
Rooms 12 double, some with shower and WC, or shower only, others with shared facilities **Facilities** sitting room, dining area **Credit cards** not accepted
Children accepted **Disabled** not suitable **Pets** not accepted
Closed 10 days Christmas **Proprietor** Mme Marie Poirier

SIXTH ARRONDISSEMENT

SAINT-GERMAIN-DES-PRES

HOTEL DE NESLE

7 rue de Nesle, 75006 Paris
TEL (01) 43 54 62 41
E-MAIL contact@hoteldenesle.com **WEBSITE** www.hoteldenesle.com

BACK IN THE 1960s, the Nesle, tucked away down a side street, was a happening place for a generation of drop-outs who dropped in and often stayed. In those days, no advance bookings were taken by Mme Busillet, its impressively proportioned proprietor. But times have changed, and it is with great regret that she now accepts, only by telephone, advance bookings ("I'm so often let down"). Her clients have changed too, as likely professionals as backpackers these days; and she no longer serves breakfast, instead directing you to Chez Paul round the corner where you can breakfast well for a few euros. But the charm of this unique hotel, amusingly decorated by her son David, remains unchanged.

The reception room, and former breakfast room, is now transformed into a country cottage fantasy, the ceiling dripping with bunches of dried flowers (and a multitude of coloured glass balls at Christmas time). The next delight is the secret garden, entered from the first floor, complete with lawn, pond and palm. As for the bedrooms, you can see many of them on the hotel's excellent website. You might choose Molière, done up like a little theatre, or Sahara, with its own miniature hammam, or Victorian dolls house Mélanie. But remember, this is basic stuff. There are *no* extras, precious little storage space, and only one WC per four rooms.

NEARBY Musée d'Orsay, Ile de la Cité; boulevard Saint-Germain.
LOCATION in a little street off rue Dauphine **PARKING** rue Mazarine **METRO** Odéon
FOOD none
PRICE €
ROOMS 20; 12 double, 5 with shower, 7 with washbasin, none with WC; 8 single, 7 with shower, one with washbasin, none with WC; 4 communal WCs.
FACILITIES reception room **CREDIT CARDS** not accepted
CHILDREN accepted **DISABLED** not suitable
PETS accepted **CLOSED** never
PROPRIETOR Mme Renée Busillet

SIXTH ARRONDISSEMENT

SAINT-GERMAIN-DES-PRES

RELAIS SAINT-GERMAIN

9 carrefour de l'Odéon, 75006 Paris
TEL (01) 44 27 07 97 **FAX** (01) 46 33 45 30

A MIXED BAG OF REPORTS, some very critical, have begun to filter through about this pricey hotel on a busy intersection at the heart of Saint-Germain. 'Irresistable, if you can afford it', is how we have previously described it: 'a sumptuous 17thC house whose mini-lift and cramped public rooms – albeit artfully mirrored and glossily decorated – give no hint of the wonderfully spacious bedrooms upstairs.' And it is true that expensive though the four-star Relais Saint-Germain undoubtedly is, what is termed a 'standard double' here would be called a 'junior suite' elsewhere. Most 'standard' rooms in Paris give you just enough room to swing a cat. The deluxe rooms are positively enormous, with two sets of French windows overlooking the street; they are embellished with stunning antiques – mostly French country – plump sofas, lovely fabrics and well-chosen prints and pictures. One is notable for its pair of stone angels culled from a medieval chapel, another for two beautiful matching bookcases. The top floor suite is a dashing yellow, with black and white prints all over the walls, a plethora of ancient sprouting beams and a tiny sun-trap terrace. But...reports of cold, unhelpful service and falling standards, as well as ones from satisfied guests, have to be passed on. Breakfast is taken either in bed, or in the adjoining 1930s café, now part of the hotel.

NEARBY boulevard Saint-Germain; Saint-Sulpice; Latin Quarter.
LOCATION boulevard Saint-Germain **PARKING** rue l'Ecole de Médecine **METRO** Odéon
FOOD breakfast
PRICE €€€€
ROOMS 21 double and twin, one suite, all with bath; all rooms have phone, modem point, TV, video, air-conditioning, minibar, hairdrier, safe
FACILITIES sitting room, bar/breakfast room **CREDIT CARDS** AE, DC, MC, V
CHILDREN accepted **DISABLED** not suitable, lift/elevator
PETS accepted **CLOSED** never
PROPRIETOR Alexis Laipsker

SIXTH ARRONDISSEMENT

SAINT-GERMAIN-DES-PRES/MONTPARNASSE

HOTEL SAINT-GREGOIRE

43 rue de l'Abbaye-Grégoire, 75006 Paris
TEL (01) 45 48 23 23 **FAX** (01) 45 48 33 95
E-MAIL hotel@saintgregoire.com **WEBSITE** www.hotelsaintgregoire..com

A CHIC LITTLE HOTEL in a tall 18thC town house, run with affable charm by manager François de Bené. Like its sister Le Tourville (page 146), Le Saint-Grégoire was designed by interior decorator Christian Badin, and here the decoration gels – dusty pink walls, maroon carpets, floral peachy curtains, and crisp white linen bedspreads and chair covers – and a warm intimate atmosphere prevails. On wintery afternoons, an open fire blazes in the *salon,* a room dotted with antiques and nick-nacks, picked up by Madame Bouvier, the owner's wife, in flea markets and antique shops. Trellis on the walls and French windows on to a tiny enclosed garden, full of flowers and ferns, make the back part of the sitting room feel more like a conservatory.

The colour scheme leads from the ground floor upstairs to equally attractive bedrooms, with beautiful antique chests of drawers, tables and mirrors; two bedrooms have private terraces. Bathrooms are mostly tiled in white and small, but well designed.

The ubiquitous cellar breakfast-room is a particularly pretty one, with woven floor, rush chairs and baskets decorating one wall.

NEARBY Musée Bourdelle; Jardin du Luxembourg; boulevard Saint-Germain.
LOCATION between rue Cherche-Midi and rue de Vaugirard **PARKING** in street **METRO** Saint-Placide/Rennes
FOOD breakfast
PRICE €€€
ROOMS 20 double and twin, all with bath; all rooms have phone, modem point, TV, air-conditioning, hairdrier
FACILITIES sitting room, breakfast room
CREDIT CARDS AE, DC, MC, V
CHILDREN accepted **DISABLED** lift/elevator
PETS accepted **CLOSED** never
PROPRIETOR M. Bouvier

Sixth Arrondissement

Saint-Germain-des-Pres

Hotel Saint-Paul

43 rue Monsieur-le-Prince, 75006 Paris
Tel (01) 43 26 98 64 **Fax** (01) 46 34 58 60
E-mail hotel.saint.paul@wanadoo.fr **Website** www.hotel-saint-paul-paris.com

We continue to be very fond of the Saint-Paul, a 17thC building that was renovated in the 1980s, and of its charming owner, Marianne Oberlin, who took over its management, along with the hotel cat, Sputnik, from her parents. The public rooms are stylish in an unfussy way with beamed ceilings, a mixture of stone and colour-washed walls, Indian rugs, *haute epoque* and good country antiques, dark pink drapes and attractive pink and green checked armchairs. Facing the entrance, a courtyard garden is set behind a glass wall, carefully tended and full of colour year-round. The cellar breakfast room is a particularly elegant variation on the theme, with high-backed tapestry chairs and round wooden tables. If the reception rooms have a rural feel, so do the bedrooms, all of which are differently decorated, with walls covered in grass cloth, or enlivened with a dash of colour in curtains and bedspreads, and carefully lit bathrooms clad in ginger or reddish marble. Our room under the eaves felt cosy, with views over the roof tops; others have four-posters or antique brass bedsteads. All in all easy-going and well run: a pleasure to stay in.

Nearby Latin Quarter; Musée de Cluny; Jardin du Luxembourg.
Location about halfway along the street, between rue Racine and rue de Vaugirard
Parking rue de l'Ecole de Médecine, rue Soufflot **Metro** Odéon
Food breakfast
Price €€€
Rooms 31; 26 double and twin, including suites, duplex and family rooms all with bath; all rooms have phone, modem point, TV, air-conditioning, minibar, hairdrier, safe **Facilities** sitting room, breakfast room
Credit cards AE, DC, MC, V
Children accepted
Disabled one room on ground floor, lift/elevator
Pets accepted **Closed** never
Proprietor Marianne Oberlin

SIXTH ARRONDISSEMENT

SAINT-GERMAIN-DES-PRES

RELAIS SAINT-SULPICE

3 rue Garancière, 75006 Paris
TEL (01) 46 33 99 00 **FAX** (01) 46 33 00 10
E-MAIL relaisstsulpice@wanadoo.fr

THIS NEWCOMER to our guide, sister of the Prince de Conti (see page 138), is a stylish hotel in one of the quiet, elegant streets that run between the church of Saint-Sulpice and the Luxembourg Gardens. Rooms are attractive in a fairly business-like way, with geometric patterned walls in some, and wrought-iron beds in all. There are two types: standard and deluxe, though the standard bedrooms are really not much smaller than the deluxe ones, and all have attractive views, either on to the classically styled internal well of the building, or on to the impressive bulk of Saint-Sulpice.

Once inside the front door, there is a reception desk on the right, and a small sitting area tucked into the other side of the lobby. The main public room is the airy and unusual breakfast room, with rather uncomfortable tables and chairs, but nevertheless cutting a dash. Our first impressions at the Saint-Sulpice made us think that we had come across a classy boutique hotel with a heart. In fact, it's less characterful and more straightforward and commercial than that, but nevertheless it makes a good address in a peaceful residential part of the Sixth Arrondissement.

NEARBY Jardin du Luxembourg; Saint-Sulpice.
LOCATION in a quiet street halfway between the Jardin du Luxembourg and Saint-Sulpice **PARKING** place Saint-Sulpice **METRO** Saint-Sulpice/Mabillon
FOOD breakfast
PRICE €€€
ROOMS 26; 23 double and twin, 3 triple, all with bath; all rooms have phone, modem point, TV, air-conditioning, minibar, hairdrier
FACILITIES sitting room, breakfast room, sauna
CREDIT CARDS AE, DC, MC, V
CHILDREN accepted
DISABLED access difficult, lift/elevator
PETS not accepted **CLOSED** never
MANAGER Eva Eriksson

SIXTH ARRONDISSEMENT

MONTPARNASSE

HOTEL LE SAINTE-BEUVE

9 rue Sainte-Beuve, 75006 Paris
TEL (01) 45 48 20 07 **FAX** (01) 45 48 67 52
WEBSITE www.paris-hotel-charme.com

ALL IS DISCRETION and understatement at this essentially simple little hotel with luxurious touches: plain cream walls, restrained patterns in the rich fabrics; beds draped in white, simple furniture mixing modern designs with country antiques, attractive pictures, fresh flowers strategically placed. A log fire burns in the classically-styled *salon*, where there is also a bar (and you can breakfast here too, if you wish).

The Sainte-Beuve always had an innate sense of style which rescued it from the rut and set it apart, along with some pampering extra services. Happily, this remains the case, despite its characterful founder, Bobette Compagnon, having sold the hotel to Jean-Pierre Egurreguy, who previously owned Brasserie Balzar. The *salon* has been redecorated but remains just as alluring, and the excellent breakfast – with bread from the master baker Mulot and newspapers, including the Herald Tribune – still arrives on a carefully laid tray and can still be ordered at any time of day until 10 pm. A selection of light dishes prepared in a neighbouring *bistrot* are also available, so that you need never leave your room. From the top floor, the winding, newly-carpeted wooden staircase makes a dizzying sight.

NEARBY boulevard Montparnasse; Jardin du Luxembourg..
LOCATION off boulevard Raspail, between places Lafou and Picasso **PARKING** in street or boulevard Montparnasse **METRO** Notre-Dame-des-Champs/Vavin
FOOD breakfast; room service
PRICE €€€
ROOMS 23 double and twin, including standard, deluxe and 2-bedroom apartments; all rooms have phone, modem point, TV, air-conditioning, minibar, hairdrier, safe **FACILITIES** sitting room, bar/breakfast room, internet booth
CREDIT CARDS AE, MC, V**CHILDREN** accepted
DISABLED access difficult, lift/elevator
PETS accepted **CLOSED** never
PROPRIETOR Jean-Pierre Egurreguy

Sixth Arrondissement

Saint-Germain-des-Pres

Hotel Saints-Peres

65 rue des Saints-Pères, 75006 Paris
Tel (01) 45 44 50 00 **Fax** (01) 45 44 90 83
E-mail hotelsts.peres.@wanadoo.fr **Website** www.esprit-de-france.com

Nearly all the bedrooms in this calmly sophisticated hotel look on to a leafy, glass-sided internal courtyard where you can breakfast or take a drink in the summer sunshine. Some of the upper bedrooms also afford a romantic view across Paris toward Saint-Sulpice, whose architect, Alphonse Daniel Gittard, built this fine town mansion in 1658 as his private residence. Gittard was architect to Louis XIV and founded the Academy of Architecture; his portrait hangs behind the reception desk. A special bedroom is No. 100 (Chambre à la fresque), the former salon, where you can contemplate the vanity of 17thC France in a vast ceiling fresco of Leda and the Swan, either from your bed or from the luxurious beignoir, which is separated from the bedroom only by a screen. It's now part of the Esprit de France group (see also the Mansart (page 36) and the d'Orsay (page 145).

For all this history, one might have expected rather more artfully decorated public rooms, and the sitting room struck us as bland and businesslike, with its pale leather armchairs and glass-topped occasional tables. Bedrooms, however, are restful and fairly spacious, and there are good paintings on the walls.

Nearby boulevard Saint-Germain; Saint-Sulpice; Jardin du Luxembourg.
Location halfway along the street, between boulevard Saint-Germain and rue de Grenelle **Parking** boulevard Saint-Germain (rue de Dragon) **Metro** Saint-Germain-des-Prés/Sèvres Babylon
Food breakfast
Price €€€
Rooms 36; 30 double and twin with bath, 4 with shower; 2 single with shower, 3 suites; all rooms have phone, modem point, TV, minibar, hairdrier
Facilities sitting room/bar, breakfast room, courtyard, garden, internet booth
Credit cards AE, MC, V **Children** accepted
Disabled lift/elevator **Pets** not accepted
Closed never **Proprietor** Paluel Martmont

SIXTH ARRONDISSEMENT

SAINT-GERMAIN-DES-PRES/LATIN QUARTER

HOTEL VILLA D'ESTREES

14 rue Git-le-Coeur, 75006 Paris
TEL (01) 55 42 71 11 **FAX** (01) 55 42 71 11
E-MAIL RDesarts@aol.com **WEBSITE** www.paris-hotel-latin-quarter.com

A BRAND NEW HOTEL, opened in November 2002. At the time of going to press we have only been able to look round, not test the hotel out by staying there, but what we saw was certainly worth recording, especially if you like your hotels very new and very *luxe*.

The front door, on a little street well placed for both the Left Bank and Ile de la Cité, leads directly into the large, rectangular lobby, which doubles as a sitting room, with the receptionist – behind a Regency desk – in one corner. The room is decorated, Empire-style, in blacks and deep reds, rather dark, rather formal and rather beautiful. The bedrooms – described as deluxe or suites – are decorated in a similarly masuculine vein, and are – as you would expect – pristine and very comfortable. The breakfast room is down stone steps in the former cellar.

In the Résidence des Arts across the road, there are a further 11 self-catering apartments, also spanking new, each with a kitchenette. You can choose from studios, suites or a top-floor apartment, ranging in price from 130 to 430 euros per night. You can breakfast at the hotel if you wish. Next door, on the corner, is a café, also belonging to the hotel.

NEARBY boulevard Saint-Germain; Notre-Dame; Latin Quarter.
LOCATION just off place Saint-André-des-Arts, on the borders of Saint-Germain and Latin Quarter **PARKING** place Saint-Michel, Ile de la Cité **METRO** Saint-Michel
RER Saint-Michel
FOOD breakfast
PRICE €€€€
ROOMS 12 double and twin, all with bath; all rooms have phone, modem point, TV, air-conditioning, safe, hairdrier; 10 self-catering studios and suites, one apartment
FACILITIES sitting room, breakfast room, internet booth in café opposite
CREDIT CARDS AE, DC, MC, V **CHILDREN** accepted
DISABLED access possible, lift/elevator
PETS not accepted **CLOSED** never
PROPRIETOR Robert Chevance

Sixth Arrondissement

Saint-Germain-des-Pres/Latin Quarter

Relais-Hotel Le Vieux Paris

9 rue Git-le-Coeur, 75006 Paris
Tel (01) 44 32 15 90 **Fax** (01) 43 26 00 15
E-mail reservation@vieuxparis.com **Website** www.vieuxparis.com

A building dating from 1480, the Relais-Hôtel le Vieux Paris was a famous Beat Generation dive where American writers such as Jack Kerouac, Allan Ginsberg and William Burroughs searched for 'life and love in Paris' as one contemporary has written in the visitors book when he paid a return visit. Nowadays the hotel is the obsession of Mme Odillard, helped by her son and daughter-in-law and the friendly chap on the reception desk, and precious little remains to remind one of those days. There are a few pieces of Beat Generation memorabilia, but they are rather out of place in the otherwise bland lobby. A cosy little sitting room with leather sofa and armchairs and a neat breakfast room with exposed stone walls and prettily laid tables make up the rest of the hotel's public spaces. Upstairs, the bedrooms have character and romantic charm, with old beams and fabric on the walls, some boldly patterned with classical motifs. Three of the suites are split-level, overlooking the Paris rooftops. While we like the Vieux-Paris, and appreciate that it's classed as a four-star hotel, and therefore priced accordingly, we remain surprised that it commands such high prices - more expensive, for example, than the Hotel de l'Abbaye (page 58).

Nearby boulevard Saint-Germain; Notre-Dame; Latin Quarter.
Location just off place Saint-André-des-Arts, on the borders of Saint-Germain and Latin Quarter **Parking** place Saint-Michel, Ile de la Cité **Metro** Saint-Michel
RER Saint-Michel
Food breakfast
Price €€€€
Rooms 19; 14 double and twin, 5 suites, all with bath or shower; suites have Jacuzzis; all rooms have phone, modem point, TV, air-conditioning, minibar, hairdrier **Facilities** sitting room, breakfast room
Credit cards AE, DC, MC, V
Children accepted **Disabled** not suitable
Pets not accepted **Closed** never **Proprietor** Odillard family

SEVENTH ARRONDISSEMENT

INVALIDES/EIFFEL TOWER QUARTER

CHAMP-DE-MARS

7 rue du Champ-de-Mars, 75007 Paris
TEL (01) 45 51 52 30 **FAX** (01) 45 51 64 36
E-MAIL stg@club-internet.fr **WEBSITE** www.hotel-du-champ-de-mars.com

A QUICK GLANCE at the smart façade of this excellent and extremely reasonably-priced two-star hotel – new to our guide this year – with its dark green paintwork and large arched windows, makes one suspect that caring hands are in place. And so they are, two pairs, belonging to Françoise Gourdal and her husband Stéphan. Having taken care with the decoration to provide a great deal more than one might expect at a hotel where two people can bed-and-breakfast for comfortably under 100 euros a night, they make sure that rooms are kept up to scratch and that guests come first. And its position, in a quiet street just round the corner from the bustle and delicious smells of the rue Cler street market, and a few paces from the green spaces of the Champ-de-Mars, is excellent.

Fabric plays a large part in the 'smart-country' decorative scheme of the hotel. In the *salon*/reception room boldly striped button armchairs co-ordinate with the deep red curtains and beige blinds, while in the breakfast room even the chairs are draped in fabric, with double tablecloths on circircular tables and ribboned pictures on the roughcast walls. Bedrooms are compact, but equally co-ordinated, with more fabric-covered chairs and matching bedheads, curtains and wallpaper friezes. Two look on to private flowered courtyards.

NEARBY rue Cler street market; Invalides; Eiffel Tower.
LOCATION in quiet side street off rue Clerbetween Invalides and Eiffel Tower
PARKING invalides **METRO** Ecole-Miltaire **RER** Invalides-Pont d'Alma
FOOD breakfast
PRICE €€
ROOMS 25 double and twin, all with bath or shower; all rooms have phone, modem point, TV, hairdrier **FACILITIES** sitting room, breakfast room
CREDIT CARDS AE, DC, MC, V **CHILDREN** accepted
DISABLED 2 ground floor bedrooms, lift/elevator **PETS** not accepted
CLOSED never **PROPRIETORS** Stéphan and Françoise Gourdal

SEVENTH ARRONDISSEMENT

SAINT-GERMAIN-DES-PRES

DUC DE SAINT-SIMON

14 rue de Saint-Simon, 75007 Paris
TEL (01) 44 39 20 20 **FAX** (01) 45 48 68 25
E-MAIL duc.de.saint.simon@wanadoo. fr

A RECENT STAY confirmed our belief that this is one of the most alluring, and consistently pleasing, small hotels in Paris, the perfect place for a special occasion such as an anniversary. First glimpsed through two pairs of French windows beyond a pretty courtyard, the Saint-Simon's interior looks wonderfully inviting; and so it is – there is a warm, beautifully furnished *salon* with the distinctly private-house feel that the Swedish proprietor seeks to maintain, and elegant yet cosy bedrooms, all individually decorated with not a jarring note. The twin bedrooms are more spacious than doubles. Everywhere you look are rich fabrics, gloriously overstuffed pieces of furniture and cleverly conceived paint effects. The kilim-lined lift is a particularly original idca.

The white-painted 19thC house backs on to an 18thC building behind, also part of the hotel, with a tiny secret garden wedged in between. Breakfasts can be had in the courtyard or in the intimate cellar bar; service is courteous, and Gun Karin Lalisse, the manager, runs the hotel with great charm and efficiency. Though prices are high, they are not unreasonable for what is offered.

NEARBY Invalides; Musée d'Orsay; Musée Rodin.
LOCATION between rue Courier and rue de Grenelle **PARKING** boulevard Raspail
METRO Rue du Bac/Solférino
FOOD breakfast, light meals
PRICE €€€-€€€€
ROOMS 34; 29 double and twin, 28 with bath, one with shower; 5 suites with bath; all rooms have phone, modem point, TV on request; some rooms have air-conditioning **FACILITIES** 2 sitting rooms, breakfast room, bar
CREDIT CARDS AE, MC, V **CHILDREN** accepted
DISABLED lift/elevator **PETS** not accepted
CLOSED never
PROPRIETOR M. Lindqvist

Seventh Arrondissement

Invalides Quarter

Latour-Maubourg

150 rue de Grenelle, 75007 Paris
Tel (01) 47 05 16 14 **Fax** (01) 47 05 16 14
E-mail info@latourmaubourg.com **Website** www.latourmaubourg.com

In a handy location by a quiet metro entrance and a taxi rank, this gracious hotel has the feel of a private house. To maintain it, Victor and Maria Orsenne, who live in an apartment on the premises with their children and their friendly dog, Faust, have recently decided to accept only couples and families and decline groups of friends. Before the Orsenne's took over in 1994, the building had been in the same family for 150 years. They have wisely left well alone, upgrading where necessary, but leaving the hotel's original proportions intact. A lovely wooden staircase, with elegant balustrades, sweeps up to the bedrooms. The best of these are entered by double doors, and have marble fireplaces, French windows and period paintings; some, including the suite, are huge. They are simply decorated, with creamy walls mixed with warmer colours for curtains and bedcovers. (You can choose between duvet or sheets and blankets; just let them know in advance.) We have had many plaudits from people who appreciate Maria's calm, friendly presence and the pension-style ambience (at night you keep your key and are given a code for the front door), although others have mentioned the need to spruce up the rooms and bathrooms.

Nearby Invalides; Eiffel Tower; Musée d'Orsay; Musée Rodin.
Location by La Tour-Maubourg metro, on the corner of boulevard de La Tour Maubourg **Parking** rue de la Constantine **Metro** La Tour-Maubourg
Food breakfast
Price €€
Rooms 10; 7 double and twin, 6 with bath, one with shower; 2 single, one with bath, one with shower; one suite/family room; all rooms have phone, modem point, TV, minibar, hairdrier **Facilities** sitting/breakfast room, internet booth
Credit cards MC, V **Children** accepted
Disabled access difficult
Pets not accepted **Closed** never
Proprietors Victor and Maria Orsenne

Seventh Arrondissement

Saint-Germain-des-Pres

Lenox-Saint-Germain

9 rue de l'Université, 75007 Paris
Tel (01) 42 96 10 95 **Fax** (01) 42 61 52 83
E-mail hotel@lemoxsaintgermain.com **Website** www.lenoxsaintgermain.com

A quiet sophistication pervades the Lenox, the more central and polished of a pair of sister hotels (see Hôtel Lenox Montparnasse, page 154). Through the entrance is a sitting area, where traditional furnishings – leather sofas and chairs, console tables and columns – are lightened by pale paint effects and friezes depicting classical scenes. Well-lit paintings, fresh flowers and potted plants add a touch of colour; rugs soften the granite floor. The clubby, art deco style bar – all wood and tan leather seats – is open from 5pm to 2am and is a congenial place to spend an evening, even though the drinks are pricey. Breakfast is served in the vaulted, brick-walled cellar.

A total renovation of most of the bedrooms has recently been completed, and they now include triple rooms as well as doubles. They are thoughtfully decorated, and their price (at the top end of our 'moderate' price band) is very fair. Ones on the first floor have splendid huge windows, original cornicing and large bathrooms. We have always found the staff friendly and welcoming, making the Lenox a sound and well-priced choice.

Nearby Musée d'Orsay; Louvre; Invalides.
Location between rue des Saintes-Pères and rue S. Bottin
Parking rue Montalembert, boulevard Saint-Germain (rue du Dragon) **Metro** rue du Bac/Saint-Germain-des-Prés
Food breakfast, light meals
Price €€
Rooms 32; 30 double, twin and triple, 2 duplex suites, all with bath; all rooms have phone, TV, air-conditioning, hairdrier, safe
Facilities sitting area, bar, breakfast room, internet booth
Credit cards AE, DC, MC, V
Children accepted
Disabled lift/elevator **Pets** accepted
Closed never **Proprietor** Michel Grenet

SEVENTH ARRONDISSEMENT

INVALIDES/EIFFEL TOWER QUARTER

SAINT-DOMINIQUE

62 rue Saint-Dominique, 75007 Paris
TEL (01) 47 05 51 44 **FAX** (01) 47 05 81 28
E-MAIL saint-dominique.reservations@wanadoo.fr **WEBSITE** www.hotelstdominique.com

PART OF THE APPEAL of this hotel, when we first came across it, was the bubbly enthusiasm of the owner/manager Monsieur Tible, who was always ready for a friendly chat or willing to help with the most trivial of problems, and was rarely absent from his post in the attractive reception-cum-sitting-room. So it was with sadness that on a return visit for this new edition, we found he had sold, and gone. His long-time assistant assured us, however, that little else had changed. A wooden spiral staircase leads down to a little breakfast room – a white-painted vault with a mixture of Lloyd loom and wicker chairs – where breakfasts are generous and attractively presented.

The small but well-equipped bedrooms are decorated in a confidently colourful style. Pretty *toile de jouy* furnishings can be seen in some rooms; in most, predominantly pine furniture, with the occasional brass bedhead.

Across a flowery courtyard, where white cast-iron tables and chairs invite summer guests to sit outside and have a drink, the annexe bedrooms tend to be smaller and more modest, but are beautifully quiet.

NEARBY Invalides; Musée Rodin; Eiffel Tower.
LOCATION between rue de La Tour-Maubourg and rue Jean Nicot **PARKING** rue de la Motte-Piquet **METRO** La Tour-Maubourg/Invalides **RER** Invalides-Pont de l'Alma
FOOD breakfast
PRICE €€
ROOMS 34; 31 double and twin, all with bath or shower, 3 single with shower; all rooms have phone, TV, minibar; some rooms have hairdrier, safe
FACILITIES sitting area, breakfast room, courtyard
CREDIT CARDS AE, DC, MC, V
CHILDREN accepted
DISABLED access difficult, lift/elevator
PETS accepted **CLOSED** never
MANAGER Karin Gachet

SEVENTH ARRONDISSEMENT

INVALIDES/EIFFEL TOWER QUARTER

THOUMIEUX

79 rue Saint-Dominique, 75007 Paris
TEL (01) 47 05 49 75 **FAX** (01) 47 05 36 96
E-MAIL bthoumieux@aol.com **WEBSITE** www.thoumieux.fr

IN THE SHADOW of the Eiffel Tower, this friendly place, once a convent, revolves around a bustling brasserie, which has belonged to the Thoumieux family since the 1930s, and is now run by Françoise Thoumieux and her husband, Jean Bassalert, with the charming Franco-American, Michael at reception. Except for the addition of mirrored walls and modern prints, the cavernous restaurant, with its black fascia, dark red velvet curtains and banquettes, seems to have changed little since its opening. It specializes in the regional cuisine of the Southwest – *foie gras, cassoulet* and the like – and honest, drinkable house wines. On Sundays, it is full to bursting with families who have been going there forever.

The hotel entrance is to the right of the restaurant, and its stylish reception can be found on the first floor. The ten bedrooms are almost all surprisingly spacious, though, despite tasteful modern furniture, they remain slightly soulless. But the welcome is so warm and friendly, and the service so personal, that 80% of clients are repeat visitors, and a large proportion of them use Thoumieux as their Paris base. Breakfast is excellent, as you would expect, and if you want a place that feels more like the sort you find outside Paris, a friendly restaurant-with-rooms, then Thoumieux makes an excellent choice. The large, airy breakfast room can be hired for functions.

NEARBY Invalides; Musée Rodin; boulevard Saint-Germain; Eiffel Tower.
LOCATION between boulevard La Tour-Maubourg and rue Amélie **PARKING** Invalides
METRO La Tour-Maubourg/Invalides **RER** Invalides-Pont d'Alma
FOOD breakfast, lunch, dinner
PRICE €€
ROOMS 10 double and twin, all with bath; all rooms have phone, modem point, TV
FACILITIES restaurant, breakfast room **CREDIT CARDS** AE, MC, V
CHILDREN accepted **DISABLED** not suitable
PETS accepted **CLOSED** never
PROPRIETORS Françoise Thoumieux and Jean Bassalert

SEVENTH ARRONDISSEMENT

SAINT-GERMAIN-DES-PRES

UNIVERSITE

22 rue de l'Université, 75007 Paris
TEL (01) 42 61 09 39 **FAX** (01) 42 60 40 84
E-MAIL hoteluniversity@wanadoo.fr **WEBSITE** www.hoteluniversite.com

THE MOOD OF THIS DIGNIFIED town-house-turned-hotel is set as soon as you step through the front door into the flag-stoned, beamed entrance, its stone walls hung with tapestries, and furnished in a masculine style, with striped velvet chairs, a grandfather clock and other dark wood antiques. The effect is rescued from being too heavy by a glimpse through glass of a tiny verdant courtyard garden.

Most of the comfortable, equally traditional bedrooms lead off grasspaper-clad corridors through velvet-padded doors.They are larger than most others we saw in this area, but not over-priced. A number have exposed beams and attractive old-fashioned wallpaper with matching bedspreads. Furniture ranges from antique wardrobes and vast carved armoires to small chaises-longues and velvet button chairs; ornate mirrors and handsome oil paintings – some portraits, others nautical – adorn the walls.

Guests can have breakfast in either of the two ground floor *salons*. The one by the front door on two levels is particularly snug and private. The cellar has been converted into a conference room with an informal, rather corporate air.

NEARBY Musée d'Orsay; Louvre; boulevard Saint-Germain.
LOCATION between rue des Saintes-Pères and rue de Beaune **PARKING** rue Montalembert **METRO** rue du Bac/Saint-Germain-des-Prés **RER** Musée d'Orsay
FOOD breakfast, light snacks
PRICE €€€
ROOMS 28; 20 double and twin, 6 single, 2 triple, all with bath or shower; all rooms have phone, modem point, TV, air-conditioning, hairdrier, minibar, safe
FACILITIES restaurant, breakfast room
CREDIT CARDS AE, MC, V
CHILDREN accepted **DISABLED** no special facilities
PETS not accepted **CLOSED** never
PROPRIETOR Mme Bergmann

Seventh Arrondissement

Invalides Quarter

Valadon

16 rue Valadon, 75007 Paris
Tel (01) 47 53 89 85 **Fax** (01) 44 18 90 56
E-mail info@hotelvaladon.com **Website** www.hotelvaladon.com

The price of a standard double room is (at present, at any rate) kept under the magical 100 euro mark, breakfast included, at this new two-star hotel opened by Victor and Maria Orsenne of the Latour Maubourg (see page 87). It's been decorated and furnished in contemporary and rather workaday style, with softly piped jazz to accompany your entrance and a neat little breakfast room at the rear. Here there is a shared fridge for guests to keep their purchases from the nearby rue Cler street market, and snack on them at any time of the day. Breakfast is available whenever you want it.

If the public parts are somewhat bland, the bedrooms are given a great lift by their colour scheme: bold black-and-white stripes are carried through curtains, valances and armchairs. Beds and linen, as at the Latour Maubourg, are of notably good quality. Each room contains three beds, a double and a single, which can be used as a day bed, or to sleep a third person. One room has a terrace, another a view of the Eiffel Tower. All in all, good value, we felt.

Nearby rue Cler street market; Invalides; Eiffel Tower.
Location in a quiet street near rue Cler between Invalides and Eiffel Tower
Parking Invalides **Metro** Ecole-Militaire **RER** Invalides-Pont d'Alma
Food breakfast
Price €
Rooms 12 double, twin and triple, 11 with shower, one with bath; all rooms have phone, modem point, TV, hairdrier, fans in summer
Facilities breakfast room, internet booth
Credit cards MC, V
Children accepted
Disabled access difficult, lift/elevator
Pets accepted **Closed** never
Proprietors Victor and Maria Orsenne

SEVENTH ARRONDISSEMENT

SAINT-GERMAIN-DES-PRES

VERNEUIL

8 rue de Verneuil, 75007 Paris
TEL (01) 42 60 82 14 **FAX** (01) 42 61 40 38
E-MAIL hotelverneuil@wanadoo.fr **WEBSITE** www.hotelverneuil.com

LOCATED IN ONE of the most alluring streets in the area, close to the gorgeous antique and fabric shops that predominate in this part of the Rive Gauche, this hotel used to be known as Hôtel Verneuil Saint-Germain. The subtle name change was by no means the only one after the hotel was taken over by Sylvie de Lattre in 1997, although the prices happily remained the same. The former rather kitsch decoration was ousted and replaced with the traditional style of an elegant private house, much more in keeping with the building's 17thC origins. Today, it is rather beautiful and enveloping.

Bedrooms, which vary in size (specify a large one), are all individually designed, some with boldly patterned wallpapers, and have antique furniture, elegant prints and pleasant lighting. The cosy sitting room is ideal for reading or relaxing. Buffet breakfasts are taken in the stone-walled cellar, which has wooden tables and comfortable seating.

According to recent visitors, the ambience at the Verneuil is happy and homely, and we agree; more reports would be welcome.

NEARBY Musée du Louvre; Musée d'Orsay; Ile de la Cité; boulevard Saint-Germain.
LOCATION between rue des Saintes-Pères and rue de Beaune **PARKING** boulevard Saint-Germain (rue du Dragon) **METRO** Saint-Germain-des-Prés
FOOD breakfast
PRICE €€€
ROOMS 26 double and twin, all with bath; all rooms have phone, modem point, TV, minibar, hairdrier, safe; some rooms have air-conditioning
FACILITIES sitting room, breakfast room
CREDIT CARDS AE, DC, MC, V
CHILDREN accepted
DISABLED lift/elevator **PETS** accepted
CLOSED never
PROPRIETOR Sylvie de Lattre

EIGHTH ARRONDISSEMENT

OPERA QUARTER

HOTEL AMARANTE BEAU MANOIR

6 rue de l'Arcade, 75008 Paris
TEL (01) 53 43 28 28 **FAX** (01) 53 43 28 88
E-MAIL beau-manoir@wanadoo.fr **WEBSITE** www.hotel-beau-manoir.com

THE TEIL FAMILY have sold their neighbouring hotels in the Opéra district, the Beau Manoir and the Lido, and the new owners have combined the two to create a larger four-star with a small change of name and the kind of facilities designed to appeal to business people: fitness centre, meeting and seminar rooms, for example. The decorative style, however, remains unchanged, still bearing the inimitable stamp of the Teils. As the name suggests, the hotel has the look and feel of a country manor, evoked downstairs by tapestry wallhangings and upholstered furniture, stone walls, dark wood panelling and furniture, and heavy damask drapes. In the cellar breakfast room, where a gargantuan buffet is on offer each morning, the manorial theme is continued with wooden tables and banquettes with leather seats, and an array of burnished copper pans and jugs.

Less masculine than the public rooms, the spacious bedrooms are decorated in strong sophisticated colours with every detail in place, from the carefully chosen porcelain lamps to the mellow wood furniture, specially made in the Massif Central. Although now technically too large to be a charming small hotel, the Beau Manoir's rustic atmosphere and delightful staff convinced us that it still has a place in this guide.

NEARBY Madeleine; Opéra Garnier; rue du Faubourg Saint-Honoré.
LOCATION between boulevard Haussmann and rue Faubourg Saint-Honoré, W of Madeleine **PARKING** private or place de la Madeleine **METRO** Madeleine
FOOD breakfast, 24-hour room service
PRICE €€€
ROOMS 60 double and twin, and suites, all with bath; all rooms have phone, modem point, TV, air-conditioning, minibar, hairdrier, safe
FACILITIES sitting room, breakfast room, bar, meeting rooms, gym, internet booth
CREDIT CARDS AE, DC, MC, V **CHILDREN** accepted
DISABLED special facilities available, lift/elevator **PETS** accepted
CLOSED never **MANAGER** M. Raux

Eighth Arrondissement

Opera Quarter

Hotel de l'Arcade

9 rue de l'Arcade, 75008 Paris
Tel (01) 53 30 60 00 **Fax** (01) 40 07 03 07
E-mail contact@hotel-arcade.com **Website** www.hotel-arcade.com

Though well-placed for theatres, the opera and ritzy shops, this part of the eighth district lacks charming yet affordable hotels, so our inspector was delighted to find this one, which opened a few years ago after a two-year renovation. The building is mid-19thC, but, with the exception of the façade and some cornicing, few period details remain. Instead, a very contemporary elegance prevails. Smart glazed doors, guarded by bay trees in tubs, lead into a discreet entrance. Gérard Gallet, who remodelled the Orient Express, is responsible for the interior: colour-washed wood panelling, a striking Delisle chandelier and a happy blend of Louis XVI-style and comfortable modern furniture.

Upstairs, pastel bedrooms and bathrooms show an equally careful attention to detail, including custom-made Swiss furniture and stylish wood-framed bedheads. The linen curtains come from England, the bathroom tiles from Sardinia. Our inspector was particularly taken with the duplexes, where a staircase leads up to the small gallery bedroom. A three-star hotel with three-star prices offering four-star comfort and services. Staff are as suave and chic as the hotel itself.

Nearby Opéra Garnier; rue du Faubourg Saint-Honoré.
Location between rue Chaveau Lagarde and rue des Mathurins **Parking** place de la Madeleine or boulevard Malesherbes **Metro** Madeleine/St-Augustin/Havre Caumartin
Food breakfast
Price €€€
Rooms 41 double and twin, single, duplex, all with bath; all rooms have phone, modem point, TV, air-conditioning, minibar, hairdrier, safe
Facilities sitting area, breakfast room
Credit cards AE, MC, V **Children** accepted
Disabled specially adapted rooms, lift/elevator
Pets accepted
Closed never **Manager** M. Kerrien

EIGHTH ARRONDISSEMENT

CHAMPS-ELYSEES

HOTEL DE L'ELYSEE

12 rue des Saussaies, 75008 Paris
TEL (01) 42 65 29 25 **FAX** (01) 42 65 64 28
E-MAIL hotel.de.l.elysee@wanadoo.fr

THE ELYSEE OCCUPIES A fine building, in this case one which straddles two streets, its multi-balconied prow tapering into the corner. Sister to the Ferrandi (page 67), it employs a similar style of period decoration. We preferred the Elysée's *salon*: elegant yet cosy, with an open fire burning in the grate on cool days; in front is the breakfast area and bar, where you sit at dainty marble-topped tables. The minute lift takes you up to bedrooms which are all different and mostly quite generous on space, although sizes vary and rooms are priced accordingly. Apart from the two suites, the best rooms are on the corner, with large windows on two sides. In these you will find pretty *toile de jouy* wallpapers and canopied beds, a small table and chairs and large antique wardrobes. Bathrooms are clad in pink marble. One correspondent describes their deluxe room as 'fetching', whilst another found theirs 'rather staid and dated...not executed with much panache'. The same correspondent, however, returns regularly to the hotel having discovered the two characterful little top floor suites, which he loves, particularly the one done out in a striking yellow floral wallpaper.

NEARBY Champs-Elysées; rue du Faubourg Saint-Honoré.
LOCATION across rue du Faubourg Saint-Honoré from Palais de l'Elysée at junction with rue Montalivet **PARKING** Rond Point des Champs-Elysées **METRO** Champs-Elysées-Clemenceau/Miromesnil
FOOD breakfast
PRICE €€
ROOMS 32; 30 single, double and twin, 25 with bath, 5 with shower; 2 suites with bath; all rooms have phone, modem point, TV, air-conditioning, minibar, hairdrier, safe
FACILITIES sitting room, breakfast room
CREDIT CARDS AE, DC, MC, V
CHILDREN accepted
DISABLED access difficult, lift/elevator
PETS accepted **CLOSED** never **PROPRIETOR** Mme Lafond

EIGHTH ARRONDISSEMENT

CHAMPS-ELYSEES

HOTEL ELYSEES-MERMOZ

30 rue Jean-Mermoz, 75008 Paris
TEL (01) 42 25 75 30 **FAX** (01) 45 62 87 10
E-MAIL elyseesmermoz@worldnet.fr **WEBSITE** www.hotel-elyseesmermoz.com

THE WORK OF A talented designer, the effect of this hotel, renovated several years ago, is fresh, pretty and full of clever touches – like painting lemon yellow the blank walls of the internal courtyard, thereby much improving the vista from the back bedrooms.

The lobby is conservatory-style, very delicate, with marble and terracotta tiled floor, painted pale green woodwork, marbled pillars, trellis, cane furniture, a glass roof and a little yellow breakfast-room tucked behind a curtain. The bedrooms are thoughtfully designed, each with a small entrance which cuts out noise from the corridor. Rooms are either blue or yellow, with fabrics from Pierre Frey including attractive wall hangings behind the bed. Desks are cleverly slipped into a V-shaped space in the pretty panelled cupboards. Bathrooms are charming, with eye-catching sea blue basins made by a new technique using fired and glazed lava, with matching blue tiles on the floor and a large mirror on the wall above the wood-panelled bath. Suites are more luxurious, recently redecorated in red with elegant bedside lamps and rich fabrics. Our favourite had what looked to be Moghul Indian touches, although the charming owner assured us it was neo-Gothic.

NEARBY Champs-Elysées; Grand Palais.
LOCATION close to junction with rue Rabelais **PARKING** Rond Point des Champs-Elysées **METRO** Franklin-Roosevelt
FOOD breakfast
PRICE €€
ROOMS 26; 21 double and twin, 5 suites, all with bath; all rooms have phone, modem point, TV, air-conditioning, minibar, hairdrier, safe
FACILITIES sitting area, breakfast room, meeting room
CREDIT CARDS AE, DC, MC, V **CHILDREN** accepted
DISABLED one suitable room, lift/elevator
PETS accepted
CLOSED never **PROPRIETOR** M. Breuil

Eighth Arrondissement

Champs-Elysees

Hotel Galileo

54 rue Galilée, 75008 Paris
Tel (01) 47 20 66 06 **Fax** (01) 47 20 67 17
E-mail hotelgalileo@wanadoo.fr **Website** www.hotel-ile-saintlouis.com

A breath of fresh air in this sometimes stuffy district, the tranquil, sophisticated little Galiléo is hotelier Roland Buffat's venture across the river to the Right Bank (see also Les Deux Iles, page 41). Some might argue that it is his most successful. The cool beige and white decoration in the calm, sophisticated, subtly lit bedrooms has recently been jettisoned in favour of a warmer combination of 'pawpaw' and white. Most are large, with attractive architectural or botanical prints, fabric-covered furniture and pristine high-tech bathrooms. Downstairs, the public rooms are also tastefully furnished, skilfully combining the traditional with the modern. So, in the congenial *salon*/entrance hall, a tapestry hangs happily alongside modern prints, antique and contemporary furniture sits felicitously side by side.

Down a pretty staircase, a small sitting area overlooks a glorious, tiny stepped garden; the trellis-framed mirror at its far end creates the illusion that it is much larger than it really is. Another cleverly placed mirror, this time decorated with pineapple lights, makes the little breakfast-room feel far from claustrophobic. Breakfast is a buffet with cereal, yogurt, eggs and freshly squeezed orange juice, as well as the usual croissants with jam.

Nearby Champs-Elysées; Arc de Triomphe.
Location between rue Vernet and ave Marceau **Parking** Champs-Elysées
Metro George V/Charles de Gaulle Etoile **RER** Charles de Gaulle Etoile
Food breakfast, room service
Price €€
Rooms 27; 23 double and twin, all with bath; 4 single, all with shower; all rooms have phone, modem point, TV, air-conditioning, minibar, hairdrier
Facilities 2 sitting areas, breakfast room, internet booth
Credit cards AE, MC, V **Children** accepted
Disabled access possible, lift/elevator **Pets** accepted
Closed never **Proprietor** Roland Buffat

Eighth Arrondissement

Champs-Elysees

Lancaster

7 rue de Berri, 75008 Paris
Tel (01) 40 76 40 76 **Fax** (01) 40 76 40 00
E-mail reservations@hotel-lancaster.fr **Website** www.hotel-lancaster.fr

It's hard to fault the Lancaster. Even the hotel's imperfect location seems to work to its advantage, as you step from the brash world of the Champs Elysées into a private house atmosphere of civilized calm and understated luxury. It's a hotel with a history: a grand *ancien régime*-style townhouse, purchased in 1930 by legendary hotelier Emile Wolf, who filled it with antiques and *objets d'art* and a starry array of guests including Noel Coward and Marlene Dietrich. Its present owner, Grace Leo-Andrieu, who also owns the Montalembert (page 144), has deftly brought the Lancaster up to date while preserving its atmosphere of unflashy glamour and carefully adding to Wolf's eclectic collection of furniture and art, much of which was acquired during the war when guests used barter to pay their bills; a system that resulted in some splendid Boris Pastoukhoff paintings.

Don't miss tea in the enchanting, pale green little Salon Berri and a ride in the original red leather lift. Most stunning of all the stunning bedrooms is the suite dedicated to Marlene Dietrich, decorated in her favourite shades of lilac. As you would expect, prices are high, but exceptionally kind, courteous staff provide impeccable and unobtrusive service. Top chef Michel Troisgros took charge of the intimate restaurant in spring 2003.

Nearby Arc de Triomphe; Champs Elysées.
Location just N of Champs-Elysées **Parking** rue de Berri **Metro** George V/Franklin D. Roosevelt
Food breakfast, lunch, dinner; room service
Price €€€€
Rooms 50 single, double and twin, 10 suites, all with bath; all rooms have phone, TV, air-conditioning, minibar, hairdrier, safe **Facilities** 2 sitting rooms, restaurant, meeting room, café/bar, garden, gym **Credit cards** AE, DC, MC, V
Children accepted **Disabled** lift/elevator
Pets not accepted
Closed never **Manager** Régis Lecendreux

EIGHTH ARRONDISSEMENT

CHAMPS-ELYSEES

HOTEL DE VIGNY

9-11 rue Balzac, 75008 Paris
TEL (01) 42 99 80 80 **FAX** (01) 42 99 80 40
E-MAIL de.vigny@wanadoo.fr **WEBSITE** www.relaischateaux.fr/vigny

THIS SMALL BUT OPULENT Relais et Château hotel occupies a striking modern building with a bowed glass front, a stone's throw from the Arc de Triomphe. Inside, the style is traditional, with an abundance of mellow wood and beautiful fabrics, but not intimidating. Deep sofas andhighly polished furniture fill the plush reception *salon*, where a log fire burns invitingly on chilly days. There's also a little library, perfect for *tête-à-têtes*, and a clubby bar/restaurant, Baretto, with leather seats and art deco details, which is open from 7 am to 11.30pm and serves drinks, as well as breakfast, lunch and dinner. The food is classic French with a modern touch.

Each immaculate bedroom is decorated in a different style, from the utterly feminine – floral fabrics and a draped canopy above the bed – to masculine leather combined with rich dark tones. Bathrooms blend marble and wood, and all the suites and one double room are kitted out with Jacuzzis and CD players. Our only quibbles are that the reception and corridors are lit by a harsh, unattractive orange light; and that some of the double rooms are small considering their sky-high prices.

NEARBY Champs-Elysées; Arc de Triomphe.
LOCATION on the corner with rue de Chateaubriand **PARKING** private or ave de Friedland **METRO** Charles de Gaulle Etoile/George V **RER** Charles de Gaulle Etoile
FOOD breakfast, lunch, dinner; room service
PRICE €€€€
ROOMS 37; 25 double and twin, 24 with bath, one with shower; one single with bath; 8 suites, 3 junior suites, all with bath; all rooms have phone, TV, air-conditioning, minibar, hairdrier **FACILITIES** sitting area, sitting room, bar/restaurant
CREDIT CARDS AE, DC, MC, V
CHILDREN accepted
DISABLED access possible in suites, lift/elevator
PETS accepted **CLOSED** never
MANAGER Charles Bourdin

NINTH ARRONDISSEMENT

OPERA QUARTER

CHOPIN

10 boulevard Montmartre (46 passage Jouffroy), 75009 Paris
TEL (01) 47 70 58 10 **FAX** (01) 42 47 00 70

DEFINITELY ONE of our top two-star hotels, with perhaps the most charming façade of all. It stands at the end of passage Jouffroy, one of the 19thC glass-and-steel roofed arcades which thread this no-frills shopping and theatre neighbourhood, and as you approach you may worry that it will be a tourist trap. Not at all. We found a warm and friendly welcome from the receptionist ("I like this job; I'm paid to smile"), and the caring hands of owner Philippe Bidal is immediately in evidence in the pretty little breakfast room, landings dressed up with a couple of chairs and a flower arrangement, and corridors clad in warm colours and lit by lights over the many pictures. Our room, No. 412, was one of the best, with coral-coloured walls and a third bed as well as simple furniture which included a desk and chairs, and a bright white bathroom. Tucked under the eaves and approached along a narrow, creaky corridor, it had the feel of an artist's garret. Set well back from the main roads, all the rooms are quiet. The continental breakfast is a cut above the average, yet reasonably priced, with hot milk for the coffee, as well as orange juice and yogurt, while downstairs a buffet is served. Double room and breakfast for well under 100 euros.

NEARBY Musée Grévin; Grands Boulevards; Opéra Garnier.
LOCATION end of passage Jouffroy, which leads off boulevard Montmartre next to Musée Grévin **PARKING** rue Chauchat **METRO** rue Montmartre/Richelieu-Druout
FOOD breakfast
PRICE €
ROOMS 36; 32 double, twin and triple, 12 with bath, 20 with shower; 4 single, one with bath, 3 with shower; all rooms have phone, TV
FACILITIES sitting area, breakfast room **CREDIT CARDS** AE, DC, MC, V
CHILDREN accepted **DISABLED** access difficult, lift/elevator
PETS accepted **CLOSED** never
PROPRIETOR Philippe Bidal

Ninth Arrondissement

Opera Quarter

LANGLOIS

63 rue Saint-Lazare, 75009 Paris
Tel (01) 48 74 78 24 **Fax** (01) 49 95 04 43
E-mail hotel-des-croises@wanadoo.fr

When we first visited the remarkable Hôtel des Croisés (now Langlois) a few years ago, it had been run by the same family for decades, during which time – and the key to its charm – it had remained largely unchanged. Then it was taken over. Improvements were made, thankfully, sympathetically. And then, in 2001, it starred in a Hollywood remake of Charade. In the film it was called the Langlois and, in honour of the movie, the owner kept the name. Though the clientele has become a bit more hip of late, the Langlois itself remains matronly, quiet and solid, with the air of a provincial town hotel.

The stone-fronted mansion is entered through double doors. The hall is baronial, with carved stone walls and an ornate wooden archway. To the right is a pretty breakfast room with faded pink Lloyd loom chairs. The original lift, with curtained windows, takes you up to the huge bedrooms, some with extraordinary ceramic fireplaces, plaster busts, big beds, leather armchairs and – the only changes – minibars and brand-new bathrooms. Under the eaves is an apartment which offers amongst the best value in Paris, with two twin bedrooms, a bathroom and kitchenette, and views of Montmartre. The hotel is handy for the Gare Saint-Lazare but is otherwise in a nondescript part of town.

Nearby Gare Saint-Lazare; boulevard Haussman; Opéra Garnier.
Location in stretch of street between square de la Trinité and rue de la Rochefoucauld **Parking** rue Pigalle **Metro** Trinité
Food breakfast
Price €€
Rooms 27; 26 with bath, one with shower; all rooms have phone, TV, minibar
Facilities breakfast room **Credit cards** AE, MC, V
Children accepted **Disabled** access difficult, lift/elevator
Pets accepted **Closed** never
Proprietor Ahmet Abut

TWELFTH ARRONDISSEMENT

BASTILLE QUARTER

PAVILLON BASTILLE

65 rue de Lyon, 75009 Paris
TEL (01) 43 43 65 65 **FAX** (01) 43 43 96 52
E-MAIL hotel-pavillon@akamail.com **WEBSITE** www.pavillon-bastille.com

A 19THC TOWNHOUSE set back from the busy road, whose interior has been designed with a capital D: perfect for the pair of Beautiful People who stood with us at the front door (you ring the bell and your luggage is swiftly taken for you), but a mite intimidating for the merely footsore. It's the type of interior which seems to cock a snoop, rather than to embrace and comfort. The only colours used throughout are blue and yellow, with lots of mirrors on walls and ceilings. The four tall steel uplighters in the sitting area are connected by toga-like draped material in a Classical pastiche, while those other prerequisites of Post-Modern architecture, the vertical line and the sensuous curve, are much in evidence. But if the decoration is mannered, the welcome and the service are not. Thoughtful touches include the complimentary wine served each evening in the reception room, the free soft drinks and beers from the minibar, the book of useful information in the bedroom, and the weather forecast posted up each morning. The copious buffet breakfast has a centrepiece of fresh fruit piled on ice. A small hotel with the amenities and service of a much larger one, and prices which are – probably due to the less popular location – extremely reasonable for what's offered.

NEARBY place de la Bastille; Opéra Paris Bastille; Gare de Lyon.
LOCATION at Bastille end of rue de Lyon **PARKING** Opéra Bastille **METRO** Bastille
RER Gare de Lyon
FOOD breakfast
PRICE €€
ROOMS 23 double and twin, all with bath; one suite; all rooms have phone, modem point, TV (video in 3 rooms), air-conditioning, hairdrier, safe
FACILITIES sitting area, bar, breakfast room, courtyard, internet booth
CREDIT CARDS AE,DC, MC, V **CHILDREN** accepted
DISABLED access difficult, lift/elevator
PETS accepted **CLOSED** never **PROPRIETORS** M. and Mme Arnaud

Thirteenth Arrondissement

Gobelins Quarter

Residence Les Gobelins

9 rue des Gobelins, 75013 Paris
Tel (01) 47 07 26 90 **Fax** (01) 43 31 44 05
E-mail reservation@hotelgobelins.com **Website** www.hotelgobelins.com

In a side street behind the famous tapestry factory, Manufacture des Gobelins, in one of the city's few unspoiled areas, this modest little hotel – or rather its delightful *patronne* – won this inspector's heart. An exuberant yet kindly Jamaican woman, Jennifer Poirier bought the hotel 18 years ago with her husband, Philippe. They renovated it, with the aim of creating a budget hotel, where they would be happy to stay themselves.

They have wisely kept the decoration simple, though downstairs, large table lamps add a touch of style to the plain entrance hall with its tiled floor and wicker furniture. From here you look out to a pretty courtyard garden, where you can keep cool in the shade of the vines if there's a heatwave. In the brilliant yellow and green breakfast room, Jennifer says she wanted to introduce some Jamaican sunshine (though she feels she might have overdone it and is considering toning down the colour). The bedrooms are all similar: large, clean, freshly painted and simply furnished.

Bursting with compliments, the visitors' book is testament to the affection which guests have for this hotel and which drives many of them to return time after time.

Nearby Manufacture des Gobelins; Mouffetard District; Latin Quarter.
Location in small street between avenue des Gobelins and boulevard Arago
Parking in street outside **Metro** Gobelins
Food breakfast
Price €
Rooms 32 double and twin, single, triple, all with bath or shower; all rooms have phone, TV **Facilities** sitting area, breakfast room, courtyard garden
Credit cards AE, MC, V
Children accepted
Disabled access possible, lift/elevator
Pets accepted **Closed** never
Proprietors Jennifer and Philippe Poirier

THIRTEENTH ARRONDISSEMENT

GOBELINS

LE VERT GALANT

41-43 rue Croulebarbe, 75013 Paris
TEL (01) 44 08 83 50 **FAX** (01) 44 08 83 69

EVEN IF YOU DON'T stay at Le Vert Galant, try to come out here for a meal at the Auberge Etchegorry next door (Tel 01 44 08 83 51), owned by the same couple. In an annexe overlooking a lush lawn, the pastel art deco-inspired bedrooms radiate calm. Ground-floor studios have French windows and kitchenettes. An attractive conservatory is filled with plants and tables and chairs for breakfast or coffee.

The *raison d'être* of the hotel is the restaurant. A rural inn in the early 19th century, it grew famous as the haunt of such celebrities as Victor Hugo, Béranger and Chateaubriand. Here, beside the now extinct River Bièvre, they were charmed by the voluptuous cabaret artiste, Mme Grégoire. Little appears to have changed in the *auberge*, decorated with bright copper pans and hams, sausages and garlic hanging from beams. Walls are half-panelled; the simple chairs have rush seats, the tables, crisp linen cloths. The cuisine is from the Basque region and includes such deliciously hearty specialities as duck *fois gras* and *confits*. But it is the atmosphere that makes this such an appealing place. Henri Laborde (Maité runs the hotel) is a genial host, who, even without English, makes his customers feel wonderfully welcome.

NEARBY square René Le Gall; Manufacture des Gobelins.
LOCATION at junction with rue des Reculettes **PARKING** free private
METRO Corvisart/place d'Italie/Les Gobelins
FOOD breakfast; lunch and dinner in restaurant
PRICE €€
ROOMS 15; 14 double and twin, all with bath or shower; one single with shower; all rooms have phone, TV, hairdrier
FACILITIES breakfast/sitting room, garden, restaurant; 5 rooms have kitchenettes
CREDIT CARDS AE, DC, MC, V **CHILDREN** accepted
DISABLED one specially adapted room **PETS** accepted
CLOSED never **PROPRIETORS** M. and Mme Laborde

Fourteenth Arrondissement

Montparnasse

Hotel Istria

29 rue Campagne Première, 75014 Paris
Tel (01) 43 20 91 82 **Fax** (01) 43 22 48 45

Back in the days when Montparnasse came to prominence, the Istria counted Man Ray, Marcel Duchamp and Sati amongst its Bohemian occupants; nowadays only Man Ray's photographs on the walls recall the past, but it is still a simple, appealing – and kindly priced – place in which to stay.

The bedrooms, small but neat with pretty bedcovers and pale grasspaper on walls adorned with black and white photographs of old Montparnasse, have all been fitted out in solid elm – bedheads, cupboards, desks, mirrors made specially for the hotel. The preponderance of wood gives the rooms a faintly Alpine air – we almost expected to see thick snow through the windows. Bathrooms (or rather shower rooms – there are only four baths) are small, but up-to-date, with pretty curved shower cubicles. Rooms on the first floor are the least expensive: they lack the grasspaper wallcovering but are otherwise the same as the rest.

Downstairs, the ground floor lobby is an attractive room mixing old with new: a Louis XIII reception desk, antique *armoire*, leather sofas, a mirrored wall, African carvings, modern paintings, soft lighting. The cellar breakfast room is similarly cosy.

Nearby blvd du Montparnasse; Jardin du Luxembourg.
Location in a side street between blvd du Montparnasse and blvd Raspai **Parking** blvd du Montparnasse **Metro** Raspail **RER** Port-Royal
Food breakfast, soft drinks available
Price €€
Rooms 26 single, double and twin, 4 with bath, 22 with shower; all rooms have phone, modem point, TV, hairdrier, safe
Facilities sitting area, breakfast room, internet booth
Credit cards AE, DC, MC, V **Children** accepted
Disabled access difficult, lift/elevator
Pets accepted **Closed** never
Proprietor Daniel Cretay

Sixteenth Arrondissement

Chaillot Quarter

Hotel du Bois

11 rue du Dôme, 75116 Paris
Tel (01) 45 00 31 96 **Fax** (01) 45 00 90 05
E-mail hoteldubois@wanadoo.fr **Website** www.hoteldubois.com

Up a short flight of stairs in the little cobbled rue du Dôme, the exterior is alluring – white stucco with black wrought-iron balconies and railings, hung with geranium-filled window boxes. This popular hotel, a step from the Arc de Triomphe, is in the same English ownership as the Queen Mary (see page 150). The winter of 1996 saw the total refurbishment of bedrooms and public rooms, and the du Bois' upgrading to three stars. The pale yellow walls with dashes of bright red in sofas, curtains and lampshades brighten the ground floor, which is furnished with reproduction antiques and paintings; its marble floor, strewn – here and there – with rugs. Light streams in through huge French windows in the only reception room, where breakfast is served at small round tables. This room has a summery feel, and plenty of sofas for relaxing.

Bedrooms are comfortable, though nothing special, with double glazing, gleaming white tiled bathrooms, and handsome co-ordinated fabrics. Prices are attractive, especially for such a dignified Right Bank location, and the atmosphere is very similar to that of its sister hotel. As for places to eat in this area, you are spoiled for choice, ranging from gourmet restaurants to jolly local bistros.

Nearby Arc de Triomphe; Champs-Elysées; Trocadéro; Musée National d'Ennery.
Location between avenue Victor Hugo and rue Lauriston **Parking** rue Lauriston or avenue Victor Hugo **Metro** Charles de Gaulle Etoile/Kléber/Victor Hugo
RER Charles de Gaulle Etoile
Food breakfast; room service
Price €€
Rooms 41; 37 double and twin, all with bath or shower; 4 single with shower; all rooms have phone, TV, minibar, safe; some rooms have modem points
Facilities breakfast/sitting room, internet booth **Credit cards** AE, DC, MC, V
Children accepted **Disabled** no special facilities
Pets accepted **Closed** never **Proprietor** David Byrne

Sixteenth Arrondissement

Champs-Elysees

Hotel Etoile-Maillot

10 rue du Bois de Boulogne, 75016 Paris
Tel (01) 45 00 42 60 **Fax** (01) 45 00 55 89
E-mail etoile.maillot@wanadoo.fr

Though the Etoile-Maillot adopts the same traditional and rather formal style of so many Champs-Elysées hotels, it stands out for its quiet elegance and for being, in an understated way, discernably a cut above its competitors, though no more expensive. Bedrooms are mostly spacious, with generous, deep and comfortable beds, handsome gilt and fabric bedheads, and equally handsome period wardrobes, chests of drawers and bedside tables, many of them inlaid with marquetry. Our inspector's bedroom was decorated with attractive 19thC English prints on the walls and a candelabra hanging from the ceiling. There was also room for a circular, marble topped table and a couple of leather chairs. The tiled and marble bathroom was large enough to accommodate the minibar, a much more appropriate place for it than amongst the period furniture in the bedroom. She reported a particularly restful night, and met some regular clients of the hotel who appreciated its location in this quiet, smart residential backwater west of the Arc de Triomphe, yet within easy reach of the business centres of Champs-Elysées and La Défense. The hotel is smaller than it seems – breakfast is served in your room – and was completely renovated in 1998.

Nearby Arc de Triomphe; Champs-Elysées; Bois de Boulogne.
Location on corner of rue Duret, which runs between ave de la Grande Armée and ave Foch **Parking** ave Foch or Porte Maillot **Metro** Argentine/Porte Maillot
RER Neuilly Porte Maillot
Food breakfast
Price €€
Rooms 27 double and twin, one suite, all with bath; all rooms have phone, TV, minibar, hairdrier **Facilities** sitting area, internet booth
Credit cards AE, DC, MC, V
Children accepted **Disabled** lift/elevator
Pets accepted **Closed** never
Proprietor Gilles Delfau

Sixteenth Arrondissement

Passy

Hotel Gavarni

5 rue Gavarni, 75116 Paris
Tel (01) 45 24 52 82 **Fax** (01) 40 50 16 95
E-mail reservation@gavarni.com **Website** www.gavarni.com

Passy – now reinvented as Passy Village – is something of a desert as far as charming small hotels are concerned, so we were delighted to stumble across this sumptuous townhouse, which has reopened after a dramatic makeover. From the moment you enter via a stylish circular sliding glass door, you know that here is something different. The ground floor has a hint of art nouveau in its striking decoration. Buttoned velvet armchairs in bright red and yellow sofas invite you to relax, surrounded by wood panelling, mirrors and colourful paintings. There is a smart wooden bar and little breakfast room beyond (although a new conservatory breakfast area is planned).

Upstairs, off corridors lit by art nouveau-style stained glass ceiling panels, you can choose between pretty, well-priced (99 euros) but tiny standard rooms, larger, more comfortable superior ones (at 150 euros) and six stunning suites (ranging between 275 and 450 euros). The last word in luxury, these have wide-screen TVs, high-tech CD and DVD players, and bathrooms with Hammam showers or Jacuzzi baths. All are beautifully done out in different styles from the feminine Versailles Suite, in blue and white *toile de jouy* with antique furniture, to the magnificent Eiffel Suite, decorated in yellow with *trompe l'oeil* effects and a view of the city's most famous landmark.

Nearby Eiffel Tower; Trocadéro; Palais de Chaillot.
Location in side street that runs between rue de la Tour and rue de Passy
Parking rue de Passy **Metro** Passy/La Muette **RER** Boulainvilliers
Food breakfast; room service
Price €€
Rooms 26; 20 double and twin, 6 suites, all with bath; all rooms have phone, modem point, TV, air-conditioning, minibar, hairdrier, safe
Facilities sitting area, bar, breakfast room, internet booth, courtyard garden
Credit cards AE, DC, MC, V **Children** accepted
Disabled access difficult, lift/elevator
Pets not accepted **Closed** never **Manager** Xavier Moraga

Sixteenth Arrondissement

Champs-Elysees

Hotel Libertel Argentine

1-3 rue d'Argentine, 75016 Paris
Tel (01) 45 02 76 76 **Fax** (01) 45 02 76 00
E-mail h2757@accor-hotels.com **Website** www.accor-hotels.com

Hotel chains rarely offer the individuality and special appeal we seek, but the Libertel chain is an exception. One of the group's 28 hotels in Paris, all well-placed, the four-star Argentine is popular with business people – fax and computer modem points in every room, one non-smoking floor – but it is attractively decorated to a high standard with an unexpected intimacy.

The building is a grand stuccoed town house, on the outside of which a bas relief commemorates the time when South America's high society occupied this quiet street. Inside, the entrance is cool and refined, with its beige and white striped walls, freshly painted woodwork and white and black stone tiled floor. Having triumphed in the choice of a stunning Egyptian motif fabric for the hall furniture, the decorator got carried away in the bar/sitting room. It is partly panelled in dark wood, and mesmerizing bright blue and dark pink striped fabric covers walls, curtains, sofas and chairs. Bedrooms are comfortable and smart – chintz fabrics co-ordinate with stripes and checks, lamps and prints reveal an architectural theme; bathrooms are done up in different types of marble. Staff are professional and caring.

Nearby Arc de Triomphe; Champs-Elysées.
Location between ave de la Grande Armée and rue Chalgrin **Parking** ave Foch
Metro Argentine/Charles de Gaulle Etoile **RER** Charles de Gaulle Etoile
Food breakfast, room service
Price €€
Rooms 40; 24 double and twin, 16 single, all with bath; all rooms have phone, modem point, TV, minibar, hairdrier, safe
Facilities bar/sitting room, 2 breakfast rooms
Credit cards AE, DC, MC, V **Children** accepted
Disabled one specially adapted room, lift/elevator
Pets accepted **Closed** never
Manager Mme Brimbeuf

Sixteenth Arrondissement

Chaillot Quarter

Au Palais de Chaillot Hotel

35 avenue Raymond Poincaré, 75116 Paris
Tel (01) 53 70 09 09 **Fax** (01) 53 70 09 08
E-mail hapc@wanadoo.fr **Website** www.chaillotel.com

The closest two-star hotel to the Eiffel Tower, is the boast of the Palais de Chaillot, which re-opened in 1996 (after renovation) under new management. The tower is just 200m away, and though the hotel is on a busy road, the bedrooms at the back are quiet.

A pair of charming brothers own and manage this tall thin town house, and masterminded its redecoration in a simple tasteful style. The ground floor, painted a sunny yellow, consists of a small reception area and breakfast room, with ceiling fans, wicker chairs and an informal atmosphere. Drawbacks are that there is no sitting room, and the only terrace is on the main road at the front.

Bold maroon textured walls on the stairs lend a masculine air, reinforced by the dark red and blue checked fabric and dark wood fittings in the bedrooms. Many are unexpectedly large: the largest (and most expensive) has a walk-in cupboard. Bathrooms and showers look pristine, tiled in white and blue, and have been thoughtfully designed so that there is a space in the shower specially for shampoo and gel. We saw few other two-stars in Paris that matched this hotel's high standard of decoration and reasonable prices.

Nearby Eiffel Tower; Trocadéro; Palais de Chaillot.
Location N of place du Trocadéro, between rue Lauriston and rue de Longchamp
Parking rue St-Didier **Metro** Trocadéro/Victor Hugo
Food breakfast
Price €€
Rooms 28; 22 double and twin, all with bath or shower, 6 single with shower; all rooms have phone, modem point, TV, hairdrier
Facilities breakfast room, internet booth, terrace **Credit cards** AE, DC, MC, V
Children accepted **Disabled** not suitable, lift/elevator
Pets not accepted **Closed** never
Proprietors Cyrile and Thierry Pien

SIXTEENTH ARRONDISSEMENT

PORTE MAILLOT

HOTEL PERGOLESE

3 rue Pergolèse, 75116 Paris
TEL (01) 53 64 04 04 **FAX** (01) 53 64 04 40
E-MAIL hotel@pergolese.com **WEBSITE** www.hotel-pergolese.com

THE ONLY HINT OF what lies in store behind the conventional late 19thC stone façade is in the black tubular ground-floor window supports and the blue steel automatic doors at the entrance. Inside, an expanse of immaculate wooden floor stretches away from you. Beyond reception is a sitting area with blue leather chairs, boxy glass tables and standard lamps on spindly metal stands. You could never call the Pergolèse cosy, but then that's not what it's about; it strives to be and is the epitome of designer chic, from the black-clad receptionist to the tower-sculpture that conceals television and minibar in every bedroom.

The designer behind the Pergolèse is Rena Dumas. Her decorative scheme is grey, contrasted with a variety of strong colours and, though pared down and functional, the bedrooms look stunning. A clever choice of warm materials includes leather tub chairs in red, blue or green, matching curtains, and beautiful ash winged bedheads. The huge beds are deeply comfortable. Just beware that you don't sever a finger on the cupboard's designer doorhandle. Bathrooms are white tiled and high-tech with stainless steel basins. As you would expect, prices are high.

NEARBY Arc de Triomphe; Champs-Elysées; Palais des Congrès.
LOCATION between ave de la Grande Armée and ave de Malakoff **PARKING** ave Foch, Porte Maillot or place Saint Ferdinand **METRO** Argentine/Porte Maillot **RER** Neuilly Porte Maillot
FOOD breakfast
PRICE €€€€
ROOMS 40; 36 double and twin, 3 single and one suite, all with bath; all rooms have phone, modem point, air-conditioning, TV, hairdrier, safe
FACILITIES sitting area, bar, breakfast room, internet booth
CREDIT CARDS AE, DC, MC, V **CHILDREN** accepted
DISABLED lift/elevator **PETS** accepted
CLOSED never **PROPRIETOR** Edith Vidalenc

SIXTEENTH ARRONDISSEMENT

CHAILLOT QUARTER

SAINT JAMES PARIS

43 avenue Bugeaud, 75116 Paris
TEL (01) 44 05 81 81 **FAX** (01) 44 05 81 82
E-MAIL contact@saint-james-paris.com **WEBSITE** www.saint-james-paris.com

IF YOUR IDEA OF heaven is to lower black-out blinds at the flick of a switch and slide between sea-island cotton sheets, Paris's only château hotel might be the choice for you – if you can afford it. The larger, but younger sister of Pavillon de la Reine (page 38) and Relais Christine (page 63), the Saint James occupies an imposing late 19thC building, in a formal walled garden where a fountain plays round the clock.

Inside, redecoration has done away with the previous modern, masculine style, and although everything is on a grand scale, from the balustraded staircase to the heavy panelled bedroom doors, arranged in galleries, the hotel has only 48 rooms. Appropriately the library bar has one wall devoted to bookcases, another to a bar. Leading off it, is a stylish dining room, with dark blue tub chairs and starched white linen tablecloths. If you overindulge at dinner, you can work it off in the frightening-looking basement gym.

Bedrooms are decorated in similar style to those of the sister hotels; many have striped wallpaper and checked curtains, softened with dried flowers and pretty prints. Bathrooms are large and luxurious.

NEARBY Arc de Triomphe; Musée de la Contrefaçon.
LOCATION at junction with place du Chancelier Adenauer **PARKING** free private
METRO Porte Dauphine/Victor Hugo **RER** Avenue Foch
FOOD breakfast, lunch, dinner; room service
PRICE €€€€
ROOMS 48 double and twin, suites and junior suites, all with bath; all rooms have phone, modem point, TV, air-conditioning, minibar, hairdrier, safe
FACILITIES sitting area, dining and meeting rooms, bar, restaurant, gym, internet booth, garden **CREDIT CARDS** AE, DC, MC, V
CHILDREN accepted **DISABLED** lift/elevator
PETS accepted
CLOSED never **MANAGER** Tim Goddard

SEVENTEENTH ARRONDISSEMENT

NORTH OF ETOILE

HOTEL DE BANVILLE

166 boulevard Berthier, 75017 Paris
TEL (01) 42 67 70 16 **FAX** (01) 44 40 42 77
E-MAIL hotelbanville@wanadoo.fr **WEBSITE** www.hotelbanville.fr

THIS 1930S TOWN HOUSE hotel offers an attractive combination of style, comfort and middle-of-the-road prices. Convenient, too, for motorists: finding your way from the Périphérique to boulevard Berthier is easy, and parking is not impossible.

The airy Art Deco building – the work of a celebrated architect, we're told – looks promising, and does not disappoint. Inside, all is tastefully decorated in muted colours, and comfortable, bordering on the luxurious. There is an elegantly furnished sitting area/bar, where a pianist often plays in the evenings. Another welcoming sitting room, with antique pieces as well as comfy sofas (which can be closed off for meetings), puts the Banville comfortably ahead of the Parisian norm in this important respect.

Murals create a garden effect in the breakfast room. The bedrooms are freshly decorated in individual styles, with thoughtfully chosen fabrics and antiques dotted throughout. Fresh flowers add a reassuring personal touch, as do such small services as having your bed turned down – a rare thing in the city nowadays. Staff are extremely friendly, and we suspect that this hotel would be far more expensive if it were on the Left Bank.

NEARBY Arc de Triomphe; Champs-Elysées; Palais des Congrès.
LOCATION on service road off boulevard Berthier, between rue A. Samain and rue de Courcelles **PARKING** boulevard Berthier, in street and garage **METRO** Porte de Champerret **RER** Péreire-Levallois
FOOD breakfast
PRICE €€€
ROOMS 41; 39 double and twin, 36 with bath, 2 with shower; 2 triple, one family room, all with bath; all rooms have phone, modem point, TV, air-conditioning, hairdrier, safe **FACILITIES** sitting area/bar, sitting room, breakfast room, internet booth
CREDIT CARDS AE, MC, V **CHILDREN** accepted
DISABLED lift/elevator **PETS** accepted **CLOSED** never
PROPRIETOR Mme Moreau

Seventeenth Arrondissment

Monceau Quarter

Hotel Eber

~ ~

18 rue Léon-Jost, 75017 Paris
Tel (01) 46 22 60 70 **Fax** (01) 47 63 01 01
Website www.hotelseber.com

Jean-Marc Eber remains as committed as ever to the little hotel he took over in the late 1980s after more than a decade practising his hotel-keeping in four-star Paris establishments.

The early 20thC house, easily missed in a quiet residential street not far from the Champs-Elysées and near the Parc Monceau, is comfortable, well cared for and prettily furnished and decorated, and M. Eber's combination of warmth and professionalism makes sure that the hotel stays well out of the rut. The public areas are tiny, but inviting – a small beamed sitting area off the reception that also serves as a bar, and a pretty little courtyard on to which some of the bedrooms lead. Breakfast may be taken in either of these places, or in your bedroom. These vary in size and ambience, and are priced accordingly – our inspector's had a little sitting room and a shower room as well as a bathroom. Some have lofty ceilings, others are small-scale; all are attractive and smart-looking since their refurbishment in 2000. Best of all is the top-floor apartment with its own private terrace, much favoured, says Monsieur Eber, by fashion directors during Paris Fashion Week.

~

Nearby Arc de Triomphe; Champs-Elysées; Parc Monceau.
Location in street which runs parallel to stretch of rue de Courcelles between avenue de Wagram and boulevard de Courcelles **Parking** rue de Courcelles
Metro Courcelles
Food breakfast
Price €€
Rooms 18; 15 double and twin, 3 duplex, 14 with bath, 4 with shower; all rooms have phone, modem point, TV, minibar, hairdrier
Facilities sitting area, bar, breakfast room
Credit cards AE, DC, MC, V **Children** accepted
Disabled lift/elevator **Pets** not accepted
Closed never **Proprietor** Jean-Marc Eber

SEVENTEENTH ARRONDISSEMENT

NORTH OF ETOILE

HOTEL DE NEUVILLE

3 rue Verniquet, 75017 Paris
TEL (01) 43 80 26 30 **FAX** (01) 43 80 38 55
E-MAIL neuville@hotellerie.net

A HOTEL CATERING MAINLY for business clientele which we include for its animated atmosphere and the personal touch supplied by its energetic young owners. A tall white *hôtel particulier* of the 19th century covered in colourful window boxes in summer, it stands in a quiet residential square within (tourists should note) easy reach of the Péripherique and with the advantage of a private garage next door. At lunchtime, the leafy, summery basement breakfast room becomes a popular meeting place for local residents and office workers, with a simple, inexpensive menu. The sophisticated bar and lounge – shades of fawn with blonde wood-panelled walls, and views on to a verdant, cleverly terraced courtyard garden – encourages guests to meet for drinks in the evenings, and the changing one-man exhibitions of paintings provides a talking-point.

Some bedrooms at the Neuville lack the allure of the public rooms but are fairly spacious, pleasant rather than characterful, with soft terracotta walls, brass bedsteads and chairs, curtains and bedspreads in autumn colours. One has a four poster with diaphanous hangings – definitely not for the businessmen.

NEARBY Arc de Triomphe; Palais des Congrès.
LOCATION in quiet square off boulevard Pereire (Nord), between place du Maréchal Juin and place de Wagram **PARKING** adjacent private garage **METRO** Pereire
FOOD breakfast, lunch
PRICE €€€
ROOMS 28 double and twin, all with bath; all rooms have phone, modem point, TV, hairdrier **FACILITIES** sitting room/bar, breakfast room, internet booth
CREDIT CARDS AE, DC, MC, V
CHILDREN accepted
DISABLED lift/elevator
PETS accepted
CLOSED never **MANAGER** Celine Albar

EIGHTEENTH ARRONDISSEMENT

MONTMARTRE

HOTEL ERMITAGE

24 rue Lamarck, 75018 Paris
TEL (01) 42 64 79 22 **FAX** (01) 42 64 10 33

WE WERE ENTRANCED when we found the Ermitage, tucked away behind Sacré-Coeur. Only a sober wall plaque announces that this is a hotel, the door opening on to a smart little gold and cream lobby, followed by a dark blue hall with deep red carpet strewn with rugs. From the reception you can see a charming kitchen with its *faience* stove from Lorraine (breakfast is prepared here and served in your room) and a little terrace beyond. Also on the ground floor: an old-fashioned parlour, decorated in green, and filled with antiques, photographs and ornaments. Par for the course so far, you may think, yet the Ermitage has a decorative surprise which starts in the hall and continues all the way up the stairs, on walls, doors, glass panels, skirtings. These are the charming, shadowy paint effects and murals of the artist Du Buc; the sketchy scenes of Montmartre, were done in 1986 when he was an old man.

Eclectic and friendly, with an atmosphere of calm familiarity, the Ermitage was the creation of Sophie Canipel's parents, who fell in love with the house some 30 years ago. Sophie took over when they retired and, in her friendly, dedicated care, the spirit of the hotel remains exactly the same. Bedrooms are by and large light and spacious, freshly decorated with floral wallpapers, lace curtains, large *armoires*. Bathrooms are tiny.

NEARBY Sacré-Coeur; Place du Tertre.
LOCATION at eastern end of rue Lamarck, close to Sacré-Coeur **PARKING** in nearby private garage **METRO** Lamarck Caulaincourt
FOOD breakfast
PRICE €
ROOMS 12; 11 double and twin, one family room; 11 rooms have bath or mini bath; all rooms have phone, hairdrier **FACILITIES** sitting room
CREDIT CARDS not accepted **CHILDREN** accepted
DISABLED 2 rooms on ground floor
PETS accepted **CLOSED** never **PROPRIETOR** Sophie Canipel

EIGHTEENTH ARRONDISSEMENT

MONTMARTRE

HOTEL PRIMA LEPIC

29 rue Lepic, 75018 Paris
TEL (01) 46 06 44 64 **FAX** (01) 46 06 66 11
E-MAIL reservation@hotel-prima-lepic.com **WEBSITE** www.hotel-paris-lepic.com

IN A BUSTLING STREET, this quirky, casual hotel has an excellent location from which to explore Montmartre. Downstairs, a sitting area with white-painted wrought-iron tables and chairs becomes the breakfast room every morning. Murals on the walls and a mass of artificial flowers and trailing vines create an out-of-doors feel. The atmosphere is airy and cheerful, and the fake flowers are charmingly kitsch rather than tacky.

Fin de siècle details are intact both downstairs, particularly in the stained glass, and in the bedrooms, some of which have wonderful high-corniced ceilings. The rooms have been completely renovated since the hotel was taken over by Mme Bourgeon two years ago, swapping their old-fashioned charm for a romantic new look, combining restful pastels in some and cheerful colours in others with boldly patterned curtains and bedspreads in co-ordinated fabrics. Fabric has also been used to swathe headboards and cover dainty chairs, and the antique plumbing has been replaced by up-to-date bathrooms. Double glazing has made the noisier street-side rooms a much more attractive proposition. Staff are pleasant, if a little breezy. Breakfasts are the minimal norm.

NEARBY Moulin Rouge; Sacré-Coeur; place du Tertre.
LOCATION between rue des Abbesses and rue Constance **PARKING** impasse Marie Blanche or rue Caulaincourt **METRO** Blanche/Abbesses
FOOD breakfast
PRICE €€
ROOMS 38; 33 double, twin and triple, 5 single, all with bath or shower; all rooms have phone, modem point, TV, hairdrier
FACILITIES sitting and breakfast areas
CREDIT CARDS MC, V
CHILDREN accepted
DISABLED lift/elevator **PETS** accepted
CLOSED never **PROPRIETOR** Martine Bourgeon

EIGHTEENTH ARRONDISSEMENT

MONTMARTRE

STYLE HOTEL

8 rue Ganneron, 75018 Paris
TEL (01) 45 22 37 59 **FAX** (01) 45 22 81 03

AN 18THC BUILDING (opened by the present owner's grandparents and little changed), not strictly speaking in Montmartre, but ten minutes' walk away, full of character and with rock-bottom prices. All the bedrooms are spacious, and some are enormous, with huge windows, wooden floors, marble fireplaces, capacious old wardrobes and a sprinkling of handsome carved double beds. The decoration is unfussy – plain painted walls, modest furnishings and, except for the antique pieces inherited by Mme Lescure from her grandparents, utilitarian furniture. Both the bedrooms and simple modern bathrooms and shower rooms (including the communal ones) are spotlessly clean.

The breakfast room has a provincial charm, with its wooden tables, potted plants and fresh yellow walls, encircled by a garland frieze. Although the ground floor lacks the style of the bedrooms, there is a pleasant courtyard and a fine staircase with wrought-iron balustrade. Perennially popular with students and Bohemian families, the Style is a great find for all low budget travellers.

NEARBY Sacré-Coeur; place du Tertre; Moulin Rouge; place de Pigalle.
LOCATION just off avenue de Clichy **PARKING** rue Caulaincourt **METRO** La Fourche/place Clichy
FOOD breakfast
PRICE €
ROOMS 36 double and twin, single, triple, 2 with bath, 15 with shower, 19 with washbasin only (communal shower rooms/WCs in corridors); some rooms have phone **FACILITIES** breakfast room, courtyard
CREDIT CARDS DC, MC, V
CHILDREN accepted
DISABLED access difficult
PETS accepted **CLOSED** never
PROPRIETOR Geneviève Lescure

ILE-DE-FRANCE

DAMPIERRE

AUBERGE DU CHATEAU

1 Grande Rue, 78720 Dampierre (Yvelines)
TEL (01) 30 47 56 56 **FAX** (01) 30 52 56 95

A TRADITIONAL INN with a calm, prosperous air which stands in the centre of a stone-built country village. The building dates back to 1650 and has always been a hostelry, probably putting up visitors to the Duc de Luynes, an influential figure in the time of Louis XIII, whose elegant château and surrounding park lie across the road. His descendants still live there.

The layout of the *auberge* bears witness to its age: floors rise and fall at will, there are low-slung beams at every turn, and rickety wooden staircases lead to the bedrooms. These are spacious and, though individually decorated, many have matching floral wallpapers and curtains; the ones at the front have a view of the château and its park; those at the rear overlook the hotel's small garden. Some have stone floors and marble-clad bathrooms. Part of the beamed dining room reaches out to a conservatory-style extension which runs along the front of the building, opening out on to a roadside terrace.

Dampierre lies in the heart of the Parc Naturel de la Haute Vallée de Chevreuse, a lovely rural area which seems very far from Paris but is, in fact, only half an hour away by car. Also nearby are châteaux worth visiting, as well as walking and pony trekking.

NEARBY Versailles; Montfort l'Amaury.
LOCATION opposite the Château de Dampierre, 36 km SW of Paris, 16 km NE of Rambouillet; ample car parking
FOOD breakfast, lunch, dinner
PRICE €
ROOMS 11 double and twin, all with bath; all rooms have phone, TV
FACILITIES sitting room, dining room, terrace, garden
CREDIT CARDS AE, MC, V **CHILDREN** accepted
DISABLED not suitable **PETS** accepted
CLOSED restaurant only, Sun dinner, Mon, Tue
MANAGER M. Blot

ILE-DE-FRANCE

ERMENONVILLE

HOTEL LE PRIEURE

6 place de l'Eglise, 60440 Ermenonville (Oise)
TEL (03) 44 63 66 70 **FAX** (01) 44 63 95 01
E-MAIL le.prieure@club-internet.fr **WEBSITE** www.hotel-leprieure.com

ONE OF OUR FAVOURITE discoveries, Le Prieuré is more a private house than a hotel. An 18thC *gentilhommerie* standing right beside the church, which shadows the attractive garden, it was taken over a year ago by a committed young couple, who fell in love with it. They have done a considerable amount of work restoring and refurbishing it, in sympathy with the impeccable style created by the previous owners, the Treillous, who lived here for more than 30 years. The redecorated bedrooms now look very fresh and pretty, with white walls, fabric draped over a few of the beds and a scattering of antiques. There are more antiques in the attractive beamed public rooms on the ground floor, including the elegant parlour, where breakfast is served. The garden is English in style, with roses and fruit trees, and a little terrace; its proximity to the church makes for a calm atmosphere. Try for one of the rooms which gives on to the garden.

Peaceful Ermenonville makes an excellent base, with the forest close by, as well as Mer de Sable outdoor leisure area, and a park from the Romantic era, full of follies, which is closely associated with Jean-Jacques Rousseau, and is his final resting-place.

NEARBY Fôret d'Ermenonville; Senlis; Chantilly.
LOCATION in Ermenonville, 40 km NE of Paris, 24 km NW of Meaux on N330; free car parking
FOOD breakfast
PRICE €€
ROOMS 8; 6 double, 2 twin, 4 with bath, 4 with shower; all rooms have phone, modem, TV, minibar **FACILITIES** sitting room, dining room, garden
CREDIT CARDS MC, V
CHILDREN accepted
DISABLED one bedroom on ground floor
PETS accepted **CLOSED** Feb
PROPRIETORS Philippe and Christine Poulin

ILE-DE-FRANCE

FLAGY

HOSTELLERIE DU MOULIN

2 rue du Moulin, 77940 Flagy (Seine-et-Marne)
TEL (01) 60 96 67 89 **FAX** (01) 60 96 69 51

A STALWART OF OUR *Charming Small Hotel Guide to France*, praised over the years by a steady flow of readers who thoroughly approve of this imaginatively converted flour mill.

The setting, with tables in the grassy garden beside the stream that still gently turns the mill wheel, is idyllic, and creates a blissfully soporific effect. Beyond the neat gardens you look out on to cultivated fields which, until the 1950s supplied the grain that was milled here. The heavy beams, wheels and pulleys of the mill dominate the cosy sitting room, and the bedrooms, named after cereals, are as quirkily captivating as you would hope in a building of this character; space is at a premium, and low beams lead some guests to move about with a permanent stoop.

The chef specializes mainly in traditional dishes, and the menu and *carte* have English translations, underlying the Moulin's popularity with British travellers. Claude Scheideker is a charming and friendly host who gives his little hotel, which he has been running for more than 20 years, an exceptionally welcoming atmosphere. And he still manages to keep his prices admirably low.

NEARBY Fontainebleu (23 km); Sens cathedral (40 km).
LOCATION in village, 23 km SE of Fontainebleu, 10 km W of Montereau; car parking
FOOD breakfast, lunch, dinner
PRICE €€
ROOMS 10; 7 double, 3 family, all with bath; all rooms have phone
FACILITIES sitting room, dining room, bar, garden, fishing
CREDIT CARDS AE, DC, MC, V
CHILDREN accepted
DISABLED access difficult **PETS** accepted
CLOSED 2 weeks Sep, late Dec to late Jan; restaurant only, Sun dinner, Mon (except Easter and Whitsun: Mon dinner, Tue)
PROPRIETOR Claude Scheidecker

ILE-DE-FRANCE

GERMIGNY L'EVEQUE

HOSTELLERIE LE GONFALON

2 rue de l'Eglise, 77910 Germigny-L'Evêque (Seine-et-Marne)
TEL (01) 64 33 16 05 **FAX** (01) 64 33 25 59

THE HOSTELLERIE, WHICH our inspector happened upon as he passed by one day, is set in a lovely wooded position on a bend of the River Marne, overlooked by a tree-shaded terrace, where a menu of mainly fish and seafood dishes is served in summer – or in the beamed dining room in cooler weather. Germigny-l'Evêque is a quiet residential village, but only 20 minutes from Euro Disney, making it a perfect spot to escape to after a rigorous day in the land of make-believe.

Bedrooms on the first floor are large, each with the luxury of a private terrace, enclosed in winter, open in summer, and decorated in part with rather kitsch 1970s style furnishings – you wonder where they managed to get them. Some of these rooms have been redecorated, while the ones above are more traditional.

Madame Collubi, voluminous and in perennial bloom, has been in charge for nearly 30 years. A great personality, who has made her own very distinctive mark on the Hostellerie, she is also a talented chef. And the irresistible combination of a lively atmosphere and excellent food is the draw for locals and visitors alike.

NEARBY Euro Disney; Montceaux.
LOCATION beside river Marne, in village, about 62 km NE of Paris, 9 km N of Meaux on D 97; car parking
FOOD breakfast, lunch, dinner
PRICE €
ROOMS 8 double and twin with bath; all rooms have phone, TV, minibar; 4 have terrace **FACILITIES** sitting room, dining room, terrace
CREDIT CARDS AE, DC, MC, V
CHILDREN accepted
DISABLED no special facilities **PETS** not accepted
CLOSED Jan; restaurant only, Sun dinner, Mon
PROPRIETOR Mme Collubi

ILE-DE-FRANCE

PROVINS

HOSTELLERIE AUX VIEUX REMPARTS

3 rue Couverte, 77160 Provins (Seine-et-Marne)
TEL (01) 64 08 94 00 **FAX** (01) 60 67 77 22
E-MAIL vieux-remparts@wanadoo.fr **WEBSITE** www.auxvieuxremparts.com

PROVINS IS A FINE medieval town, well placed for a stop between Paris and Burgundy. Like Chartres, the town, once the third largest in France, rises from fields of corn, its splendid ramparts enclosing superb medieval buildings and pretty houses whose gardens are filled with roses. The hotel, situated in the oldest quarter, the insular, carefully preserved Ville Haute, is surrounded by half-timbered buildings which give it the air of a grandiose film set. In summer the town plays host to medieval festivals and pageants when the streets are clogged with visitors, but at night: '*on n'entendait pas un chat*' – utter silence.

The Hostellerie is rather sprawling and has an emphasis on business clientele, so that the atmosphere is polished and professional rather than intimate. Public rooms are mostly in the ancient core of the building, including the refectory-style dining room, where guests can choose from a rich, extensive and regularly changing menu of very French dishes. An excellent breakfast is served in a room beneath the eaves. Bedrooms are comfortable in a superior-Novotel kind of way, and seven brand new ones have been created since our last edition of the guide. The hotel has been in the Roy family since 1858, and M. Roy could not be more helpful.

NEARBY Saint-Loup-de-Naud; Rampillon.
LOCATION in the Ville Haute, 90 km SE of Paris, 48 km E of Melun on N19; car parking
FOOD breakfast, lunch, dinner; room service
PRICE €€
ROOMS 32 double, twin and family, all with bath or shower; all rooms have phone, TV, minibar
FACILITIES sitting room, dining room, bar, meeting rooms, terrace, garden
CREDIT CARDS AE, DC, MC, V
CHILDREN accepted
DISABLED 2 rooms on ground floor, lift/elevator
PETS accepted **CLOSED** never
PROPRIETOR Xavier Roy

FIRST ARRONDISSEMENT

BEAUBOURG QUARTER

HOTEL BRITTANIQUE

20 avenue Victoria, 75001 Paris
TEL (01) 42 33 74 59 **FAX** (01) 42 33 82 65
E-MAIL mailbox@hotel-brittanique.com **WEBSITE** www.hotel-brittanique.com

THE HOTEL'S SMART FAÇADE is matched by the tone of the reception area and sitting room. The style here is glossy, primarily British with naval touches in the model ships and seascapes. The colours are warm, mainly red, with leather sofas and dark wood tables on which French and English language newspapers appear each morning. Breakfast, served in a small, cheery room, is copious, including ham and cheese. Bedrooms are comfortable and in good decorative order (recent refurbishment has taken place), but banal compared to the charm and atmosphere of the public rooms – which is so often the case.

NEARBY Marais; Les Halles; Notre-Dame; Pompidou Centre; Ile Saint-Louis. **LOCATION** in the stretch of street parallel to quai de la Megisserie, W of place du Châtalet **PARKING** Hotel de Ville (rue de Lobau) **METRO** Châtelet **RER** Châtelet/Les Halles **FOOD** breakfast; room service **PRICE** €€€ **ROOMS** 40; 33 double and twin, 28 with bath, 5 with shower; 7 single, 3 with bath 4 with shower; all rooms have phone, modem point, TV, minibar, hairdrier, safe **FACILITIES** sitting room, breakfast room **CREDIT CARDS** AE, DC, MC, V **CHILDREN** accepted **DISABLED** access difficult, lift/elevator **PETS** not accepted **CLOSED** never **PROPRIETOR** M. Danjou

BEAUBOURG QUARTER

GRAND HOTEL DE CHAMPAIGNE

13 rue des Orfèvres, 75001 Paris
TEL (01) 42 36 60 00 **FAX** (01) 45 08 43 33
E-MAIL champagne@hotelchampaigneparis.com **WEBSITE** www.hotelchampaigneparis.com

BUILT IN 1562 (the date is recorded on a wooden pillar in the lobby) theGrand Hôtel de Champaigne (note the unusual spelling) is a glossy, somewhat overwrought version of a character hotel. There's character in spades in the building itself – in its time a monastery and an inn – with impressively large and grand public rooms on the ground floor, and six further floors of twisting corridors and cosy, oddly shaped, beamed rooms. Each floor is meant to represent a different period in French history; in reality they are all boldly coloured with patterned fabrics, ties, tassles and canopies and an assortment of furniture, some antique. Good breakfast.

NEARBY Marais; Les Halles; Notre-Dame; Pompidou Centre; Ile Saint-Louis. **LOCATION** on corner of rue Jean-Lantier, between rue de Rivoli and Quai de la Megisserie **PARKING** Hôtel de Ville (rue de Lobau) **METRO** Châtelet/Pont-Neuf **RER** Châtelet-Les Halles **FOOD** breakfast **PRICE** €€€ **ROOMS** 43 double, twin and single, all with bath or shower; all rooms have phone, modem point, TV, air-conditioning, hairdrier; some rooms have minibar **FACILITIES** sitting room, bar, breakfast room **CREDIT CARDS** AE, DC, MC, V **CHILDREN** accepted **DISABLED** access difficult, lift/elevator **PETS** accepted **CLOSED** never **PROPRIETOR** M. Herbon

FIRST ARRONDISSEMENT

BEAUBOURG QUARTER

HOTEL PLACE DU LOUVRE

21 rue des Prêtres-Saint-Germain-l'Auxerrois, 75001 Paris
TEL (01) 42 33 78 68 **FAX** (01) 42 33 09 95
E-MAIL hotel.place.louvre.@wanadoo.fr **WEBSITE** www.esprit-de-france.com

OUR PREVIOUS VISIT was marred by an extremely flustered and unhelpful receptionist; not so on this occasion, although the hotel suffers from the same rather impersonal chain mentality as its sisters, the Saints-Pères, Parc Saint-Séverin, d'Orsay and Mansart, all included in these pages, all with something special to offer but all lacking on the personality front. The Place du Louvre stands right next door to the Relais du Louvre (see page 35), but being on the corner, it benefits from better views, not only of Saint-Germain-l'Auxerrois opposite, but across to the Louvre as well. Decoration is of the smart modern variety, and, we felt, rather soulless, with a ubiquitous cellar breakfast room.

NEARBY Marais; Musée du Louvre; Ile de la Cité; Samaritaine store (rooftop view). **LOCATION** in quiet side street parallel to Quai du Louvre **PARKING** opposite **METRO** Pont-Neuf/Louvre-Rivoli **RER** Châtelet/Les Halles **FOOD** breakfast **PRICE** €€ **ROOMS** 16 double and twin, all with bath, 4 single with shower; all rooms have phone, modem point, TV, hairdrier **FACILITIES** sitting area, bar **CREDIT CARDS** AE, DC, MC, V **CHILDREN** accepted **DISABLED** access difficultlift/elevator **PETS** not accepted **CLOSED** never **MANAGER** M. Chevalier

TUILERIES QUARTER

HOTEL TAMISE

4 rue d'Alger, 75001 Paris
TEL (01) 42 60 51 54 **FAX** (01) 42 86 89 97
E-MAIL hoteldelatamise@worldonline.fr

AFTER THE DEPARTURE of the friendly Spanish manager, Monsieur Antonio, the Tamise lost some of its charm for us, and its air of faded gentility is a little more faded now. It must be said that it is one of the more low-key hotels in this guide, hardly attracting attention in any quarter, but still, we feel, merits an entry for its genuine Edwardian feel. A mirrored entrance hall with potted plants and tessallated floor opens on to a lovely little *salon* on one side and a breakfast room on the other. A tiny wrought-iron and gilt lift takes you up to fairly dull bedrooms with skimpy beds.

NEARBY Tuileries; rue de Rivoli; Musée du Louvre; place de la Concorde. **LOCATION** in a street off rue de Rivoli, opposite Tuileries. **PARKING** place Marché Saint-Honoré, place Vendôme **METRO** Tuileries **FOOD** breakfast **PRICE** €€ **ROOMS** 18; 14 double and twin with bath; 4 single with shower; all rooms have phone, TV **FACILITIES** sitting room, breakfast room **CREDIT CARDS** AE, DC, MC, V **CHILDREN** accepted **DISABLED** not suitable, lift/elevator **PETS** accepted **CLOSED** never **PROPRIETOR** M. Bellec

SECOND ARRONDISSEMENT

OPERA QUARTER

HOTEL FAVART

5 rue de Marivaux, 75002 Paris
TEL (01) 42 97 59 83 **FAX** (01) 40 15 95 58
E-MAIL favart.hotel@wanadoo.fr **WEBSITE** www.hotel-paris-favart.com

WITH BREAKFAST included (unusually for Paris hotels) in the inexpensive room price, the Favart makes a good choice for those looking for accomodation for two for a fraction over 100 euros a night. But you will also have to enjoy , as we do, the old-fashioned ambience – swirling patterned carpets and all – of the grand ground floor, with its columns, mirrors, velvet armchairs and sweeping staircase with Spanish-style wrought-iron balustrade. Bedrooms are old-fashioned too, without the allure of the lobby, but with grand touches, such as sweeping curtains and paintings on the walls. Some of the mirrored and tiled bathrooms are charming.

NEARBY Opéra Garnier; Grands Boulevards; La Madeleine.
LOCATION a short street off boulevard des Italiens **PARKING** boulevard des Italiens **METRO** Richelieu-Druout **FOOD** breakfast **RER** Opéra-Auber **PRICE** €€
ROOMS 37 double, twin and single, all with bath or shower; all rooms have phone, TV, hairdrier **FACILITIES** sitting room, bar, breakfast room **CREDIT CARDS** AE, DC, MC, V **CHILDREN** accepted **DISABLED** no special facilities **PETS** accepted **CLOSED** never **PROPRIETOR** M. Champetier

BEAUBOURG QUARTER

HOTEL VICTOIRES OPERA

56 rue Montorgueil, 75002 Paris
TEL (01) 42 36 41 08 **FAX** (01) 45 08 08 79
E-MAIL hotel@victoiresopera.com **WEBSITE** www.hotelvictoiresopera.com

ALL CHANGE at what used to be the Grand Hôtel Besançon, including the name. Total refurbishments of old hotels are par for the course, but of ones that are spanking new – unusual. But that's just what the new owners did when they bought the Besançon, sweeping away the reproduction furniture and fittings in favour of a sleek, white-walled contemporary look, and bumping up to four stars in the process. It's not personal, but it's stylish and comfortable, and altogether rather successful. And there are other points in its favour, not least the location: pedestrianized rue Montorgeuil, lined with colourful flower and vegetable stalls

NEARBY Marais; Les Halles; Notre-Dame; Pompidou Centre; Ile Saint-Louis.
LOCATION on corner of rue Jean-Lantier, between rue de Rivoli and Quai de la Megisserie **PARKING** Hôtel de Ville (rue de Lobau) **METRO** Châtelet/Pont-Neuf **RER** Châtelet-Les Halles **FOOD** breakfast **PRICE** €€€€ **ROOMS** 20; 18 double, twin and suites, 2 single; all rooms have phone, modem point, TV, air-conditioning, minibar, hairdrier **FACILITIES** sitting room, bar, breakfast room **CREDIT CARDS** AE, DC, MC, V **CHILDREN** accepted **DISABLED** 2 specially adapted rooms, lift/elevator **PETS** accepted **CLOSED** never **MANAGER** Hakim Boudaa

Fourth Arrondissement

Beaubourg Quarter/Marais

Hotel Beaubourg

11 rue Simon Lefranc, 75004 Paris
Tel (01) 42 74 34 24 **Fax** (01) 42 78 68 11
E-mail htlbeaubourg@hotellerie.net **website** www.hotelbeaubourg.com

Just round the corner from the Pompidou Centre, this is a straightforward hotel in a converted 17thC building. Although the interior verges on the bland, there are enough attractive touches to keep up one's interest, and we had a warm welcome, a comfortable night and a modest bill at the end. First impressions are favourable, with the beamed reception/sitting area and wide corridor beyond enormously enhanced by the use of a sunny yellow wallcovering, leather sofas and chairs, and soft lighting. There is also a stone-vaulted *cave* breakfast room, plainly furnished, and a courtyard garden, full of trailing plants, over which some of the bedrooms look. Opt for one of these or the ground-floor room with its own terrace.

Nearby Pompidou Centre; Les Halles; Marais; Notre Dame.
Location in side street off rue du Renard **Parking** Pompidou Centre **Metro** Rambuteau **RER** Châtelet/Les Halles **Food** breakfast **Price** €€ **Rooms** 28 double and twin, 24 with bath, 4 with shower; all rooms have phone, modem point, TV, air-conditioning, minibar, hairdrier **Facilities** sitting area, breakfast room, courtyard **Credit cards** AE, DC, MC, V **Children** accepted **Disabled** one room on ground floor, lift/elevator **Pets** accepted **Closed** never **Proprietor** Mme Morand

Marais

Hotel du Bourg Tibourg

19 rue du Bourg Tibourg, 75004 Paris
Tel (01) 42 78 47 39 **Fax** (01) 40 29 07 00
E-mail hotel@bourgtibourg.com **website** www.hoteldubourgtibourg.com

You enter another world when you walk through the door of this handsome old, but – from the outside – ordinary-looking town house. Decorated in romantic Moorish style, the latest addition to the Costes empire has the feel of an Arabian boudoir, with its tasselled sofas and arched chairs placed beside antique and lacquered furniture, dim lighting and an atmosphere rich with the heady aroma of scented candles. A mini and more affordable version of his flagship Hôtel Costes, it was – like that hotel – designed by Jacques Garcia. His hallmarks are everywhere from the leopard-print furniture in the cellar breakfast room to the overblown bedrooms, with huge fringed lamps and daring combinations of printed and striped fabrics. Our inspector found the staff remarkably off-hand.

Nearby Pompidou Centre; place des Vosges; Musée Carnavalet; Notre Dame.
Location in side street between rue de Rivoli and rue Sainte-Croix-de-la-Bretonnerie **Parking** Hôtel de Ville **Metro** Hôtel de Ville/Saint-Paul **RER** Châtelet/Les Halles **Food** breakfast **Price** €€€ **Rooms** 31 double and twin, single suite, all with bath or shower; all rooms have phone, modem point, TV, air-conditioning, minibar, hairdrier, safe **Facilities** sitting area, breakfast room **Credit cards** AE, DC, MC, V **Children** accepted **Disabled** lift/elevator **Pets** accepted **Closed** never **Proprietor** M. Costes

FOURTH ARRONDISSEMENT

ILE DE LA CITE

HOTEL HOSPITEL

Hôtel-Dieu, 1 place du Parvis Notre-Dame, 75004 Paris
TEL (01) 44 32 01 00 **FAX** (01) 44 32 01 16

GO PAST RADIOLOGY, opthalmology and geriatrics, then up to the top floor of the Hôtel-Dieu hospital, which serves central Paris, to find a quirky little hotel mainly patronized by patients and their families, but also by budget-conscious (and hypochondriac?) tourists. A huge colonnaded building surrounding a long garden, it was built in the 19th century as part of Baron Haussmann's grand design for the city. If you have ever been in a modern private hospital, that's what the bright, comfortable rooms feel like, some of them with views of the cathedral. There are no public rooms, so breakfast is served in your bedroom. If you're not put off by the faint whiff of antiseptic, the welcome is friendly and personal, and the location and prices almost unbeatable.

NEARBY Notre-Dame; Sainte Chapelle; Ile Saint-Louis; Latin Quarter.
LOCATION on the N side of the square in front of Notre-Dame **PARKING** private or place du Parvis Notre-Dame **METRO** Cité **RER** Saint-Michel Notre-Dame **FOOD** breakfast; room service **PRICE** € **ROOMS** 14 double and twin, single, triple, all with bath; all rooms have phone, TV, safe **FACILITIES** none **CREDIT CARDS** AE, MC, V **CHILDREN** accepted **DISABLED** specially adapted rooms, lift/elevator **PETS** not accepted **CLOSED** never **MANAGER** Mme Catherine Jarrige

MARAIS

HOTEL DE LA PLACE DES VOSGES

12 rue de Birague, 75004 Paris
TEL (01) 42 72 60 46 **FAX** (01) 42 72 02 64
E-MAIL hotel.place.des.vosges@gofornet.com **WEBSITE** www.hotelbeaubourg.com

SET IN A QUIET STREET only 25 metres from one of the loveliest squares in Paris (but please note that, despite its name, it is not in the place des Vosges), this simple 17thC house is entirely in harmony with the surrounding area. The *salon* is suitably traditional and rustic in style; bedrooms used to have less character, with basic furnishings and fittings, but Renata Sibiga, the delightful new owner, is injecting some excitement and style into them, as well as replacing bathrooms. Many rooms are small, but all are remarkably peaceful. The family room has two extra beds, and several others have one extra bed which acts as a couch if you don't need it. The lift could be the world's smallest. There is a certain homely charm about the place, and if you're on a budget but want a great location, this is a good bet. Reports continue to praise it for its terrific value and service.

NEARBY Musée Carnavalet; Musée Picasso; Ile Saint-Louis.
LOCATION in short street off rue Saint-Antoine leading to place des Vosges **PARKING** rue Saint-Antoine **METRO** Saint-Paul **FOOD** breakfast **PRICE** €€ **ROOMS** 16 double and twin, triple, family, 11 with bath, 5 with shower; all rooms have phone, modem points, TV, hairdrier **FACILITIES** sitting area, breakfast room **CREDIT CARDS** AE, DC, MC, V **CHILDREN** accepted **DISABLED** not suitable, lift/elevator **PETS** accepted **CLOSED** never **PROPRIETOR** Renata Sibiga

FOURTH ARRONDISSEMENT

MARAIS

HOTEL SAINT-PAUL-LE-MARAIS

8 rue de Sévigné, 75004 Paris
TEL (01) 48 04 97 27 **FAX** (01) 48 87 37 04
E-MAIL stpaulmarais@hotellerie.net **WEBSITE** www.hotel-paris-marais.com

THIS POPULAR, WELCOMING HOTEL in a converted 17thC convent has a stylish lobby decorated in warm colours, with an inviting curved bar in one corner. Through French windows, you glimpse the little patio garden that comes into its own in summer, and behind reception, the smiling face of the friendly receptionist. Some handsome new fittings and furniture in wild cherry wood (shaped bedheads, wardrobes, mirrors, chairs and desks), gauzy curtains and pretty bedspreads have given the standard bedrooms a fresh look. There are also two superior doubles with Jacuzzi baths, and two spacious triples. A hearty buffet breakfast is offered each morning in the pleasant cellar breakfast room.

NEARBY place des Vosges; Musée Carnavalet; Musée Picasso.
LOCATION just N of rue de Rivoli **PARKING** rue Saint-Antoine **METRO** Saint-Paul **FOOD** breakfast **PRICE** €€ **ROOMS** 27; 12 double, 5 twin, 2 triple, all with bath or shower; 8 single with shower; all rooms have phone, modem point, TV, air-conditioning, hairdrier, safe **FACILITIES** bar/sitting area, breakfast room, internet booth, patio garden **CREDIT CARDS** AE, DC, MC, V **CHILDREN** accepted **DISABLED** not suitable, lift/elevator **PETS** accepted **CLOSED** never **MANAGER** Michèle Leguide

MARAIS

HOTEL DU SEPTIEME ART

20 rue Saint-Paul, 75004 Paris
TEL (01) 44 54 85 00 **FAX** (01) 42 77 69 10
E-MAIL hotel7art@wanadoo.fr

NOT JUST A HOTEL, but a bar, gallery, shop and hotel rolled into one. From the outside, it looks like a typical Marais shopfront, its windows filled with a wonderfully eccentric mix of miniature figures, representing famous film stars and jazz musicians, and gleaming *espresso* machines. Inside, through a mirror-tiled entrance, is a cosy beamed bar with ceiling fans and potted palms, navy velvet banquettes, café chairs, marble-topped tables, a real fire, and the reason behind its name – framed posters for old movies, everywhere. The posters, figures and coffee machines are all for sale. The bar is open until midnight and for breakfast. Bedrooms are simple and unexceptional, but the attic room has plenty of space. The ambience is matched by the friendly staff.

NEARBY place des Vosges; Musée Carnavalet; Hôtel de Ville.
LOCATION between rue Charles V and rue Neuve Saint-Pierre **PARKING** rue Saint-Antoine **METRO** Saint Paul/Pont Marie/Sully Morland **FOOD** breakfast **PRICE** € **ROOMS** 23; 22 double and twin, all with bath or shower; one single without shower or WC; all rooms have phone, TV, safe; some rooms have modem point **FACILITIES** bar/breakfast room, cellar meeting room, internet booth **CREDIT CARDS** AE, DC, MC, V **CHILDREN** accepted **DISABLED** access difficult **PETS** accepted **CLOSED** never **PROPRIETOR** M. Michel

Fifth Arrondissement

Latin Quarter

Hotel Residence Henri IV

50 rue des Bernadins, 75005 Paris
Tel (01) 44 41 31 81 **Fax** (01) 46 33 93 22
E-mail reservation@residencehenri4.com **Website** www.residencehenri4.com

If you are looking for somewhere to stay where you can do some limited self-catering, you might consider this hotel, set at the end of a quiet cul-de-sac. Each room contains a minute kitchenette, consisting of hob, microwave, fridge and storage space which can be hidden away behind a pull-down screen. The apartments have a large comfortable sofa bed in the sitting room, so that a family of four could fit in. The rooms used to be bland, but have been redecorated with more style. They also have splendid period features, including ornate ceilings and panelled walls. Some retain marble fireplaces and pretty painted plaster figures on the walls. Staff are helpful and friendly.

Nearby Panthéon; Musée de Cluny; Notre-Dame; Sainte-Chapelle.
Location between rue Monge and rue des Ecoles **Parking** place Maubert **Metro** Maubert Mutualité **RER** Saint-Michel **Food** breakfast **Price** €€ **Rooms** 12; 5 double, one single, 6 apartments, all with bath; all rooms have phone, modem point, TV, minibar, hairdrier, safe, kitchenette **Facilities** sitting area, breakfast room **Credit cards** AE, DC, MC, V **Children** accepted **Disabled** one room on ground floor, lift/elevator **Pets** not accepted **Closed** never **Proprietor** Corinne Brethous

Latin Quarter

Hotel de Notre-Dame

19 rue Maître Albert, 75005 Paris
Tel (01) 43 26 79 00 **Fax** (01) 46 33 50 11
Email hotel.denotredame@libertysurf.fr **Website** www.notre-dame-hotel.com

The hotel's frontage has large plate glass windows with attractive views down the street towards the *quai*, while the smart reception room has a marble floor, stone walls and a mixture of old and new furniture. We found the reception staff helpful and friendly. Bedrooms have been renovated quite recently. Some have a Japanese-style partition between bedroom and bathroom. They are however very quiet, especially those which look on to an internal courtyard rather than the street – although the street-facing rooms are larger, with French windows opening on to pretty window boxes.

Nearby Musée de Cluny; Notre-Dame; Ile Saint-Louis.
Location near rue Lagrange end of street **Parking** rue Lagrange **Metro** Saint-Michel/Maubert-Mutalité **RER** Saint-Michel **Food** breakfast **Price** €€ **Rooms** 34 double and twin, 33 with bath, one with shower; all rooms have phone, modem point, TV, minibar, hairdrier, safe **Facilities** sitting area, breakfast room **Credit cards** AE, DC, MC, V **Children** accepted **Disabled** access difficult, lift/elevator **Pets** not accepted **Closed** never **Proprietor** M. Fouhety

Fifth Arrondissement

Latin Quarter

Hotel du Pantheon

19 place du Panthéon, 75005 Paris
Tel (01) 43 54 32 95 **Fax** (01) 43 26 64 65
E-mail reservation@hoteldupantheon.com **website** www.hoteldupantheon.com

Like its sister and neighbour, the Grands Hommes, this comfortable 18thC mansion has recently emerged from a total refurbishment, which has added a touch of *élan* to what was a solid, dependable hotel. The bedrooms in particular are unrecognizable: previously pedestrian and bland, they now look stylish and inviting, with jazzy wallpapers and curtains, teamed with checked or striped headboards and quilts, and with pristine white tiled bathrooms. Some rooms have four-posters, some have beams, but the ones to try for overlook the Panthéon directly opposite. The best thing about this hotel is still its position; the view is one of the city's greatest, especially at night. Our reporter found the staff most helpful.

Nearby Panthéon; Saint-Etienne-du-Mont; Sorbonne; Musée de Cluny.
Location on S side of square, between rue Clotaire and rue d'Ulm **Parking** rue Soufflot **Metro** Cardinal Lemoine/Place Monge **RER** Luxembourg **Food** breakfast **Price** €€ **Rooms** 35; 34 double and twin, one single, all with bath; all rooms have phone, modem point, TV, air-conditioning, minibar, hairdrier **Facilities** sitting area, breakfast room **Credit cards** AE, DC, MC, V **Children** accepted **Disabled** lift/elevator **Pets** not accepted **Closed** never **Proprietor** Mme Moncelli

Latin Quarter

Relais Saint-Jacques

3 rue de l'Abbé de l'Epée, 75005 Paris
Tel (01) 53 73 26 00 **Fax** (01) 43 26 17 81
E-mail nevers.luxembourg@wanadoo.fr **website** www.relais-saint-jacques.com

Not to be confused with the homely two-star Hôtel Saint-Jacques (see page 56), the Relais is a plush four-star, which, despite its over-decorated interior, is extremely comfortable, well-run and competitively priced. An interior designer has had a field day here, starting with the polished marble entrance, through the 1920s bar and Louis XV salon to the immaculate bedrooms, individually named and decked out in a different fabric. Our inspector was rather taken aback by the 'speaking' lift (it tells you – rather unnecessarily she thought – which floor you've arrived at). Breakfast is served in a pretty conservatory.

Nearby Luxembourg Gardens; Panthéon; boulevard Saint-Germain.
Location in side street off boulevard Saint-Michel, near junction with rue Gay-Lussac **Parking** rue Soufflot **Metro** Saint-Michel **RER** Luxembourg **Food** breakfast; 24-hr room service **Price** €€€ **Rooms** 23 double and twin, single, triple, all with bath; all rooms have phone, modem point, TV, air-conditioning, minibar, hairdrier, safe **Facilities** sitting room, bar, breakfast room **Credit cards** AE, DC, MC, V **Children** accepted **Disabled** one specially adapted room, lift/elevator **Pets** not accepted **Closed** never **Proprietor** M. Bonneau

Fifth Arrondissement

Latin Quarter

Hotel Sorbonne

6 rue Victor Cousin, 75005 Paris
Tel (01) 43 54 58 08 **Fax** (01) 40 51 05 18
E-mail reservation@hotelsorbonne.com **Website** www.hotelsorbonne.com

The straightforward budget hotel, the Cluny Sorbonne, has dropped the prefix from its name and reopened in this new incarnation. The summer-yellow lobby has become deep green; the beamed ceiling above now trendily painted. Here a cool receptionist surveys the scene from behind a huge desk. The little sitting/breakfast room looks very cosy, decorated in an equally strong shade – but here it's red – with rattan chairs and an open fireplace. A few stylish touches make it upstairs to the bedrooms: particularly in the solid wooden bedheads, wrought-iron light fittings and the picking out of architraves and panelling in different coloured paints. Best of all, the Sorbonne's prices are almost as reasonable as they were.

Nearby Sorbonne; Panthéon; Saint-Etienne-du-Mont; Musée de Cluny.
Location in side street off rue Soufflot, opposite Sorbonne **Parking** rue Soufflot
Metro Cluny-la-Sorbonne **RER** Luxembourg **Meals** Breakfast, room service
Price €€ **Rooms** 37 double and twin, all with bath or shower; all rooms have phone, TV **Facilities** sitting area, sitting/breakfast room **Credit cards** AE, MC, V
Children accepted **Disabled** lift/elevator **Pets** not accepted **Closed** never
Proprietor M. Lopez

Latin Quarter

Hotel des Trois Colleges

16 rue Cujas, 75005 Paris
Tel (01) 43 54 67 30 **Fax** (01) 46 34 02 99
E-mail hotel@3colleges.com **Website** www.3colleges.com

In the university heartland, this hotel has a historically important location on the site of the crossroads at the centre of the ancient Roman town; maps verifying this cover the walls. In the pretty glass-roofed *salon*, among Lloyd loom chairs, ancient pots are on display – finds from archaeological digs here. Even the original well is visible in a corner. Its real attraction was the simple *salon de thé* next door, an integral part of the hotel, which has been closed since the manageress left to have a baby. Although at the time of writing.a replacement for her hadn't been found, the hotel hopes that the closure will not be permanent as the simply decorated tearoom was a popular meeting place for students, teachers and tourists alike. The bedrooms, with their white formica and wood fixtures are pedestrian. Staff are very friendly and attentive.

Nearby Panthéon; Sorbonne; boulevard Saint-Michel; Musée de Cluny.
Location between rue V. Cousin and boulevard Saint-Michel **Parking** rue Soufflot
Metro Luxembourg **RER** Luxembourg **Food** breakfast **Price** €€ **Rooms** 44; 36 double and twin, 2 triple, all with bath or shower; 6 single with shower; all rooms have phone, modem point, TV, hairdrier **Facilities** sitting room, internet booth
Credit cards AE, DC, MC, V **Children** accepted **Disabled** lift/elevator **Pets** accepted
Closed never **Proprietors** M. and Mme Wyplosz

Sixth Arrondissement

Montparnasse

L'Atelier Montparnasse

49 rue Vavin, 75006 Paris
Tel (01) 46 33 66 00 **Fax** (01) 40 51 04 21
E-mail hotel@ateliermontparnasse.com **Website** www.ateliermontparnasse.com

A tiny hotel whose homely and cosy atmosphere, engendered by its new owner, Victoria Bourjault, reflects something of the laid-back, artistic legacy of the area. The entrance has a magnificent mosaic floor, with a painting of Bernard Bouin's *On the Road* dominating the reception. The smallish but comfortable and neat bedrooms (there is a junior suite, Foujita, on the top floor) are notable for their highly original mosaic bathrooms. Each mosaic – representing a famous painting, by Modigliani, Gaugin, Foujita and others, have recently been renovated with the help of the mosaicist, who was the mother of the hotel's first owner.

Nearby boulevard du Montparnasse; Jardin du Luxembourg.
Location between boulevard Montparnasse and boulevard Raspail **Parking** in street or boulevard Montparnasse **Metro** Vavin **Food** breakfast **Price** €€
Rooms 17, all double and twin, all with bath; all rooms have phone, modem point, TV, minibar, hairdrier **Facilities** sitting room, breakfast room **Credit cards** AE, DC, MC, V **Children** accepted **Disabled** lift/elevator **Pets** accepted **Closed** never **Proprietor** Victoria Bourjault

Saint-Germain-des-Pres

Hotel Crystal

24 rue Saint-Benoït, 75006 Paris
Tel (01) 45 48 85 14 **Fax** (01) 45 49 16 45
E-mail hotel.crystal@wanadoo.fr **Website** www.hotels-paris-reservation.com

Set in a little street filled with typical Left Bank *bistrots* and restaurants, this is a hotel which – for the best reasons – has become less and less characterful as it has become smarter and smarter over the years. The owners have striven hard to keep it in tip-top shape, resulting in a hotel which is neat as a pin, clean, well-run, pleasant without being in any way remarkable. The quiet rooms have all been renovated recently, with pretty fabrics, reproduction furniture, and smart bathrooms.Downstairs from the business-like lobby (with helpful uniformed staff manning the reception desk) there is a large vaulted and exposed stone cellar breakast room, with tables prettily draped in pink.

Nearby boulevard Saint-Germain; Jardin du Luxembourg; Musée d'Orsay.
Location in a short street between boulevard Saint-Germain and rue Jacob **Parking** boulevard Saint-Germain (rue du Dragon) **Metro** Saint-Germain-des-Prés **Food** breakfast **Price** €€€ **Rooms** 26; 17 double and twin, 4 single, 4 triple, one suite; 20 rooms with bath, 6 with shower; all rooms have phone, modem point, TV, minibar, hairdrier, safe **Facilities** sitting room, breakfast room **Credit cards** AE, DC, MC, V **Children** accepted **Disabled** access possible, lift/elevator **Pets** accepted **Closed** never **Manager** Danielle Adda

SIXTH ARRONDISSEMENT

MONTPARNASSE

HOTEL DANEMARK

21 rue Vavin, 75006 Paris
TEL (01) 43 26 93 78 **FAX** (01) 46 34 66 06
E-MAIL paris@hoteldanemark.com

EVERYTHING ABOUT this smart hotel is deliberately stylish: the triple-arched, electric blue frontage, the striking modern art, the smart reception area and sitting room with attractive contemporary furniture, wall and table lights. In the past we complained that bedrooms were less impressive than the ground floor, but the hands-on owner, Jean Nurit constantly strives to keep his establishment in tip-top shape, and has recently improved them greatly with warmer curtains and bedcovers, and complettely refurbished rooms on the top floor. Each floor has its own pleasing colour scheme.

NEARBY boulevard du Montparnasse; Jardin du Luxembourg.
LOCATION between boulevard Raspail and rue Notre-Dame-des-Champs **PARKING** in street or boulevard du Montparnasse **METRO** Vavin **FOOD** breakfast **PRICE** €€ **ROOMS** 15, all double and twin, 14 with bath, one with Jacuzzi; all rooms have phone , modem point, TV, minibar, hairdrier **FACILITIES** sitting room, breakfast room **CREDIT CARDS** AE, DC, MC, V **CHILDREN** accepted **DISABLED** lift/elevator **PETS** accepted **CLOSED** never **PROPRIETOR** Jean Nurit

SAINT-GERMAIN-DES-PRES

HOTEL JARDIN DE L'ODEON

7 rue Casimir-Delavigne, 75006 Paris
TEL (01) 46 34 23 90 **FAX** (01) 43 25 28 12

THERE'S NOTHING startling about this safe, three star hotel in the same quiet street near the Odéon theatre as the Hôtel Delavigne (see page 65), except perhaps the jagged and swirling pattern on the *salon* sofas and armchairs and the stiffish prices. The 1920s *leitmotif* extends from the green marble floor and elegant, high-backed black chairs in the breakfast area to the posters, paintings and logo. The chairs crop up again in the pristine bedrooms, as do the posters and pictures, adding a much needed fillip to an otherwise standardized room. Some rooms open on to the pretty courtyard garden, and there is also a bar in the large reception lobby – which acts as sitting room and breakfast room as well – from where you can catch sight of the greenery.

NEARBY Jardin du Luxembourg; boulevard Saint-Germain; Latin Quarter.
LOCATION in a short street between rue Monsieur-le-Prince and place de l'Odéon **PARKING** rue l'Ecole-de-Médecine **METRO** Odéon/Saint-Michel **RER** Luxembourg **FOOD** breakfast **PRICE** €€€ **ROOMS** 41; 34 double and twin, 5 triple, all with bath; 2 single with shower; all rooms have phone, modem point, TV, minibar, hairdrier, safe **FACILITIES** sitting area, breakfast area, courtyard garden **CREDIT CARDS** AE, MC, V **CHILDREN** accepted **DISABLED** access possible, lift/elevator **PETS** accepted **CLOSED** never **MANAGER** Anne-Sophie Bossut

SIXTH ARRONDISSEMENT

MONTPARNASSE

HOTEL DES MARRONNIERS

[illegible]

TEL (01) 43 25 30 60 **FAX** (01) 40 46 83 56

THE ALLURE OF THE Marronniers lies in its situation, tucked away from the bustle of Saint-Germain between a quiet courtyard in front and a lovely garden behind. The ground floor particularly has the feel of a country hotel, its flowery conservatory – Empire-style curtains, white wrought-iron furniture – opening on to the garden beyond. In the contrastingly dark basement, stone vaulted cellars form a sitting room and breakfast room. Bedrooms are passable, some brightly decorated, and vary in size; ask for one with a view across the roof-tops and the steeple of Saint-Germain-des-Prés. We remain of the opinion that the hotel has lost its bloom, although it still retains a long list of faithful clients.

NEARBY boulevard Saint-Germain; Musée d'Orsay; Louvre; Ile Saint-Louis.
LOCATION near junction with rue de Seine **PARKING** rue Mazarine, boulevard Saint-Germain **METRO** Saint-Germain-des-Prés/Mabillon **FOOD** breakfast **PRICE** €€€
ROOMS 37 double, twin and single, all with bath or shower; all rooms have phone, TV **FACILITIES** conservatory, sitting room, breakfast room, garden **CREDIT CARDS** MC, V
CHILDREN accepted **DISABLED** lift/elevator **PETS** not accepted **CLOSED** never
PROPREITOR M. Henneveux

SAINT-GERMAIN-DES-PRES

LE RELAIS MEDICIS

23 rue Racine, 75006 Paris

TEL (01) 43 26 00 60 **FAX** (01) 40 46 83 39

E-MAIL relais-medicis@wanadoo.fr **WEBSITE** www.123france.com

THIS GORGEOUS LITTLE HOTEL was opened in 1992 by the owners of the sought-after Relais Saint-Germain (see page 78), but inexplicably never became as successful as they had envisaged. In 1996 it was taken over by a husband-and-wife team, Monsieur and Madame Chérel, professional hoteliers who appear to have been successful in turning around its fortunes. Its 16 stylishly comfortable, beamed bedrooms, decorated in the style of different impressionist painters and all with luxurious marble bathrooms, are arranged around a pretty courtyard. On the ground floor everything is small-scale and dainty: a narrow entrance, a soothing little pink and green breakfast room and welcoming *salon* with dramatic red walls. Here they are covered with thoughtfully hung paintings. Prints or sepia photographs fill the walls elsewhere.

NEARBY Latin Quarter; Musée de Cluny; Jardin du Luxembourg.
LOCATION just off place de l'Odéon between rue Corneille and rue Monsieur-le-Prince **PARKING** rue l'Ecole-de-Médecine **METRO** Odéon **FOOD** breakfast **PRICE** €€€ **ROOMS** 16 double and twin, all with bath; all rooms have phone, TV, air-conditioning, minibar, hairdrier **FACILITIES** sitting room, breakfast room, courtyard
CREDIT CARDS AE, DC, MC, V **CHILDREN** accepted **DISABLED** lift/elevator **PETS** not accepted **CLOSED** never **PROPREITOR** M. and Mme Jean-Marie Chérel

SIXTH ARRONDISSEMENT

SAINT-GERMAIN-DES-PRES

HOTEL MILLISEME

21 rue Jacob, 75006 Paris
TEL (01) 43 25 30 60 **FAX** (01) 40 46 83 56
E-MAIL reservation@millesimehotel.com **WEBSITE** www.millesimehotel.com

LITTLE SISTER of the Aubusson (see page 61), this glossy hotel opened in 1997, bringing a touch of Côte Sud to rue Jacob. Shades of ochre, yellow and terracotta are carefully coordinated throughout, offset by wood and tiled floors, potted plants and a mixture of wrought-iron and painted furniture. Its best feature is a charming courtyard, glimpsed through French windows as you walk in: it makes a calm spot in which to sit. Though fresh-looking and comfortable, the bedrooms remain standard hotel rooms, reminiscent (in atmosphere rather than looks) of the Aubusson's. The cellar breakfast room is particularly pretty.

NEARBY boulevard Saint-Germain; Musée d'Orsay; Notre-Dame; Latin Quarter. **LOCATION** near junction with rue de Seine **PARKING** rue Mazarine, boulevard Saint-Germain **METRO** Saint-Germain-des-Prés/Mabillon **FOOD** breakfast **PRICE** €€€ **ROOMS** 22; 21 double, twin and triple, one single, all with bath; all rooms have phone, modem point, TV, air-conditioning, minibar, hairdrier, safe **FACILITIES** sitting area, breakfast room, internet booth, courtyard **CREDIT CARDS** AE, DC, MC, V **CHILDREN** accepted **DISABLED** one specially adapted room **PETS** accepted **CLOSED** never **MANAGER** Romain Trollet

SAINT-GERMAIN-DES-PRES

HOTEL DE L'ODEON

13 rue Saint-Sulpice 75006 Paris
TEL (01) 43 25 70 11 **FAX** (01) 43 29 97 34
E-MAIL hoteldelodeon@wanadoo.fr **WEBSITE** www.paris-hotel-odeon.com

DOMINATING EACH BEDROOM in this pleasant hotel is a different, but equally stunning, bed; it may be antique brass with inset pictures, a four-poster upholstered in tapestry, twin beds decorated with inlay and painted figures or a pretty wooden sleigh. There are antiques and mirrors to match. Housed in a beamed 16thC building, the *salon* is filled with antique and repro pieces; torch lights and paintings hang on the walls. Only the patterned carpet and tasteless fluorescent sign look out of place. There is a tiny, colourful garden and a breakfast room, beyond which are the new bedrooms. Quieter, but smaller, these rooms have modern brass beds and pretty painted cupboards, but less character than the old. The reception staff are friendly and welcoming.

NEARBY boulevard Saint-Germain; Jardin du Luxembourg; Ile de la Cité. **LOCATION** between rue de Condé and rue de Tournon **PARKING** place Saint-Sulpice **METRO** Odéon/Mabillon **FOOD** breakfast **PRICE** €€€ **ROOMS** 29; 21 double and twin, 4 single, 3 triple, one family, all with bath or shower; all rooms have phone, modem point, TV, air-conditioning, hairdrier, safe **FACILITIES** sitting area, breakfast room, internet booth **CREDIT CARDS** AE, DC, MC, V **CHILDREN** accepted **DISABLED** access possible, lift/elevator **PETS** accepted **CLOSED** never **PROPREITOR** M. Pilfert

SIXTH ARRONDISSEMENT

LUXEMBOURG QUARTER

HOTEL PERREYVE

63 rue Madame, 75006 Paris
TEL (01) 45 48 35 01 **FAX** (01) 42 84 03 30
E-MAIL perreyve@club-internet.fr

A PRETTY, early 20thC building across the street from the Regent's Hôtel (see page 140) in calm, dignified rue Madame. Both hotels share an appealing location close to the green spaces and amusements of Jardin du Luxembourg and all the Rive Gauche has to offer, and until recently both were similar in their simple sobriety and their price. The Regent's has been modernized and refurbished but at the little changed Perreyve, travellers on a budget will find courteous staff, a homely, dignified, old fashioned *salon*, and small and very simple, but clean bedrooms. Bathrooms are fairly unexciting, but, again, spotlessly clean.

NEARBY Jardin du Luxembourg; Saint-Sulpice; boulevard Saint-Germain.
LOCATION between rue Chevalier and rue de Vaugirard **PARKING** Saint-Sulpice **METRO** Saint-Sulpice **FOOD** breakfast **PRICE** €€ **ROOMS** 30; 27 double and twin, 2 single, one single, 13 with bath, 17 with shower; all rooms have phone, TV, hairdrier **FACILITIES** sitting room, breakfast room **CREDIT CARDS** AE, DC, MC, V **CHILDREN** accepted **DISABLED** not suitable, lift/elevator **PETS** not accepted **CLOSED** never **MANAGER** René Doumergue

SAINT-GERMAIN-DES-PRES

HOTEL PRINCE DE CONTI

8 rue Guénégaud, 75006 Paris
TEL (01) 44 07 30 40 **FAX** (01) 44 07 36 34
E-MAIL princedeconti@wanadoo.fr

AN UPMARKET, welcoming hotel which is perhaps too carefully designed, co-ordinated and generally coerced to generate much character, but nonetheless its bedrooms are very smart and comfortable. No. 61, for example, is a large room handsomely decked out in red and green Empire-style medallion wallpaper with chairs, carpet, curtains in matching colours. The ottoman at the end of the bed is a welcome extra touch. No. 42 is a pretty single, in pink *toile de jouy* with green furniture and a grey and black marble bathroom. The hotel has an identical twin close by, the Prince de Condé (39 rue de Seine; tel (01) 43 26 71 56), the only difference being that it boasts a luxury suite with Jacuzzi. Good breakfast.

NEARBY boulevard Saint-Germain; Ile de la Cité; Musée du Louvre.
LOCATION between rue Mazarine and quai de Conti **PARKING** rue Mazarine **METRO** Odéon **FOOD** breakfast **PRICE** €€ **ROOMS** 26; 21 double and twin, 19 with bath, 2 with shower; all rooms have phone, modem point, TV, air-conditioning, minibar, hairdrier, safe **FACILITIES** sitting room, breakfast room, bar, courtyard **CREDIT CARDS** AE, DC, MC, V **CHILDREN** accepted **DISABLED** access possible, lift/elevator **PETS** not accepted **CLOSED** never **PROPRIETORS** M. and Mme Touber

SIXTH ARRRONDISSEMENT

SAINT-GERMAIN-DES-PRES

HOTEL LE RECAMIER

3 bis Saint-Sulpice, 75006 Paris
TEL (01) 43 26 04 89 **FAX** (01) 46 33 27 73

IN A QUIET CORNER of place Saint-Sulpice – with its fine barn of a church, fountain, some serious fashion shops and buzzing café – this is a tiny, old-fashioned two-star hotel that seems to have hardly changed in looks in the last 30 years or so. New to the guide, it was the bird-of-paradise wallpaper in the entrance hall that caught our eye as we passed, and to be honest, it's probably – along with the location and the little *propre* sitting room – the hotel's best feature. There is a simple breakfast room for simple breakfasts, and simple bedrooms, with floral wallpaper, candlewick curtains and bedspreads and bamboo tables and chairs. Washing facilities are tucked here and there. Try for one of the rooms overlooking the church; see if you can spot the little vegetable garden on the roof.

NEARBY Jardin de Luxembourg; Saint-Sulpice; boulevard Saint-Germain.
LOCATION in a corner of place Saint-Sulpice **PARKING** place Saint-Sulpice **METRO** Saint-Sulpice **FOOD** breakfast **PRICE** €€ **ROOMS** 30; 29 double and twin, one single, all with bath, shower or bidet; all rooms have phone, TV **FACILITIES** sitting room, breakfast room **CREDIT CARDS** MC, V **CHILDREN** accepted **DISABLED** access difficult, lift/elevator **PETS** not accepted **CLOSED** never **PROPRIETOR** Gilbert Dauphin

LUXEMBOURG QUARTER

HOTEL LE REGENT

61 rue Dauphine, 75006 Paris
TEL (01) 46 34 59 80 **FAX** (01) 40 51 05 07
E-MAIL hotel.leregent@wanadoo.fr **WEBSITE** www.francehotelguide.com

FOR ONCE A HOTEL where the bedrooms exceed the reception rooms. The lobby, with its mirrored walls, banks of houseplants and bright lighting lacks much character, but the recently renovated bedrooms are more interesting, all different, with unusually pretty bathrooms. Rooms at the back on the fifth and sixth floors have a view of Notre-Dame; larger ones have sitting areas. On the sixth floor, the large rooms at the front have their own tiny terraces. One has a lovely blue-and-white tiled bathroom; another has a damson pink tiled floor, with *toile de jouy* wallpaper in the bedroom.

NEARBY boulevard Saint-Germain; Latin Quarter; Notre-Dame; Sainte Chapelle.
LOCATION between rue Saint-André-des-Arts and rue Christine **PARKING** rue Mazarine **METRO** Odéon **FOOD** breakfast **PRICE** €€ **ROOMS** 25, 20 double and twin, 16 with bath, 4 with shower; 5 single, all with shower; all rooms have phone, modem point, TV, air-conditioning, minibar, trouser press (in large rooms), hairdrier, safe **FACILITIES** sitting area, breakfast room **CREDIT CARDS** AE, MC, V **CHILDREN** accepted **DISABLED** lift/elevator **PETS** accepted **CLOSED** never **MANAGER** M. Cretey

SIXTH ARRRONDISSEMENT

LUXEMBOURG QUARTER

REGENT'S HOTEL

44 rue Madame, 75006 Paris
TEL (01) 45 48 02 81 **FAX** (01) 45 44 85 73
E-MAIL regents.hotel@wanadoo.fr

THIS USED TO BE a plain, respectable two-star establishment with a low-key welcome, staid breakfast room, and drab brown corridors. Since our last visit, however, a new proprietor has taken charge and has given the hotel a much-needed facelift, without greatly increasing the prices. The sitting room is a bit like a smart suburban house, with floor-length blue curtains, tall potted plants, three-piece suite and glass-topped coffee table. Well located, close to the welcome open space of the Jardin du Luxembourg, there is also a flowery courtyard garden – with flowering plants in tubs and trellis on the walls for climbers – where you take breakfast on sunny mornings.

NEARBY boulevard Saint-Germain; Latin Quarter; Notre-Dame; Sainte Chapelle.
LOCATION midway along rue Madame between rue Chevalier and rue de Vaugirard **PARKING** Saint-Sulpice **METRO** Saint-Sulpice **FOOD** breakfast **PRICE** €€ **ROOMS** 34 25 double, twin and triple, 5 single, 4 family, all with bath; all rooms have phone, TV, hairdrier **FACILITIES** breakfast room, sitting area, courtyard garden **CREDIT CARDS** AE, DC, MC, V **CHILDREN** accepted **DISABLED** one room on ground floor, lift/elevator **PETS** accepted **CLOSED** never **PROPRIETOR** M. Aymard

SAINT-GERMAIN-DES-PRES

HOTEL SAINT-GERMAIN-DES-PRES

36 rue Bonaparte, 75006 Paris
TEL (01) 43 26 00 19 **FAX** (01) 40 46 83 63
E-MAIL hotel-saint-germain-des-pres@wanadoo.fr **WEBSITE** www.hotel-paris-saint-germain.com

A SMALL HOTEL WITH ALL THE TRAPPINGS, which stands out for charm and individuality, if not for notably good taste or coherence of interior design. Its bedrooms are all furnished in a hotchpotch of styles and colours; some have brightly coloured velvet bedheads, others have vigorously floral wallpaper and fabric, which seems to overwhelm them; one suite has a solid four-poster, parquet floor, heavy wood furniture and tapestry-clad walls, and a Parisian scene in the bathroom. At the far end of the large *salon*-cum-breakfast-room a bank of fresh flowers introduces a riot of colour; unfortunately it fails to mask a chocolate-box mural in powdery pastels, depicting early 20thC life in Saint-Germain. What you will find here is a friendly smile behind the reception desk and plenty of personal attention.

NEARBY Musée d'Orsay; Louvre; boulevard Saint-Germain; Ile de la Cité.
LOCATION between rue Jacob and rue de l'Abbaye **PARKING** boulevard Saint-Germain **METRO** Saint-Germain-des-Prés **FOOD** breakfast **PRICE** €€€ **ROOMS** 30; 28 double and twin, 2 suites, all with bath or shower; all rooms have phone, modem point, TV , minibar, hairdrier, safe; 15 rooms have air-conditioning **FACILITIES** *salon*/breakfast room **CREDIT CARDS** AE, MC, V **CHILDREN** accepted **DISABLED** no special facilities **PETS** accepted **CLOSED** never **PROPRIETOR** M. Nouvel

SIXTH ARRRONDISSEMENT

SAINT-GERMAIN-DES-PRES/LATIN QUARTER

HOTEL SAINT-ANDRE-DES-ARTS

66 rue Saint-André-des-Arts, 75006 Paris
TEL (01) 43 26 96 16 **FAX** (01) 43 29 73 34
E-MAIL hsaintand@wanadoo.fr **WEBSITE** www.123france.com

A ONE-OFF. If there are any beatniks left, this is the hotel for them. In the meantime, it endears itself to backpackers and academics who prefer the simple life. The house, in one of the liveliest streets in the district, dates from the late 16th century and has a charming old shop front as a façade, a splendid choirstall in the entrance and a listed staircase. After our latest visit, we felt that, despite a fresh lick of paint in the bedrooms, the common parts looked so shabby that we could no longer give the hotel a full entry. Prices are still unbeatable, and Monsieur le Goubin still plays jazz and chats about Sartre and philosophy.

NEARBY rue de Buci street market; boulevard Saint Germain; Latin Quarter. **LOCATION** in a street leading off place Saint-Michel between boulevard Saint Germain and the Seine **PARKING** place Saint-Michel **METRO** Odéon/Saint-Michel **RER** Saint-Michel **FOOD** breakfast **PRICE** € **ROOMS** 33 single, double and twin, triple, family, all with bath or shower; all rooms have phone **FACILITIES** breakfast room **CREDIT CARDS** MC, V **CHILDREN** accepted **DISABLED** not suitable **PETS** accepted **CLOSED** never **PROPRIETOR** M. le Goubin

SAINT-GERMAIN-DES-PRES

LA VILLA

29 rue Jacob, 75006 Paris
TEL (01) 43 26 60 00 **FAX** (01) 46 34 63 63
E-MAIL hotel@villa-saintgermain.com **WEBSITE** www.villa-saintgermain.com

ELEGANT RUE JACOB is filled with richly stocked interior design and antique shops, which makes La Villa stand out all the more. Designed within an inch of its life to be ultra modern, ultra cool, its triple arched glass façade reveals a lobby with all the sophisticated minimalism, sensuous curves and hard edges that contemporary design requires. Upstairs, laser lights beam the room numbers on to the carpet in front of each door; behind them we find more unremitting modernity, softened by very soothing lights on dimmers, and glossy, high-tech bathrooms with stainless steel sinks set into frosted glass surrounds. Prices are high; service is polished.

NEARBY boulevard Saint-Germain; Musée d'Orsay; Louvre; Notre-Dame. **LOCATION** at junction with rue Bonaparte **PARKING** boulevard Saint-Germain (rue du Dragon) **METRO** Saint-Germain-des-Prés **FOOD** breakfast, room service **PRICE** €€€€ **ROOMS** 32; 29 double and twin, 3 suites, all with bath; all rooms have phone, modem point, TV, air-conditioning, minibar, hairdrier, safe **FACILITIES** breakfast room, bar, internet booth, jazz bar **CREDIT CARDS** AE, DC, MC, V **CHILDREN** accepted **DISABLED** access difficult, lift/elevator **PETS** accepted **CLOSED** never **MANAGER** Valerie Dude

SEVENTH ARRONDISSEMENT

SAINT-GERMAIN-DES-PRES

HOTEL DE L'ACADEMIE

32 rue des Saints-Pères, 75007 Paris
TEL (01) 45 48 36 22 **FAX** (01) 45 44 75 24
E-MAIL academiehotel@aol.com **WEBSITE** www.academiehotel.com

A SMART HOTEL in an elegant 18thC building, rather stiffly decked out in a dark green and blue colour scheme. To our mind, the gilded Empire-style furniture and Classical statues strike a rather pompous note, but this is perhaps unfair because, despite the preponderance of swags and tassles, gilt and velvet, the colours are rich, the seating areas and breakfast room softly lit and cosy. Bedrooms are thoughtfully decorated with individual furniture and objects, and bathrooms well-planned. The term 'junior suite' denotes a small sitting area and a Jacuzzi.

NEARBY Musée d'Orsay; boulevard Saint-Germain; Musée du Louvre..
LOCATION in the stretch of street between quai Malaquais and boulevard Saint-Germain **PARKING** boulevard Saint-Germain (rue du Dragon) **METRO** Saint-Germain-des-Prés **RER** Musée d'Orsay **FOOD** breakfast **PRICE** €€€ **ROOMS** 33; 20 double and twin with bath, 5 with Jacuzzi; 8 single with shower; all rooms have phone, modem point, TV, minibar, hairdrier, sare; half have air-conditioning **FACILITIES** sitting room, bar, breakfast room **CREDIT CARDS** AE, DC, MC, V **CHILDREN** accepted **DISABLED** lift/elevator **PETS** accepted **CLOSED** never **PROPRIETOR** Gérard Chekroun

SAINT-GERMAIN-DES-PRES

HOTEL DE BEAUNE

29 rue de Beaune, 75007 Paris
TEL (01) 42 61 24 89 **FAX** (01) 49 27 02 12

IT IS EASY TO WALK past this narrow 18thC house with its crumbling façade, and not notice that it's a hotel. But, once inside, the warm little interior envelopes you wholeheartedly. The dark red moirée walls and plain wood floor, bare but for one small runner, are part of the fairly new decorative scheme created by the delightfully eccentric Madame Cholale. Beyond reception is a bar/breakfast area where banquettes are piled with cushions and guests can have coffee or breakfast at café tables. Bedrooms and bathrooms are adequate; some are surprisingly spacious and some share the idiosyncratic character of the ground floor.

NEARBY Musée d'Orsay; quai Voltaire; Musée du Louvre; boulevard Saint-Germain.
LOCATION between rue de l'Université and rue de Verneuil **PARKING** rue Montalembert **METRO** rue du Bac/Solférino **RER** Musée d'Orsay **FOOD** breakfast **PRICE** €€ **ROOMS** 19 double and twin, all with bath or shower; all rooms have phone, TV, minibar, hairdrier, safe **FACILITIES** bar/breakfast room **CREDIT CARDS** AE, DC, MC, V **CHILDREN** accepted **DISABLED** not suitable, lift/elevator **PETS** accepted **CLOSED** never **PROPRIETOR** Mme Cholale

SEVENTH ARRONDISSEMENT

SAINT-GERMAIN-DES-PRES

HOTEL BERSOLY'S SAINT-GERMAIN

28 rue de Lille, 75007 Paris
TEL (01) 42 60 73 79 **FAX** (01) 49 27 05 55
E-MAIL hotelbersolys@wanadoo.fr **WEBSITE** bersolys-paris-hotel.com

A 17THC FORMER convent in a great location for sightseeing. From the street, the reception/*salon* looks cosy and inviting; a little beamed room with a stone floor and green walls, table lamps which cast a soft light, and sofa and chairs covered in a cheerful fabric. A pleasant place to wait, though its size causes problems if too many guests arrive at the same time. Sadly the warmth of the room did not extend to our welcome, which was distinctly cool. Each of the bedrooms – generally somewhat small too – has been thoughtfully tricked out in a favourite colour of the impressionist painter it is named after. Furniture is traditional; bathrooms, tiny and-functional. Breakfast is served in a vaulted cellar, split into two rooms.

NEARBY Musée d'Orsay; quai Voltaire; Musée du Louvre; boulevard Saint-Germain. **LOCATION** between rue du Bac and rue des Saints-Pères **PARKING** rue Montalembert **METRO** rue du Bac/Saint-Germain-des-Prés **RER** Musée d'Orsay **FOOD** breakfast, room service **PRICE** €€ **ROOMS** 16 double and twin, all with bath or shower; all rooms have phone, TV, air-conditioning, ceiling fan, hairdrier, safe **FACILITIES** sitting area, breakfast room **CREDIT CARDS** MC, V **CHILDREN** accepted **DISABLED** lift/elevator **PETS** accepted **CLOSED** 2 weeks Aug **PROPRIETOR** Sylvie Carbonnaux

SAINT-GERMAIN-DES-PRES

HOTEL DE LILLE

40 rue de Lille,75007 Paris
TEL (01) 42 61 29 09 **FAX** (01) 42 61 53 97
E-MAIL hotel-de-lille@wanadoo.fr

THE RECEPTION area is sparse, but quite smart in a no-nonsense, business-like way, with art deco touches such as a marble floor, blue tub chairs and black-and-white pictures. Green pot plants in the window add a splash of colour. Spiral stairs lead down to a large vaulted breakfast room which feels distinctly 1970s rather than '30s with its padded wicker chairs and glass-topped tables. Bedrooms have echoes of both these decades, some with '30s veneered furniture, others with bamboo tables and chairs. They are mostly small, with matching bedcovers and curtains. Top floor rooms are beamed. Bathrooms are not new, but adequate. The hotel's location is excellent for sightseeing, on the Left Bank, but close to the islands and the Right Bank.

NEARBY Musée d'Orsay; boulevard Saint-Germain; Musée du Louvre. **LOCATION** between rue de Verneuil and quai Voltaire **PARKING** rue Montalembert **METRO** rue du Bac/Saint-Germain-des-Prés **RER** Musée d'Orsay **FOOD** breakfast **PRICE** €€ **ROOMS** 20; 13 double and twin, all with bath or shower; 6 single with shower; one triple with bath; all rooms have phone, TV, hairdrier, safe **FACILITIES** sitting area, bar, breakfast room **CREDIT CARDS** AE, DC, MC, V **CHILDREN** accepted **DISABLED** lift/elevator **PETS** accepted **CLOSED** never **PROPRIETOR** M. Margouilla

SEVENTH ARRONDISSEMENT

SAINT-GERMAIN-DES-PRES

HOTEL MONTALEMBERT

3 rue de Montalembert, 75007 Paris
TEL (01) 45 49 68 68 **FAX** (01) 45 49 69 49
E-MAIL welcome@montalembert.com **WEBSITE** www.montalembert.com

THE DECORATION OF THIS RITZY, costly hotel has been cleverly conceived and immaculately realized down to the last designer detail. Bannisters, lights and doorhandles, as well as principal pieces of furniture, have all been specially crafted in wrought iron, cast bronze, sycamore wood and leather. A bold navy and white striped fabric recurs on restaurant chair backs and duvets. The honey-marbled entrance looks stylish and important; the equally chic café/bar has a sitting area round an open fire at one end. Bedrooms are furnished with beautiful wooden beds and antiques or sleek black modern furniture. Bathrooms are impeccable. All very serious.

NEARBY Musée d'Orsay; boulevard Saint-Germain; Musée du Louvre.
LOCATION between rue de l'Université and boulevard Saint-Germain **PARKING** next door **METRO** rue du Bac **RER** Musée d'Orsay **FOOD** breakfast, lunch, dinner; room service **PRICE** €€€€ **ROOMS** 56; 51 double and twin, 5 suites, all with bath; all rooms have phone, modem point, TV, video, air-conditioning, minibar, hairdrier, safe **FACILITIES** bar/restaurant, sitting area, meeting rooms, internet booth **CREDIT CARDS** AE, DC, MC, V **CHILDREN** accepted **DISABLED** lift/elevator **PETS** accepted **CLOSED** never **MANAGER** M. Bonnier

INVALIDES/SAINT-GERMAIN-DES-PRES

HOTEL DE NEVERS

83 rue du Bac, 75007 Paris
TEL (01) 45 44 61 30 **FAX** (01) 42 22 29 47
E-MAIL hoteldenevers75@aol.com

WE RECOMMEND THIS QUIRKY little hotel for the young and strong. It occupies a tall thin 17thC house with no lift and a wrought-iron staircase that seem to go up forever: and you're bound to have to carry your own bags. It was redecorated a couple of years ago and has an individual appeal, particularly in the tiny entrance with beams, one wall of rough stone and another mirrored to create the illusion of space. Close your eyes to the suspect artwork on the landings (where well-placed chairs invite you to sit and regain your breath) because if you can puff your way to the top, the bedrooms there have more than a little garret charm. Nos 10 and 11 have terraces; two on the first floor have huge windows. Good value.

NEARBY boulevard Saint-Germain; Musée d'Orsay; Musée Rodin.
LOCATION between rue de Grenelle and rue de Varenne **PARKING** rue du Bac **METRO** rue du Bac **RER** Musée d'Orsay **FOOD** breakfast **PRICE** €€ **ROOMS** 12; 11 double and twin with bath or shower, one single with shower; all rooms have phone, TV, minibar **FACILITIES** sitting area **CREDIT CARDS** not accepted **CHILDREN** accepted **DISABLED** not suitable **PETS** accepted **CLOSED** never **PROPRIETOR** M. Hamrioui

SEVENTH ARRONDISSEMENT

INVALIDES QUARTER

HOTEL D'ORSAY

91 rue de Lille, 75007 Paris
TEL (01) 47 05 85 54 **FAX** (01) 45 55 51 16
E-MAIL hotel.orsay@wanadoo.fr **WEBSITE** www.esprit-de-france.com

A FAVOURITE OLD HOTEL of ours, the Solférino, closed down a few years ago and has now been merged with the fairly straightforward, reasonably priced Hôtel Orsay next door. Both buildings were recently given a thorough make-over, under the ownership of the Esprit de France group (which also owns the Saints-Pères and the Mansart on pages 81 and 36). We feel a pang of nostalgia as we stand in what was the charming yellow breakfast room of the Solférino, but that's life. The Orsay's bedrooms have been redecorated in pastel shades with pretty floral fabrics and attractive bathrooms in white and boldly coloured Italian tiles. Public areas are stylish, if lacking character, We felt it offered value for money.

NEARBY Musée d'Orsay; boulevard Saint-Germain; Musée du Louvre.
LOCATION in stretch of street between boulevard Saint-Germain and rue de Solfériino **PARKING** rue du Bac **METRO** Assemblée Nationale **RER** Musée d'Orsay **FOOD** breakfast **PRICE** €€ **ROOMS** 41 double and twin, all with bath; all rooms have phone, modem point, TV, minibar, hairdrier **FACILITIES** sitting room, breakfast room, internet booth **CREDIT CARDS** MC, V **CHILDREN** accepted **DISABLED** lift/elevator **PETS** not accepted **CLOSED** never **MANAGER** David Chevalier

SAINT-GERMAIN-DES-PRES

HOTEL DU QUAI VOLTAIRE

19 Quai Voltaire, 75007 Paris
TEL (01) 42 61 50 91 **FAX** (01) 42 61 62 26
E-MAIL info@quaivoltaire.fr **WEBSITE** www.quaivoltaire.fr

A HOTEL SINCE 1850, the Quai Voltaire has numbered Oscar Wilde, Wagner, Baudelaire and Pissaro amongst its guests. Its charm lies in its simplicity – it has changed little over the years – with spacious bedrooms mostly decorated with old-fashioned wallpapers and plain curtains. Each is different and varies in size; those at the rear are quiet, while those at the front have a fabulous view across the Seine to the Louvre. However, you pay a steep price for that view, both in terms of money (considering how basic the rooms are) and of noise – the windows are not soundproofed. It 's shabby and needs careful updating without losing its charm.

NEARBY Musée d'Orsay; boulevard Saint-Germain; Musée du Louvre.
LOCATION bordering the Seine, mid-way between Pont-Royal and Pond du Carrousel **PARKING** quai Anatole France **METRO** rue du Bac **RER** Musée d'Orsay **FOOD** breakfast **PRICE** €€ **ROOMS** 33; 25 double, 6 single, 2 triple, 27 with bath, 4 with shower, 2 with washbasin (no WC); all rooms have phone, TV on request, hairdrier **FACILITIES** breakfast room, sitting room **CREDIT CARDS** AE, DC, MC, V **CHILDREN** accepted **DISABLED** access difficult, lift/elevator **PETS** accepted **CLOSED** never **PROPRIETOR** André Etchenique

Seventh Arrondissement

Invalides/Eiffel Tower Quarter

Hotel de Suede

31 rue Vaneau, 75007 Paris
Tel (01) 47 05 00 08 **Fax** (01) 47 05 69 27
E-mail hoteldesuede@aol.com **Website** www.hoteldesuede.com

We receive only plaudits for the Hôtel Suède, and it's time we bumped it up to a long entry; only reasons of space have held us back in this edition. It's a popular, traditional, good-value hotel in the embassy district, also close to the shops of rue du Bac and the Bon Marché and Conran stores. Pleasant bedrooms, recently renovated, and with new bathrooms, have high beds and velvet chairs; some overlook the gardens of the Prime Minister's official residence. Downstairs the decoration is less interesting. Walls are panelled in an orange-ish wood veneer, which clashes with the grey carpet and gold velvet chairs. Small courtyard garden.

Nearby Musée d'Orsay; boulevard Saint-Germain; Musée du Louvre.
Location in stretch of street between rue de Varenne and rue de Babylone **Parking** rue du Bac **Metro** Sevres-Babylone/ Saint-Francois-Xavier **RER** Musée d'Orsay **Food** breakfast **Price** €€ **Rooms** 39; 35 double and twin, all with bath or shower; 4 single with shower; all rooms have phone, TV, air-conditioning, hairdrier, safe **Facilities** sitting room, bar, breakfast room **Credit cards** AE, DC, MC, V **Children** accepted **Disabled** lift/elevator **Pets** accepted **Closed** never **Manager** Carole Gonelle

invalides/Eiffel Tower Quarter

Hotel Le Tourville

16 avenue de Tourville, 75007 Paris
Tel (01) 47 05 62 62 **Fax** (01) 47 05 43 90
E-mail hotel@tourville.com **Website** www.hoteltourville.com

A plush four-star, under the same ownership as Le Saint Grégoire (page 79), also designed by interior decorator Christian Badin. A brave combination of colours in the reception/*salon* – mint and dark green, royal blue, vivid orange – doesn't create harmony in this otherwise smart room. We liked the mix of antique and chic modern furniture, and the old books and sculptures dotted around. Superior double rooms are particularly elegant, with white linen covers and black marble and grey tiled bathrooms. There are some lovely antiques in the bedrooms, but the odd table or bedside cabinet crops up looking as if it has come from a DIY store.

Nearby Invalides; Musée Rodin; Eiffel Tower.
Location between boulevard La Tour-Maubourg and avenue del La Motte-Picquet **Parking** avenue de Tourville **Metro** Ecole-Militaire/La Tour-Maubourg **RER** Invalides-Pont de l'Alma **Food** breakfast **Price** €€€ **Rooms** 30; 28 double and twin, 2 suites, all with bath; all rooms have phone, TV, air-conditioning, hairdrier **Facilities** sitting room, bar, breakfast room **Credit cards** AE, DC, MC, V **Children** accepted **Disabled** lift/elevator **Pets** accepted **Closed** never **Proprietor** M. Bouvier

SEVENTH ARRONDISSEMENT

INVALIDES/EIFFEL TOWER QUARTER

HOTEL DE LA TULIPE

33 rue Malar, 75007 Paris
TEL (01) 45 51 67 21 **FAX** (01) 47 53 96 37
E-MAIL hotelde latulipe@wanadoo.fr **WEBSITE** www.hoteldelatulipe.com

PAINTED YELLOW and with its windows shaded by awnings, this hotel looks jolly from the outside, and doesn't disappoint within. In fact, with its charming Provençal-style breakfast room and exposed stone and beams in the fairly simple bedrooms, it brings a touch of the Côte Sud to Paris. Built in the mid 17th century for the wife of Louis XIV's gunpowder-keeper, after which it had a spell as a convent, it has been owned for the past 16 years by a charming actor and his wife. The five rooms that lead off the pretty, overgrown courtyard are modest, but private and appealing, at least in summer (in winter they may be a trifle damp).

NEARBY Invalides; Musée Rodin; Eiffel Tower.
LOCATION between rue Saint-Dominique and rue de la Université **PARKING** Invalides **METRO** La Tour-Maubourg/Invalides **RER** Invalides-Pont de l'Alma **FOOD** breakfast **PRICE** €€ **ROOMS** 22; 21 double and twin all with bath or shower; one single with shower; all rooms have phone, modem point, TV, minibar, hairdrier, safe **FACILITIES** sitting area, breakfast room, courtyard garden **CREDIT CARDS** AE, MC, V **CHILDREN** accepted **DISABLED** one specially adapted room **PETS** accepted **CLOSED** never **PROPRIETOR** M. and Mme Fortuit

INVALIDES QUARTER

HOTEL DE VARENNE

44 rue de Bourgogn, 75007 Paris
TEL (01) 43 54 01 70 **FAX** (01) 43 26 17 14
E-MAIL hotel.varenne@wanadoo.fr **WEBSITE** www.paris-hotel-varenne.com

YOU STUMBLE UPON this little hotel through its agreeable overgrown 'secret' garden. The pleasing entrance has cream walls, white-painted panelling and a corniced ceiling, a tiled floor and well-placed mirrors and plants. Breakfast room and bedrooms are spruce, if simple, with big modern paintings and solid wood tables and chairs in the former and floral bedspreads, plain walls and comfy bedrooms chairs in the latter, Bathrooms are mostly spacious, and the staff are friendly and helpful. On sunny days you can take breakfast in the garden at white wrought-iron tables and chairs covered in pretty floral cloths and padded seat cushions.

NEARBY Invalides; Musée Rodin; Eiffel Tower.
LOCATION close to Invalides, between rue de Varenne and rue de Grenelle **PARKING** Invalides **METRO** Varenne/Invalides **RER** Invalides-Pont de l'Alma **FOOD** breakfast **PRICE** €€ **ROOMS** 24; 20 double and twin, all with bath; 4 single with shower; all rooms have phone, TV, modem point, hairdrier, safe **FACILITIES** sitting area, breakfast room, courtyard garden **CREDIT CARDS** AE, MC, V **CHILDREN** accepted **DISABLED** one specially adapted room **PETS** accepted **CLOSED** never **PROPRIETOR** Maurice Janin

EIGHTH ARRONDISSEMENT

CHAMPS-ELYSEES

HOTEL CHAMBIGES ELYSEES

8 rue Chambiges, 75008 Paris
TEL (01) 44 31 83 83 **FAX** (01) 40 70 95 51
E-MAIL chamb@paris-hotels-charm.com **WEBSITE** www.paris-hotels-charm.com

WITH THE PURCHASE OF this lavish small hotel, the Teil family, the most acquisitive hotel-keeping dynasty in Paris, has moved into a new district, the so-called 'Golden Triangle' between avenues Champs-Elysées, George V and Montaigne. As with their other hotels (see pages 71 and 74), the Teils gutted the original building and refurbished throughout, covering the walls with pale wood-panelling made in the Auvergne and carefully-chosen fabrics. In keeping with the location, this hotel seems grander: paintings and mirrors in heavy frames, rich patterned materials and luxurious marble bathrooms. For such a central hotel, it has plenty of space for sitting: an elegant *salon*, intimate bar and flowery patio garden.

NEARBY Champs-Elysées; Grand Palais; Petit Palais; the Seine.
LOCATION between rue du Boccador and rue C. Marot **PARKING** Champs-Elysées **METRO** Alma-Marceau **FOOD** breakfast **PRICE** €€€ **ROOMS** 34; 21 double, twin and triple, one single, all with bath; all rooms have phone, modem point, TV, air-conditioning, minibar, hairdrier, safe **FACILITIES** sitting room, bar/breakfast room, internet booth, garden **CREDIT CARDS** AE, DC, MC, V **CHILDREN** accepted **DISABLED** specially adapted rooms, lift/elevator **PETS** accepted **CLOSED** never **PROPRIETORS** Teil family

CHAMPS-ELYSEES

HOTEL ELYSEES MATIGNON

3 rue de Ponthieu, 75008 Paris
TEL (01) 42 25 73 01 **FAX** (01) 42 56 01 39
E-MAIL elyseesmatignon@wanadoo.fr **WEBSITE** hotelparischampselysees.com

A PERFECT RECREATION of the art deco period from the sweep of the reception desk and the mosaic-tiled floor in the little entrance to the large square basins in the bathrooms where every square inch is tiled. There is a pretty gilded fountain on the left as you come in, but the *pièce de résistance* is the lift, a narrow cage with a decorated opaque glass exterior door. It looks stunning and is the genuine article, but hardly practical when a family of four arrives with all their luggage. The bedrooms tend to be small, with dark, if carefully chosen, fabrics. The hotel has an arrangement with the bar next door, which is under different management and a lively nightspot, allowing guests to have breakfast there.

NEARBY Champs-Elysées; Grand Palais; Petit Palais; ave Montaigne.
LOCATION between ave Matignon and rue Jean Mermoz **PARKING** ave Matignon or Rond-Point des Champs-Elysées **METRO** Franklin D. Roosevelt **RER** Charles de Gaulle Etoile **FOOD** breakfast **PRICE** €€ **ROOMS** 23; 19 double and twin, all with bath or shower; 4 junior suites with bath; all rooms have phone, TV, air-conditioning, minibar, hairdrier, safe **FACILITIES** sitting area **CREDIT CARDS** AE, DC, MC, V **CHILDREN** accepted **DISABLED** access difficult, lift/elevator **PETS** accepted **CLOSED** never **PROPRIETOR** M. Michaud

Eighth Arrondissement

Champs-Elysees

Hotel Franklin Roosevelt

18 rue Clément-Marot, 75008 Paris
Tel (01) 53 57 49 50 **Fax** (01) 47 20 44 30
E-mail hotel@hroosevelt.com **Website** www.hroosevelt.com

The Franklin Roosevelt has changed hands since we last visited it, going up several notches in luxury and price in the process. The renovated bedrooms are now furnished with mahogany doors, antiques, Persian rugs and calico wallcoverings. Most have lost their calm murals, of which we were fond. Guests can choose between fairly spacious 'superior' rooms, with big bathrooms, eight even larger 'de-luxe' rooms and three stunning sixth-floor suites. Downstairs, there is a sedate *salon*, a clubby English-style bar, and a conservatory breakfast room, overlooking the terrace with a *trompe l'oeil* garden and beautiful camellias in tubs. Staff can be cool.

Nearby Champs-Elysées; Grand Palais; Petit Palais; ave Montaigne.
Location between rue Marbeuf and rue de La Trémoille **Parking** rue François 1er, rue Marbeuf or ave George V **Metro** Franklin D. Roosevelt/Alma-Marceau/George V **Food** breakfast **Price** €€€€ **Rooms** 45 double and twin, all with bath or shower; all rooms have phone, TV, minibar, hairdrier, safe; some rooms have modem points and air-conditioning **Facilities** sitting room, bar, breakfast room, patio garden **Credit cards** AE, MC, V **Children** accepted **Disabled** access difficult, lift/elevator **Pets** accepted **Closed** never **Manager** M. Ghorbal

Champs-Elysees

Hotel Residence Lord Byron

5 rue Chateaubriand, 75008 Paris
Tel (01) 43 59 89 98 **Fax** (01) 42 89 46 04
E-mail lordbyron@escapade-paris.com **Website** www.escapade-paris.com

In an area of grand hotels and exorbitant prices, the Lord Byron – slightly more illustrious sister of the Mayflower next door (see page 150) – stands out for its personal service and, by local standards, reasonable prices. The elegant entrance and formal sitting room are decorated to a high standard in traditional style, with a fleet of delicate chairs, upholstered in velvet or checked silk. With the exception of the suites, bedrooms tend to be smallish, but are modern and comfortable, with bold floral fabrics, traditional-style furnishings and spotless bathrooms. Annexe bedrooms – across a flower-filled garden – offer peace and quiet. The garden is the hotel's greatest asset and lovely in summer.

Nearby Arc de Triomphe; Champs-Elysées; Musée Jacquemart-André.
Location between rue Washington and rue Lord Byron **Parking** ave de Friedland, Champs-Elysées or rue de Berri **Metro** George V/Charles de Gaulle Etoile **RER** Charles de Gaulle Etoile **Food** breakfast **Price** €€ **Rooms** 31; 23 double and twin, 6 suites, all with bath or shower; 2 single with shower; all rooms have phone, modem point, TV, minibar, hairdrier, safe **Facilities** sitting/meeting room, breakfast room, garden, internet booth **Credit cards** AE, MC, V **Children** accepted **Disabled** lift/elevator **Pets** accepted **Closed** never **Proprietor** Mme Benoit

EIGHTH ARRONDISSEMENT

CHAMPS-ELYSEES

HOTEL MAYFLOWER

[illegible] Chateaubriand, 75008 Paris
TEL (01) 45 62 57 46 **FAX** (01) 42 56 32 38
E-MAIL mayflower@escapade-paris.com **WEBSITE** www.escapade-paris.com

A FRIENDLY HOTEL in the same ownership as the Résidence Lord Byron next door (see page 149), with a similarly refined and relaxed atmosphere. The bar/*salon* is a restful place to put up your feet at the end of a tiring day. Bedrooms are pretty, with chintz fabric and limed or stained wood furniture, but some on the street are noisy and cramped. Those on the courtyard side have large bathrooms and are pricier, but still value for money, considering the location. The cellar breakfast room is a refreshing variation on the theme: it is done out like an ocean liner with a seascape mural on one wall, and not a rough-stone wall or copper pot in sight.

NEARBY Arc de Triomphe; Champs-Elysées; Musée Jacquemart-André.
LOCATION between rue Washington and rue Lord Byron **PARKING** ave de Friedland, Champs-Elysées or rue de Berri **METRO** George V/Charles de Gaulle Etoile **RER** Charles de Gaulle Etoile **FOOD** breakfast **PRICE** €€ **ROOMS** 24; 18 double and twin, all with bath; 6 single with bath or shower; all rooms have phone, TV, minibar, hairdrier, safe **FACILITIES** bar/sitting room, breakfast room **CREDIT CARDS** AE, MC, V **CHILDREN** accepted **DISABLED** lift/elevator **PETS** accepted **CLOSED** never **PROPRIETOR** Mme Benoit

OPERA

HOTEL QUEEN MARY

9 rue de Greffulhe, 75008 Paris
TEL (01) 42 66 40 50 **FAX** (01) 42 66 94 92
E-MAIL hotelqueenmary@wanadoo.fr **WEBSITE** www.hotelqueenmary.com

THE TELL-TALE SIGNS that this hotel is British owned, apart from the name and the carriage lamps that flank the front door, are the trouser press and decanter of sherry in every room and the full English breakfast available each morning. Following a meticulous renovation, this well-appointed three-star, decorated throughout in cream, pale yellow and peach, or yellow combined with blue, is kept well up to scratch. But, despite this and some attractive original cornicing, it lacks panache. Bedrooms – single, standard and superior double – are fresh and comfortable, but uniform, with reproduction furniture. In summer, you can sit out on the pretty terrace.

NEARBY Madeleine; Opéra Garnier; place Vendôme; Jardin des Tuileries.
LOCATION between rue des Mathurins and rue de Castellane **PARKING** place de la Madeleine **METRO** Havre Caumartin **RER** Auber **FOOD** breakfast; room service **PRICE** €€ **ROOMS** 36; 30 double and twin, one suite, all with bath; 5 single with shower; all rooms have phone, TV, air-conditioning, minibar, hairdrier, safe; some rooms have modem points **FACILITIES** sitting room, bar, breakfast room, terrace, internet booth **CREDIT CARDS** AE, MC, V **CHILDREN** accepted **DISABLED** access possible, lift/elevator **PETS** accepted **CLOSED** never **PROPRIETOR** David Byrne

EIGHTH ARRONDISSEMENT

OPERA

HOTEL ROYAL OPERA

5 rue de Castellane, 75008 Paris
TEL (01) 42 66 14 44 **FAX** (01) 42 6648 47
E-MAIL royal@paris-hotels-opera.com **WEBSITE** www.paris-hotels-opera.com

REASONABLY PRICED HOTELS in the eighth *arrondissement* are almost a contradiction in terms, so we were delighted to find this little two-star with a youngish clientele in a side street just north of the Madeleine. Its best feature is a trendy yellow and green breakfast room with a huge arched window looking on to the street and attractive architectural prints on the walls. Upstairs, past a smart little reception area, the bedrooms are perfectly comfortable, equipped with the kind of amenities you'd expect from a three- rather than a two-star, but – like so many Paris hotel rooms – with disappointingly anodyne decoration.

NEARBY Opéra Garnier; boulevard Haussmann; rue du Faubourg Saint-Honoré.
LOCATION between rue de l'Arcade and rue Tronchet **PARKING** rue Chauveau Lagarde or place de la Madeleine **METRO** Madeleine/Havre Caumartin **RER** Auber **FOOD** breakfast **PRICE** €€ **ROOMS** 30; 15 double, 15 twin, 15 with bath, 15 with shower; all rooms have phone, TV, minibar, hairdrier, safe; some rooms have air-conditioning **FACILITIES** breakfast room **CREDIT CARDS** AE, DC, MC, V **CHILDREN** accepted **DISABLED** lift/elevator **PETS** accepted **CLOSED** never **PROPRIETOR** M. Léger

CHAMPS-ELYSEES

HOTEL SAN REGIS

12 rue Jean-Goujon, 75008 Paris
TEL (01) 44 95 16 16 **FAX** (01) 45 61 05 48
E-MAIL message@hotels-sanregis.fr **WEBSITE** www.hotel-sanregis.com

JUST A STILETTO'S STEP from avenue Montaigne, home to Christian Dior, Valentino and other great names of fashion, the elegantly opulent San Régis has been patronized by couturiers since it opened in 1923. On the ground floor is a smart little restaurant, lined with faux books, an English-style bar and winter garden. Only the hectically floral carpet in the *salon* was not to our taste, and upstairs, carpets and wallpaper clashed in some corridors. Bedrooms have richly coloured, though sometimes over-patterned, fabrics, deep sofas, antiques and impeccable bathrooms – every one equipped with a phone, so you can order a glass of champagne as you soak. Staff are wonderfully attentive, but you are paying for it.

NEARBY Champs-Elysées; ave Montaigne; Grand Palais; Petit Palais.
LOCATION between ave Franklin D. Roosevelt and place François 1er **PARKING** impasse d'Antin **METRO** Franklin D. Roosevelt/Champs-Elysées Clemenceau **FOOD** breakfast, lunch, dinner; room service **PRICE** €€€€ **ROOMS** 44; 42 double and twin and suites, all with bath; 2 single with shower; all rooms have phone, TV, air-conditioning, minibar, hairdrier **FACILITIES** sitting area, sitting room, restaurant, bar **CREDIT CARDS** AE, DC, MC, V **CHILDREN** accepted **DISABLED** not suitable, lift/elevator **PETS** not accepted **CLOSED** never **PROPRIETOR** M. Georges

NINTH ARRONDISSEMENT

OPERA QUARTER

HOTEL DE BEAUHARNAIS

51 rue de la Victoire, 75009 Paris
TEL (01) 48 74 71 13 **FAX** (01) 44 53 98 80

TUCKED AWAY down a long, rather dull street, this is a quaint budget establishment, dominated by its splendid owner, Madame Bey. On our visit, she proudly flung back the sheets to reveal pristine mattresses, and insisted on lifting the loo seats and the pedal bin lids. "I am German," she announced, "and I like everything to be completely clean." Rooms are furnished with an eclectic mix of Victorian antiques, some delightfully over-the-top – for instance a massive wooden bedstead, a collection of Venetian glass wall lights, and a large number of ornate and over-sized mirrors. Downstairs, there is a recently created reception area. The excellent breakfast coffee is another source of pride: "It is very good," she states, "because I make it as at home, you understand?"

NEARBY Opéra; Grands Boulevards; La Madeleine; Gare Saint-Lazare.
LOCATION N of rue Lafayette, between rue de la Chaussée and rue Lafitte **PARKING** in street **METRO** Chaussée d'Antin **FOOD** breakfast **PRICE** €€ **ROOMS** 17; 11 double and twin, 5 single, one family, all with shower, 13 with WC; most rooms have hairdrier **FACILITIES** breakfast room **CREDIT CARDS** not accepted **CHILDREN** accepted **DISABLED** access difficult, lift/elevator **PETS** accepted **CLOSED** never **PROPRIETORS** Mme and Mlle Bey

OPERA QUARTER

HOTEL DU LEMAN

20 rue de Trévise, 75009 Paris
TEL (01) 42 46 50 66 **FAX** (01) 48 24 27 59
E-MAIL lemanhot@aol.com **WEBISTE** www.hotelduleman.com

IVY CLIMBS the trellis-work between the windows and flower-filled baskets hang from the balconies on the pretty exterior of this hotel. Inside, the marble-floored entrance is uncluttered with diverse objects including an Egyptian sculpture and a slim uplighter, both strategically placed. The bedrooms are decorated in muted shades, with stained wood bedheads and small functional bathrooms, and though tasteful, are impersonal. The most congenial rooms are those on the sixth floor, where sloping walls and beams give them some character. The cellar breakfast room has rough-stone walls and looks like a hundred others in the city, only more kitsch, with café tables and chairs, and some garish paintings.

NEARBY Folies Bergères; Gare du Nord; Opéra Garnier; Montmartre; Musée Grévin.
LOCATION between rue Richer and rue Saint-Cécile **PARKING** in street or rue Richer, rue Bleue **METRO** rue Montmartre/Cadet/Bonne-Nouvelle **FOOD** breakfast, brunch **PRICE** €€ **ROOMS** 24 double and twin, all with bath; all rooms have phone, modem point, TV, minibar, hairdrier, safe **FACILITIES** sitting area, breakfast room **CREDIT CARDS** AE, DC, MC, V **CHILDREN** accepted **DISABLED** access difficult, lift/elevator **PETS** accepted **CLOSED** never **PROPRIETOR** Emanuelle Le Grand

Ninth Arrondissement

Opera Quarter/Montmartre

Hotel Riboutte-Lafayette

5 rue de Riboutté, 75009 Paris
Tel (01) 47 70 62 36 **Fax** (01) 48 00 91 50

There is nothing pretentious about this modest, inexpensive two-star, around the corner from the Folies-Bergères and more like a hotel in the provinces than one in the centre of Paris. In the homely reception area there is space to sit at tables on rush-seated chairs, or to relax in deep cane sofas. The glow from several pretty table lamps accentuates the warm ambience, and care has been taken with flower arrangements and little pieces of china on display. Presiding over it all is the delightful Claudine Gourd, manager here since 1972, and her faithful old Scottie, Chipie. Bedrooms tend to be small and unexceptional, though ones at the top have beams, and some have pleasing pieces of painted furniture.

Nearby Gare du Nord; Opéra Garnier; Grands Boulevards.
Location S of square de Montholon, between rue de La Fayette and rue Bleue **Parking** in street or square de Montholon, cité de Trévise, rue Richer **Metro** Cadet **RER** Auber **Food** breakfast; room service **Price** € **Rooms** 24; 18 double and twin, 5 triple, all with bath or shower; one single with shower; all rooms have phone, TV, hairdrier **Facilities** sitting room, breakfast area **Credit cards** AE, MC, V **Children** accepted **Disabled** not suitable, lift/elevator **Pets** accepted **Closed** never **Proprietor** M. Pannard

Opera Quarter/Montmartre

Hotel de la Tour d'Auvergne

10 rue de la Tour-d'Auvergne, 75009 Paris
Tel (01) 48 78 61 60 **Fax** (01) 49 95 99 00
E-mail contact@oteltourdauvergne.com **Webiste** www.hoteltourdauvergne.com

The hotel's smart façade is matched by the tone of the reception area and sitting room. The style here is glossy, primarily British with naval touches in the model ships and seascapes. The colours are warm, mainly red, with leather sofas and dark wood tables on which French and English language newspapers appear each morning. Breakfast, served in a small, cheery room is copious, including ham and cheese. Our inspector's verdict on her room was less enthusiastic: although comfortable (but not spacious), clean and in good decorative order, with all the normal extras, she felt let down by its banality compared to the charm and atmosphere of the public rooms - which is so often the case.

Nearby Gare du Nord; Opéra Garnier; Grands Boulevards.
Location between rue de Rochechouart and rue Rodier **Parking** in street or square d'Anvers **Metro** Anvers/Cadet **RER** Gare du Nord **Food** breakfast **Price** €€ **Rooms** 25; 18 double and twin, 4 single, 3 triple, all with bath or shower; all rooms have phone, TV, hairdrier, safe **Facilities** sitting area/bar, breakfast room **Credit cards** AE, DC, MC, V **Children** accepted **Disabled** not suitable, lift/elevator **Pets** accepted **Closed** never **Proprietor** M. Duval

Fourteenth Arrondissement

Montparnasse

Hotel Lenox Montparnasse

15 rue Delambre, 75014 Paris
Tel (01) 43 35 34 50 **Fax** (01) 43 20 46 64
E-mail hotel@lenoxmontparnasse.com **Website** www.hotellenox.com

If the frequently neglected area of Montparnasse appeals to you, with its bohemian heritage and famous brasseries, this well-priced hotel is a good bet. One-time sister of the alluring Lenox Saint-Germain (see page 88), but now under a new owner, it has an excellent location, a stone's throw from La Coupole, the huge, buzzing 1920s brasserie. Most of the large modern bedrooms lack atmosphere, but are about to be refurbished. The most attractive have beams and fireplaces. If you can stretch to it, go for one of the handsome top-floor mini-suites. Of the public rooms, we particularly liked the congenial bar, where you can have light meals as well as drinks. Breakfast is the skimpy norm, but staff are courteous and kind.

Nearby Jardin du Luxembourg; Cimetière du Montparnasse; Tour Montparnasse. **Location** between boulevard du Montparnasse and boulevard Edgar Quinet **Parking** private **Metro** Vavin/Edgar Quinet **Food** breakfast, light meals; room service **Price** €€ **Rooms** 52 double, twin, single and mini-suites, 44 with bath, 8 with shower; all rooms have phone, modem point, TV, minibar, hairdrier **Facilities** sitting area, bar, meeting room **Credit cards** AE, DC, MC, V **Children** accepted **Disabled** access possible, lift/elevator **Pets** accepted **Closed** never **Proprietor** M. Dupasquier

Montparnasse

Hotel Raspail Montparnasse

203 boulevard Raspail, 75014 Paris
Tel (01) 43 20 62 86 **Fax** (01) 43 20 50 79
E-mail raspailm@wanadoo.fr **Website** www.charming-hotel-paris.com

A hotel on the busy boulevard Raspail that harks back to the 1920s – the cultural heyday of Montparnasse. Beneath the original marquise and garland of carved roses, the entrance is through heavy glass doors with chrome Art Deco handles, which swing open automatically to let you in to an airy reception/sitting room. Here scarlet leather and grey velvet tub chairs cluster around small tables, on which rest spindly black lamps. The design is the work of celebrated decorator Serge Pons. Fabulous photographs line the walls, and art and sculpture is sometimes exhibited. Bedrooms in different colours pay homage to individual artists: Cézanne, Chagall, Modigliani and Picasso, among others. Chic, but hard-edged, it appeals to business types.

Nearby Jardin du Luxembourg; Cimetière du Montparnasse; Tour Montparnasse. **Location** at southern junction of boulevard Montparnasse and boulevard Raspail **Parking** Hôtel de Ville **Metro** Vavin **RER** Port Royal **Food** breakfast **Price** €€ **Rooms** 38; 33 double and twin, 5 single, all with bath or shower; all rooms have phone, modem point, TV, air-conditioning, minibar, hairdrier, safe **Facilities** bar/sitting area, meeting room **Credit cards** AE, MC, V **Children** accepted **Disabled** lift/elevator **Pets** not accepted **Closed** never **Proprietor** Christiane Martinent

Fifteenth Arrondissement

Eiffel Tower Quarter

Hotel du Bailli de Suffren

149 avenue de Suffren, 75015 Paris
Tel (01) 56 58 64 64 **Fax** (01) 45 67 75 82
E-mail bailli.suffren.hotel@wanadoo.fr **Website** www.hotel-baillitoureiffel.com

Small but significant details lift this hotel, named after a famous admiral, above the three-star norm. The *salon* is filled with well-chosen antiques, and pictures and sculptures that are for sale. The owner clearly wants to please: an open book invites comments and there are questionnaires in the bedrooms; robes are provided. Bedrooms and bathrooms all have different colour schemes (we preferred the pale to the dark), and bedside lights are on dimmers. Double rooms can combine to form apartments. Breakfast is served in a pleasant pink and green room. Drawbacks are that the area is rather unappealing, and, while we were there, the huge television blared constantly in the *salon*.

Nearby Eiffel Tower; UNESCO; Ecole Militaire; Invalides.
Location between rue Pérignon and rue Bellart **Parking** rue François Bonvin **Metro** Ségur/Sèvres Lecourbe/Cambronne **Food** breakfast; light meals **Price** €€
Rooms 25; 15 double and twin, 5 triple, all with bath; 5 single with shower; all rooms have phone, modem point, TV, hairdrier, safe **Facilities** sitting room, breakfast room, internet booth **Credit cards** AE, DC, MC, V **Children** accepted **Disabled** lift/elevator **Pets** accepted **Closed** never **Proprietor** M. Tardif

Eiffel Tower Quarter

Hotel Paris Saint Charles

37 rue Saint-Charles-36 rue Rouelle, 75015 Paris
Tel (01) 45 79 64 15 **Fax** (01) 45 77 21 11
E-mail H1928@accor-hotels.com **Website** www.mercure.com

This acceptable two-star is in a residential neighbourhood some way from the centre that seems dull today, but has a history. It was part of an early-19thC new town called Beaugrenelle, created on the Grenelle agricultural plains by a speculator, Léonard Violet, who built himself a château (now a fire station) next to the square named after him. Several streets to the north, the Paris Saint Charles used to be the Charles Quinze but is now part of the Mercure chain. It has quite a pleasing entrance, filled with pine furniture and dark blue leather chairs, which help to counter the sterile effect of a white-tiled floor. The bedrooms are modest but comfortable, with modern bathrooms and contemporary pictures that brighten the simple decoration. There's a basement breakfast room, and – best of all – a terrace garden.

Nearby square Violet; Eiffel Tower; Les Invalides; Ecole Militaire; Passy.
Location S of boulevard de Grenelle, on corner **Parking** rue George Bernard Shawor rue du Théâtre **Metro** Dupleix/Charles Michels **Food** breakfast **Price** €€
Rooms 30; 25 double and twin, all with bath or shower; all rooms have phone, modem point, TV, minibar, hairdrier **Facilities** sitting area, breakfast room, garden **Credit cards** AE, DC, MC, V **Children** accepted **Disabled** lift/elevator **Pets** accepted **Closed** never **Manager** Claire Fournerie

SIXTEENTH ARRONDISSEMENT

PORTE SAINT-CLOUD

HOTEL BOILEAU

81 rue Boileau, 75016 Paris
TEL (01) 42 88 83 74 **FAX** (01) 45 277 62 98
E-MAIL boileau@noos.fr **WEBSITE** www.hotel-boileau.com

EXHIBITORS AT THE Porte de Versailles exhibition centre are among the regulars at this simple hotel just across the Seine. It only has two stars, but it bears the hallmark of a caring owner. Elegant antiques, including busts, a display cabinet and marble-topped chest, are scattered through the public areas, which have terracotta-tiled floors and half-panelled walls in pale wood. There's a tiny bar and cheerful yellow and red breakfast room. Though nothing special, the bedrooms (some of which are in an annexe) look fresh and bright, with painted furniture and new bathrooms; the best also have large casement windows and are gloriously light.

NEARBY Bois de Boulogne; Parc des Princes; De Coubertin stadium.
LOCATION between boulevard Exelmans and avenue de Versailles, near junction with rue Charles Marie Widor **PARKING** in street or in avenue de Versailles **METRO** Exelmans/Porte de Saint-Cloud/Chardon Lagache **FOOD** breakfast **PRICE** € **ROOMS** 30; 17 double, 4 twin, 3 triple, 6 single, all with bath or shower; all rooms have phone, TV, hairdrier **FACILITIES** sitting area, breakfast room, bar, meeting room **CREDIT CARDS** AE, DC, MC, V **CHILDREN** accepted **DISABLED** not suitable **PETS** accepted **CLOSED** never **MANAGER** Fabrice Royer

PASSY

LE HAMEAU DE PASSY

48 rue de Passy, 75016 Paris
TEL (01) 42 88 47 55 **FAX** (01) 42 30 83 72
E-MAIL hameau.passy@wanadoo.fr **WEBSITE** www.hameaudepassy.com

THIS HOTEL'S BEST FEATURE is its situation in a secluded little courtyard, planted with trees and flowers, and set back from rue de Passy and its traffic noise, but still conveniently close to the shops and restaurants in the liveliest part of this district. The old shuttered façade would be attractive but for the glass-encased spiral staircases which have been tacked on to it. These lead to modern bedrooms (a lift serves some too), all faintly soulless, but airy and bright with white rough-cast walls and painted wooden furniture. On the ground floor there's a place to sit within the reception area and a breakfast room. Recent reports have been complimentary, particularly about the courteous and helpful staff.

NEARBY Eiffel Tower; Trocadéro; Cimitière de Passy.
LOCATION between rue Vital and rue Massenet **PARKING** rue de Passy **METRO** La Muette/Passy **RER** Boulainvilliers **FOOD** breakfast **PRICE** €€ **ROOMS** 32; 29 double and twin (3 can be triple), 19 with bath, 10 with shower; 4 single, 3 with bath, one with shower; all rooms have phone, modem, TV, hairdrier **FACILITIES** sitting area/bar, breakfast room, garden **CREDIT CARDS** AE, DC, MC, V **CHILDREN** accepted **DISABLED** one specially adapted room, lift/elevator **PETS** accepted **CLOSED** never **PROPRIETOR** Mme Brepson

SIXTEENTH ARRONDISSEMENT

CHAILLOT QUARTER

HOTEL MAJESTIC

29 rue Dumont d'Urville, 75116 Paris
TEL (01) 45 00 83 70 **FAX** (01) 45 00 29 48
E-MAIL management@majestic-hotel.com **WEBSITE** www.majestic-hotel.com

DON'T JUDGE THIS HOTEL by its ugly, modern façade, because the interior justifies its name. In reception, a fine black and white marble floor is strewn with rugs. Upstairs, heavy doors open off landings on to vast, comfortable bedrooms, many with dark red carpets, old-fashioned chintzes, king-size beds, pre-war furniture and huge bathrooms. The public rooms are equally formal, with velvet chairs, potted plants and *trompe l'oeil* doors. A slightly faded old lady of a hotel, where you can imagine eating cucumber sandwiches and sipping tea with a great aunt. The penthouse apartment is vast, with its own terrace.

NEARBY Arc de Triomphe; Champs-Elysées; Trocadéro.
LOCATION between rue Jean Giraudoux and rue de Belloy **PARKING** avenue Foch or Champs-Elysées **METRO** Kléber/Boissière **RER** Charles de Gaulle Etoile **FOOD** breakfast **PRICE** €€€€ **ROOMS** 30; 27 double and twin, 2 suites, one apartment, all with bath; all rooms have phone, modem point, TV, air-conditioning, minibar **FACILITIES** sitting rooms **CREDIT CARDS** AE, DC, MC, V **CHILDREN** accepted **DISABLED** lift/elevator **PETS** accepted **CLOSED** never **MANAGER** M. Garnier

PASSY

HOTEL TROCADERO LA TOUR

5 bis rue Massenet, 75016 Paris
TEL (01) 45 24 43 03 **FAX** (01) 45 24 41 39
E-MAIL trocadero-la-tour@magic.fr **WEBSITE** www.trocadero-la-tour.com

IN THE RESIDENTIAL DISTRICT of Passy, the Trocadéro la Tour cuts an eccentric figure with its green marble floor, wood-panelled walls, hunting prints, leather sofas and chairs, and *Herald Tribune* in the rack. This is the old Hôtel Massenet, which has recently changed its name but little else. The bedrooms cast off this masculine air; typically they are decorated in subtle colours with cream and gold furniture, chandeliers and brocade or chintz curtains and bedspreads. There's a private celadon-coloured sitting room, dotted with antiques, and a traditional bar that's open round the clock. Guests eat breakfast in a creamy yellow room with delicate mouldings and country style chairs, or on the charming sliver of a terrace when the weather is clement. Pleasant staff see to their needs.

NEARBY Eiffel Tower; Trocadéro; Cimitière de Passy.
LOCATION between rue Vital and rue de Passy **PARKING** rue de Passy **METRO** La Muette/Passy **RER** Boulainvilliers **FOOD** breakfast **PRICE** €€ **ROOMS** 41; 31 double and twin, 10 single, all with bath or shower; all rooms have phone, modem point, TV, minibar, hairdrier; some rooms have air-conditioning **FACILITIES** sitting room, breakfast room, bar, internet booth, terrace **CREDIT CARDS** AE, DC, MC, V **CHILDREN** accepted **DISABLED** lift/elevator **PETS** accepted **CLOSED** never **MANAGER** Mme Moisan

Seventeenth Arrondissement

Beaubourg Quarter

Hotel Champerret Heliopolis

13 rue d'Heliopolis, 75017 Paris
Tel (01) 47 64 92 56 **Fax** (01) 47 64 50 44
website www.champerret-heliopolis-paris-hotel.com

A surprising little hotel, decorated in beige and blue, sporting rust-coloured leather sofas, gold cushions and a line of multi-coloured cacti, with a refreshingly eclectic style. Though not large, the inviting reception acts as a sitting area and bar as well; guests eat breakfast perched on blue bar stools at the attractive pale wood bar, or sunk into one of the comfy sofas. Arranged around a tiny but pretty fern-filled courtyard, the bedrooms, in contrast to the ground floor, are disappointingly ordinary and spartan (all identically decorated in the same colour as the ground floor), but worth enduring for the low prices.

Nearby Arc de Triomphe; Champs-Elysées; Palais de Congrès.
Location between ave de Villiers and rue Guillaume Tell **Parking** in street or boulevard Berthier **Metro** Porte de Champerret/Péreire **RER** Péreire-Levallois **Food** breakfast, room service **Price** €€ **Rooms** 22; 12 double and twin, 8 single, 2 triple, all with bath or shower; all rooms have phone, modem point, TV, hairdrier **Facilities** bar/sitting/breakfast area, patio garden **Credit cards** AE, DC, MC, V **Children** accepted **Disabled** lift/elevator **Pets** accepted **Closed** never **Proprietor** Catherine Rennie

Champs-Elysees

Hotel Etoile Park

10 avenue Mac-Mahon, 750017 Paris
Tel (01) 42 67 69 63 **Fax** (01) 43 80 18 99
website www.etoilepark.com

The sort of hotel that is full of exhausted tourists who like the fact that it is no more than a stone's throw from the Arc de Triomphe. The decoration could be described as 'modern functional', with, as in so many Paris hotels, public areas that are far more appealing than the bedrooms. Here, the sitting area in the lobby is distinctly elegant, with two groups of attractive matching sofas and armchairs on marble floors, sophisticated blinds at the windows, Japanese-style screens, modern art on the walls, and warm light cast from large table lamps. A well-stocked bar with high stools completes the picture. The neat, glossy breakfast room, its walls lined with prints, is pleasant too. The bedrooms, many with sponged walls, are okay, but a bit dull.

Nearby Arc de Triomphe; Champs-Elysées; Palais de Congrès; La Défense.
Location in one of the avenues radiating from the Arc de Triomphe **Parking** Arc de Triomphe **Metro** Charles-de-Gaulle-Etoile **RER** Charles-de-Gaulle-Etoile **Food** breakfast **Price** €€ **Rooms** 21 double and twin, 17 with bath, 6 with shower; 5 single with shower; 2 family; all rooms have phone, modem point, TV, minibar, hairdrier, safe **Facilities** sitting area, bar, breakfast room, internet booth **Credit cards** AE, DC, MC, V **Children** accepted **Disabled** lift/elevator **Pets** accepted **Closed** never **Manager** Mme Leridon

SEVENTEENTH ARRONDISSEMENT

NORTH OF ETOILE

HOTEL FLAUBERT

19 rue Rennequin, 750017 Paris
TEL (01) 46 22 4 35 **FAX** (01) 43 80 32 34
E-MAIL paris@hotelflaubert.com **WEBSITE** www.hotelflaubert.com

A WARM WELCOME from hotel's owners, Patrick and Françoise Schneider, and a luxuriant courtyard garden are the distinguishing features of this otherwise unexceptional hotel. Despite the abundance of flowers and plants in the tiled reception area, its windows hung with festoon blinds; the patio, literally overflowing with plants, as well as a wooden staircase and a little bridge, comes as a delightful surprise. Standing in the centre of the building, many of the 41bedrooms open on to it. They have been recently redecorated, with floral bedspreads and matching curtains.

NEARBY Arc de Triomphe; Champs-Elysées; Palais de Congrès; La Défense.
LOCATION in a street off avenue Wagram, 10 minutes walk from the Arc de Triomphe **PARKING** avenue Wagram**METRO** Ternes **RER** Charles-de-Gaulle-Etoil/'Péreire **FOOD** breakfast **PRICE** €€ **ROOMS** 41 single, double and triple, all with bath or shower; all rooms have phone, modem point, TV, minibar, hairdrier **FACILITIES** sitting area, breakfast room **CREDIT CARDS** AE, MC, V **CHILDREN** accepted **DISABLED** lift/elevator **PETS** accepted **CLOSED** never **PROPRIETORS** Patrick and Françoise Schneider

NORTH OF ETOILE

HOTEL REGENT'S GARDEN

6 rue Pierre-Demours, 750017 Paris
TEL (01) 45 74 07 30 **FAX** (01) 40 55 01 42
E-MAIL hotel.regents.garden@wanadoo.fr **WEBSITE** www.hotel-paris-garden.com

IT HAS AN ENGLISH NAME, but this is a typically French hotel in a handsome shuttered mansion built by Napoleon III for his doctor. It is set well back from the road and, as you might expect from a glance at the exterior, has a glorious, large garden at the back, where ivy scales the walls, trees and flowering shrubs flourish, and tables and chairs are set out in summer. The interior has been done out in an appropriately country house style, with faded chintzes in the comfortable, still elegant *salon.* No one bedroom is the same; all are refined, with chandeliers and Second Empire chairs, upholstered in velvet or satin; some are vast, with two double beds; some, a little down at heal; all have modern bathrooms. If you are arriving by car, try to get here before 7pm when you should have no trouble parking in one of the eight spaces in the hotel's forecourt.

NEARBY Arc de Triomphe; Champs-Elysées; Palais des Congrès.
LOCATION betweem place Tristram-Bernard and rue Marcel-Renaud **PARKING** outside hotel or in street **METRO** Ternes **RER** Neuilly-Port Maillot/Charles-de-Gaulle-Etoile **FOOD** breakfast **PRICE** €€€ **ROOMS** 39 double and twin, all with bath; all rooms have phone, modem point, TV, air-conditioning, minibar, hairdrier **FACILITIES** sitting room, breakfast room, garden **CREDIT CARDS** AE, DC, MC, V **CHILDREN** accepted **DISABLED** lift/elevator **PETS** accepted **CLOSED** never **PROPRIETORS** Condy family

ILE-DE-FRANCE

ANGERVILLE

HOTEL DE FRANCE

2 place du Marché, 91670 Angerville (Essonne)
TEL (01) 69 95 11 30 **FAX** (01) 64 95 39 59
E-MAIL hotel-de-france3@wanadoo.fr **WEBSITE** www.hotelfrance3.com

THREE COTTAGES HAVE BEEN knocked together around a lovely enclosed paved garden to make this appealing hotel, part of which was a *relais de poste* as far back as 1715. The outside is drenched in ivy; the inside, decorated in rustic fashion, giving it a cosy, welcoming atmosphere. Beams, tiled floors, stone walls, wooden stairs and antiques abound, and in winter a log fire burns not just in the sitting room but in the dining room too. Great care has been invested in the decoration of the bedrooms: each is different with stunning, mainly checked, fabrics, metal four-posters and subtle colours. Anne-Marie Tarrene presides over the kitchen, specializing in her own delicate version of *cuisine du terroir*.

NEARBY Etampes; Chartres; château de Méréville; château de Farcheville.
LOCATION 15 km S of Etampes on N20, in market square; car parking **FOOD** breakfast, lunch, dinner **PRICE** €€ **ROOMS** 17 double, twin and single, with bath or shower; all rooms have phone, TV **FACILITIES** sitting room, dining room, meeting room, courtyard garden **CREDIT CARDS** AE, MC, V **CHILDREN** accepted **DISABLED** access possible, lift/elevator **PETS** accepted **CLOSED** restaurant only, Sun, Mon **PROPRIETORS** Anne-Marie Tarrene and Claude Faucheux

BARBIZON

HOTELLERIE DU BAS-BREAU

22 rue Grande, 77630 Barbizon (Seine-et-Marne)
TEL (01) 60 66 40 05 **FAX** (01) 60 69 22 89
E-MAIL basbreau@wanadoo.fr **WEBSITE** relaisetchateaux.fr/basbreau

HALF OF EUROPE'S political grandees have been guests at this handsome and luxurious (Relais et Châteaux) inn. Seen from the road it looks small and chocolate box cute, but it extends back some 300 metres, and includes two separate buildings. Of the rooms in the inn itself, one includes the Hirohito suite – sometime residence of the Japanese emperor. In the more modern building, which is set amid the beautifully tended flower gardens, rooms are decorated with restrained luxury in mind. Rich fabrics, discreet and subtle colours, capacious sofas, and up-to-date accoutrements, such as the Bang and Olufsen televisions. The dining room has a reputation for excellent food, including delicious breakfasts, with plenty of choice.

NEARBY Fontainebleu; Vaux-le-Vicomte.
LOCATION in Barbizon, 60 km SE of Paris, 10 km NW of Fontainebleau, off N7 **PARKING** ample, including private garage **FOOD** breakfast, lunch, dinner; room service **PRICE** €€€ **ROOMS** 20 double and twin and suites, all with bath; all rooms have phone, modem point, TV, air-conditioning, minibar, hairdrier, safe **FACILITIES** sitting room, dining room, bar, terrace, garden, swimming pool, tennis court **CREDIT CARDS** AE, DC, MC, V **CHILDREN** accepted **DISABLED** no special facilities **PETS** not accepted **CLOSED** never **PROPRIETORS** M. and Mme Fava

ILE-DE-FRANCE

FONTAINE CHAALIS

AUBERGE DE FONTAINE

22 rue Grande, Fontaine Chaalis, 60300 Senlis (Oise)
TEL (03) 44 54 20 22 FAX (03) 44 60 25 38
E-MAIL contact@cjfontaine.com WEBSITE www.cjfontaine.com

A PLAIN WHITE FLAT-FRONTED building, formerly an *epicerie*, in a smart, isolated village in the middle of a forest, where the youthful owners have worked hard to create a simple, homely *auberge*. The bedrooms are beamed, comfortable and pleasantly higgledy-piggledy with good beds and terrific cast-iron baths. The public rooms are similarly traditional in style, particularly the dining room, where there are more beams, a chequerboard tiled floor, red upholstered chairs and tables covered with white linen cloths. The highly-regarded kitchen is Jérôme's province, and produces a range of splendid fish dishes. Outside there is a shady paved terrace and a playground, just one sign of the Durands' child-friendliness.

NEARBY Abbaye Royale de Chaalis; Senlis; Compiègne; Chantilly.
LOCATION 9 km SE of Senlis on D330A and D126, then left in village **PARKING** car park **FOOD** breakfast, lunch, dinner **PRICE** € **ROOMS** 8; 6 double and triple with bath or shower; 2 family with bath; all rooms have phone, modem point, TV **FACILITIES** sitting room, dining room, terrace, garden **CREDIT CARDS** MC, V **CHILDREN** welcome **DISABLED** not suitable **PETS** accepted **CLOSED** one week Feb, first 2 weeks Nov; restaurant only, Tue Nov to Mar **PROPRIETORS** Jérôme and Céline Durand

SAINT-GERMAIN-EN-LAYE

HOTEL LA FORESTIERE

1 avenue Kennedy, 78100 Saint-Germain-en-Laye (Yvelines)
TEL (01) 39 10 38 38 FAX (01) 39 73 73 88
E-MAIL .hotel@cazaudehore.fr WEBSITE www.cazaudehore.fr

THE REAL CHARM OF THIS sophisticated Relais et Château hotel is its romantic woodland setting. Arriving at the yellow painted house with brown shutters, trees and shrubs growing hard up against the front door and a riot of roses in the garden, it's hard to believe that you're still in a suburb of Paris. Bedrooms are as plush as you would expect though some of the decoration goes a tad over the top. The restaurant, 'Cazaudehore', has an excellent reputation and a fine cellar, and in summer tables are arranged along the garden paths, overlooking the immaculate flower-bordered lawns. In winter diners are warmed by an open fire. A walk along bridle paths takes you to Château de Saint-Germain-en-Laye. Staff are particularly helpful.

NEARBY Château de Saint-Germain-en-Laye; Château de Malmaison; Versailles.
LOCATION in Saint-Germain-en-Layes off N184, 21 km NW of Paris; car parking **FOOD** breakfast, lunch, dinner **PRICE** €€€ **ROOMS** 30; 25 double and twin, 5 suites, all with bath; all rooms have phone, TV, minibar, hairdrier, safe **FACILITIES** sitting room, restaurant, bar, conference room, garden **CREDIT CARDS** AE, MC, V **CHILDREN** accepted **DISABLED** lift/elevator **PETS** accepted **CLOSED** restaurant only, Mon **PROPRIETOR** Philippe Cazaudehore

ILE-DE-FRANCE

SAINT-GERMAIN-EN-LAYE

LE PAVILLON HENRI IV

19-21 rue Thiers, 78100 Saint-Germain-en-Laye (Yvelines)
TEL (01) 39 10 15 15 **FAX** (01) 39 10 15 15
E-MAIL pavillonhenri4@wanadoo.fr **WEBSITE** www.pavillonhenri4.fr

IN THIS STYLISH SUBURB with sweeping views of Paris, as far as the Eiffel Tower, this hotel occupies a distinguished lodge, which has witnessed more romantic times than ours. Built by Henri IV, it was the birthplace of Louis XIV, before being transformed into a small hotel in the grand style, popular in the 19th century with the great and the good. Alexandre Dumas wrote part of *The Three Musketeers* here, and Offenbach claimed that the tranquil atmosphere helped him to compose several operettas. Today the dainty pastel Louis XVI furniture fits perfectly with the style of the rooms. Even the renowned kitchen has been touched by history: it was here in 1830 that Collinet, a former *chef-patron*, invented *béarnaise* sauce.

NEARBY Château de Saint-Germain-en-Laye; Château de Malmaison; Versailles.
LOCATION in Saint-Germain-en-Layes off N184, 21 km NW of Paris **PARKING** private car park **FOOD** breakfast, lunch, dinner; room service **PRICE** €€€ **ROOMS** 42; 30 double, twin and suites, all with bath; 12 single, 3 with shower, 9 with bath; all rooms have phone, modem point, TV, minibar **FACILITIES** sitting room, dining room, meeting room **CREDIT CARDS** AE, DC, MC, V **CHILDREN** accepted **DISABLED** lift/elevator **PETS** accepted **CLOSED** never **PROPRIETOR** Charles Eric Hoffman

SENLIS

HOSTELLERIE DE LA PORTE BELLON

51 rue Bellon, 60300 Senlis (Oise)
TEL (03) 44 53 03 05 **FAX** (03) 44 53 29 94

A HOSTELRY SINCE THE 16th century, found down a cobbled street in this lovely medieval town, the Porte Bellon has a modest two stars, but provides the closest accommodation to the historic centre. The interior is homely and very French, with much heavy wooden furniture. At the heart of the hotel, the restaurant is appropriately traditional, and exceedingly popular for its terrific food. The cosy but simple bedrooms in the old building have recently been revamped, and now have en-suite bathrooms. They may not be so peaceful, but they have more character than the ones in the annexe. Probably not the kind of hotel where you'd spend a week's holiday, but it makes a useful stop-over. Don't miss the splendid 12thC cathedral whilst you're here, just five minutes' walk away.

NEARBY Cathédrale de Notre-Dame; Musée de la Vénerie; Château de Chantilly.
LOCATION in town, just SE of place du Parvis; car parking **FOOD** breakfast, lunch, dinner **PRICE** € **ROOMS** 19; 18 double and twin, one appartment, all with bath or shower; all rooms have phone, TV, minibar **FACILITIES** bar/sitting area, meeting room **CREDIT CARDS** MC, V **CHILDREN** accepted **DISABLED** lift/elevator **PETS** accepted **CLOSED** mid-Dec to mid-Jan **PROPRIETOR** M. Patanotte

INTRODUCTION

In the following pages we present, as a new departure for this *Charming Small Hotel Guide*, descriptions of 68 special restaurants in Paris. They follow exactly the same order as the hotels: beginning with the 1st Arrondissement and ending with towns in Ile-de-France in alphabetical order.

What's the criteria for this selection? Simple – they are all noteworthy addresses that we would like to pass on to our readers: places that we have particularly enjoyed, and places that we feel have the same quality of charm, individuality and value for money as the hotels that we recommend and which we know you appreciate. The inspectors are Brent Gregston and Sharon Sutcliffe. Brent, American, and Sharon, English, are both travel and food writers who live in the French capital, know it back to front and have, we believe, created the most stimulating selection of eating places in Paris that you can find anywhere.

The majority of the restaurants are comfortable rather than luxurious, pretty and atmospheric rather than formal, with an emphasis on good regional cooking. A few are smart and expensive, but in our opinion, worth it. We don't stray into the territory of *haute cuisine* and three Michelin stars – it's not our style. Instread, these are the kind of places you dream of finding in Paris: honest and welcoming, serving good food (it might be solidly traditional or subtly inventive) at fair prices.

The restaurants in this section are, in our opinion, the most interesting that Paris has to offer. For a larger selection we recommend this guide's sister publication, *Charming Restaurant Guides, France.*

PRICES

As with our hotels, we have used price bands for the restaurants to indicate how much they cost. Restaurants vary widely in what they offer: some have just a couple of set menus; others offer menus ranging from cheap to expensive, plus an extensive *carte*. In devising our price bands we have calculated the cost of an average three-course meal for one person, without wine. Very few of our recommendations will break the bank; several will leave your wallet hardly scathed.

The price bands are as follows:

The cost of an average three-course dinner for one without wine

less than 30 euros	€
30–50 euros	€€
over 50 euros	€€€

RESTAURANTS

Paris 1st

1st Arrondissement

Au Pere Fouettard

9 rue Pierre-Lescot, 75001 Paris
Tel 01 42 33 74 17
Metro Etienne-Marcel

Traditional wine bar steeped in the nostalgia of old Les Halles. Man-sized slabs of terrine, bowls of mussels and huge steaks are a perfect match for the larger-than-life atmosphere. Unfortunately, the wine list is crammed with the kind of spelling mistakes which appear to be a trademark of many of Paris' wine bars. Still, the service is good-humoured and the delicious home-made tarts, loaded with fruit, are reminiscent of those for which Alsace is famous. (In Alsace, Le Père Fouettard is a kind of bogeyman who accompanies Saint Nicholas on visits to naughty children.) As we went to press, one person could eat two courses here for around 12 euros. Wines were, on average, 3 euros a glass.

Price €
Closed Christmas Day
Credit cards AE, V

1st Arrondissement

Djakarta Bali

9 rue Vauvilliers, 75001 Paris
Tel 01 45 08 83 11
Metro Halles

The only Indonesian restaurant of note in the French capital, Djakarta Bali is run by a sister and brother team. Service is so pleasant and attentive that one has the impression of an invitation to a private house. The Hanafis are quick to point out that the Indonesian archipelago is made up of over three thousand islands so their food is predictably varied in style and they try to make it as authentic as possible. The *Nasi Goreng* (spicy fried rice with chicken, shrimps and vegetables) is outstanding, as are the various *satés.* The reasonably-priced wines make eating at this pretty restaurant light on the pocket.

Price €–€€
Closed Mon
Credit cards MC, V

Paris 1st/2nd

1st Arrondissement

Il Palazzo

Normandy Hotel, 7 rue de l'Echelle, 75001 Paris
Tel 01 42 60 91 20 Fax 01 42 60 45 81
Metro Palais-Royal

The huge Napoleonic dining room with its 7-metre-high ceiling complete with painted fresques makes Il Palazzo a fitting neighbour for the Louvre and Palais Royal. Contemporary touches have recently been added such as the massive light-reflecting steel domes and the purist lines of Bernardaud porcelain. "I'm developing a classical but modernistic style of Italian cuisine," says chef Thierry Barot. His food is certainly creatively presented: the *compotée* of sardines takes the form of a tin of sardines; the lobster, shellfish and vegetable stew is layered into glass jars in the manner of a traditional preserve. Each Saturday, from 1.30 pm to 5.30 pm, the pastry chef lays on an all-you-can-eat dessert buffet based on chocolate in winter and fruit in summer: 27.50 euros as we went to press.

Price €€
Closed Sun Mon; Aug
Credit cards AE, DC, MC, V

2nd Arrondissement

Passy Mandarin

6 rue d'Antin, 75002 Paris
Tel 01 42 61 25 52 Fax 01 42 60 33 92
Metro Opéra

Two minutes from the Opera and Place Vendôme, this charming, elegant Chinese restaurant has earned itself a solid reputation for quality and commitment to authenticity. Owner Vong Vai Kuan had already made a name for himself with the immensely popular Chez Vong at Les Halles. Here the decoration is even more refined and the service just as attentive and courteous. All of the dishes here are faultless, particularly the perfect, caramelised Peking duck. As well as Cantonese and other regional Chinese dishes, there is a selection of Thai specialities.

Price €€–€€€
Closed Sun in Aug
Credit Cards AE, DC, MC, V

Paris 3rd

3rd Arrondissement

Chez Jenny

39 bd du Temple, 75003 Paris
Tel 01 42 74 75 75
Metro Republique, Filles du Calvaire, Temple or Oberkampf

There are two main attractions at this hugely popular, historic brasserie located just off buzzing Place de la République: the superb marquetry by celebrated cabinetmaker Charles Spindler, and the enormous platters of seafood and choucroute ferried around the vast dining room by waitresses in Alsatian costume. What makes the choucroutes so special is that instead of the usual boiled ham-hock they carry a whole knuckle of roasted pork taken from the rows of spits by the door. This is one of the few Parisian restaurants to have a useful no-smoking area.

Price €€
Closed never
Credit cards AE, DC, MC, V

3rd Arrondissement

Le Hangar

12 Impasse Berthaud, 75003 Paris
Tel 01 42 74 55 44
Metro Rambuteau

Hidden in an alley, just steps from the Pompidou and honking horns, this is a friendly refuge with a terrace and minimalist, art gallery interior. The simple, classic food is all about attention to detail and the time of year – say a *gaspacho d'avocats*, cool squash soup or quivering pan-fried *foie gras* with puréed potatoes. Desserts are the forte here and you must choose between the signature *gateau au chocolate fondant*, a superb chocolate soufflé, or *crème catalan*. Generous wine prices start at 9 euros a bottle (mostly from the Loire and Languedoc). It fills up quickly so reserve if possible. Find Le Hangar by walking north of the Pompidou on the east side of rue du Renard, taking the first right after Rambuteau.

Price €
Closed Sun, Mon; three weeks in Aug
Credit cards none

PARIS 3RD/4TH

3RD ARRONDISSEMENT

LE PAMPHLET

38 rue Debelleyme, 75003 Paris
Tel 01 42 72 39 24
Metro Filles du Calvaire or St Sébastien Froissart

DESPITE HIS RAPID rise to fame, the chef at this rustic little restaurant, stashed away in a winding street in the Marais, has kept a level-headed approach to success. Dishes on the succinct menu are still based on products that arrive fresh every morning and, happily, the beamed 17thC dining room with its round tables conducive to conversation remains free of any attempt at modernisation. In his small, impeccable kitchen Alain Carrère works on the best produce from his native south-west: tuna from Saint-Jean-de-Luz, farmhouse pigeons, Salers beef and sheep cheese from the Pyrénées.

PRICE €
CLOSED Sat, Sun and Mon lunch
CREDIT CARDS MC, V

4TH ARRONDISSEMENT

L'ALIVI

27 rue du Roi de Sicile, 75004 Paris
Tel 01 48 87 90 20
Metro St Paul

IN THE HEART of the Marais lies a small corner of 'Ile de Beauté'. With its wooden tables, beams, thick stone walls, polyphonic music and Corsican newspapers it is worth seeking out just for the cultural experience. Gruff service from the waiters perfectly reproduces the atmosphere at one of the island's splendid ferme-auberges. As rustic as the decoration, the food is true shepherd's fare – hearty country soup, *tarte aux herbes*, roasted kid and a fine selection of Corsican cheeses. Top Corsican wines.

PRICE €€
CLOSED Sun eve
CREDIT CARDS MC, V

Paris 4th

4th Arrondissement

Brasserie de l'Isle St-Louis

55 quai de Bourbon, 75004 Paris
Tel 01 43 54 02 59 Fax 01 46 33 18 47
Metro Pont-Marie

NOTHING HAS CHANGED in this brasserie for decades, certainly not the menu or the stuffed swan above the bar. The view from the tables outside looking up to Notre-Dame's soaring buttresses hasn't changed in centuries. The homey interior sports hunting trophies and endearing Alsatian bric-â-brac. Tourists rub elbows at the long tables with French rugby fans and residents of the little island. The hearty Alsatian menu offers *tarte à l'oignon* as a starter and the succulent *jarret de porc aux lentilles* or *choucroute garni as a main*. Wines are reasonable (from 13 euros a bottle) but skip the overpriced coffee and ice cream. Instead, walk across the street and buy your own.

Price €
Closed Wed, Thur lunch; Aug
Credit cards MC, V

4th Arrondissement

Le Rouge Gorge

8 rue St Paul, 75004 Paris
Tel 01 48 04 75 89
Metro Sully-Morland

AT THE HEART of the antique dealers' quarter, this small wine bar, all wooden beams and exposed stone, exudes Parisian charm. François Briclot makes each and every client feel like part of the family as he lines up sample bottles on your table. Wine themes change every three weeks; recently there was an interesting Corsican white by esteemed producer Etienne Suzzoni. The tasty food complements the wine and is copiously served, particularly the large bowl of *rillons confits* from Hardouin that you can delve into at will. Wines are also available for take-away. You can eat here (wine excluded) for as little as 16 euros.

Price €–€€€
Closed Sun eve; two weeks Aug
Credit cards MC, V

PARIS 4TH/5TH

4TH ARRONDISSEMENT

AU SOLEIL EN COIN

21 rue Rambuteau, 75004 Paris
Tel 01 42 72 26 25
Metro Rambuteau

UNPRETENTIOUS and inexpensive, this 'sunny corner' functions as a friendly neighbourhood canteen. There is a blackboard where local residents write announcements – concerts, offers to sell or exchange, looking for love, and so on. The short and sweet menu begins with a starter, perhaps *salade d'haricots verts et pétoncles marinées* or *huitres tièdes aux poireaux et à la vanille*. To follow you might well be offered the *Gigot poêlé aux herbes* or *blanquette de veau à l'ancienne*. The home-made desserts don't disappoint.

PRICE €
CLOSED Sat lunch, Sun; Aug
CREDIT CARDS AE, DC, MC, V

5TH ARRONDISSEMENT

BISTROT COTE MER

16 boulevard St Germain, 75005 Paris
Tel 01 43 54 59 10
Metro Maubert-Mutualité

IT'S NO WONDER that this affordable Left Bank 'seaside' bistro is always full. Given the often exorbitant price of fish restaurants in Paris, the *prix-fixe* menus here offer real value for money. In terms of atmosphere, the blue and yellow dining room feels like a family-run pension. In fact, it is supported by Michelin-starred chef Michel Rostang (his daughter started and runs it). First courses such as *ravioles de Romans au homard*, could be followed by a relatively simple main course of plump filet of Saint Pierre (John Dory) or a more rustic *gratin de macaroni au vieux jambon*. The *tarte souflée au chocolat amer* is an intense third act.

PRICE €–€€
CLOSED never
CREDIT CARDS AE, V

Paris 5th

5th Arrondissement

Chez Henri

9 rue de la Montagne Sainte Geneviève
75005 Paris
Tel 01 43 29 12 12
Metro Maubert-Mutualité

Chez Henri stands at the crossroads between the Latin Quarter and Boulevard Saint Germain and rue Monge, famous for its market. With its turn-of-the-century decoration, complete with brown banquettes, bevelled mirrors and long-aproned waiters, this is the snug, archetypal bistrot you were hoping to find. Menus don't come much more traditional than here, with *canard à l'orange, boeuf bourguignon, blanquette de veau, gigot de sept heures*, bone-marrow toasts, lemon tart and *confiture de vieux garçon*.

Price €–€€
Closed never
Credit cards MC, V

5th Arrondissement

Cote Seine

45 quai des Grands Augustins, 75005 Paris
Tel 01 43 54 49 73
Metro St Michel

Standing on the banks of the Seine, between ever vibrant Place St Michel and the oldest bridge in Paris, this little bistro looks as if it has emerged from a fifties' film-set. Black and white photos of classic movie stars line the walls and the red moleskin banquettes lend an air of Paris in an earlier decade. Ladies come to this romantically-located bistro as much to admire the dark good looks of owner Remus Nica as for the food, which is best described as decent but nothing special. The rump steak with fat homemade fries and old-fashioned beef bourguignon stand out from an otherwise unadventurous menu. Ask for the window-seat from which you will be able to dine with a view of Notre-Dame.

Price €€
Closed Mon lunch
Credit cards AE, V

PARIS 5TH

5TH ARRONDISSEMENT

MARTY

20 avenue des Gobelins, 75005 Paris
Tel 01 43 31 39 51 Fax 01 43 37 63 70
Metro Gobelins

LOCATED NEXT TO the historic Gobelins tapestry workshops, Marty opened in 1913 as a coaching inn and has become a veritable institution. Its authentic 1930s decoration, complete with leopardskin upholstery, is a talking point amongst diners. The chef comes from the illustrious Tour d'Argent and his experience shows not only in the range of brasserie classics (juicy thick-cut fillet steak with *frites, navarin* of lamb) but also in more contemporary offerings such as the crisp filo pastry basket filled with colourful spring vegetables. The people at the next table confirmed the freshness and quality of their heavily-laden seafood platters. As we went to press menus ranged from 33 to 90 euros

PRICE €€–€€€
CLOSED never
CREDIT CARDS AE, DC, MC, V

5TH ARRONDISSEMENT

MAVROMMATIS

5 rue du Marché des Patriarches, 75005 Paris
Tel 01 43 31 17 17
Metro Censier-Daubenton

WITH ITS RATHER understated decoration - a classic blend of wood and neutral colours, enlivened by black and white photos of old Cyprus and a few discreetly-placed silvery olive trees, Mavrommatis is light years away from the tourist-trap Greek canteens of the nearby Quartier Latin. The food is as select as the clientele. *Mega pikilia* features no less than ten traditional starters, but the warm octopus salad with lemon and olive oil is also hard to resist. Main courses include *sheftalia,* minced lamb pancakes, and the colourfully-named Cypriot 'resistance fighter' leg of lamb. The wine list includes what is probably the best retsina outside Greece, but possibly a more original choice would be the full-bodied Domaine Mercouri.

PRICE €€
CLOSED Sun eve, Mon; Aug
CREDIT CARDS MC, V

PARIS 5TH/6TH

5TH ARRONDISSEMENT

LES VIGNES DU PANTHEON

4 rue des Fossés Saint-Jacques, 75005 Paris
Tel/Fax 01 43 54 80 81
Metro Luxembourg

A LITTLE RESTAURANT full of character next to the Panthéon. It seems to have stepped out of another era, with its painted ceiling, wood-panelled walls lined with bevelled mirrors, old tiled floor and original zinc bar. Just the place in which to linger over dinner and lose yourself in deep conversation: time seems to stand still here. This impression is confirmed by a menu that includes such ageless bistro classics as bonemarrow on toast, *úufs meurette*, smoked herrings with warm potatoes, kidney in mustard sauce and tripe. The time-travel experience is completed with a choice of soul-comforting desserts such as home-made profiteroles, *crème caramel* served in a deep, earthenware terrine, wine-soaked prunes and *Óle flottante*. Prices are reasonable and Marie-Josèphe Malière extends a warm, smiling welcome.

PRICE €–€€
CLOSED Sat, Sun (but open Sat eve on request)
CREDIT CARDS V

6TH ARRONDISSEMENT

LES BOOKINISTES

53 quai des Grands Augustins, 75006 Paris
Tel 01 43 25 45 94 Fax 01 43 25 23 07
Metro St Michel

OPENED IN 1994, this offshoot of Guy Savoy's gastronomic empire attracts a crowd of faithful followers, not least due to the superb location. A self-proclaimed supporter of genuine farm produce – "supermarkets are vectors of trends and false prophets of pleasure" – he correspondingly offers a range of relatively simple dishes based on seasonal products: grilled *andouille* with cauliflower cream, Salers beef and a wonderful shepherd's pie made with oxtails… and for dessert the perennial almond and hazelnut macaroon with chestnut ice-cream or chocolate tart. The wood and steel decoration in the spacious, sun-coloured dining room aims to reflect a combination of past (the historic area) and present (Savoy's innovative cuisine).

PRICE €€
CLOSED Sat lunch, Sun
CREDIT CARDS AE, DC, MC, V

PARIS 6TH

6TH ARRONDISSEMENT

LE PARC AUX CERFS

50 rue Vavin, 75006 Paris
Tel 01 43 54 87 83 Fax 01 43 26 42 86
Metro Vavin

CRAYONS ARE ON THE TABLE so diners can doodle in this skylit Montparnasse bistro, a former artist's atelier that still feels private thanks to a cosy mezzanine and interior courtyard. Young Corsican chef Martine Maille-Battestini shows plenty of sun-kissed flair in her short Mediterranean menu with starters such as *mousse de courgettes aux safran* and main courses such as *râble de lapin aux pruneaux et haricots tarbais au jus* or a *tajine d'agneau aux olives niçoises*. Many of her desserts are graced by home-made ice cream – *au lait d'amande and au caramel* – or *sorbet à la mirabelles*. Owner Paul Hayat is a wine connoisseur and his wine list shows it, in fact it's a model of value for money.

PRICE €€
CLOSED Aug
CREDIT CARDS MC, V

6TH ARRONDISSEMENT

LA TABLE D'AUDE

8 rue de Vaugirard, 75006 Paris
Tel 01 43 26 36 36 Fax 01 43 26 90 91
Metro Odeon

THE SEASONALLY CHANGING menu of chef Bernard Patou spans the cuisine of Aude, a departement in the Languedoc region stretching between the Massif Central and the Mediterranean. He and his wife, Veronique, deliver their regional fare inside a tiny, cosy restaurant near the Luxembourg gardens. They will happily introduce you to the earthy pleasures of an *Aude chicken facon grand-mère, coq au vin*, or an exemplary *cassoulet de Castelnaudary* (white beans, grilled pork sausages, duck or goose *confit*) married to powerful, berry-filled wines such as Minervois, Fitou, Corbières. In winter, there is *pigeon paté* and *sanglier* (wild boar). A we went to press the weekday lunch menu was 12 euros.

PRICE €
CLOSED Sun; Aug
CREDIT CARDS AE, V

Paris 6th/7th

6th Arrondissement

Wadja

10 rue de la Grande-Chaumière, 75006 Paris
Tel 01 46 33 02 02
Metro Vavin

THE DECORATION HERE was the latest thing – in 1930. You could not ask for a pleasanter patronne or a better, cheaper, market fresh lunch menu (*cuisine du marché*). The wine list is informative – and complete with maps – but you can also just ask for a recommendation. A la carte takes over in the evenings: try starting with a *fricassée de pleurotes et pancetta rotie* or *terrine de carnard sauvage et figues* followed by a garlicky *gigot â sept heures* or *blanquette de lotte minute et croustillant d'oignons carmélisés*. Dessert could be a simple baked apple with honey, or something fancier such as *tiramisu à la menthe poivrée*. The three-course lunch menu at 13.15 euros is one of the best for value on the Left Bank.

Price €
Closed Sat-Sun; Aug
Credit cards MC, V

7th Arrondissement

L'Affriole

17 rue Malar, 75007 Paris
Tel 01 44 18 31 33 Fax 01 44 18 91 12
Metro Invalides

ON A NARROW STREET just off the Seine, behind a 1930s façade, lies this quirky bistro, usually packed with locals who appreciate the kitchen's finesse coupled with a sense of adventure. Start with the *feuilletés d'escargots* before moving on to a richly flavoured *chausson de lapin aux oignons et romarin*, or a *vapeur de raie, compotée de choux et girolles*. The coffee, served with *petit fours*, is practically a dessert unto itself. The bread is from Poujauran, the favourite baker of French presidents.

Price €–€€
Closed Sun to Mon; two weeks in Aug
Credit cards MC, V

PARIS 7TH/8TH

7TH ARRONDISSEMENT

LA FONTAINE DE MARS

129 Rue St-Dominique, 75007 Paris
Tel 01 47 05 46 44 Fax 01 47 05 11 13
Metro Ecole Militaire

THIS ARCHETYPAL PARIS BISTRO is complete with lace curtains, checked-gingham table cloths, attentive waiters, fabulous food – and locals who treat it like home. Follow their example and tuck into the *plat de jour fois gras chaud et lentilles*, *magret de canard au miel des Pyrénées* or *turbot sauce hollandaise*. The house speciality, *véritable cassoulet au canard confit*, is the real thing and so is the *île flottante Fontaine de Mars*. On the wine list is an excellent Cahors house wine at 11 euros.

PRICE €€–€€€
CLOSED New Year's Eve, Christmas
CREDIT CARDS AE, MC, V

8TH ARRONDISSEMENT

ASIAN

30 avenue George V, 75008 Paris
Tel 01 56 89 11 00 Fax 01 56 89 11 01
Metro George V or Alma Marceau

WELCOME TO A WORLD of super chic, oriental relaxation. This is a new concept at one of the most coveted addresses in Paris, a few steps from the Champs Elysées. The de-stress experience begins with the long entrance hall where birdsong and gentle music lead you to the airy, elegant bar furnished with teak, soft light emanating from luminous columns. Downstairs, the restaurant is just as smart and offers dishes from throughout the Asian world. Go Chinese with a crispy 'sour' royal bream, Vietnamese with crab dumplings, Thai with the plump salt 'n' pepper giant prawns or bass fillet in banana leaves. Japan is represented with a *sashimi* and sushi menu. The market menu was 58 euros as we went to press- wines are in our lower and middle price bands.

PRICE €–€€
CLOSED Sat lunch
CREDIT CARDS AE, DC, MC, V

Paris 8th

8th Arrondissement

Cafe Jacquemart-Andre

158 Boulevard Haussmann, 75008 Paris
Tel 01 45 62 04 44
Metro Miromesnil

Built in the Belle Epoque's most magnificent boulevards, this 1870 dreamhouse evokes the Second Empire and the exquisite world of Charles Swann, the protagonist of Proust's Remembrance of Things Past. It is now a museum strong on the French and Italian Renaissance. The charm of its sumptuous café pulls in loçal residents as well as museum goers, and is surely the only place where you can eat with a Gobelin tapestry at your elbow. While waiting for your salad to arrive (served with smoked salmon or breast of duck), look up at the trompe l'oeil ceiling by Tiepolo – and its gallery of 17thC faces staring down at you from a painted banister. As we went to press, the *plats de jour* were ten to 16 euros.

Price €
Closed for dinner every day; lunch 11.30am-5.30pm
Credit cards V

8th Arrondissement

Le Copenhague

142 avenue des Champs-Elysées, 75008 Paris
Tel 01 44 13 86 26 Fax 01 42 25 83 10
Metro Ch. de Gaulle Etoile

It may come as a surprise to stumble across a Danish restaurant right at the top of the Champs Elysées but Le Copenhague has been there so long that it is now part of the scenery. Regulars have always found it consistent. The first-floor restaurant commands a magnificent view of the 'most beautiful avenue in the world'; downstairs the airy patio is a pure delight in spring and summer. Chef Georges Landriot, formerly of the prestigious Goumard, serves precisely executed dishes that have earned the restaurant its well-deserved reputation for quality. Fish is the star attraction, particularly the *saumon à l'unilateral*. The wine list features an incredible number of top names at emminently reasonable prices.

Price €€-€€€
Closed Sat lunch, Sun; two weeks Aug
Credit cards AE, MC, V

PARIS 8TH

8TH ARRONDISSEMENT

L'ENVUE

39 rue Boissy d'Anglas, 75008 Paris
Tel 01 42 65 10 49
Metro Concorde

BETWEEN PLACE DE LA CONCORDE and La Madeleine, ultra-fashionable, ultra contemporary L'Envue is the latest place to be seen. Opened in summer 2002, it immediately attracted followers from the nearby Embassies and chic shoppers from rue du Faubourg Saint Honoré and Rue Royale. Owner Valerie Balard created her elegant rose, grey and mauve decoration from ideas gleaned in Greece, Italy and Germany and poached the chef from jet-set darling Costes. He definitely has the edge for minimalist but delicious dishes such as the *langoustine ravioli* and the beef fillet with perfect *pont neuf* potatoes. The *Tout en Vue* snack or starter menus offer a prettily presented range of four appetizers served with a glass of wine. As we went to press, breakfast was 12 euros; snacks 7; four appetisers with wine were 26 euros.

PRICE €–€€
CLOSED never
CREDIT CARDS AE, DC, MC, V

8TH ARRONDISSEMENT

LE GRENADIN

44-46 rue de Naples, 75008 Paris
Tel 01 45 63 28 92 Fax 01 45 61 24 76
Metro Europe

INNOVATION, CREATIVITY, AND MODERNITY are the bywords here. Chef Patrick Cirotte trained with three-star Guy Savoy and Taillevent, then worked as the personal chef to music giant Eddy Barclay. Don't be put off by the rockstar-style decoration, Cirotte's talent for making the most of prime products makes a visit here well worthwhile. He manages to create happy marriages from radically different textures and flavours in such dishes as haddock and avocado on granny smith *coulis*, sea bream in chocolate sauce, rhubarb crumble with curry ice-cream and his signature *chef-d'oeuvre*, the *millefeuille minute*.

PRICE €€–€€€
CLOSED Sat lunch, Sun, Mon eve; one week in July, one week Aug
CREDIT CARDS AE, MC, V

PARIS 9TH

9TH ARRONDISSEMENT

L'ALSACO

10 rue Condorcet, 75009 Paris
Tel 01 45 26 44 31
Metro Poissonnière

IT MAY BE THE SIZE of a railroad car, but this jovial Alsatian Winstub does better *choucroute garni* than any grand brasserie. The poached sausages and roast and steamed pork, nestling in a bed of nicely acid *sauerkraut*, are a carnivore's dream. A mug of Alsatian beer is the classic accompaniment. Equally satisfying is the *bäckaofa*, a thick, three-meat stew. For a lighter meal, ask the ruddy-faced waitresses for a *flammenkueche*, an Alsatian 'pizza' topped with bacon, cream, onions and cheese. The wine cellar offers 150 of Alsatian's best wines (Ostertag, Domanine Faller, Trimbach, and so on) and potent *eau de vie*.

PRICE €
CLOSED Sat lunch; last two weeks July, Aug
CREDIT CARDS MC, V

9TH ARRONDISSEMENT

CASA OLYMPE

48 rue St Georges, 75009 Paris
Tel 01 42 85 26 01
Metro St Georges

IN AN AREA where a number of small restaurants vie for attention on a busy street, this one is particularly good value. Local regulars crowd in at lunchtime to soak up the convivial atmosphere and enjoy Olympe's down-to-earth cooking. Many of the dishes are inspired of her Corsican origins, such as the herb-crusted leg of lamb which arrives at the table whole, still sizzling in its oven dish. Not that Olympe is any stranger to sophistication: she used to be the darling of the jet-set at her former establishment in the 15th Arrondissement. Now notoriously media-shy, she still attracts a faithful following of in-the-know Parisians.

PRICE €€
CLOSED Sat, Sun; Christmas and New Year; one week in May, three weeks in Aug
CREDIT CARDS AE, MC, V

PARIS 9TH

9TH ARRONDISSEMENT

CHARTIER

7 rue du Faubourg-Montmartre, 75009 Paris
Tel 01 47 70 86 29
Metro Rue Montmartre

NO VISIT TO PARIS is complete without a visit to Chartier. Two centuries ago this was a *bouillon*, a workers' serving. Bought by Edouard Chartier in 1896 this cavernous restaurant still caters to anyone on a tight budget or who is looking for basic fare such as house pâté, snails, egg mayonnaise, steak and chips, *sole meunière*... The decoration is listed – revolving doors, antiquated mirrors and brass coat stands – nothing has changed since the beginning of the 20th century. It's as popular as ever - diners still have to share a table and wait to be seated. Noisy, boisterous and immortal.

PRICE €
CLOSED never
CREDIT CARDS MC, V

9TH ARRONDISSEMENT

LA PETITE SIRENE DE COPENHAGUE

47 rue Notre-Dame-de-Lorette, 75009 Paris
Tel 01 45 26 66 66
Metro St Georges

THIS FRANCO-DANISH BISTRO is the sort of quintessential *bonne address* that Parisians share with friends. Come here for the best smoked salmon served in Paris. The perfectionist chef Peter Thulstrup, who has worked at the Crillon and La Tour d'Argent, limits the menu to a few starters such as the *omelette norvègienne à l'anis,* and mains such as *fricadelles au curry, lotte aux betteraves, selle d'agneau aux pruneaux*. The excellent wine list includes a margaux chateau Palmier and a 1988 chassagne Montrachet. Reservations are a must here in the evening.

PRICE €€
CLOSED Sun, Mon; 3 weeks in summer
CREDIT CARDS none

Paris 9th/10th

9th Arrondissement

Le Roi du Pot-au-Feu

34 rue Vignon, 75009 Paris
Tel 01 47 42 37 10
Metro Havre-Caumartin

THIS PLACE IS SO FIRMLY ROOTED in tradition that it feels timeless. Trends will come and go, but Parisians will always eat *pot-au-feu* in that pre-war interior with slow-motion waiters. The classic beef and vegetable stew, served with pickles and grain mustard, is a substantial and appetising meal that forms a nice duo with a house *gamay d'Anjou*. But you can add a starter, say the greaseless *bol de bouillon* or *l'os à moelle* (bone marrow) on toast and/or a desert: *crème caramel*, *tarte Tatin*, *mousse chocolate* or the more adventurous *sorbet pomme au calvados*.

Price €
Closed Sun; 15 Jul-15 Aug
Credit cards MC, V

10th Arrondissement

Chez Michel

10 rue de Belzunce, 75010 Paris
Tel 01 44 53 06 20 Fax 01 44 53 61 31
Metro Gare-du-Nord or Poissonière

RARE IS THE CHEF who straddles the line between tradition and invention with the finesse of Thierry Breton. Given the low price (30 euros as we went to press) of his gourmet menu, he also merits the title of a public benefactor. He gleefully experiments with the best ingredients in a classic bistro setting near the Gare du Nord train station. The result can claim to be a sort of new regional cuisine. Dishes such as *lasagnes de chèvre et artichaut breton au pistou*, and *milllefeuille de betteraves et foie gras poêlé* are genuinely original. For dessert, try the traditional *Kouing Amman*, a stack of ultra-thin pastry leaves filled with butter and sugar. Be sure to book.

Price €€
Closed Sun, Mon; Christmas week; Aug
Credit cards MC, V

Paris 11th

11th Arrondissement

Astier

44 rue Jean-Pierre Timbaud, 75011 Paris
Tel 01 43 57 16 35
Metro Parmentier or Couronnes

With its firmly-established reputation as a true bargain, Astier epitomizes the great-value Paris neighbourhood bistrot. Every weekday, devoted regulars sit elbow to elbow in the nondescript dining room for the sake of this copiously served, tasty, traditional food. Not the place to come if you don't have a healthy appetite. Astier's menu depends on the season and what was available at market. If you're lucky you will find freshly-caught sole, calf liver with bilberries or rabbit in mustard sauce with a side-basket of thick-cut chips. But leave some room to delve into the platter of cheeses that will take up most of your table. The wine list offers some excellent bottles at reasonable prices. As we went to press, the cheapest menu was 19.50 euros.

Price €
Closed Sat, Sun; Easter, Aug, Christmas
Credit cards MC, V

11th Arrondissement

Auberge Pyrenees-Cevennes

106 rue de la Folie Mericourt, 75011 Paris
Tel 01 43 57 33 78
Metro Republic

An eclectic crowd comes here with one thing in common: a (big) appetite for French *terroir* soul food from Lyon and the Southwest. For a starter try the *caviar du Puy* (green lentils in vinaigrette) or *Lyonnais endive salads* topped with chunky bacon. The humble *cassoulet* is elevated to a pedestal here along with perfectly aged *entrecôte* and *Sabodet* sausage. The runny Saint-Marcellin cheese is exquisite. Good value wines from Morgon. Among desserts, the *Tarte Tatin* takes pride of place. Possibly the only restaurant in Paris with hams and sausages hanging from the ceiling.

Price €–€€
Closed Sat lunch, Sun; 15 Jul to 15 Aug
Credit cards V

Paris 11th

11th Arrondissement

Blue Elephant

4[illegible] rue de la Roquette, 75011 Paris
Tel 01 47 00 42 00
Metro Bastille

Fabulous Thai 'village' on busy rue de la Roquette next to Bastille. Massive bunches of imported orchids, teak walls and furniture, waterfall complete with giant carp and waitresses in vibrant silk render the enchantment real. The whole concept is in line with the taste one would expect of the elegant antiquarian owner Karl Steppe. Head Chef Nopporn Siripark specializes in Royal Thai Cuisine featuring classics and personal creations such as the red and green curries, delicious banana flower salad, Thai fish cakes, prawn and lemongrass soup, jasmin tart and the unusual sweet 'n' sour dessert, Sod Sai. Most ingredients are imported direct from Thailand and degrees of spiciness are indicated by elephant symbols. The impeccable wine list is put together by international expert Manuel de la Motta Veiga. Several regional Thai festivals are celebrated throughout the year.

Price €€
Closed Sat lunch
Credit cards AE, DC, V

11th Arrondissement

Le Passage

18 passage de la Bonne-Graine, 75011 Paris
Tel 01 47 00 73 30
Metro Ledru-Rollin

It is snugly hidden in the elbow of an alley only steps from the busy Bastille crossroads. Technically, it is a wine bar – with a formidable list of Rhone Valley and Burgundy crus; it would take hours to read the wine list – so ask for advice. The Breton owner finds room on his menu for the eight verions of the earthy *andouillette*, served grilled, as well as trendier dishes like seafood risotto or pasta. The trio of *pots de crème* makes a perfect finale. To find the passage, walk south from the crossroads of Charonne and Ledru-Rollin, on the right-hand side of Ledru-Rollin Renard, taking the first left.

Price €
Closed Sat lunch, Sun
Credit cards V

PARIS 12TH

12TH ARRONDISSEMENT

LA BICHE AU BOIS

45 avenue Ledru Rollin, 75012 Paris
Tel 01 43 43 34 38
Metro Quai de la Rapée

A CANDIDATE for the title of best-value-for-money in Paris, this small restaurant near the Gare de Lyon is always full. Parisians come for the copiously served, home-style cooking and decent wines, but also to be part of the ambient *bonhomie*. Nowhere else in town will you encounter this quality and choice at such a bargain price. The Biche really comes into its own during the game season, when you will often find grouse, venison, partridge and wild boar on the menu. Always on offer are the state-of-the-art *coq au vin, bœuf bourguignon*. A huge platter of perfectly-ripened cheeses plus dessert are included in the price. Booking is essential. As we went to press the single menu cost just over 20 euros.

PRICE €
CLOSED Sat, Sun; end July to third week of Aug
CREDIT CARDS AE, DC, MC, V

12TH ARRONDISSEMENT

L'OULETTE

15 place Lachambeaudie, 75012 Paris
Tel 01 40 02 02 12
Metro Bercy

L'OULETTE WAS A PIONEER in this now super-trendy area of the capital and has a faithful following of diners. The widely-spaced tables guarantee confidential conversation and the warm but unobtrusive service and imaginative takes on the cooking of South-West France keep Parisians coming back. The generous evening menu includes two half bottles of very decent white and red wine. From the à la carte menu choose from duck terrine with *foie gras* in *Jurançon* jelly, *millefeuille de sardines*, duck *confit* and for dessert, the featherlight apple *tourtière*. The informed wine list features a number of quality sherries, and coffee is chosen from a menu arranged by country.

PRICE €–€€
CLOSED Sat lunch, Sun
CREDIT CARDS AE, DC, MC, V

PARIS 12TH

12TH ARRONDISSEMENT

LA SOLOGNE

104 avenue Daumesnil, 75012 Paris
Tel 01 43 07 68 97 Fax 01 43 44 66 23
Metro Daumesnil

AS THE NAME SUGGESTS, this classic stalwart next to the fountains of Place Daumesnil serves *cuisine de terroir*, particularly from the eponymous region. Think Sologne, think game goes the saying, and here the chef really comes into his own during the game season. Wild boar, duck, partridge, hare, venison… Didier Maillet offers the whole range, except pheasant. "It is impossible to find good-quality pheasant today, so we just refuse to sell it." He used to have a wine shop, so he knows all the best producers and now his wine list offers such rareties as Overnoy's Arbois Pupillin 85, a Rayas 97 and a superb Fixin Domaine Fougeray de Beauclair 98.

PRICE €–€€
CLOSED Sat lunch, Sun
CREDIT CARDS AE, MC, V

12TH ARRONDISSEMENT

LES ZYGOMATES

7 rue de Capri, 75012 Paris
Tel 01 40 19 93 04 Fax 01 44 73 46 63
Metro Daumesnil or Michel-Bizot

THE ZYGOMATIC MUSCLES of the lower cheek are used for two of pleasurable activities – smiling and chewing – and this bistro is a place to do both. It was a delicatessen in the 1920s, which explains the pre-war interior of marble counters, painted etched glass, and polished, walnut-moulded windows and doors. Starters include a luscious goat-cheese cannelloni. Typical of main dishes is the *crêpinette de faison farci au chou et foie*, a roll of sliced pheasant, with crispy skin on the outside, stuffed with cabbage and duck liver. As we went to press there was a 14-euro lunch menu.

PRICE €€–€€€
CLOSED Sat lunch, Sun; Aug
CREDIT CARDS V

PARIS 13TH

13TH ARRONDISSEMENT

L'AVANT-GOUT

26 rue Bobillot, 75013 Paris
Tel 01 53 80 24 00 Fax 01 53 80 00 77
Metro Place d'Italie

THIS IS THE BEST RESTAURANT in Butte-aux-Cailles, a village-like enclave of small houses and gardens and arguably the most charming unknown neighbourhood in Paris. Noisy and crowded, it's not a place for quiet reflection, but for savouring, in convivial communion, the inventive cuisine of chef Christophe Beaufront. A starter might be *tajine des legumes à la graine de fenouil*, followed by the house speciality, *pot-au-feu de cochon aux épices* or, in season, *sanglier à sept heures*. The wine list is original and affordable. Lunch menu for 14 euros as we went to press.

PRICE €–€€
CLOSED Sun, Mon; first week of Jan and May; three weeks Aug
CREDIT CARDS V

13TH ARRONDISSEMENT

CHEZ GLADINES

30 rue des Cinq-Diamants, 75013 Paris
Tel 01 45 80 70 10
Metro Corvisart

THIS BASQUE RESTAURANT is a friendly neighbourhood *table de quartier*, always crowded and incredibly cheap. The house speciality is an immense salad with a citrus vinaigrette served in an earthenware bowl. You choose what to add: *jambon de Bayonne*, duck, potatoes, and so on. Or you can go for Basque chicken, *piperade* or, in winter, *pot-au-feu*, accompanied by full-blooded wines from the south-west. Finish with a slice of sheep's cheese or the fine home-made desserts, such as a cherry-flled *Gateau de Basque*. You can eat here for around ten euros without wine. Dinner menu 16 euros as we went to press.

PRICE €
CLOSED never
CREDIT CARDS none

PARIS 14TH

14TH ARRONDISSEMENT

LA COUPOLE

102 bd du Montparnasse, 75014 Paris
Tel 01 43 20 14 20 Fax 01 43 35 46 14
Metro Vavin

GENERATIONS OF PARISIANS have dined, danced and romanced at La Coupole which is as much a part of the history of Montparnasse as the Bohemian poets, musicians and artists who made it their own at the turn of the 20th century. Despite its huge size, this 'food hall' fills up with a crowd of Parisians, suburbanites and tourists every meal time. The wait for a table often exceeds half an hour in the evening, but still they come to people-watch, admire the art deco and experience one of the liveliest restaurants in Paris. Be sure that this is the charm of La Coupole, rather than interesting food. As in all brasseries, seafood tops the bill but the extensive menu also offers such timeless favourites as snails, onion soup, *foie gras*, *steak tartare* and *châteaubriand*.

PRICE €€
CLOSED Sun
CREDIT CARDS AE, DC, MC, V

14TH ARRONDISSEMENT

LA CREOLE

122 bd du Montparnasse, 75014 Paris
Tel 01 43 20 62 12
Metro Vavin

THIS IS THE NEAREST you will get to the French Caribbean without leaving Paris. Smiling, friendly waitresses clad in colourful *damas* and lace, white wrought-iron or wicker furniture and huge bouquets of vibrant tropical flowers offer a faithful reproduction of the Antilles. Peep though the curtain of green plants which all but obscure the windows and you might just remember you are in Paris. Owner Charlie will explain the differences between the dishes of Martinique and Guadeloupe from a menu that includes such stalwarts as *féroce*, stuffed crab, cod fritters, *chatrou* (octopus stew) and a delicious *colombo* (lamb or pork curry. Charlie is president of the Rum Academy so can be relied upon to unearth that old vintage you have been longing to try.

PRICE €–€€
CLOSED never
CREDIT CARDS AE, DC, MC, V

Paris 15th

15th Arrondissement

Le Belisaire

2 rue Marmontel, 75015 Paris
Tel 01 48 28 62 24
Metro Convention

Just the kind of place you were hoping to stumble upon in this tiny street at the heart of Paris' most extensive Arrondissement. The essential elements of the quintessential old bistro are still there –polished wooden floors and bar, art deco lighting, mirror panels, snowy-white tablecloths – but Matthieu Garrel, the 31-year-old Breton chef, has rejuvenated the menu, lending an innovative touch to the classics: saffron mussels, black sausage *nems*, green pepper *vichyssoise, feuilleté d'andouille*, *artichokes barigoule* with *foie gras*, and for dessert… chocolate and pepper cake.

Price €
Closed Sat lunch, Sun; three weeks Aug
Credit cards V

15th Arrondissement

Bistro 121

121 rue de la Convention, 75015 Paris
Tel 01 45 57 52 90 Fax 01 45 57 14 69
Metro Boucicaut

Formerly a favourite haunt of Orson Welles and François Mitterand, Bistro 121 has kept the warm atmosphere and rich mahogany tones of its original decoration designed by the ubiquitous Slavik. It now caters for an almost exclusively Parisian clientèle, particularly from the residential 15th Arrondissement. Chef Igor Sterenfeld serves a blend of *cuisine du terroir* and lighter, more contemporary dishes. According to the season his menu may include such monuments as *tête de veau sauce gribiche* or *pot au feu*, but also *gratin de langoustines* or *artichauts Lucullus*.

Price €€
Closed never
Credit cards DC, MC, V

Paris 15th

15th Arrondissement

Le Bistrot de Cancale

90 93 bd de Vaugirard, 75015 Paris
Tel 01 43 22 30 25 Fax 01 43 22 45 13
Metro Montparnasse Bienvenüe

A RECENT ADDITION to the Breton enclave around Montparnasse station, this outsized *bistrot* extending over three levels plus a terrace, is distinguished by the quality of its fish dishes. Young chef Gaël Allais started out working with three-star Olivier Roellinger in his native Brittany where he learned how to select the very best of the day's catch. The ultra-fresh seafood platters at the Cancale feature oysters, shrimps, prawns, cockles and a whole crab, or you can go for the elite of the oyster world: a dozen Belons on the half-shell. The lunchtime menu is unbeatable value for the area, and includes a starter or dessert and main course plus a choice of wine, beer or cider.

Price €
Closed Sun and Sat in Aug
Credit cards AE, MC, V

15th Arrondissement

Ty Breiz

52 Boulevard de Vaugirard, 75015 Paris
Tel 01 43 20 83 72
Metro Pasteur or Montparnasse

IN THE SHADOW of Tour Montparnasse, the City of Light's only skyscraper, you will find this homey, wood-panelled *creperie*, one of the best cheap eateries in Paris. Lacey, thin buckwheat pancakes (*galettes*) are served, simply with salted Breton butter, or filled with ingredients. One house speciality is *la Normande* (chicken, crème sauce and mushrooms). Earthenware bowls of bubbling cider or thick *lait Ribot* (Breton buttermilk) are happy partners. For dessert, don't miss *la crêpe de froment Ty Breiz*, stuffed with apples, whipped cream and homemade ice-cream.

Price €
Closed Sun, Mon
Credit cards MC, V

PARIS 16TH

16TH ARRONDISSEMENT

BRASSERIE DE LA POSTE

54 rue de Longchamp, 75016 Paris
Tel 01 47 55 01 31
Metro Trocadero

ONLY A COUPLE OF BLOCKS from place Trocadero and stunning views of the Eiffel Tower, this is a friendly haven in a much-visited, upmarket area. An elegant bar dominates the entrance to the polished, 1930s wood and mirrored interior. A crowd of locals and suits pay homage to a seasonal menu ranging from *huîtres fines de claires* and *choucroute garni* in winter to a summer *salade d'herbes folles* and *Saint-Jacques à la provençale*. *Steak tartare* and the house *foie gras* are constants as well as a superb *crème brûlée* and on weekends all you can eat for 18.5 euros.

PRICE €–€€
CLOSED never
CREDIT CARDS AE, V

16TH ARRONDISSEMENT

LE CHALET DES ILES

Lac du Bois de Boulogne, 75016 Paris
Tel 01 42 88 04 69 Fax 01 45 25 41 57
Metro Pte Dauphine

A SHORT BOAT RIDE takes you to this glass-fronted haven on an island in the Bois de Boulogne. Originally built as a hunting lodge for Empress Eugenie, the restaurant features a wide terrace where you can dine with a view over the lake with the Eiffel Tower in the distance while peacocks strut around the lawn. Probably the most romantic setting in the capital. Tables overlooking the lake are distributed on a first-come-first-served basis, so come early. Food is expensive, but interesting, with a hint of the Pacific Rim, a relatively new concept in France: Prawn Colombo, Salmon steak marinated in saké.

PRICE €–€€
CLOSED Sun evening in winter
CREDIT CARDS AE, V

PARIS 16TH

16TH ARRONDISSEMENT

LES JARDINS DE BAGATELLE

Parc de Bagatelle, Route de Sèvres à Neuilly, 75016 Paris
Tel 01 40 67 98 29
Metro Pte Dauphine

SUMMER OR SPRING are the best times to enjoy a leisurely lunch at delightful Bagatelle park deep at the heart of the Bois de Boulogne. Tables are set out in the shade of the century-old trees next to the delightful scented rose garden. Chef Alain Raichon comes from the Jura, so expect to sample traditional regional dishes such as chicken with morels cooked in *vin jaune*. He also makes his own *foie gras*. Combine eating here with a visit to the park's folly, built in just 64 days as a bet between Marie-Antoinette and her brother-in-law, the Comte d'Artois.

PRICE €€–€€€
CLOSED evenings mid-Sept to 1st May; 24 and 31 Dec
CREDIT CARDS AE, MC, V

16TH ARRONDISSEMENT

LE PETIT RETRO

5 rue Mesnil, 75116 Paris
Tel 01 44 05 06 05 Fax 01 44 05 06 05
Metro Victor Hugo

A BAR AND TWO TINY rectangular rooms are all there is to this turn-of-the-century bistro. The classic bistro food has some whimsical touches such as the *oeufs pochés a la crème de chorizo* or the *raviole de crabe au curry*. The *blanquette de veau à l'ancienne* is, in the best tradition, satisfyingly robust and tender. Dessert lovers will adore the *rioche rotie au miel et glace au pain d'épices*. An interesting choice of wines and perky service add to the pleasure.

PRICE €
CLOSED Sat lunch, Sun, three week in Aug
CREDIT CARDS none

PARIS 16TH/17TH

16TH ARRONDISSEMENT

LE SCHEFFER

22 rue Scheffer, 75116 Paris
Tel 01 47 27 81 11
Metro Trocadero or Passy

A HAPPY, FAMILY-RUN *bistro de quartier* hides behind red-and-white chequered curtains on a sidestreet off place Trocadero. Simple and unpretentious, it serves sturdy bistro classics to a crowd of often packed-in regulars, many of whom, alas smoke. Starters run from a *terrine de lapin aux pleurotes* to *salade d'epinard frais oeuf poché*, while main courses feature a first-rate *navarin d'agneau aux petits legumes, filets de rouget* and *foie de veau*, either *rosé au vinaigre de Xéres* or *au miel d'acacia*. Some of the desserts pack an alcoholic punch: try *cerises à l'eau de vie* or prunes soaked in either cassis or armagnac.

PRICE €
CLOSED Sun; Christmas, New Year
CREDIT CARDS none

17TH ARRONDISSEMENT

LA FOURCHETTE DES ANGES

17 rue Biot, Paris, 75017 Paris
Tel 01 44 69 07 69
Metro Place-de-Clichy

ONLY A FEW METRES from the honking horns of Place Clichy, the 'angels' fork' is a very popular bistro, which has kept its soul intact - simple, charming and still relatively cheap. Unroll your papyrus scroll menu beneath grinning plaster-of-Paris cupids and look for starters such as *cassolette de ravioles* or *millefeuille de légumes à la mozzarella*. Mains include *émincé de bœuf* and *magret de canard aux figues*. For dessert, there is a truly divine *poire pochée au caramel épicé*. Reservations advised, particularly in the evening.

PRICE €-€€
CLOSED Sun; Aug
CREDIT CARDS MC, V

PARIS 17TH/18TH

17TH ARRONDISSEMENT

OLIVIER & CO

8 rue de Lévis, 75017 Paris
Tel 01 53 42 18 04 Fax 01 53 42 18 15
Metro Villiers

OLIVIER BAUSSAN shot to fame with his Provençal-style boutiques dedicated to Mediterranean olive oils made by top small producers. Now he has opened his first bistro/shop in the chic 17th Arrondissement. Run by Mario Pontarolo, formerly a sommelier at the Tour d'Argent, the restaurant is an ode to all things olive-based. Before you eat he will run you through a tasting of a selection of oils which you can follow up with a simple choice of three *tians*. The stuffed bell peppers and artichoke and fennel mousse are particularly recommended. For dessert, the pineapple in hibiscus syrup.

PRICE €
CLOSED Sun, Mon, Tue, Wed eve; three weeks in Aug
CREDIT CARDS AE, V

18TH ARRONDISSEMENT

AU BON COIN

1 rue des Cloÿs, 75018 Paris
Tel 01 46 06 91 36
Metro Larmarck-Caulaincourt

FROM THE OUTSIDE, you would never guess that this ordinary-seeming café is an awarding winning ('Bouteille d'Or') bistro. The third-generation owner, Jean-Louis Bras, is its heart and soul, gathering the *produits du marché* each morning for a couple of tasty *plats du jour* (*saucisson de Lyon à beaujolais, tartiflette*) and pairing them with just the right, ready-to-drink *vins de soif*. Prepare to meet local people who call this café home for at least part of the day.

PRICE €
CLOSED Sat dinner, Sun; Aug
CREDIT CARDS MC, V

20TH/AROUND PARIS

20TH ARRONDISSEMENT

LE ZEPHYR

1 rue du Jourdain, 75020 Paris
Tel 01 46 36 65 81
Metro Jourdain

THIS ART DECO GEM is well worth seeking out in the up-and-coming 20th Arrondissement. You can combine the lunch menu - one of the best value for money in Paris – with a walk in either the Buttes Chaumont or Parc Belleville, two of Paris' loveliest parks. The food displays original touches without being off-the-wall: witness the *canard sauvage roti au miel de lavande* accompanied by a *polenta épicée*. Desserts are classic – go for the *fondant tiède au chocolat sauce vanille* or whichever *crème brulée* is on offer (with coffee and cardoman or figs and cinnamon ice-cream). The wine list is good, if not thrilling. It fills up most evenings with neighbourhood residents, so best to reserve ahead.

PRICE €–€€
CLOSED Sat lunch, Sun; Aug
CREDIT CARDS AE, DC, MC, V

OUTSIDE PARIS ILE-DE-FRANCE – BARBIZON

AUBERGE DU GRAND VENEUR

63 rue Gabriel-Séailles, 77630 Barbizon
Tel 01 60 66 40 44 Fax 01 64 14 91 20

THIS RUSTIC, utterly quaint hunting lodge makes a perfect stop in the tiny village of Barbizon, a place that exerted a powerful charm over 19thC painters including Corot and Millet. It is dominated by a massive fireplace on which the chef prepares the house speciality, *grillade* (grills). *Gibier,* game, is usually on the menu from October to February. After eating, you can walk through the vast forest of Fontainebleau. Service is friendly.

PRICE €€–€€€
CLOSED Wed eve, Thurs; first week of Jan, first three weeks of Aug
CREDIT CARDS AE, V

AROUND PARIS

FONTAINEBLEAU

LE CAVEAU DES DUCS

[illegible]
Tel 01 64 22 05 05 Fax 01 64 22 05 05

JUST AROUND THE CORNER from the château of Fontainebleu, you can dine beneath the arches of magnificent 18thC cellars with furniture to match. José Perreire's *cuisine du marché* features plenty of seafood, and Mediterranean influences in dishes such as *alliance de saumon et de sandre à la bisque de langoustines* and *mijoté de baudroie à la provençale*. Or you can choose heartier fare such as *magret de carnard mulard au vinaigre de cidre et pommes caraélisées*. Portions are generous.

PRICE €–€€
CLOSED first two weeks of Aug, first week of Jan
CREDIT CARDS AE, V

MOISSY CRAMAYEL

LA MARE AU DIABLE

Parc Plessis Picard, 77550 Moissy-Cramayel, Seine et Marne
Tel 01 64 10 20 90 Fax 01 64 10 20 91

THIS CHARMING 15THC manor house/hotel, which used to belong to the writer George Sand, lies just 30 minutes from Paris via the N6. A visit can easily be combined with looking around the romantic candle-lit Château Vaux-le-Vicomte. The extensive, wooded gardens provide an idyllic setting for summer dining, but when the weather grows colder the ideal place to be is in the historic beamed dining room next to the log fire. The menu carries mainly seasonal produce, so you may find lobster salad, sander cooked in bacon, sea bass in meat juices, lamb with tarragon and of course the flagship dishes: pan-fried *foie gras* with cider and honey, and duck flamed in armagnac. Michèle Eberwein is a charming hostess.

PRICE €€
CLOSED Sat lunch, Sun; Aug
CREDIT CARDS AE, V

AROUND PARIS

LE PERREUX-SUR-MARNE

BLUE MARNING

44 quai de l'Artois, 94170 Le Perreux-sur-Marnem, Val de Marne
Tel 01 43 24 11 05

ONE COULD NOT WISH for more romantic a setting just a ten-minute drive from the city. This glass-fronted summer house stands literally on the Marne river opposite lovely Ile aux Loups. Portuguese owners Aurea and Manuel Alves have made such an effort to integrate the restaurant into its natural surroundings that they had part of it built around a tree that now towers above. The first course of grilled sardines is always a good bet in season; or try the salted codfish with red peppers. Ask Manuel for one of his excellent Portuguese wines kept for special customers. Don't miss the picturesque port of Nogent-sur-Marne just a short stroll away along the riverbank. In winter, you eat in the old beamed house across the road.

PRICE €€
CLOSED Wed; annual holiday closure depends on the weather forecast
CREDIT CARDS V

VERSAILLES

LE BOEUF A LA MODE

4 rue au Pain, 78000 Yvelines
Tel 01 39 50 31 99 Fax 01 30 21 27 66

TOURISTS VISITING the palace of Versailles tend to overlook the city itself and its superb farmer's market – its main attraction for French visitors, who come from far and wide to shop here. This tiny, traditional bistro is right on the marketplace and benefits from the market's cornucopia. Fresh produce shows up in dishes such as the *farci de pommes au chevre et noix, pave de veau en roquefort* and *filets de daurade aux baies roses*. For dessert, go for the *crème caramel* or a *crumble aux pommes et fruits rouges*. As we went to press the two course lunch menu, with wine and coffee included, cost 22 euros.

PRICE €
CLOSED never
CREDIT CARDS V

Hotel & Restaurant names

In this index hotels and restaurants are arranged in order of the most distinctive part of their name: very common prefixes such as 'Hôtel', 'Grand Hôtel', 'Hostellerie', 'Auberge', 'Relais', 'Le/La' and 'Au' are omitted, but more significant elements such as 'Villa' and 'Pavillon' are retained.

A
Abbaye, Hôtel de l' 58
Académie, Hôtel de l' 142
L'Affriolé 174
L'Alivi 167
L'Alsaco 178
Amarante Beau Manoir, Hôtel 94
Angleterre, Hôtel d' 59
l'Arcade, Hôtel de 95
Artus, Hôtel 60
Asian 175
Astier 181
L'Atelier Montparnasse 134
Aubusson, Hôtel 61
L'Avant-Gout 185

B
Bailli de Suffren, L'Hôtel du 155
Balcons, Grand Hôtel des 62
Banville, Hôtel de 114
Bas-Bréau, Hôtellerie du 160
Bateau Jolia 48
Beaubourg, Hôtel 128
Beauharnais, Hôtel de 152
Beaune, Hôtel de 142
Le Belisaire 187
Bersoly's Saint-Germain, Hôtel 143
La Biche au Bois 183
Bistrot 121 187
Le Bistrot de Cancale 188
Bistrot Coté Mer 169
Blue Elephant 182
Blue Marning 195
Le Boeuf à la Mode 195
Boileau, Hôtel 156
Bois, Hôtel du 107
Au Bon Coin 192
Les Bookinistes 172
Bourg Tibourg, Hôtel du 128
Brasserie de l'Isle St-Louis 168
Brasserie de la Poste 189
Bretonnerie, Hôtel de la 39
Brittanique, Hôtel 125

C
Café Jacquemart-André 176
Caron de Beaumarchais, Hôtel 40
Casa Olympe 178
Le Caveau des Ducs 194
Le Chalet des Isles 189
Chambiges Eysees, Hôtel 148
Champ-de-Mars 85
Champaigne, Grand Hôtel de 125
Champerret Héliopolis, Hôtel 158
Chartier 179
Château, Auberge du 120
Chez Gladines 185
Chez Henri 170
Chez Jenny 166
Chez Michel 180
Chopin, Hôtel 101
Christine, Hôtel Relais 63
Le Clos Médicis, Hôtel 64
Le Copenhague 176
Cote Seine 170
La Coupole 186
La Créole 186
Crystal, Hôtel 134

Hotel & Restaurant names

D

Danemark, Hôtel 135
Degrés de Notre-Dame, Hôtel and Restaurant 49
Delhy's Hôtel 66
Delavigne, Hôtel 65
Deux Iles, Hôtel des 41
Djakarta Bali 164
Duc de Saint-Simon, Hôtel 86

E

Eber, Hôtel 115
Elysée, Hôtel de l' 96
Elysées Matignon, Hôtel 148
Elysées-Mermoz, Hôtel 97
L'Envue 177
Ermitage, Hôtel 117
Esmeralda, Hôtel 50
Etoile-Maillot, Hôtel 108
Etoile Park, Hôtel 158

F

Favart, Hôtel 127
Ferrandi, Hôtel 67
Flaubert, Hôtel 159
Fleurie, Hôtel 68
Fontaine, Auberge de 161
La Fontaine de Mars 175
Forestière, Hôtel la 161
La Fourchette des Anges 191
France, Hôtel de 160
Franklin Roosevelt, Hôtel 149

G

Galileo, Hôtel 98
Gavarni, Hôtel 109
Globe, Hôtel 69
Gobelins, Résidence les 104
Le Gonfalon, Hostellerie 123
Grand Veneur, Auberge du 193
Grandes Ecoles, Hôtel des 51
Grands Hommes, Hôtel des 52
Le Grenadin 177

H

Le Hameau de Passy 156
Le Hangar 166
Henri IV, Hôtel Résidence 131
Hospitel, Hôtel 129
L'Hôtel 70

I

Il Palazzo 165
Istria, Hôtel 106

J

Jardin de l'Odéon, Hôtel 135
Les Jardins de Bagatelle 190
Jeanne d'Arc, Grand Hôtel 42
Jeu de Paume, Hôtel du 43

L

Lancaster 99
Langlois 102
Latour-Maubourg, Hôtel 87
Left Bank, Hôtel 71
Léman, Hôtel du 152
Lenox Montparnasse, Hôtel 154
Lenox Saint-Germain 88
Libertel Argentine 110
Lille, Hôtel de 143
Lord Byron, Hôtel Résidence 149
Louis II, Hôtel 72
Louvre, Le Relais du 35
Lys, Hôtel du 73

M

Majestic, Hôtel 157

Hotel & Restaurant names

Au Manoir Saint-Germain-des-Prés 74
Mansart, Hôtel 36
La Mare au Diable 194
Marronniers, Hôtel des 136
Marronniers, Pension les 75
Marty 171
Mavrommatis 171
Mayflower, Hôtel 150
Médicis, Le Relais 136
Melia Colbert, Hôtel 53
Milliséme, Hôtel 137
Montalembert, Hôtel 144
Moulin, Hostellerie du 122

N

Nesle, Hôtel de 76
Neuville, Hôtel de 116
Nevers, Hôtel de 144
Nice, Hôtel de 44
Notre-Dame, Hôtel de 131

O

l'Odéon, Hôtel de 137
Olivier & Co 192
Orsay, Hotel d' 145
L'Oulette 183

P

Au Palais de Chaillot Hôtel 111
Le Pamphlet 167
Panthéon, Hôtel du 132
Le Parc aux Cerfs 173
Parc Saint-Séverin, Hôtel 54
Paris Saint Charles, Hôtel 155
Le Passage 182
Passy Mandarin 165
Pavillon Bastille 103
Le Pavillon Henri IV 162
Pavillon de la Reine 38
Au Pere Fouettard 164
Pergolèse, Hôtel 112
Perreyve, Hôtel 138
Le Petit Retro 190
La Petite Sirene de Copenhague 179
Place du Louvre, Hôtel 126
Place des Vosges, Hôtel de la 129
Porte Bellon, Hostellerie de la 162
Le Prieuré, Hôtel 121
Prima Lepic, Hôtel 118
Prince de Conti, Hôtel 138
Auberge Pyrénées-Cevennes 181

Q

Quai Voltaire, Hôtel du 145
Queen Mary, Hôtel 150

R

Raspail Montparnasse, Hôtel 154
Recamier, Hôtel le 139
Le Régent, Hôtel 139
Regent's Garden, Hôtel 159
Régent's Hôtel 140
Riboutté-Lafayette, Hôtel 153
les Rives de Notre-Dame, Hôtel 55
Le Roi du Pot-au-feu 180
Le Rouge Gorge 168
Royal Opéra, Hôtel 151

S

Saint-André-des-Arts, Hôtel 141
Saint-Dominique 89
Saint-Germain, Le Relais 77
Saint-Germain-des-Prés, Hôtel 140

Hotel & Restaurant names

Le Saint-Grégoire, Hôtel 78
Saint Jacques, Hôtel 56
Saint-Jacques, Relais 132
Saint James Paris 113
Saint-Louis, Hôtel 45
Saint-Louis Marais, Hôtel 46
Saint-Merry, Hôtel 47
Saint-Paul, Hôtel 79
Saint-Paul-Le-Marais, Hôtel 130
Saint-Sulpice, Relais 80
le Sainte-Beuve, Hôtel 81
Saints-Pères, Hôtel des 82
San Regis, Hôtel 151
Le Scheffer 191
Septième Art, Hôtel du 130
Au Soleil en Coin 169
La Sologne 184
Sorbonne, Hôtel 133
Style Hôtel 119
Suède, Hôtel de 146

T
La Table d'Aude 173
Tamise, Hôtel 126
Thoumieux 90
Timhotel Jardin des Plantes 57
Tour d'Auvergne, Hôtel de La 153
Le Tourville, Hôtel 146
Trocadéro la Tour, Hôtel 157
Trois Collèges, Hôtel des 133
Tuileries, Hôtel des 37
Tulipe, Hôtel de la 147
Ty Breiz 188

U
Université 91

V
Valadon 92
Varenne, Hôtel de 147
Verneuil 93
Le Vert Galant 105
Victoires Opéra, Hôtel 127
Vieux Remparts, Hostellerie aux 124
Vieux Paris, Relais-Hôtel le 84
Les Vignes du Pantheon 172
Vigny, Hôtel de 100
La Villa 141
Villa d'Estrees, Hôtel 83

W
Wadja 174

Z
Le Zéphyr 193
Les Zygomates 184

Menu decoder

A selection of the words and phrases that visitors find hardest to understand on Paris menus:

Abats	offal
Agneau	lamb
Aiglefin, aigrefin, eglefin	haddock
Aiguille	needlefish, garfish
Ail	garlic
Airelles	cranberries, whortleberries, bilberries
Allache	large sardine
Alsacienne, à la	with choucroute, ham and frankfurter sausages
Ananas	pineapple
Andouillettes	small chitterling sausages, usually served hot with mustard
Ange de mer, angelot	angel fish, resembling skate
Anguille	freshwater eel
Arachide	peanut
Araignée de mer	spider crab
Arapède	limpet
Ardennaise, à l'	usually with juniper berries
Arlésienne à l'	fish or meat with tomatoes, onions and olives
Armoricaine à l'	fish or lobster with brandy, white wine, herbs, tomatoes and onions
Baie de ronce	blackberry
Bar, badèche, cernier, bézuque, loup de mer	sea bass
Barbadine	passion fruit
Barbue	brill
Basquaise	with tomatoes, peppers and rice
Baudroie	monkfish
Bécasse, bécasseau	woodcock
Bécassine	snipe
Beignets	fritters
Belon	breton oyster
Bergère, à la	chicken or meat with ham, mushrooms, onions and potatoes
Betterave	beetroot
Bifteck	steak
Blanchaille	whitebait
Boeuf	beef
Bonite	bonito fish, resembling tuna
Bordelaise, à la	in red wine sauce with shallots, tarragon and bone marrow
Boudin noir	black pudding
Bouillabaisse	mediterranean fish stew
Boulangère, à la	oven baked, with potatoes
Boule de neige	sponge or ice-cream covered with whipped cream
Bourgeoise, à la	braised meat or chicken with bacon, carrots and onions
Bourride	white fish stew
Brandade de morue	dried salt cod mousse
Bretonne, à la	in onion sauce with haricot beans

Menu decoder

Bretonneau	turbot
Brochet	pike
Brochet de mer	barracuda
Broufado	beef stew with vinegar, capers and anchovies
Cabillaud	cod
Caille, cailleteau	quail
Camarguaise, à la	with tomatoes, garlic, herbs, orange peel olives and wine or brandy
Canard, caneton,	duck
canardeau	cranberry
Canneberge	sardine
Cardeau, celan	plaice
Cassoulet	pork, mutton or lamb, cooked with haricot beans, bacon and sausage
Cèpe	wild mushroom
Cerise	cherry
Cervelas	smoked pork sausage with garlic
Cervelle	brain
Champignon	mushroom
Chasseur	with wine, mushrooms and shallots
Chèvre	goat
Chevreuil	venison
Chicon	chicory
Chou-fleur	cauliflower
Chou-navet	swede
Ciboule	spring onion
Citrouille	pumpkin
Civet	thick meat stew, thickened with blood
Clafoutis	baked cherry batter pudding
Colimaçon	snail
Colin	hake
Coquillages	shellfish
Coquille Saint-Jacques	scallops
Cornichon	gherkin
Cotriade	fish stew with onions, potatoes and cream
Couissinet	cranberry
Crécy, à la	soup with carrots
Crème Anglaise	egg custard
Crépinette	small flat sausage, encased in caul
Crevette	shrimp, prawn
Croque Monsieur	toasted ham and cheese sandwich
Crudités	raw vegetables
Cuisseau	leg of veal
Cuisses de grenouille	frogs' legs
Darne	thick fish steak
Daube	braised meat in red wine, herbs, carrots and onions
Daurade, dorade	sea bream
Dieppoise, à la	fish, often sole with shellfish, in white wine sauce
Dinde	turkey
Ecrevisse	crayfish
Encornet	squid

Menu decoder

Epinard	spinach
Escargot	snail
Espadon	swordfish
Esprot	sprat
Esquinade	spider crab
Estouffade	pot-roasted fillet
Exocet (poisson volant	flying fish
Faisan, faisandeau	pheasant
Faséole	kidney beans
Faux-filet	sirloin steak
Fermiére, à la	meat or chicken braised with vegetables
Flétan	halibut
Fraise	strawberry
Framboise	raspberry
Galantine	loaf-shaped chopped meat, fish or vegetables set in natural jelly
Galette	breton buckwheat pancake
Garbure	soup with root vegetables and bacon
Gibier	game
Gigot	leg of lamb
Grecque, à la	mushrooms, aubergines and other vegetables poached in oil and herbs
Grenade	pomegranate
Groseille	redcurrant
Hareng	herring
Homard	lobster
Huître	oyster
Ile flottante	soft meringue on egg custard sauce
Italienne, à la	with pasta, tomato and mushrooms
Langue	tongue
Lapin	rabbit
Lièvre	hare
Lotte de mer, baudroie	monkfish
Lyonnaise, à la	with onions
Maquereau	mackerel
Marcassin	young wild boar
Merlan	whiting
Merluche	hake
Mirabelle	small yellow plum
Mode, à la	marinated meat braised in wine with bacon, calf's foot and vegetables
Mouclade	mussel stew
Moules	mussels
Mûre	mulberry
Myrtille	bilberry
Navarin	lamb stew with onions and potatoes
Navet	turnip
Niçoise, à la	with tomatoes, anchovies, olives and garlic
Normande, à la	with apples, cream, cider or calvados
Palombe	woodpigeon
Palourde	clam or cockle
Pamplemousse	grapefruit
Panais	parsnip

Menu decoder

Perdreau	partridge
Persil	parsley
Pintade	guinea fowl
Pipérade	scrambled egg with red peppers, onions and tomatoes
Plie	plaice
Pochade	freshwater fish stew with carrots and raisins
Poireau	leek
Pomme	apple
Pomme de terre	potato
Pot-au-feu	boiled beef with turnips, leeks, carrots and pumpkin
Poulet	chicken
Poulpe	octopus
Poussin	baby chicken
Pouvron	sweet pepper
Praire	clam
Prune	plum
Pruneau	prune
Quenelle	poached, chopped fish or white meat, like dumplings
Raie	ray, skate
Ramereau, ramier	woodpigeon
Rave	turnip
Reine, à la	with chicken
Rillettes	shredded, potted meat
Ris	lamb or veal sweetbreads
Rognon	kidney
Rosbif	cold, rare beef
Rouget	red mullet
Salmis	game casserole
Sanglier	wild boar
Soupe au pistou	vegetable soup with basil paste
Tarte Tatin	upside down apple pie
Thon	tuna
Truffado	potatoes with garlic, bacon and cheese
Veau	veal
Vigneron, à la	in wine sauce,with grapes

Confirming a booking

It is well worth booking a room in advance for the peak holiday seasons. Nowadays, many chambres d'hôtes have a fax that makes confirmation of a telephone reservation easier. The following is a simple letter that can be amended as needed:

Dear Sir, Madam,

I would like to book a room for two from ..... to ..... (dates) for ..... nights. Could you confirm the booking and the price of the room as soon as possible?

Yours faithfully,

....

(name)

Monsieur, Madame,

Je voudrais réserver une chambre pour deux personnes à partir du ..... au ..... pour ..... nuits. Veuillez confirmer la réservation et le prix de la chambre dès que possible?

Nous vous prions d'agréer l'expression de nos sentiments distingués,

....

(name)

Special offers

Buy your *Charming Small Hotel Guide* by post directly from the publisher and you'll get a worthwhile discount. *

Titles available:	Retail price	Discount price
Austria	£10.99	£9.50
Britain	£12.99	£11.50
France	£11.99	£10.50
France: Bed & Breakfast	£10.99	£9.50
Germany	£11.99	£10.50
Greece	£10.99	£9.50
Ireland	£9.99	£8.50
Italy	£11.99	£10.50
Mallorca, Menorca & Ibiza	£9.99	£8.50
Southern France	£10.99	£9.50
Spain	£11.99	£10.50
Switzerland	£9.99	£8.50
USA: New England	£10.99	£9.50
Venice and North-East Italy	£10.99	£9.50

Please send your order to:

Book Sales,

Duncan Petersen Publishing Ltd,

31 Ceylon Road, London W14 OPY

enclosing: 1) the title you require and number of copies

2) your name and address

3) your cheque made out to:

Duncan Petersen Publishing Ltd

*Offer applies to this edition and to UK only.

Visit charmingsmallhotels.co.uk

Our website has expanded enormously since its launch and continues to grow. It's the best research tool on the web for our kind of hotel.

Exchange rates

As we went to press, $1 bought 1.25 euros and £1 bought 1.47 euros